THE
GORDON
MACQUARRIE
SPORTING
TREASURY

THE GORDON MACQUARRIE SPORTING TREASURY

Stories by
Gordon MacQuarrie

Compiled and edited by Zack Taylor

WILLOW CREEK PRESS

MINOCQUA, WISCONSIN

Published by Willow Creek Press
P.O. Box 147
Minocqua, Wisconsin 54548

Designed by Patricia Bickner Linder

For information on other Willow Creek titles, call 1-800-850-9453

Library of Congress Cataloging-in-Publication Data
MacQuarrie, Gordon, 1900-1956.
    The Gordon MacQuarrie sporting treasury : stories by Gordon MacQuarrie ; compiled and edited by Zack Taylor.
       p.   cm.
   ISBN 1-57223-032-0
   1. Hunting stories, American. 2. Fishing Stories, American.
I. Taylor, Zack. II. Title.
PS3563.A3293A6 1998
813' .54--dc21   98-39214
                          CIP

CONTENTS

DEDICATION

This book is dedicated to my wife, Melissa,
who never objected to ducking days, boats
galore, dollars spent on decoys rather than
drapes and whose laughter stirs me still.

— Z.T.

INTRODUCTION

WHY A TREASURY

So many forces shape a man: My father, a good and honest man with a sense of humor that never deserted him; My grandmother's chauffeur who taught me to surf fish and the lure of lonely beaches; My grandfather who died the year I was born. His fishing rods were left in a bedroom. I still revere and idolize this man I never knew. Those rods talked to me. I was too little to know where grandpa went with those rods or what he fished for, but I vowed to find out. I did find out.

So it was with Gordon MacQuarrie. His stories shaped my teenage years. I yearned for the life he led. I delighted in his passions. I envied his friendships and warm ways. I wanted to be like him and live the life he lived. I did live the life he lived.

Almost three decades ago, I got the greatest job on earth. Boat Editor of *Sports Afield* magazine. (I used to get press releases from the Coast Guard addressed to the Boast Editor. I didn't take it personally.) The job gave me the ability to roam where I wanted, to hunt and fish, write stories, working out of my home, not an office. MacQuarrie was unknown then, swept into oblivion by the march of time. I determined to restore him to his rightful place. I determined to give to other young men and women what he had given to me. This book is the culmination of that effort.

So far there have been no objections.

— Zack Taylor

MacQuarrie —
The Writer

By my calculations, Gordon MacQuarrie wrote some 75 stories and articles that appeared in all the main outdoor magazines. His first was published by *Outdoor Life* in September 1931. His last, in *Sports Afield*, ran after his death. In the early years of 1931 to 1937 he was averaging a piece about every two months, no doubt trying to supplement a reporter's meager income across the dark days of the depression. World War II again spurred his output and in the six years after 1940 he again averaged one piece every couple of months. I'd speculate that the war years put a crimp on everyone's traveling and, hunting and fishing less (and closer to home), he put the time in front of the typewriter. The bulk of his work was published in *Sports Afield* and *Field & Stream*, but *Outdoor Life* got a share as did lesser known magazines like *Hunting and Fishing*, *National Sportsman* and *The Outdoorsman*. His most famous article was "Gertrude, the Wonderful Duck" about a mallard hen who built her nest on a piling in the Milwaukee River in the heart of downtown Milwaukee. First published in *Sports Afield* in September of 1945, Gertrude went around the world on the wire service, was made into children's books, adopted for TV and vied with headlines of Hitler's death and the fall of Berlin.

Many writers agonized to perfect a style that seemed as effortless as MacQuarrie's. But he, apparently, belted out his little masterpieces with ease. He, say those who knew him best, was aware he could spin a yarn with the best of them, and spin them he did.

He is one of four writers of his day still in print. It's pretty heady company to rank with Archibald Rutledge, Havilah Babcock and Nash Buckingham.

GORDON MACQUARRIE

by Ellen MacQuarrie Wilson

G ordon MacQuarrie was born in Superior, Wisconsin, July 3, 1900. He died November 10, 1956 in Milwaukee of a heart attack, his first real illness. He was the son of William MacQuarrie and Mary Elizabeth Stevenson MacQuarrie. Both the Stevenson and MacQuarrie families were Scottish in origin and had come to the United States by way of Canada.

He was graduated from Superior Central High School and attended the Superior State Teachers College for two years before attending the University of Wisconsin where he received a degree in journalism in 1923. He earned his way through college as a drummer with a dance band which played in the northern Wisconsin-Minnesota-Michigan area, and around the state university at Madison.

Upon graduation MacQuarrie joined the *Superior Evening Telegram* as a reporter. After two years he became city editor, and in 1927 managing editor. He left Superior in April 1936 to become outdoor editor of the *Milwaukee Journal.* He had been a guest columnist for the *Journal* and was widely known through stories in the leading sportsmen's magazines. He continued with the *Journal* for 20 years, a popular and prominent figure.

He was married to Helen Peck in 1927. She was the daughter of Al Peck, a Superior automobile dealer, who became the model for the first President of the Old Duck Hunters' Association, a fictitious organization MacQuarrie invented for literary purposes, although the two men actually were close and frequent companions. [MacQuarrie's first wife died in 1952.

They had one daughter, Mrs. T. H. Wieder, now deceased].

After the death of Al Peck, the Old Duck Hunters series was discontinued for several years until a close attachment was formed with Mr. Harry Nohr, postmaster of Mineral Point, Wisconsin. He became the second Mr. President and the series was continued until 1956.

During his years with the *Journal,* MacQuarrie traveled an estimated 40,000 miles a year covering his special field. He developed an immense personal following with his unique blend of information and entertainment.

Northwest Wisconsin remained his favorite area and the scene of most of the Old Duck Hunters stories. It was there on the Eau Claire chain of lakes that his father, a carpenter for the Superior school system, built a log cabin while MacQuarrie was still in his teens. In the early days it was a sixteen-mile walk to the cabin from the nearest railroad stop. The cabin became his lifelong retreat, figuring in many of his stories.

In 1953, MacQuarrie married Ellen Gibson, then a reporter for the *Journal.*

Physically, he was a wiry, red-headed man with a down-to-earth attitude and a quick, salty wit. He entered the field of outdoor writing when it was at a low point; most stories were poorly written, with little or no imagination. With his light humor, careful character delineation, story sense, and descriptive ability he helped raise the level of the entire field. He was a pioneer, and a dedicated conservationist when it was neither fashionable nor polite to be one.

The Stories

TROUT TOWN

I have chosen this story to begin with. Here is the first of the Mr. President yarns, only here he is called "The Fellow I Often Fish With." Not much sparkle there: There will be time enough for The Old Duck Hunters, Incorrigible, to evolve.

Now MacQuarrie needs a companion on his journey. He should be older. He is. He should be wise. He is. He should be of sober mien and lofty purposes. Hah! This Fellow I Often Fish With is full of the devil. A prankster. A bald-faced liar on occasion. A man who will never lose his sense of youthful veneration. An envied friend to the end. He will be a man worth knowing.

And about MacQuarrie himself? Well, how many people do you know who boast of having "a speaking acquaintance with several spruce trees of splendid character." Hmmm. This thing could get interesting. It will.

By the way, anyone know what a dandiprat is?

Trout Town comes alive at sundown. From beneath overhanging banks, sunken logs and sheltering rocks come the adult citizenry to chase the dandiprats out of the riffles and accept whatever hatch the evening has to offer.

This is the witching hour for the dry fly angler. He wipes his hot forehead with kerchief about his neck, lights a fresh bowl of tobacco, looks well to his terminal tackle, and so is prepared for the day's denouement.

It is truly the magic hour. A favorite fly is selected. It may be a hideous No. 6 Jungle Cock or a dapper No. 14 Pink Lady. The fly is knotted on. The angler advances to the tail of his pool. The somber curtain of night creeps up in the east. The knotted fly is held up to the light of the west to make sure that all is well — and the play begins.

Then the little "slaps" of playful six-inchers give way to businesslike "ker-plunks" as more powerful tails hit the surface. A street of water, during the midday seemingly as empty as a deserted city, becomes an avenue of fish life, with its inhabitants eager for the evening hatch — and maybe the angler's fly.

We've all been there. We know the hour, the day, the pool. And it is the very staff of life to an angler.

I just got back from Trout Town. It was three nights ago, but the memory of it has been with me ever since. I can still see the Brule, lifeless except for small fish, become suddenly quiet, as though resting from the day's work of running down to Lake Superior. I can still see the shower of brownish flies that seemed to come from nowhere. I can still see the first good brown trout shoulder his way to the surface.

Here are furtive beauty, dynamic life, wild courage. Here is a place to test the sureness of a trembling hand. Here is opportunity to match one's beloved enemy on his own terms, taking the bitter with the sweet and victories with defeats. Here, if anywhere, a fisherman looks up at the sky and down at the stream and thanks his gods for being a fisherman.

The Fellow I Often Fish With was with me that evening. Throughout the sizzling afternoon we had conspired and perspired to ensnare brother trout from his cool retreat in the bottom of the river. We might just as well have rested beneath the pines and saved our strength, but the Other Fellow is not made of such stuff. "If they're hard to get, they're more fun getting," he avowed about two hours after we had started, with little to show.

Each of us had a couple of small rainbows. I was counting heavily on the business of the evening, and I knew that he, too, had this in mind.

"Let's take a rest until it cools off," I suggested. "It's obvious there's nothing doing. There probably will be later on."

"Young man," he young-manned, "you still have much to learn of the ways of trout. There remains before you at least one big lesson in moral sacrifice that, I am sorry to say, you have not learned yourself. You must realize that trout fishing is a pilgrimage of the spirit — a test of what character you still possess after fishing with me. It is a game in which you give much to gain much.

"I have always found that he who suffers in the bright sun will often reap his reward at dusk. But I have found, too, that he who lolls in the shade during the working hours, or the time of penance, as it were, generally receives no such rich evening reward. Maybe it is because I am superstitious, but I have no mortal use for a fisherman who will try to reap the pleasures of the evening rise without first having prepared his soul and humbled himself by ceaseless effort when the fish riseth not."

"Well spoken, Sir Izaak!" I applauded. "I shall remain by thy side in this fishless river, though we never see a trout, or feel its pull, even unto the end of this day's fishing."

So I stayed, and made a virtue of a necessity, for he had my cigarettes and wouldn't give them back. Furthermore, he had my evening lunch in his fishing pocket. He usually sees to it that things are arranged that way.

But the hot day passed — and even on a hot day, when trout are listless, there are things to do if one will look around. The birds are always on hand, and the queer lights and shadows on the trees, especially the spruces, are worthy of a passing glance. On the side of a spruce where the sun strikes there is a smile, and the tree is positively gloomy on the shady side. I have a speaking acquaintance with several splendid spruce trees of great character and individuality along the Brule. There are also fish places to look for and bottoms to explore — knowledge to be filed away in the mind for future reference. And there is, above all, the anticipation of something better later in the day.

I had a wonderful experience that night. I have seen hundreds of rises on many waters. On the Namakagon I have seen browns, at high noon, start feeding suddenly, with no sign of a hatch, continue for twenty minutes or so, and stop just as suddenly as they started. On the Iron I have seen water, the surface of which was devoid of all signs of a rise, yield twelve or fourteen big trout within an hour. And on the Brule there is always a trout turnout sometime during the day. It may be fair, good or poor, but always something. That's why so many anglers go back to it again and again.

I am sure my experience was unusual, even if it were only because I had not had such an experience before. Others may have — perhaps all anglers have had many similar days.

The sun retreated behind the spruce steeples, and I got ready. The Other Fellow was upstream 200 yards. We fish too fast on the Brule, we dry-fly fellows, and I had planned to overtake him within a few minutes; but as things turned out, I did not see him until near dark.

Now, about 150 yards below the ranger's cabin in the state park, outside the town of Brule, there is a 100-yard stretch of beautiful water, shallow in the middle and deeper at both banks, especially the right bank. You stand in the shallower water and work the deep water easily. And if you are careful, you don't forget the shallow directly ahead of you and maybe a little to the right. Sometimes it yields surprising fish.

I was halfway up this wide, comparatively slow stretch, to the point where a 75-foot spruce sticks out from the right bank over the river. This tree spreads over a fairly fast run, and just below and above are deep pools. All along the bank there are dense bushes and old logs rooted into the bank, the bank itself being concave. The browns just love it. There was a small brown fly showing, and I grabbed one. Just a little dusty brown fellow to me, but he indicated a Brown Bivisible, which is my favorite fly anyway. Some day I shall buy a big book with colored plates and scientific descriptions of flies, and will plan, carefully and cautiously, to learn how to imitate the hatch on the water. Some day, I say, I shall do that, and I will know the names of the flies, too. But I know that when the hour of dusk has come and there is a fish to be caught, lying in the riffles ahead of me, I will tie on a No. 12 Brown Bivisible and mark myself forevermore as an unprincipled opportunist, clinging with superstitious weakness to the past.

Some day I shall try something else. And some day, too, I shall learn how to tie a double water knot so that I may fasten broken or shortened leaders together and thus confound all anglers who knoweth not how to tie a double water knot. Yes, yes; no doubt, no doubt . . .

The browns were ravenous. Can more be said? I have never seen anything like it — yes, I have, on private ponds and one night, years ago, before I began fishing for trout. Now I know they were trout, because I know there are millions of trout in the Brule.

The next day I told two men about it. I was pretty much fired by my experience. One of them was an old hand at the dry fly game. The other was a lake fisherman — and a good one — who has his first-day fling at the Brule annually, gets nothing, year in and year out, and then quits cold. After hearing my story that "it looked like it was raining," the lake fisherman suggested an examination by an alienist. The veteran of the floating fly smiled. He knew all about that kind of thing. To him I told it all.

I tried the lower pool — right at the place where the dark water slides out from beneath the spruce-tree branches. Had I been wise, I should have worked the tail of the pool, but I am not wise under such circumstances. I am a feckless fool, a-tremble with anticipation and utterly unable to be cool, calm and collected. The hungry browns were brimming over the upper end of the pool, and there I went.

One forgets himself more completely, at such a time, than at any other moment of his life. I was no longer a person with a rod, a reel, a line, a leader and a fly, all hitched together. I became, with my paraphernalia, a single, purposeful unit.

The first cast fell short of the overhanging branches, and the fly was wafted to the dark water. I could see it well in the falling light, its white neck of hackle looming like a little lighthouse. It floated three or four feet and then disappeared. No impulsive rush, no flash of fish, no slap of tail. That fish knew his business. A little fly — he would not bother to exert himself too much for it. I set the hook, and he was on with a strong, sudden wiggle that told me I need not implant the hook more firmly.

Into the bank he went, away from the channel where he had been feeding. Away from the dinner table and under a mass of brush and driftwood. I horsed him out and backed into midstream as quietly as possible, trying not to disturb the place more than necessary. The trout did not break water until I had him in the middle of the river, when he thrashed vigorously as I tried to bring him to net. He was a brown. I knew that by his fight — dogged, persistent, cagey, but lacking the brilliant madness of the fight a hooked rainbow makes. One can gauge the fight of a brown, but never that of a rainbow. I netted him. He was a good foot long.

The matted fly was whipped dry and sent forth again, to the same spot.

Fish were rising there as though nothing had happened, and one was coming upward with the persistency of a fiddling cricket. The fearlessness of the trout that evening was something I had never seen before. The steadily feeding brown would show his entire body in his rise, but made little commotion. Over him I floated the fly, time and again, and though he kept feeding he paid no heed to the artificial. Several times he rose when the fly was not a foot from him. I finally quit him, fearing to lose other chances.

I tried to the right of the pool, in water a little shallower. A smaller fish was taken there. A few minutes later, thinking to rest the head of the pool, I dropped the fly in the shallower water of midstream, directly in front of me. It was taken immediately, and this third trout was nearly as large as the first — all browns. Three without moving very far from one spot.

I was doing famously; so I returned to the cagey one that was so particular about his supper. He had been feeding all the time I caught the other two. On my previous trials I had cast the fly about five feet ahead of him and had let it drift down. This time, on an impulse, I let it drop as close to his dining table as I could, and it came down in the right place with a little splat. He grabbed it two seconds after it struck, and was off to the concave bank. The same old story — he was persuaded to come out into the middle of the stream — and there I ran him ragged.

Further effort at that spot failed. But I felt that the pool above would be as good or better. Perhaps there were six or eight good fish rising in that pool. Maybe more. Now I was more careful, and more confident. I was beginning to feel I had the situation pretty well in hand. I took a couple of 10-inchers out of the tail of the pool, fought them away from the bank and creeled them without disturbing the other feeding fish in the least.

I have yet no explanation for the indifference of the browns to my presence that night. They must have seen me. I can only conclude that they had spent a warm day on the bottom of the stream and were making up for lost time by particularly heavy feeding.

One energetic fish occupied the center of the pool, and I tried for him. He took the fly without much fuss, but I knew his pedigree the minute he did — a rainbow.

Have you ever attended a prize-fight and sat, listless, through three of four tame preliminaries, then awaited the final bout with melancholy foreboding? Maybe the man next to you has told you that the whole card has been framed. You look around for your hat and coat and begin to wonder where you parked your car. Then, under the glow of the floodlights, two demons incarnate are unleashed and you lean forward, like the savage you are, and howl with the mob for a knock-out.

That rainbow made me lean forward and howl for a knock-out. For a split second he did not know what he had, and then he went crazy. He leaped once, and two seconds later leaped again, twenty feet downstream, on a slack line.

One does nothing with a hooked rainbow for about thirty seconds. The rainbow has everything his way. He was all over the pool, under the bank, out in the open, and back to his pool before I felt I had a chance to net him. When he had settled down, I slowly worked him toward me, stripping in line. I looked for a bigger fish than the first brown. He was hardly as big — but what a fighter!

The Other Fellow came splashing downstream to me. He was getting ready to quit. By his swagger I knew he had caught fish. I asked him to avoid the pool, and he made a long detour, coming up in back of me. He had seven, browns and rainbows, and he was a happy man. I asked him, a veteran of many a trout season, if he had ever seen such a rise. He said he had, but not often. As we spoke a fish rose almost at my knee. They were everywhere — fearless and greedy.

While he stood there I tossed the fly into the far corner of the head of the pool, near a bush that hung out over the river. It was getting darker, and I thought the fly had landed in the bush. I gave a tentative pull, and the fly remained wherever it was. A more vigorous pull, then a jerk, and I got an answering jerk that was a complete surprise. Three more jerks came out of the bush, and in my eagerness I jerked too hard. Fly, leader and line came back to me and were tangled almost inextricably.

"That was a fish," I said as calmly as I could.

"Looked to me like you were stuck in a tree," said the Other Fellow.

He lit matches in order to help me untangle the snarl, but it was of no use. I told him to try the pool, not omitting the corner, while I retreated to a rock, where I sat down and rigged up anew. It took me fully twenty minutes in the half-light, and while I did so the Other Fellow took a couple of little rainbows from the pool. I knew that he had not disturbed the corner, and that he felt I had actually been snagged on a bush. He marched off upstream, telling me he would wait ten minutes for me just above the pool.

I approached within range of the corner with a profound respect for whatever was in it. In place of the minute bivisible, I had attached a No. 8 nondescript with white body and brown hackle, a good juicy mouthful of a fly. I did not bother to oil it, as it was almost dark and I planned to keep it dry for what little fishing remained by whipping it.

The first cast did the trick. I measured out enough line barely to miss the bush. A rush and splash, and I had hold of the river bottom. The fish leaped and writhed. I could barely see him, but he looked big and felt bigger. I guessed him to be another rainbow — maybe a two-pounder. I am convinced he was the same fish I had on before and was highly pleased with myself. My plan was working well, though I have realized since that it was pure luck that my outfit had become snarled, else I would have rushed him with another offering and might have scared him away.

I took him out of the pool, gradually, and got him into the center of the stream. There was no horsing this fellow. He had to be cajoled. Once he got back under the bank, but luck was with me and I took him away from that dangerous place. Then he went downstream, and I followed, not wishing to pay out line in the gathering darkness. I kept him as close to me as I could. I wondered if my little net would hold him and looked for a sand beach where I might land him. There was none. It must be the net or nothing. I worked him in front of me and then let him drift down toward me. The first sweep of the net did the trick, and I lifted him out of the water.

Curled up in the net, his nose and tail just barely missed touching the rim. No more fishing now. Occasional "kerplunks" told me the fish were still feeding, but the day was over. The Brule had been more than kind to me, and I was anxious to show the Other Fellow what had been lying in that corner.

I found him above me, at a place where the river makes a little island, and in the weak light I held up my big trout. It didn't have to be very light to see that fellow. He was big enough to loom in the most meager light. The fish measured about 20 inches, perhaps a little more. He was a dark-hued brown, and may have weighed from two to two and a quarter pounds.

"There, mister," said I, "is the fish I told you was in that corner. And you passed him up for a couple of little ones. You'll listen to me next time."

"Gosh, that is a nice fish," he replied.

"He'll go a half-pound — easy!"

DOWN WENT McGINTY

You have here the start of another MacQuarrie trait. He befriends things. Here the tattered little fly he finds, the McGinty, performs for him in such a giant fashion, that he befriends it, sings songs about it, terms it "a fighting fool." Mr. President (he isn't that yet but is getting there) puts it down to "The Luck of the Irish." In goes McGinty to the hallowed felt pads of his fly book among the other "aristocrats." McGinty will be a pal to the end.

Remember the spruce trees?

I found it firmly stuck in a bushy branch — that warrior McGinty fly — after I had waded precariously through the deep hole over which the branch drooped. It wasn't my McGinty until that moment. My own fly had fastened to the same branch and when twitches failed to loosen it I hitched up my canvas jacket to protect the camera in its pocket, and, like an old lady crossing a muddy street on a rainy day, made my way slowly through the pool.

The pool, ordinarily, is not to be waded, but the Brule was low and I barely made it, with only a trickle slipping over the wader top and darting down my leg to prove once more how cold the stream can be. It was getting late even then and I groped to locate my marooned Coachman. My hand felt a fly and I twisted it out of the bark. It was Mr. McGinty himself — yellow vest, black waistcoat, red socks and all. I retrieved the Coachman, made a retreat out of the pool, and sent forth grateful acknowledgement to Chief Winnebojou and the aboriginal headmen of Wisconsin who are supposed to look after things on the Brule.

"If this," I ruminated, "isn't a sign from above, nothing is."

Three hours before I had donated my last McGinty to the gentleman I was fishing with, and from all indications he was using it with wonderful results. He had offered to give it back when he creeled his fourth rainbow and I was still tying and untying Turle knots on flies they wouldn't even smell. I had made some foolish remark about "that bee never catching anything anyway," and I didn't want to back water.

It had been a remorselessly hot day. The Piscatorial Prevaricator and I had chosen the afternoon to penetrate a relentless jungle in quest of favored waters. Sopping with perspiration we had plunged into the river where the regrettable transaction took place. He had set off upstream with it, fishing it wet and I followed, one hundred yards behind, using dry flies, wet flies, and Republican flies, which are neither wet nor dry, but only get a little damp and dry out in the first good breeze.

When I passed him, upward bound myself, he reported the McGinty's record.

"I'd give it back in a minute if you wanted it," he said.

"Oh, keep it, that's all right," I replied. "They must be taking something else."

"Sure, they must be, they must be," he came back, rather hurriedly, I thought, and added, "They're taking it if I can get it down far enough to 'em. Can't whip it much but gotta let it soak and get good and wet. Then they hit it. It's tied right for a deep wet fly, too — not too much hackle on it. Just like the McGinty in the old song — you know, 'Down went McGinty to the bottom of the sea.'"

He actually attempted to hum a few bars of the song and there I left him, the ingrate, and it was not until the McGinty of the pool came in to my life that I felt the slightest flicker of that hope which stirs honest fishermen to further crusades.

As I was saying, it was growing darker. If I were to come in that night with anything I had to set to work right away and the fading light discouraged more tying and untying. It was Mr. McGinty or nothing. He had to go down and come up with something if his latest owner hoped to overcome, with fishy spoil, the taunting thrusts of his companion. I thought of Casey at the bat, not forgetting his woeful failure, but McGinty came through in such a way as to more than wipe out the blot against the immortal Casey. It seems a fact that what one Irishman can't do, another one will, and between them they can do almost anything.

Now for the fishing. The Brule at evening. Mellowed, waning light pouring down through the pines, revealing the stream with a gentle gray delineation like a perfectly exposed photographic negative. A persistent fiddling of crickets. Here and there an early firefly with his lantern aglow. A white-throat saying the same old thing over again, and the river itself, musing thoughtfully under the deep banks and purling quietly in the swifter places. The magic dusk seems to lay a hand on the impulsive current, as though to stay it, for a moment, in its short but tumultuous journey to Lake Superior.

It had to be downstream fishing from then on. The homeward route lay that way, and I was compelled to take it, although I would have preferred to proceed farther upstream and work Mr. McGinty like a dry fly, letting him drift down to me. But I had to make the best of things.

Mr. McGinty — I think he was a No. 10 — sailed out over a little pool, one of those baby pools where the stream nudges the bank coyly, and only hesitates before continuing on to linger for a real caress in a deeper, stiller pool. On the Brule there are "holes," which are not so idyllic but just as descriptive. Mr. McGinty, with characteristic Irish stubbornness, fastened himself in an overhanging branch, but a slight movement released him and he fell into the water with a little splash. I had soaked him well and he floated for hardly an instant before making his dive to the bottom, or thereabouts.

I tell everyone who asks — and many who don't — that the trout that went after McGinty was eighteen inches long. He struck like twenty-four inches and Mr. McGinty hit right back, a sock in the teeth that fastened the brook trout for good. He put up a noble contest. Mr. McGinty hung on, through thick and thin, fast water and dead water, but it was a lot darker when I finally slid the net under his beaten victim. An eighteen-inch brook trout —

is there any fish so beautiful, so symmetric, so perfect in all respects? All honor to the browns and the hell-for-leather rainbows, but the native American trout in his own bailiwick is the most gallant and lovely of fishes. Once on a time, the Brule, like the Nipigon, was the home of — but I must omit the raptures.

About the native trout. The next morning I showed him to a fisherman. Cold and bright he was as I seized him from the refrigerator and held him up.

"Guess he'll go eighteen, eh?" I remarked.

The fisherman looked me straight in the eye and declared:

"Hell, he'll go twenty-two if he's an inch."

Gentlemen, there is the true manifestation of all that is praiseworthy in an angler. That trout would have done well to pass sixteen inches!

In the interim between the first round and the next I hurriedly applied restoratives to Mr. McGinty. I brushed back his bedraggled wings. I rubbed his stomach. I let him rub his shoes in the rosin and whispered to him to work the old left hook. At the bell he was tired but dead game.

Nothing happened right away and I worked along rather fast for it was getting darker. There is a pool, a real pool, at this place, that fishermen call Rainbow Bend. It is deep and slow, with a slight surface ruffle in the center from the shaft of current flowing into it.

McGinty, the embattled personification of some fly-tier's dream, landed at the head of the pool and there was enough slack in the line to let him reel groggily into the deeper water. The trout waiting for him must have thought he was punch drunk and ready for the haymaker, but McGinty came to life, and the counter punch he hung on that trout's jaw hooked the trout securely. The fish rallied, however, for he was as tough as McGinty and for the next five minutes he made me think I had hooked a big rainbow that had forgotten to return to the lake after the spring spawn.

He did not break water, but many big rainbows sometimes go the entire route without coming to the top, although it is usual for them to leap. Even the little dandiprats, four or five inches long, will leap like dolphins — only a lot faster and fiercer.

McGinty was compelled to do a lot of infighting in the second tussle, for the trout eventually got back into his own corner and for a few minutes he had the leader wrapped around something on the bottom. I waited to see if he would free himself, but finally risked everything on one jerk. McGinty remained with me and once more I had the trout out in open water and much more tired.

Once in the net I found him to be another native, and practically the same size as the first! I doubt if there was a difference of $1/2$-inch in their length, and their weight was about the same. But poor McGinty — ah, McGinty, what they had done to you that evening! While he may have won both his fights by knockouts he looked anything but the smartly-colored little fellow that had pricked my finger as I groped for my own fly on the over-hanging branch. His feathers were torn and tattered, his dashing vestments reduced to mere silk ravelings and his red tail was completely gone! The price of victory as ever, had been dear to McGinty on the Brule that evening. The path of glory was leading to the grave, no doubt about that, but McGinty still bore a resemblance to a trout fly and I sent him back to the wars.

I was traveling rapidly downstream by that time, in order to overtake the ichthyological ingrate of my angling days, and the trout that saw McGinty reeling his way, a battered nondescript, without well defined mark or manner, tossed hurriedly into this pool and yanked summarily out of that pool, probably laughed at such artlessness. But McGinty, whose water-soaked togs were carrying him deeper and deeper, still had a scrap left in him, although he could not have been fighting under his true colors. He didn't have any more colors. I found out the old spirit was still there at the foot of a long series of rapids through which I had hastened. McGinty was sent forth into the tail of the last rapid and was joined in battle with lightning speed by a rainbow. No doubt about what kind of a trout he was. No feinting or clever footwork about that fellow. He simply struck and ducked, and as he did McGinty let go with the old left hook and his first punch was the beginning of the end. The rainbow proceeded to show me he was a match for any upstart Irishman and he writhed out of the water several times with McGinty hanging to him. It is not hard to envision him now, heaving skyward with nose straight up and body writhing. It was a sore test for McGinty, after the other two battles, but he was equal to the task. The rainbow was a pretty fish, somewhat shorter than the natives, but, perhaps, a trifle heavier.

But McGinty — poor McGinty.

What was left of his wings looked like water-soaked cobwebs. I lit a match to inspect the complete damage and found the hook even slightly bent outward. There had been a brave neck of hackle at the beginning. That was gone, or so confused with the remnants of wings as to be just the same as gone, and the body was worn and torn through so as to reveal the slender shank of the hook.

McGinty I carefully laid away between two felts to dry out and rest from his labors. He was in aristocratic company in the lid of that box, for many another fly had I wet or oiled before McGinty turned the tide. Handsome bivisibles, aristocratic fan-winged Coachmen, a glorified Parmacheene Belle, and a host of other plutocrats looked fine in the glow of the match, but none so belligerently fine as McGinty as I reverently stuck him into the felt pad and snapped the cover shut.

Waiting at the car was the other fellow. He had seven, all good fish, all caught on my McGinty — but none so large as my three.

"You can have four of 'em," he proffered.

His conscience was bothering him.

"What?" I cried. "Take another man's fish from him? I wouldn't do that any more than I'd take his last fly!"

Then I showed him my three and told him the story of McGinty's last stand.

"That's it," he declared. "Mine were all caught on the McGinty and you had to send it down to get results."

"I apologize for what I said about McGinty." I said. "He's a fightin' fool and deserves a lot of credit."

"It's the luck of the Irish," he replied. "It was simply McGinty's day to go down and he went down with a vengeance. Down went McGinty and up came Mr. Trout."

He was humming that as we backed out of the parking place and straightened away for home.

Ducks? You Bat You!

This is the start of the adventure. It is MacQuarrie's first duck hunt. And by now he has invented Mr. President and the Old Duck Hunters' Association, Inc.

What tales there are to be told! Humor, frolic, friendship, in all manner of expression of the outdoors. And appreciation. Deep appreciation of the color, the excitement, the thrill of ducks at dawn and deer and leaping trout and the look and the feel of a stream. All to brighten our lives.

Years ago, I wrote an introduction to "Ducks? You Bat You!" and said, possibly carried away with my youth and my zest for MacQuarrie's yarns, that they "come to grips with life; what to get out of it, and what it means."

Now, after many years do I still think these simple tales of trout fishing and duck shooting hold within them the meaning of life?

You Bat You!

Tonight is the end of summer. A needle-fine rain is pelting the shingles. Autos swish by on wet concrete. Until now summer has been in full command. This full, cold rain is the first harbinger of autumn.

Maybe the cold rain started me off. A flood of recollections of my first duck-hunting trip crowds everything else from my mind. Just such a rain — only colder — was falling from northern Wisconsin skies that night in late October, many years ago, when the President of the Old Duck Hunters' Association, Inc., rapped at my door.

It was an impatient rap. I found him standing in the hall, quizzical, eager, in his old brown mackinaw that later was to become his badge of office. As always, only a top button of the mackinaw was fastened. His brown felt hat dripped rain. Below the sagging corners of the mackinaw were high tan rubber boots. He danced a brief jig, partly to shake off the rain and partly to celebrate an impending duck hunt.

"Hurry up!" he said.

"Where?"

"You're going duck hunting."

That was news. I had never been duck hunting. Not once in a varied life devoted to fishing and hunting had I ever hunted ducks. For some reason, ducks had not appealed to me. They had been just something that flew over a lake where I was fishing late in the year. I didn't know it then, but I was much like a person who has grown to maturity without having read *Robinson Crusoe*.

"Shut the door!" a voice cried from within my house.

It was my wife, the daughter of the President, the only person who awes Mr. President. He shuffled through the door with alacrity and took a tongue-lashing for sprinkling water on the floor.

"Who's going duck hunting?" demanded the lady, adding, "And who says who can go duck hunting? Isn't it enough that he spends all his idle moments fishing?"

"It's like this," began Hizzoner. "I told him last summer that now, since he was more or less one of the family, I ought to take him duck hunting. He's been at our house eating ducks and currant jam for years. Why shouldn't he contribute to the — er — groaning board?"

"I see," said the daughter of the President cannily. "You want someone to row the boat."

"I do not!" he replied indignantly. "I even borrowed a gun for him."

"You'll find he won't row. He won't even put up curtain rods. He looks like a dead loss for both of us."

"I'll take a chance on him."

From a closet she helped me resurrect heavy clothing, including an old sheepskin coat. When I was ready, the President advised his only heir that he would return the body safely some time the next evening. It was then about

8 PM. The lady whom I had wed only some four months previously sat down resignedly with a magazine. Her parting injunction was: "Mallards. Get some mallards."

A loaded car was at the cub. Wedged in a corner of the back seat beside a duffle and a crate of live duck decoys was a huge figure that answered to the name of Fred. Later I was to learn that better duck shots have seldom displayed their wares on any of our local waters.

Down sandy highway No. 35 with the rain streaking the windshield, off to the right at the store in Burnett County, over the humpbacked hills, then into a yard beyond which a light from a house gleamed among huge oak trees. As we drove up, a floodlight came on, as though someone within the house had been waiting for us.

It was Norm. Always there is a Norm for duck hunters who really mean it, some vigilant sentinel of the marshes who phones to say, "The flight is in." Norm was apprehensive. As we stored things in our allotted cabin we did not have to be reminded by him that it was growing colder. The rain was abating, and a northwest wind was rocking the oaks. "Little Bass may be frozen over," said Norm. "You should have come when I first phoned, two days ago. The temperature has fallen from 55 to 40 since sunset."

We occupied the cabin. There were two full-sized beds. Norm built up a roaring jack-pine fire in the little air-tight stove. There was much palaver along instructional lines for my benefit. Later my two benefactors prepared for bed.

"We'll give you the single bed," said the President magnanimously. "Fred and I are used to sleeping together. We'll put this extra blanket between the beds. Whoever gets cold and needs it can just reach over for it. Goodnight."

In five minutes they were asleep. Outside the wind rose. Even before I fell asleep, only half-warm, I contemplated the probability of grabbing that blanket. Later I woke. I was somewhat congealed. I reached for the blanket. It was gone. I tried to fall asleep without it, but the cold was steadily growing worse.

Teeth chattering, I got up, lit a kerosene lamp and discovered the blanket carefully tucked around the two sleeping forms in the other bed. Sound asleep and snoring gently lay my two kind old friends. I wouldn't for the world snake that blanket off their aging bones. Not me!

I piled all available clothing on top of my own thin blanket and tried again to sleep. At times I almost succeeded, but it was along toward 3:30 AM when I got up, lit a fire in the stove and thawed out. Then I dozed in an old rocking chair, to be awakened soon by a loud thumping on the single wall of the cabin.

It was Norm delivering his summons to his hunters. I turned up the wick on the lamp. The President and Fred awakened languorously. The President sat upright, threw his legs over the edge of the bed and studied the top of the table where the blanket had rested.

"Just looking for scratches in the varnish," he said. "Dreamed last night I heard someone reaching for that blanket. Wasn't you, was it? Surely a young man with your abounding vitality wouldn't be needing an extra blanket?"

"Why, we've got the blanket ourselves," chimed in Fred. "Now isn't that funny? Do you know, I had a dream too. Dreamed I was cold in the night and got up and took the derned blanket."

Since then I have learned to get that extra blanket in a hurry.

In Norm's kitchen there was a beaming platter of eggs and bacon. When it was empty, the platter was refilled with sour-cream pancakes, such as people often talk about but seldom can get. And after that a big white coffee pot was passed around as the Old Duck Hunters' Inc., washed down layer after layer of toast.

Outside it was bitter cold. The first real arctic blast had helped to dry the sand roads. Where it did not dry them the cold froze them, so that the car lurched and bumped along the ruts. There was the faintest hint of dawn as the car turned through a cornfield, plunged over rough ground a hundred yards and came to a stop near the base of a long point thrusting into the middle of a narrow, shallow lake.

This point on Little Bass Lake was — and still is — one of the most sought-after ducking points in northwest Wisconsin. Situated north of Big Yellow, this shallow lake with its swampy shores is a natural haven for ducks escaping bombardment on the bigger lake.

From a nearby patch of scrub-oak the President hauled at something until, in the faint light, I saw he had hold of a duck boat. I helped him drag it to the water. He paddled off through thin ice inshore to spread the decoys in open water. While he was busy at this morning ritual, the searing slash of duck wings came down to us a half-dozen times. Fred called to him to hurry, but no one hurries the President when he is making a set.

Finally he came ashore and occupied the small scrub-oak blind alongside mine. Even then he was not content to sit and wait, as was Fred in the nearby blind, but counted over and over again the wooden decoys. And was dissatisfied when he had thirty-two. "Anyone knows you've got to have an uneven number. Why, thirteen is better than any even number!" he chafed.

I just sat. Said I to myself, "So this is duck hunting." Just sit and wait.

Then there was a searing roar in back of us. I was about to raise my head to see what it was, but the mittened hand of Mr. President seized my shoulder and pulled me down to the sand floor of the blind. He himself seemed to be groveling in the sand, and from the nearby cover where Fred skulked I heard him stage-whisper: "Don't move. They're flying in back to look us over."

Twice again the sound of many wings cleaving the frosty air was borne down to us. At no time did I dare look up. The sound faded, disappeared entirely, the swelled again, louder and louder. When it seemed it could grow no louder, it changed to a hissing diminuendo. That sound was my first introduction to the music of stiff, set wings on a long glide down.

"Now!" Maybe it was Fred who said it, maybe it was Mr. President.

Before I had thrust my head over the parapet of scrub-oak Fred's 32-inch double had sounded and the President, who shot a pump in those days, had fired once and was grunting and straining to operate the action for the next shot. He had to catch that old corn-sheller of his just right to make it throw the empty out and a new shell in. Always, whether it worked smoothly or not, the President gave off a groaning, whining sound between shots, like an angry terrier held back from a square meal. He got off three shots before I could make out a low-flying squad of dark objects high-tailing across the lake.

"Bluebills," said the President.

On the open water beyond the rushes and in the quieter water on the very thin ice were five objects. I dragged the duck boat from its thicket and retrieved them. One of them had green on its wings. "What the — ?" said Fred. "Look, Al! One greenwing among those bluebills."

So this was duck hunting. Well, not bad. Not bad at all. Indeed not!

The sounds of swift wings and booming guns were good sounds. The smell of burned powder was a good smell. The feel of those birds, warm in a bare hand, was a good feeling. My toes had been cold; now they were tingling. I knew those five ducks would go best with wild rice and currant jelly. They made a nice little pile at our feet in the blind.

After a while Gus Blomberg, who owned the point and lived in a house five hundred yards back of us, came down through the oaks to see what was going on. He took a chew of snuff and said: "Halloo-o-o! How iss it, eh? Nice docks, you bat you!"

Great guy, Gus. Fred gave him a dollar. That was for the use of his point. Gus said "Tenk you," and also, "How 'bout leetle coffee at noon, eh? Goes good cold day. You bat you!"

Gus went away. The President stood up occasionally and beat his mitts together to warm his fingers. Fred just sat. He had enough fat to keep him warm. I never saw him wear gloves in a blind, even on frightfully cold December mornings. All Fred wore was his old shooting jacket and a cigarette. He could keep his cigarette lit in a cloudburst.

Other ducks came in. Some went on, and some stayed. After a while it occurred to me that I might try a shot at a duck myself.

"Haven't you had your gun here all this time?" asked the President. And he meant it; he had been too busy to think of anything but that early-morning flight. He took me back to the car and unearthed a short-barreled hammer-lock, the fore piece of which was held firm by close-wrapped wire.

"It's the best I could find around the neighborhood," he said. "The choke has been sawed off. Don't shoot at anything unless it's on top of you."

So I had a gun. This duck-hunting business was getting better and better.

Back in the blind, Fred had a couple more down. A flock of four bluebills came in. They were trusting souls. They neither circled nor hesitated.

They came spang in, from straight out in front, low. They set their wings. I picked out one and fired — both barrels. One fell at the second shot.

My first duck! Lying out there on the thin ice, white breast up, dead as a door-nail. The President and Fred had declined to shoot. They were furthering the education of a novice. They were, in fact, letting the duck-hunting virus take full effect. They laughed at me and pounded me on the back and kidded me, and all day after that they seemed to get an awful kick out of just looking at me and ginning.

About noon it began to snow. The wind fell off. The decoys froze in tightly. Fred stirred and said, "Coffee!" Hizzoner explained to me that it was necessary to pull in the blocks before leaving the blind. I was glad for the exercise. After coffee and some of the other things had been duly consumed, we returned to the blind, Fred to his motionless waiting. Hizzoner to his quick, bird-like neck craning.

The President usually saw the ducks first and signaled Fred. It did not perturb Fred much. The only sign of excitement from him was a gradual drawing-in of his neck, turtle-like. Then he would stamp out the last quarter-inch of his cigarette and wait. At the crucial moment he didn't stand to fire; he just straightened out his legs and sort of rared up. He was by far the best duck shot I have ever seen.

Maybe I killed another duck; I am not sure. From then on I shot with the others. They had let me have my chance. I had killed a duck. It had been an easy shot. They knew that. So did I. But they did not speak of it. They just kept grinning, for they must have known I had been ordained to love the game and they were glad to help a natural destiny work itself out.

They grinned when I threw myself into the small chores that beset the duck hunter. Dragging the duck boat from the thicket for a pick-up, cutting new boughs for the blind, walking around the sedgy shore of Little Bass to pick up a cripple that had drifted over, driving back for a package of cigarettes for Fred.

To all these tasks I set myself eagerly. They came as part of the game. Those two rascals had frozen me the night before; but they had introduced me to something new and something good, and I was grateful.

Since then, while hunting with these two I have felt this obligation to do my part. Both are many years older than I, and they have appreciated it, but, of course, never mentioned it. They would prefer to guy me with mild rebuke, criticize my shooting and otherwise continue the good work already well begun.

Of such stuff are the recollections of that first ducking trip. Diverse images, grateful peeks back at two wise and capable practitioners of what has become for me the most dramatic thing in outdoor sports.

The outdoors holds many things of keen delight. A deer flashing across a burn, a squirrel corkscrewing up a tree trunk, a sharptail throbbing up from the stubble — all these have their place in my scheme of things. But the magic visitation of ducks from the sky to a set of bobbing blocks holds more of beauty and heart-pounding thrill than I have ever experienced afield with rod or gun. Not even the sure, hard pluck of a hard-to-fool brown trout, or the lurching smash of a river smallmouth has stirred me as has the circling caution of ducks coming to decoys.

The afternoon wore on. Shortly before quitting time Gus came back, to stand with Fred for a chance at a few mallards. He took a brace and was satisfied. Mr. President said he thought he'd take a walk around the north end of Little Bass "just for the fun of it." Gus said he might find a mallard or two if there was open water, "but you got to sneak opp on dem. You bat!"

"You bat you, too, Gus," said the President. He buttoned the second button on the brown mackinaw and headed into the swirling flakes.

Fred lit a cigarette. We waited. Collars and mittens were now soggy with snow water. Fred's magic cigarette somehow managed to stay lit and in the waning light glowed more brightly. From the north end of the lake came four reports, muffled by the distance and the snow.

"Ay hope iss dem mollard," said Gus. "Al, he like dem mollard, you bat you!"

We were picked up and packed up when the President returned. The President had two mallards, of course. He dropped them in the car trunk with the other birds and unbuttoned the top button of the old brown mackinaw. We stood in the snow and said good-by to Gus. Added to his brace of birds were three more that Fred gave him. He turned and walked away through the rasping corn-stalks with a final, "You bat you!"

The President addressed me: "How'd you like it?"

In those days I was very young. It took me a long time to try to say what I felt. I have never succeeded yet, I simply babbled.

We drove out of the cornfield, stopped to yell good-by to Norm, who came out to his back door to wave, and then headed for the main highway. I drove. Fred reposed in the back, comfortable as the clucking ducks against whose crate he leaned. At my side sat the President. The light from the cowl partly illuminated his strong, sharp features.

Finally I said: "Wish you had let me in on this earlier in the season. There won't be another duck weekend after today."

The President flicked cigar ashes and replied: "I thought of that, but decided to break it to you gently. Too much of a good thing is bad for a growing boy."

When the White-Throats Sing

Most of MacQuarrie's titles are home runs. This one softens my heart. Imagine two grown men, eager to get to their fishing, taking delight in hearing a song sparrow sing. "Old Sam Peabody, Peabody, Peabody." (So my bird book describes the song.) Mr. President squeezing his son-in-law's arm every time the sparrow's notes rise above the roar of the Brule. If that isn't touching, or what!

Enter another of MacQuarrie glad tidings. I have called it "the sweet savoring of life." I cannot improve on that. Enjoying each moment and all things in it. It isn't a theme MacQuarrie invented. It runs through all the world's great religions, after all. But you don't expect to find it so gloriously portrayed in a common old outdoor magazine. Yet, there it is. And there will be more to come!

"Mebbe," said the President of the Old Duck Hunters' Association, "I am all wrong, but I think I'm right!"

We had been sitting in front of his place of business, arguing about when trout hit best. To climax an hour or more of wrangling he had said, "They do best for me when the white-throats sing."

I asked why.

"Because that's when I think they'll hit."

There is nothing to be done about a man like that. Though heavily freighted with the science of trout, he will toss it out the window to play a hunch.

Homeward-bound, I had come by his business place and spied him in a new car in the showroom. I was intent on the brisk walk ahead, and my mind was made up. I would just hike along smartly and be gone with a wave of the hand.

I saw his brown eyes following me. I tried to get by, but he let out a "Hey!" that went right through the showroom windows. And there I was in the car beside him, meek as any house dog.

The conversation went through wet flies, dry flies, soft rod, stiff rod, early season, late season — right down to the strange rainbow run up north Wisconsin's Brule, of which so little is known. I had done most of the talking when the palaver was confined to, shall we say, theory. Only along toward the meatier portions of the conference did he speak up. Then, flicking cigar ashes, he had announced: "They'll hit when the white-throats sing."

"I must be getting on," I said.

"Just sit there and wait," he said. "I'll be leaving for home pretty soon."

I sat, even though "pretty soon" to the President of the Old Duck Hunters may be in the next five minutes or next January. His knack for getting people to wait for him amounts to genius.

It was well-nigh two hours after the legal time of 6 PM. when we drove to my door. Two hours devoted to rambling and heated discourse on trout.

He called for me the next mid-afternoon, and we headed for the river that strikes down from Douglas County, Wisconsin, to Lake Superior.

It was one of those May days. It might have snowed. But it was 75 above. Lilacs were in blossom. The sky was blue and bland. The air reeked with earth smells.

Mister President wheeled through Lake Nebagamon and east along the county trunk. Thence across the iron bridge over the Brule to the trivial, barely visible road that bears north — past a logs-on-end house. Down this road he let the car nose its own way in the ruts, not even getting out to chop away down-stuff, but just driving through with many a crunch of limbs against metal. The farther you go on this road the closer the brush crowds it.

There is a little turn-around at the end of this road. If you cramp the wheels sharply enough, you can swing around and face out — a great help after dark. There is also a rough board table handy for leaning a rod against. And, best of all, there is at this place a grand dull roar, caused by the Brule running downhill through boulders. A fisherman would know what it meant the first time.

Men who know me will tell you that I am inclined to reckless haste in any campaign on this stream. They will tell you that I practically fall apart spiritually once I am within earshot of the Brule. And that I have been known to go to it so recklessly as to step into it without remembering that I took off my trousers — but forgot to put on waders.

It is so. I irked Mister President with my unseemly haste, for he sat and declared: "Look here. When I come to fish the Brule above the stone dam, I do not wish to be waited on by a committee for the local drive. I do not wish anyone to try and sell me anything. I do not want to buy a set of the Encyclopedia Universillia, or a patent can opener, or a new kind of potato peeler. I will not be driven to this river like a mule. Nor will I leap into it like a damn bullfrog!"

Deliberately he drew on waders. Deliberately he strung up the rod with the 16-inch cork grip — an invention long neglected by rod makers. He forced me to sit while he checked pockets for the sinews of war, turned the key in the car and finally announced, "Now!"

Even then he did not plunge headlong down the steep path. He stood and listened where the path dipped sharply. At first, all I heard was the keener roar of the river. Then he squeezed my arm, and above the roar of the river I heard it! Somewhere down in that trough a white-throat sang. He must have been a way downstream, but it is hard to say. It was the sad, brave salute of the wilderness sparrow for the place on earth he loved the best. It rose at intervals from the deep valley. Some parts of it would be lost in the singing river, and some parts of it would rise triumphantly in the air and come strongly to our ears.

"Ain't he a guy?" said Mister President, chuckling.

Mere words cannot make that picture live again. Nor can words duplicate the sounds, the smells, the very tastes of the Brule valley in May.

Each time the bird sang, Mister President would squeeze my arm. Then, if ever, I saw deep into this old and good man, Mister President, so keenly tuned to the real life about him.

"The little beggar," he said softly. "Once I kept one in my back yard for a week with bread crumbs and seeds. Thought he'd stay and build a home. Not him! Never yet was a white-throat didn't know a trout stream was the best place on earth to live."

The Old Duck Hunters parted there. I was a long time pondering the music, thinking of those who said he sang *"Poor Canada . . . Canada . . . Canada."* And of those who said he was really saying *"Peabody . . . Peabody . . . Peabody."* So do men fight to claim this mite of feathers for their own, and why not? Music like his has never been matched for simple beauty.

I wet my waders in the Brule. Many times have the Old Duck Hunters come to this place. You might say that such places never change, that the same old boulders and turns and banks are everlasting in one man's life. It is a lie to say that. Such places change as much as friends, as much as hunting dogs, as much as sunsets, or as much as spring, which is never quite the same, praise be.

This is good water. The hasty man does not know it well. He does not know of the straight-north road from east of the Winnebojou bridge. The hasty man knows much of the Brule State Park camp just below this stretch — below the old stone dam. The hasty man has no business on a trout stream, anyway; so why fret about him?

Once I knew a man beset with business cares who came to the little turn-around at the end of this road and camped for three months in a trailer. He was as happy a man as I ever knew. He caught up with himself there.

He had a danged old five-dollar rod that I borrowed once. He had his trailer backed under a tall pine. He had a nervous breakdown when he arrived in the spring, and he had the color and zest of a wild Indian when he left in September.

Old Doc Brule cured him. He went to sleep to the river's lullaby and woke up to the song of its birds. He built himself back by slogging up and down the Brule's rocky backbone. He caught and ate more trout than mortal man is entitled to these days. He looks back to it today as his second boyhood.

Letting myself down that watery stairway, I thought of him. Of how lucky he had been to find this place. Of the danged old rod he owned which drove me to distraction that day I broke mine. Of the books he had read in that pine-shaded trailer and how, every time I saw him, he was browner and tougher, and grinned wider and wider.

The river was in splendid order that afternoon. Within the week it had rained very hard, such a rain as would raise the average river to a terrific stage. The Brule was up about two inches; that was all. The Brule is never apoplectic. Down below the town of Brule it may run a bit red where rains sluice off clay banks. But never does it grow dirty up there above the stone dam — never. Where are streams like that this day?

My fly was a Jock Scott of trout proportions and salmon-fly construction, an item right difficult to get nowadays. The first fish it turned was a thoughtful brown which investigated but did not touch. It merely rose, bowed and vanished in the wings.

Very well. The afternoon was young. Two hours later that spotted gentleman would feel differently. There'd be a brash rainbow or brookie somewhere soon. Especially would there be a native if I could work that gaudy little soaker over into the right bank where there was a cool drip from the hillside and some rocks to hold the coolness before it oozed away in the current.

The cool spot fooled me. No native came forth, but rather a tough rainbow — ten inches of solid muscle, fighting in the current before his doorstep like a two-pounder. He was netted. There must be a local boy, a true native son of the Brule in that rocky cool spot. Must be . . .

A lucky first cast put the Scotsman close in against the edge of rocks, where the spring water dribbled down from the bank. The water was quiet there, and by virtue of a slack line the fly stood stock-still. "That fatal pause," the President has always called it when a fly lingers miraculously in slack water, though on the verge of swift water.

The brookie took it with the joyous abandon of his kind — an abandon which the Old Duck Hunters long ago agreed among themselves is one good reason for his scarcity. Let the men of trout look into this a bit. Warming water is indeed one answer. Gullibility is another, but you seldom hear it mentioned. My brookie was a bit bigger than the rainbow, a purplish fellow, but in no ways as darkly radiant as his cousins fifteen miles upstream that spend their days beneath the alders and feed principally on insects.

In the fast water of this part of the Brule there are some deep holes. They lie behind stubborn boulders. It is well to hug the shore while wading here. One wrong step, and the river just reaches up and takes a man in. Sometimes, before spitting him out, the Brule will fetch him along twenty or thirty feet, bumpily and abrasively. A friend of mine invariably refers to one good rip here as "the place where I swim the Brule every time I wade it."

Some of the elderly faithful will tackle this stretch only out of a canoe, such as might be piloted by those old Brule familiars: Carl Miller, Johnny Degerman, or John LaRock. Indeed, there are times when the stoutest wading men would prefer to be seated in the fore end of a canoe, knowing that their fate was in the hands of a stalwart abaft wielding a 12-foot spruce pole shod with steel.

Mister President, though long since qualified for such delightfully easy fishing, has always insisted upon working this stretch standing on his own two legs. He likes to come to terms with a river.

Back of one of those big boulders I met the inevitable. The river bottom betrayed me. Where I thought there had been solid bottom there was only water. The casual reader of this screed need not be perturbed. My fate was certain, but not serious. The river grabbed me by the seat of the pants, kicked me along about ten feet and sloshed me gently into the side of another boulder. I went ashore and peeled.

It was two hours to sunset. I built a fire, more smudge than flames, for the mosquitoes were moving. Although wet as a Labrador, I was quite warm. I have always felt flattered at being kicked around by a river as decent as this one. You have no idea how often I have been flattered!

When my clothes were half dry and thoroughly smoked, I put them on and went at it again. The magic hour was at hand. On the high bank of the Brule it was still full daylight, but down in the trough was the beginning of darkness. That is the time! That is the time when big old trout, thick through the shoulders, come cautiously out from beneath banks and brush tangles, and a man looks carefully to that part of his tackle extending from the line-leader knot to the knot that links fly to gut.

In this place the evening feeders will invariably be browns. I nailed one of a good pound and a half from a spot where I have taken a dozen like him. He was a pushover. I knew him as I knew his relatives, which I had eaten. He was ready to feed. It was darkening. Anything reasonably like trout feed would satisfy him. The Jock Scott, No. 6, was good enough. He took it and dived for his cave down under that bank. I horsed him out into midstream, where he was at a disadvantage, and then, by virtue of the stout leader rather than any boasted skill, I ran him ragged. I think he was finally glad to flop into my net. Anyway, I was glad!

There was another one, ten minutes later, which deceived me badly. He was of about the same vintage, a good Brule brown, called "lunker" in some waters. He too came forth willingly to battle and took the beaten Jock Scott so quickly that he was back under the snags and tying me up on a root before I knew what was happening.

Never mind. Losing one Jock Scott is part of an evening on the Brule. I have lost many more than one. I have come away from there so sorely beaten that I have seriously considered giving it all up. That I would be back the next night after work is, of course, understood by all men who love fly rods.

One night on this particular stretch of the Brule, with George Babb, the greatest trout-getter who ever arched a fly in my bailiwick, I had hold of a brown that swam into my vision like a muskalonge . . . But this is just getting on into a fisherman's conversation, which is a one-sided affair, with a fellow hanging on to another fellow's coat lapel and talking his head off.

There was not much time left. But there was still time to look down a straight, flat stretch of the Brule and see the final light of the sun make the water gray. There was still time to make out a snagged fly in a spruce, climb the tree and save the fly, for it was one of my scarce-as-hen's-teeth Jock Scotts.

And there was still time to mark the yearling doe as she froze — a statue on the bank at my right, befuddled, I think, by my immobility and the smell of citronella and oil of pennyroyal which drifted down to her. She held her ground even when I snorted, a trick for stopping deer which is done with the tongue against the roof of the mouth.

I worked down through the flat stretch, and at the end of it I found Mister President. I had expected to catch him a bit upstream. He was stretched out on top of the bank by the stone dam. The wind hits in there; so the mosquitoes had not scourged him. He was on his back, asleep, his rod at his side and his creel a few feet away.

I looked inside the creel. There wasn't a sign of a fish in it. From nearby came the regular rhythm of Mister President's snoring. The river, up and down stream, was a misty ribbon, losing itself in the night. And then, as I tiptoed so as not to waken him, there came from somewhere down around Rainbow Bend the song of eternal sweetness as a sleepy white-throat gave his final benediction to the day.

NATIVE SON

This is another new one to the MacQuarrie collection.

The words on my college degree say I attended Colgate University in upstate New York, majoring in English. What the authorities didn't know (and I wasn't about to tell them), was that Nick, my hunting partner, and I really majored in Grouse Hunting. We each got a Ph.D. in grouse hunting, rearranging our schedules so we could spend afternoons following "The Brown Birds," as we called them.

So I have a self-confessed weakness for the subjects of this story. And it's true what MacQuarrie says, you've got to concentrate one hundred percent waiting for that explosive take-off that chills the blood. Don't point the gun. Don't think about anything. Don't worry about tree limbs, leaves, obstructions. Just get the lead in the air as fast as possible and hope for the best. Noble subject. Noble sport.

Things have come to a pretty pass when a man feels he must preface a piece on partridge with a description of the bird.

That is the way it is, thanks to that ubiquitous exotic, the ring-neck pheasant.

The partridge of the northern states, from New England west through parts of the Dakotas, is the forgotten man of the upland game birds. The experts call him *Bonasa unbellus*. Many call him ruffed grouse. And some of the old-timers call him just plain old pa'tridge.

He is the original brown bomber. He is the fan-tailed drummer who gets on a down log and beats his short wings in a kettle drum roll. He is the shawl-necked grouse, legs feathered like fur chaps. He is born and mates and lives and dies usually within an area a mile square. He is the gourmet's delight and the gunner's Nemesis.

He is as American as pumpkin pie and hickory smoked bacon.

It's partly the fault of the species. *Bonasa* goes through unexplained cycles of life and death. The men of wildlife research estimate the cycle of ups and downs may spread over eight to 11 years. They are not sure yet.

But they are pretty sure that when partridge are at their peak the best thing to do is go out and collect the crop. They hold that partridge headed for the toboggan chute of the cycle will recover faster from the die-off if they are heavily hunted. That is one of the newer creeds of modern game management. Get 'em when they're high up on the population graph, say the experts.

The trouble with Johnny Partridge is when he is good he is too good to be true. The present new crop of shotgun fans thinks of him as something Grampaw lies about. The present generation declines to fret about cycles when they can go not very far away and burn nitro in favor of those gorgeous pheasant cocks. The pheasant is expedient. The local boy — a true native son — is almost forgotten.

Johnny Partridge certainly is a bit farther away from the big towns. Certainly he is a bit harder to come at. But as a game bird he is to the pheasant as Joe Louis is to the preliminary boy.

The way to get at partridge is thus-wise:

Forget about dogs unless you are certain of some genius dog which has grown up with partridge. Put on the briar-proof pants and the far-going boots. Choose the shotgun with the fairly open bore. Take a course in gymnastics to harden up. Then drive north.

Thing to do is go north and ask questions. Inevitably the partridge man will be directed to the all-out partridge authority of the local community. This worthy will size up the interloper, nibble his fine cut speculatively, and then if the omens are good he may break down and tell all.

He may tell about the 500 miles of old logging grades and tote roads in Sawyer County, Wisconsin. All the lake states have 'em. Thousand of miles of these trails run through the cutover, remnants of Paul Bunyan days. Surprisingly, many of them are still wide open to passage by man. Some of them are still excellent auto roads.

Let not the man of the corn fields depend upon the full choke gun in the partridge woods. It is brush shooting, calling for something that throws a big, open pattern. Skeet bores are popular. The various patent, adjustable choke devices are gaining many friends. The tried and true double-bore with right barrel improved cylinder and left barrel modified is just about perfect for me. Any full choke barrel will spotter birds.

Brush loads are used, though they are erratic. These trick loads with dividing partitions in the shot end, just seem to throw pellets every which way. They haven't much more pattern than a calico cat. In the case of the beginner willing to tempt providence they may serve as well as anything.

Clothing is important. This is no place for the heavy woollens. Save them for the deer season. In 30 years of partridge hunting I have worn about everything, beginning the game with what came to hand. My partridge rig today is for going places. Boots are moccasin-built, 11 inches high, with one pair of soft wool socks. Trousers are the pliable khaki thornproof kind with elastic bottoms which are tucked into boots. Shirt is flannel if the day be cool, khaki cotton otherwise. Jacket is light with pockets galore. It just so happens I never saw a good partridge dog though I've seen dozens of dogs hunt partridge. For every good partridge dog there are a hundred good quail dogs.

The partridge asks quite a bit of a dog. He will not lie to a point like the bobwhite quail. He likes to get away from danger. Like the fast running pheasant, the partridge "will ruin a good bird dog." Silly, isn't it? But that's the way it is.

Things being as they are, by far the greater number of partridge hunters go about their chores without dogs. In lieu of a dog they try to keep themselves on constant edge for the nerve-shattering roar of the bird taking off.

No game bird in America takes the air with such thunder. The flushed bobwhite quail offers a mere whisper of drumming wings as compared to the partridge. The husky pheasant's getaway, while noisier than that of the quail, is far less nerve-racking than that of the partridge. The pheasant's get-away is a leathery flapping of wings. The partridge roars away.

Hunters flushing their first partridge have become so upset they fired both barrels into the air. The impact of those roaring wings is rather terrific on a jittery fellow. The short round wings of Johnny Partridge are definitely low-gear wings. He is always in low gear when flying — and his foot is always down to the floor board.

Way to hunt 'em is to proceed with the certain knowledge that sooner or later somebody will set off a firecracker 15 yards up front, during which you are supposed to spot the bird, plant both feet at the best angle, figure the swing and lead through the brush and touch off the trigger. Like the feller says, it ain't easy but it's fun.

The best of the oldsters of this game just prod along with their eyes fixed on nothing in particular, constantly thinking of partridge. That is really it — constantly thinking of partridge. And if there are any amateur photographers in the audience let them prepare to keep their eyes stopped down to about f/32 for depth of focus.

Hunting partridge is no time to admire the russet and bronze of autumn. Let that wait.

A guy who looks for partridge on the ground, in hope of busting him there, ought to be hung. It's dishonorable. These pot hunters go by the name of ground-swatters. Their niche in the sports picture is right beside the boy who kills deer at night with a jack light.

Watch a veteran partridge hunter and you'll see him constantly moving so as to keep dense brush and big trees out of a possible line of shot. He knows when to back up, to turn aside, and when to smash quickly through "dirty" stuff so as to get out of it and into the clear and ready for a shot. The very best of the partridge hunters often drop birds by shooting before the gun butt reaches their shoulder. It is just that nip and tuck.

That is one good reason for hunting partridge alone. The distractions of conversation hamper concentration. Far better to say farewell to a comrade and meet him for the noon sandwich at some appointed rendezvous. Going it alone a man can get down to business. Furthermore, when he swings and pulls he may do so without fear that an odd pellet or two will strike his partner. Twosomes in the partridge woods do poorly.

Partridge hunting is as good as detective story reading for a let-down. It demands a different kind of effort than bread and butter chores. It gets a man out.

Come late October when the leaves are heaping the curbs in the cities, it is a fine thing to toss gear into the car trunk and head for the shaggy haunt of br'er.

The man kneeling in autumn leaves dressing his first partridge should know that he is of the elect, that he has entered that Valhalla of sport where the best is hard to get, and the getting the best part of it.

Let him remove the craw of this glorious native son and smell it. Yes, smell it! Never yet has there been a partridge that was not a dainty feeder. Mostly the craw will contain seeds and leaves and gravel and more often than not it will be redolent with the odor of wintergreen and clover.

Only on the way back should a partridge hunter permit himself to let down.

Then, if he has hunted hard, if he has been licked a little bit, he is entitled to let the shaggy old woods take him in. Then, when the feet drag and he is thirsty and hungry, he may let Johnny Partridge catapult up ahead of him and make no move to level a barrel.

Let the man who is new to it pause a minute on a rise and see the blood red sun of Indian summer sink into the far hill. Let him, going down the next hill, stop again and bathe those feet in a cool creek. Let him reach round with a hand to the game pocket if he has been lucky and feel the weight of Johnny Partridge there, every ounce of him white meat, every feather of him as American as the spots on a brook trout.

CANVASBACK COMEBACK

"Character smelted and shaped by hard work, many worries and a dominant determination to be a decent human being." That says it all. That sums up Mr. President, and all of MacQuarrie's heroes in fact.

All MacQuarrie's writing is good stuff. Professional. Accurate. Researched down to fine detail. But when he had this old man in his sights, the writing was uplifted. It moved to a higher plane. Hence the lyric descriptions. The snorting good humor. The pranks and ripostes. All turned up a notch or two. Or maybe three.

All because of this man who was "determined to be a decent human being."

It was a bad night for driving north and west through Wisconsin. Beyond the windshield, through stabbing sleet and snow, the President of the Old Duck Hunters' Association waited. So I kept a-going.

Mister President would be draped before an open fire. He'd be wearing the worn gray carpet-slippers and the sweater vest with the bulged lower pockets where he stuck his thumbs. Outside the cedar-planked cabin the storm would be hammering while he dozed.

I was ninety miles from this happy rendezvous, tooling a car through a storm that was making seasonal history, and making Mister President's duck-hunter soul gladder by the minute. I should have known better than to delay the start-off. But at 6 PM it is too late to do anything about that sort of thing. The only possible course was to blast on through. The President was waiting up.

Near Loretta-Draper, Wisconsin, I stopped at Flambeau Louie Johnson's and in twenty minutes (a) consumed a warm meal, (b) heard once more of my shortcomings because I had failed to land that 40-pound muskie last summer, and (c) promised Edie Johnson on my honor I'd take it slow and easy up that fire-lane road. Those two good friends came to the door to look anxiously after me as the car surged up the bill into the storm, heading for Highway 70, the fire lane, Clam Lake, Cable, Drummond — and the Middle Eau Claire Lake of Bayfield County, where Hizzoner smoked and dozed and waited.

There was new warmth in me when I left. All of it was not from Edie Johnson's superfine Scandinavian coffee, either. It was an inward warmth engendered by the certain knowledge that two good people would have restrained me by force if they had thought they could get away with it. Truth is, I enjoyed that drive. Revived by food, I had just one thing in mind — the sudden flood of light on the little cabin stoop when Mister President swung open the door at the sound of my motor.

That trip had some fierce and splendid moments. The fire lane straight north from Loretta-Draper is no playground for a hard-road driver. It demands a man of the Model T vintage, inured to highway trickery and the feel in the seat of the pants that prevents skids. The fire lane, now open to all, penetrates the wildest country I know in Wisconsin. There are no houses by the wayside to fall back on. You push up in there and take your own chances.

I felt my way at a cautious 20 per. It grew colder. Thank heaven, I know that fire lane. I know where the quick, sharp turns lie in wait for the reckless driver, where the narrow little bridges are, and where a man has to take the snowy hills in a steady-pulling second gear to save himself from sliding backward into a ditch.

Big trees went down in that night's wind. Afterward the wildlife experts said the blow leveled enough white cedar to take care of north Wisconsin's overgrown deer herd through the ensuing winter. It was fun. I love storms and lonely roads.

Twice I got out and whaled away with an ax to clear the road. On the twisting north end of the fire lane, slogging toward Cable, speed was cut to 15 miles per hour. What if I was late? Wasn't the Old Man waiting? Wasn't this blast just what the doctor ordered?

The plot was bluebills, maybe canvasbacks! It had been a long time since the Old Duck Hunters had hung a bag of cans. The scene was to be the broad, shallow south end of the Middle Eau Claire Lake, which the natives call Libby Bay. The scenario had been written weeks in advance by Mister President, who is a genius at guessing what weather does to duck flights. He was to be there with the necessary equipment, and I was to drive in on him.

It required three hours to make Cable, a journey ordinarily achieved in half that time. The town was asleep in the storm. I didn't have the heart to wake up the McKinneys and demand more coffee. But the worst was over. The treacherous fire lane was behind me. The snow was deepening, but I was now on black-topped Highway 63. The road was strewn with limbs torn off and hurled willy-nilly. A few of them had to be thrown aside. Others I just drove around.

When I made the left turn to the west at Drummond, the snow was six inches deep and still coming. No more sleet now. Just snow. That kind of snow can't last in this country on that kind of wind. The wind was north and west, a cold-wave wind. A bad snow wind here would have to be from the northeast. It was very cold. I could feel the sharper air working through the car doors, and turned the heater up to full blast.

The roadside trees at my turn-in were carrying terrific burdens. The brittle jack-pines were hard hit, many of them broken and hundreds of them bent so badly by wet snow that they have never recovered, but continue to thrive in the tenacious way of the fire pine at odd, sharp angles.

I parked the car at the hilltop as a precaution against having to buck snow uphill later, grabbed a duffel bag and a shotgun and plowed toward the lighted windows. It was late: so there was no good reason why Hizzoner should be up. The anticipated challenge from the stoop was not realized, but as I came up the picture was still a proper one for a conclave of the Old Duck Hunters.

Through the door window I saw Hizzoner dozing in the big chair before the open fire — just as he should have been. Sure enough, he wore the old gray sweater vest and the worn gray slippers. The little crooked pipe had fallen from his hand and lay beside him on the floor. Flames from the fire threw shadows against the warm cedar walls and ceiling.

I stepped from icy cold into peaceful warmth, stamped my feet and heard the verdict as he leaped up: "I knew you'd be damfool enough to try it! Do you realize this is the worst November blow to hit this country since 1930?"

He fumed. Didn't I know that main highways were blocked with drifted snow and deadfalls? Didn't I know that by morning it would be as cold as a monkey in Iceland? Didn't I know that the thermometer was 20, and dropping?

"Your Honor," I pleaded, embracing his lean, hard shoulder, "shut up and pour me a cup of coffee."

He lost no time. Before I had gear assorted, the rich aroma filled the kitchen and the big living room. With the coffee was half a breast of duck and a batch of biscuits, the like of which Mister President can whip up while efficient lady cooks of this generation are pouring through a cookbook for a recipe.

The duck was a big fellow. The breast was big as a mallard's, but it was not a mallard.

"Canvasback," explained Mister President. "Straight from heaven knows where. They've been plumping into Libby Bay like they never have in ten years. Canvasback . . ." There was adulation in his voice, "Canvasback . . . I've been living on 'em since I came, four days ago. They slid in ahead of this blow. They've got Libby Bay plastered with floating celery they've dug up. They come to the bay in the morning, fill up and haul back to the quieter pot-holes. Canvasback . . ."

No finer tribute was ever paid the long-faced can than the gleam in Mister President's eye that late, stormy night.

He drove me to bed under the scarlet blankets. Then he asked, "You got enough shells for the both of us?" An old joke with him.

I said, "More'n enough," and barely caught his reply, "So you think," before drifting off as the wild wind screamed over the ridge pole.

The wind was still pouring it on when he switched on the light and held his little alarm clock a foot from my eyes. It read 4:30 AM.

"Get up, you pup," he said firmly.

The snow had stopped. He predicted the wind would blow itself out during the day, but that we would have a mighty fast ride before it to the point blind by the Hole in the Wall.

In the blowy dark we went down the hill. He uncovered the motor, and I shoved off. One turn brought a volley that drowned out the roar in the tossing pines. By instinct and habit he cut the boat sharp from the shore and headed with the wind toward Libby Bay.

He was indeed right. Never had I had such a surging ride to the duck point which we call the Hole in the Wall. The wind was in complete charge. The lake shore, speeding past, was a mere dark line of trees on the broad white beach where snow was drifting deeply. Without that wind to churn the waters and prevent a freeze-up, we never would have got away from shore. As it was, the whole lake was open.

In pitch-dark against the lee shore he drove the boat into a scattering of shore willows. It was automatic with me to crawl over the prow, pull the nose up farther and lay hands on gear.

Mister President pulled on trout waders deliberately. He is no man to become hurried when the time nears and excitement grows. He holds that "with a little sweet oil and diplomacy a man can skin a cat alive." Never in his mature life has he tossed a hurried set-up of boosters on the waters, then leaped into the blind to sit and hope. When he gets through, they are spread correctly.

He laid them in the formation which he has learned is best for the deep divers, a semi-horseshoe of decoys with the bulk of them at the toe of the shoe and a long lead line of decoys running straight out to form one long arm of the shoe, parallel to the direction of the wind. It was coming daylight when he had completed this careful rite. He joined me in the blind, pulled off the waders for more freedom and worked three shells into his automatic. As yet there was no light for seeing. We could make out the far shore of Libby Bay, but that was about all. We could hear the waves bickering in front of us and the pines moaning behind us. It was a fine morning.

Daylight was stubborn. It came tentatively over the far eastern shore of

Libby Bay. But it did not like what it saw. It hesitated, then grudgingly conceded itself a victim to the turning of the spheres, and Mister President said, "Look!"

He needn't have said it. I had been trying to decide if that black mass in midbay was ducks or jut some quirk of the eerie morning light on tossing water. It would be there, and it wouldn't be there. One minute it would be ducks. Then it would be gray light and gray waves.

"They'd rather stay in the pot-holes, but they can't resist that celery," he whispered.

All seasoned blindsmen whisper when they smell the smoke of battle. It was just habit with him, although the ducks couldn't have heard him if he had yelled through a megaphone.

The first shock troops rode over us from behind on the screaming wind. They were not seen until they had almost taken off our hats and were far beyond the decoys. No use in listening for wings on such a morning. It was eyes or nothing.

"They spent the night on the thoroughfare, and came straight from it, hungry as wolves," Mister President guessed.

Our Hole in the Wall is a 40-acre backset off Libby Bay proper, with one good blunt-nosed point. It is a fine place when the wind is right. This morning the wind was perfect — right at our backs.

The first fair targets came like fighter planes spang into the wind; blazing through the Hole in the Wall for quieter waters, which they can find hereabouts in hundreds of pot-holes and many rivers and creeks. The performance was instinctive with the Old Duck Hunters. He took his side, and I took mine, those low incomers on a 35-mile blast are not missed often. Not canvasback!

"Five," he remarked as they drifted off in the waves. "One for you and four for me."

I know full well that two of them were mine. But he insisted he nailed three with his first two shots, and then picked a crossing shot with his final shell. Who am I to quarrel with the leader of the Old Duck Hunters? All were canvasback, and mighty welcome visitors to these waters which their ancestors had used for thousands of years. Welcome indeed! Northern canvasback, broad in the bill and broad in the breast. Just the kind of canvasback a man should be collecting here so late in the season. The lake was completely ours. Not another hunter was around. The thermometer was around 10 above. Our blind protected us well, as do all late-season blinds fashioned by Hizzoner. He had even built a low wooden bench which was propped against the back wall. He sat there on the bench, a grand old patriarch in the storm. Beneath the rim of his shapeless brown hat there was white to match the snow in the dented hat crown. And in the furrowed collar of the old brown mackinaw there was more white, where the snow lit and stuck.

Sixty years old. And it was 10 above, with a wind . . . A drop stood on the end of his nose. A happy light gleamed in the sharp brown eyes. There was an alertness about him, as indicated by the quick right hand, ever ready to shake off the scuffed leather mitt.

Often have I looked at him in blinds such as this. From the smooth-bottomed rubber larrigans to the top of the ancient brown hat there was character. Character smelted and shaped by hard work, many worries and a dominant determination to be a decent human being.

He was aglow that morning; he was a part of the morning. I have seen him equally excited at the first arbutus on the chill forest floor of April. I have seen him so while fighting a good fish, still-hunting a buck, or planting a pine tree.

"The natives think the season is over," he gloated. "They think everything's gone through."

Hurtling flocks of bluebills tore loose from the rafted birds, and after the first few bunches had dusted across the decoys it was no longer necessary for the President to lay a warning hand on my knee. He was out for canvasback, to show me a come-back bag limit on a precious species which has made prodigious gains these past few years.

The big graybacks kept coming. In that kind of shooting a man can cultivate a careless rhythm to his swing. No need to stiffen. Almost every bird was centered. Such plenitude insures that most important conditioning factor of wing-shooting — relaxation.

At the noon hour Oscar fought across in his outboard from the far side of the bay to investigate the shooting at the Hole in the Wall. Oscar is a trapper of remarkable skill, a man who knows where otter play, yet refuses to trap them. He is a man who might some day stumble on to the last wolverine in Wisconsin. It would be a rare remnant of a species. He is fairly sure there is one of them in the wilderness of the nearby Totogatic country.

No duck hunter, Oscar. Rather is he a pack-sack and gum-boot man of the purest ray serene. He sat between us on the bench for an hour, ate a sandwich and munched an apple. Twice he borrowed the Old Man's automatic and took his share of the birds using his watery front yard for a restaurant.

When he departed in the afternoon, he hardly had to turn over the motor or touch the tiller, except to steer. Once beyond the quiet water inshore, his sturdy skiff was picked up and blown across the bay to his own far point.

"She'll die out by sundown," Mister President opined. "Can't blow longer. The wind is getting tired."

"I'd better walk around the shore and pick 'em up while there's still daylight," I suggested.

"The boat'll be easier — quicker."

But I wanted to stretch legs and set out, despite his warning that it would be a good four miles coming and going. Back among the shore pines and stripped of the heavy hunting jacket, I fought through six to eight inches of snow, concealed down-stuff and whipping brush.

First, the long way around the Hole in the Wall. Then up the sharp hill, panting, where I could look across water and down upon the lone, patient figure in the snowy blind. I went through the popple blow-down to the pine stand and the place where we drag up the boat to boil a dish of tea on good bass days. And so around through low tamarack country to the east side of Libby Bay. The waves had thrown every duck up on the beach. Some had been tossed on their backs by the waves, so that they stood out starkly.

They were a load. I was glad I had shed the heavy hunting jacket, and glad my boots had good treads on the bottoms, so that they gave me footing in the snow. An extra rawhide boot-lace saved the day. By tying the ducks together with it I could tote them with fair comfort.

As I came up in back of the blind, pretty tired, I saw the perfect finish. A single canvasback laced through the Hole in the Wall. The President waited until the duck was well over the land before firing, and then dropped it neatly far back of the blind, where I picked it up.

True to his prediction, the wind faltered at pick-up time. When we headed back, it was gusty, but the determined strength was out of the storm. The clouds were growing ragged. Before we made shore on the long run there were a few stars visible. A still, cold night coming up, he forecast.

The fireplace ashes were harboring coals. I brought them alive with birch bark and pine knots. Welcome heat surged through the big room. Mister President set the thermometer out on a jack-pine, and said it was crowding zero already. The stars were blazing and beautiful.

"How come," I said over the last cup of coffee, "you took a chance on that last bird? We might have had a limit already, you know."

"I counted 'em."

"But it might have been darned easy to count 'em wrong."

He was weary now. Five days of early rising were showing up on the peerless leader of the Old Duck Hunters. The reaction was setting in. Nodding a bit, he said: "I allus make allowances. A limit apiece — on canvasback."

"You sure hit it right. You shot half of 'em, and I shot half of em."

The warm room felt awfully good to him. He was almost asleep in the big chair, but declined to come full awake and challenge me. He just grinned, eyes half closed and said, "Oh sure . . . sure."

THAT RIVER . . . THE BRULE

Gordon MacQuarrie fished all over North America from "Anchorage to Key West," as he put it. Part of his job was to know and report on the conditions in all the streams of the Midwest. But it's hardly a secret the one stream he held as first among equals was the Brule. He returns to it again and again in his writing. Mr. President loved it as much as MacQuarrie and the river was never far from their thoughts.

This is another one that appears here in book form for the first time.

That river — that Brule — sweeping for 66 miles from the heart of Douglas County, Wisconsin to lake Superior. I've already said too much about it. Those who didn't know it before are finding it out. I must be cautious, but it is hard to even think of it without accompanying rhapsody. But maybe it's not a bad thing to fall in love with a river.

If this most famous of Wisconsin trout streams is to have a biographer I ask no better job than to be that biographer. Let's see, now. I've been fishing it for 25 years. Part of it's running through me most of the time, like a well-remembered old song. Its loveliness, its trout, its perfect wildness even though millions have gone into homes along its bank, constitute a modern-day miracle. Thirty miles from Superior-Duluth this ancient highway of the fur traders today is a piece of the splendid heritage which has fallen into the laps of this generation. It should be guarded well.

But there is a story and it must be told. It is about Old Mountain, a legendary rainbow that lives in the Brule. He and his brother, the far-famed

Mule, worked in harness for several winters for Paul Bunyan when he was logging out of Lake Nebagamon, with headquarters in George Babb's barber shop in Nebagamon. George, one of this country's finest dry-fly fishermen, can tell you more. If you ever meet him — and you will if you are a fisherman — you will hear many, many things.

Now, about Old Mountain and the Mule. Paul Bunyan employed them on various jobs. During a log jam they'd hitch up to it and pull the key logs apart. That saved money on dynamite. They were also useful in placing themselves at the mouths of feeder creeks and backing up water. Then, when they had quite a lake, Bunyan would give the signal. They'd swim out of the way and the full tide of water would come down, bringing the timber into the main stream. That eliminated the need for expensive dams. To this day there have never been more than four logging dams the full length of the creek. The four or five tons of table scraps they consumed daily, was a mere nothing. The Gillagilee birds would have eaten them anyway.

Well, sir, these two fish got along splendidly until they got into an argument over some trollop of a trout that came up from Lake Superior one spring to spawn. The resulting battle continued for several days and so great was the disturbance that Big Lake was formed, giving the otherwise narrow stream its one wide stretch of still water. After that battle Old Mountain preempted the upper part of the stream and the Mule took up his dwelling down below.

They haven't spoken since, excepting the day President Coolidge arrived to spend the summer on the Brule. That day the Mule came up-stream and the river rose two feet. Coolidge was sore about it because the fishing was bad for three days. No one has invited the Mule back since.

You who have stood on the bank of your favorite river at dawn, know about the exhilarating thrill. We were three, George, myself, and Paul (not Bunyan) who said he just came for the ride and finished the day in a blaze of glory by hooking Old Mountain himself. We started from Stone's bridge on the upper river, a bridge that's launched a thousand anglers in any two years you want to name.

George and I were rigged up and went to it while Paul, who had never before used a fly-rod, bided his time. We got several small strikes, mostly from native brook trout which are numerous up stream. It was evident they were hitting freely. George is one of those rare Brule experts who can handle a boat with one hand and fish with the other. Try it sometime. We kept a number of the 9- and 10-inchers for the noon snack.

I'm waiting for the big ones," quoth Paul, the uninitiated. "I propose to bring home some meat. You chaps can play around."

After awhile he went to sleep, which stamps him as of the true philosophic breed of which fishermen are made. I halted to watch George in action.

George Babb is a fisherman. That morning he was swinging an eight-foot. four-ounce rod and was dry fly-fishing in a boat going down-stream. And after you see it done don't let anyone ever tell you dry flies can't be fished down-stream. Maybe it cannot be done when you are wading, but in a boat, drifting with the current, it is managed very well by all the upper Brule fishermen. His No. 10 Coachman, which he uses more than half the time, fell like thistledown.

Babb for a short time once held the world's record for brown trout. He was a 14-pounder, taken at night. After that they began getting bigger ones in western streams. His ability to hook rising fish is uncanny. Years of training have sharpened his eye.

"Bend your wrist when you see 'em," cried George to me after I had lost one.

"But how do you see 'em?"

"Watch for 'em."

Thus endeth the lesson.

I drank in the morning air and watched, with supreme contentment, the piscatorial perfection which George Babb has attained through 35 years of angling and guiding on the Brule.

He places a fly where you or I would never essay a try. His is a vigorous style, with plenty of power in the back cast and worlds of finesse in the forward cast. He found the trout feeding inshore, under tangled, overhanging branches and went right in after them. Every cast, almost, was accompanied by the risk of becoming hung up but this happened seldom and when it did he usually freed the fly by a freakish roll of the line which snapped the fly back and free. He seemed to know by instinct how much room he had behind him. I never saw him look back. Perhaps he knows all the spots on the Brule by heart. His fishing he accompanies by a constant and interesting flow of trout lore. It seems as though all his mental faculties are engaged in making conversation the while he fishes automatically. It does seem a fact that all good fishermen spend a lot of time fishing. They keep their lines wet.

George kept plying his paddle and rod while I set about to emulate him. The results were anything but successful. Trying to send out a fly with a man like George around is a bit difficult. One may be a fair performer at any branch of sport but when placed side by side with a real expert, morale and style often suffer. The Hon. Babb, however, is very kindly under ordinary circumstances and resorts only to his milder methods of oral castigation when fishing with amateurs, like myself.

I went on with my casting. Paul slept until I awakened him and offered him my place in the bow. He peeped into the creel. A dozen or so small fish were caught by that time.

"Ho hum," he yawned. "Calling on old Paul to come to the rescue. Never cast a fly in his life but he brings home the bacon. Gimme 'at'ere pole, son."

"Now you'll see some fishing," cried George. "I'm pulling in my outfit to teach that fellow a few rudiments."

I retired to the stern to run the boat so that George could come up amidship and conduct another class in icthyological pursuit. Everything in his long years of angling went into the sincere discourse which he poured into Paul's ear with an earnest constancy which would do credit to a machine gun. The whole expressive arsenal of the veteran angler's vocabulary exploded with delightful detonations on Paul's unheeding ear drums. And, don't think that George Babb cannot teach one how to handle a fly rod. If he can't, no one can. With him it is an art and the success of a pupil is his greatest pleasure. Paul was rigged with two wet flies, a Western Bee and a Black Gnat, but paid not the slightest attention to the implorings of his adept teacher. That man had the audacity to persist in fishing with reckless amateurishness before the eyes of the old master of the Brule. Another would have been consigned to the river but these two were old friends of the wars.

Paul clung to his seat in the bow and actually made considerable progress, under George's tutelage. He was doing well when we stopped at the mouth of a small creek at George's command.

"Stay here, I'll be right back," said George as he vanished in the cedars.

In a few minutes he was back with a couple handfuls of watercress.

"That's for our Brule salad." he explained.

We proceeded. The trout were still on the feed. George himself admitted they were "taking well" although we hooked no more large ones. None of those brought to net were over 11 or 12 inches but all possessed the fierce doggedness that comes to trout living in the frigid Brule. In the hottest summers the river is entirely unfit for swimming. A ducking while wading is more than a wetting. The cold goes right to the marrow.

We came to a place where the river made a fairly sharp turn to the left, over a mild rapids. A log, perhaps 15 feet long, projected out from the bank at the turn. Along its edge the water curled and eddied. I stopped the boat 50 feet away, up-stream and across from the log.

"There's one in there, George," said I, in the wisdom of my years.

It was beautiful to see him drop his fly six inches from the log. He had judged the flow of the water well for the dry Coachman was carried downstream almost parallel with the log. It might have fallen off the log into the water, so easily did it come to rest. It bobbed to nearly the end of the log, a fleck of brown and white against the shadowed water beside the log. The trout came from beneath the end of the projection. George struck before I saw the fish and a split second after the strike, the trout broke water in a shimmering curve. It was a Lochleven, weighing about two pounds. In a few moments, due to expert handling, it was creeled.

At noon we stopped for two hours, ate fried trout and Brule river salad, the component parts of which are a mysterious to me as the ingredients of George's line dope. Some day I hope to extract both secrets. On down-stream we continued, through rapids and slow stretches and so on, through an ever-changing valley of pines and cedars, trickling creeks, shadowed pools.

Paul caught a number of fairly good fish, to his complete delight. By the time we slid under the high railway trestle at Winnebojou the Brule valley was darkening and the chill of the river was being felt a little. Warm jackets were in order, although I knew in the open the sun was still warm. The Brule has a way of sending forth its chill at sundown. It is not long after that when vaporous mist-wraiths commence their all-night dance over its surface. He who fishes at night must prepare for that, even in midsummer. But whatever slight discomfort it may bring, one may reconcile himself with the knowledge that it is that cold, pure water that makes it one of the country's greatest trout streams.

Up the railway at Winnebojou we skidded the boat to the waiting trailer, lashed it into place and prepared for departure homeward.

"You'll learn, Paul," said George with paternal accent as he handed over the entire creel, refusing to keep any for himself. "In fact, I'm quite proud of you. For one day you've done well. Next time you'll know a little bit about it."

For answer the new-born angler pursed his lips and whistled with solemn intonation the first strain of "Nearer My God to Thee."

Pickering Falls for the Brule

This is a new one, unread except for the readers of the August, 1935 Outdoor
Life. *It's a wonderful story. It illustrates another MacQuarrie strength (dispirited
souls might call it a weakness), his penchant for pranks. I have no doubt somebody
turned up like Pickering, moved away and sung the praises of his new trout waters.
MacQuarrie and his pals took him to the Brule. Then the writer's imagination
began to kick into action. What if the man named Pickering hooked into a big fish?
What if . . . Pete, riled by new placed loyalties . . . ? What if he gave the canoe a little
hike at the right moment . . . ? And there you have Pickering, owner of six rods, ten
reels and 3,000 flies, coming out of the Brule in a "grand surge, like a sea lion."*

D rowsing with my feet on the desk on a sleepy July afternoon, I
look up to see Paul standing breathlessly beside me.
"Pickering," he pants. "Harold G. Pickering is in town."
The soles of my shoes hit the floor with a bang. I reach for my coat.
Paul, anticipating my response, is already halfway to the door and we meet on
the stairs.

"You are sure," I inquire, "that Harold Gregg Pickering is in town?"

"Even at this moment," he replies.

"Where?"

"Follow me!"

It is only a few steps to Superior's most attractive hotel. In this hotel, as
in many others, there is a long, narrow room, with a mahogany counter running almost its full length. Before this counter there is a brass rail and strewn

along it are sundry persons. At the end of the counter is a small but earnest group, with hats pushed back and vests unbuttoned.

Harold Gregg Pickering himself is in the center of this fraternal group. He is a middle-sized man with a mint julep. He is speaking.

"... and just as I got him to the top of the water," he is saying, "he gave one last desperate wrench and was free — the biggest native ever seen in any pond on the Megantic."

Paul and I join the group and listen to the tale of Pickering, the wandering angler, who, 10 years ago, quit his law practice on the Brule River in Wisconsin and resumed it on the Neversink, the Willowemoc, the Beaverkill, and the waters of the Megantic Club in Maine.

It has been 12 long months since the eagle eye of Harold Gregg Pickering has feasted upon the faces of his friends in Superior and he is somewhat changed. For one thing, he is not going fishing on the Brule this trip, as he has only a few days and his schedule is full. Paul and I exchange meaning glances. The group slowly breaks up, and finally there are only four of us — Pickering, Paul, myself, and one solid citizen by the name of Eugene West, who is, of course, called Pete.

Pickering has flown from New York to California and has dropped in at the Superior on his way back to New York. His wife, also a confirmed angler, is with him. But she is firm; there is to be no fishing.

"You ever read the papers?" Paul asks Pickering.

The defendant answers that occasionally he does.

"Then you know all about these kidnapping cases, eh?" continues Paul.

The light of reason dawns in the eye of Harold Gregg Pickering.

"Doggone!" he says. "Not a bad idea! And would you mind running upstairs now and telling my wife I am to be kidnapped, specifying the day and hour and — er — the time for the return of the victim?"

Paul goes upstairs with the tidings and delivers his message to Susan Pickering. She stands in the doorway and says:

"I was afraid of that. I'd like to go but I can't. Make it Monday then by noon, and have him back by 9 PM."

The hour of noon Paul's automobile, which also holds Pete and myself, draws up at the hotel. In the door stands Harold Gregg Pickering, vice-president of the Anglers' Club of New York.

"Get your stuff," says Paul.

Pickering conscripts two bellhops and, before our bulging eyes, the uniformed lackeys drag down from upstairs the following assortment of tackle: 6 rods, 10 reels, all loaded, 5 huge fly boxes, and a big, papa fly case, with little compartment drawers all enameled in white, containing, so help me, nothing less than 3,000 flies.

"Shame," says Solid Citizen Pete West as he lifts the stuff into the car, "that you didn't bring your fishing tackle."

The wonder and the glory of that fishing paraphernalia passeth the understanding of a common angler like myself. To see it brought forth in all its splendor is like spending an hour in the greatest sporting goods store in the world. No detail has been omitted. The rods are the handmade kind. The flies are tied, by famous tyers. The assortment of accessories is endless. For it must be known Harold Gregg Pickering is no ordinary man. When he sets out to enjoy fishing he goes the limit. He dwells among the elect. He fishes with the great Hewitt.

It is a joyous ride to the appointed place on the Upper Brule where two river canoes of a friend await our coming. The kidnapped barrister gazes with reminiscent eye upon the stream of his desire. It is hot and the river weeds are already choking the slow places in the river. But we must see to it that the Brule does not disappoint one who has come so far to woo her.

Of the Brule much has been said — but not too much. The angling men of all nations have tasted its offerings and found them good. The Upper River, cedar-lined, alternating fast with slow stretches, is the answer to a calendar artist's dream. The feel of it was high in our blood as we got into the canoes, Pete and Paul in one and Pick and myself in another. Pick selected for his weapon a 3-ounce wonder, 8 feet long, and before we were 50 feet from the dock he was stretching out line over honey water.

Solid Citizen Pete West was in the bow of the other boat, businesslike, deliberate. Pete is an angler of no mean repute. The hectic swirls of commerce have never completely engulfed him. Whenever he feels he's making too much money he goes fishing.

I knew before we had gone 100 yards it was to be one of those days. The July sun was relentless. The water was cold to the hand but there is no surface life. The birds were stilled. Until nightfall the trout would take their siesta and would refuse to be disturbed.

Pete and Paul and I felt sort of responsible for Pick. We had to see to it that he caught fish. The Brule must acquire no evil name from the tongue of an old sweetheart.

It was after a stop had been made upstream a way that Solid Citizen West suggested it might be well to drop the masks and agree the fishing was lousy. Pick agreed, gently, and opined he had enjoyed much better fishing 50 miles from New York City. Paul snickered and asked him what he meant by such calumny. After that the party was on. Within minutes Pete was engaged in a battle to the death with Pick over the relative merits of the Brule and "any damn crick the other side of the Appalachians."

The meeting was to be a success, after all, I decided. Pickering divested himself of his jacket, rolled up his sleeves, and orated at large and at length on the fecundity of the Megantic Club waters in Maine, the waters of the Windbeam Club near New York, the Neversink, the Esopus, the Beaverkill, and a lot of others. The forest rang with his denunciation of his once beloved Brule and the woolly West. In its way it was a clash of Titans, with Pick upholding the Hewitt-delicate-as-hell contingent and Pete declaiming on behalf of the five-ounce-sock-it-to-'em boys.

"You've got to have faith," lectured Pete. "No fisherman can catch fish when he feels they are not in the river. I'll grant this is a rotten day but don't tell me this stream is fishless. If I had a dime for every trout in the Brule, I'd be richer'n Henry Ford."

"They used to be here, you mean," said Pick, the sap of brotherly combat mounting in him.

"I insinuate nothing," went on Solid Citizen West. "I blew your nose for you when you were a kid and I kicked your pants when you skipped school. All my life I've watched over you and now you tell me the Brule is fishless.

Next thing you'll be casting aspersions on my home life."

It was the best meeting of the Happy Home Club in many a year. The only things lacking were a couple oak chairs to throw through the window.

Pete suddenly aroused himself from the cedar trunk on which he sat and strode toward the canoe.

"Come with me, Pickering," he thundered, "and I'll show you something about this river you've forgotten." Pickering, confident, arrogant, followed. He took the bow seat of Pete's canoe. Paul and I followed close behind.

"I'll show you whether there are fish in this river," stormed Pete. Upstream he forged, advising Pickering where to cast his fly, now slowing down to work into better position for a tricky spot, now speeding up through dead water, which lay listless and uninviting. The sun slid downhill behind the spruces. The coolness of the water arose into the air. But still came no fish to the fly of Harold Gregg Pickering.

We were far upstream now, and nearing a deep pool. The water, a glistening mirror in the midday sun, was now a promising pool. Solid Citizen West was very careful. The pool was his best shot. He tried now to put his man in the place where a big one lurked. There was no hope for a large mess, as the hour was late and we had a long way to go back. Cautiously Pete worked his canoe toward the pool.

"Remember," he goaded, "no bum casts. You lay it out there and you'll see something you have never seen on the Neversink — or any other kind of sink, including kitchen!"

"Them words were gospel 15 years ago," returned Pickering. "But times have changed, Peter. The ol' Brule ain't what she used to be."

The solid citizen winced. From our canoe, hanging back to watch the show, Paul and I saw that Pete's dander was way up. This was most unusual, as Solid Citizen West usually has complete control of his dander.

West was giving Pickering every chance. Hardly a ripple came from his paddle. A cream-colored line squirted through the tip of Pickering's 3-ounce Leonard. At the end of a 15-foot leader was a No. 10 Brown Bivisible, sparsely tied. His execution was good. The fly streaked back and forth like a dragon fly, halted abruptly in midflight and settled softly to the quiet pool.

Sometimes both Pete and I have broken our hearts over the pool, but it is money water any day of the year — only, woe to him who telegraphs the least sign of his presence.

The fly floated, drifted downward imperceptibly with the slow current. A huge fish nose came through the surface 3 feet in front of it and seized something. It was a deliberate rise to another fly, but perhaps the trout had not seen Pickering's fly. There was still a chance. But Pickering had to be careful. He was. He let the fly and leader float slowly back, taking no chance with retrieving it earlier and frightening the fish with the pick-up of the line. It seemed hours before it was back near the boat. He stripped in line and worked the rod again. No word was spoken by anyone. The big fellow rose again in the same place. The second cast dropped a yard in front of him, the leader curving away from the rise. It was perfect. The moment had arrived.

The fish rose by the side of the almost motionless fly. Pickering was about to retrieve it in disgust but Pete whispered hoarsely, "don't move it!"

The fly floated another foot. Then it was gone and Pickering's right wrist was suddenly tensed. The rod answered with a heavy throbbing and from the rear of the boat Solid Citizen West shouted:

"Socko!"

Pete plunged his paddle into the water and made for the center of the pool. The water was deeper there, and it was a safer place to be with such a fish on the line. The brown darted for the bank but Pickering snubbed him away. Pickering's little rod was marvelously alive. Paul and I moved in closer, but not too close. This was to be a battle. Pickering's leader tapered to 4X but he could win if he was careful. The brown leaped but once and we saw him — 4 pounds, perhaps. Too big to jump more.

Pete's face was aglow with happiness, not so much for himself as for the vindication which his own river had given him. He shrieked advice but did not forget to handle the boat. Pickering, inwardly excited, but matter-of-fact as always in time of great stress, played a masterful hand. There was a lull in the battle and Pete, with trembling hand, reached for the net.

"Pick," said Pete, "I want to ask you just one question before we net that boy."

"Go ahead," replied the attorney.

"Will you admit now that there ever was a brown like that in the Neversink?"

Pickering was busy with his work but he made shift to answer.

"Well, Pete," he explained, in his best legal manner, "I've seen some just as big. This one's a beauty but I've seen some that — "

He never finished the sentence. Before any of us knew what was happening the side of the canoe began tipping and Pickering, who had been standing, the better to see the fish, was swaying from side to side. The canoe was rolling dangerously. Pickering's face was a picture of mingled surprise and apprehension. Once, in a fierce reach for balance, he almost regained his equilibrium but the pull of the fish was too much and, finally resignedly, dramatically, he performed the most nearly perfect parabola I have ever seen and went over the side into 10 feet of ice-cold water.

Miraculously, the canoe remained on an even keel and Solid Citizen West escaped a ducking. The surface of the pool was split in a moment with the emerging head and shoulders of Harold Gregg Pickering. His feet must have pushed hard against that rocky bottom for he came half out of water in a grand surge, like a sea lion. His hat was gone. He blew water like an artesian well. His hair fell over his eyes in a bedraggled lick. I retrieved the rod — fishless now — and then picked up the other articles that had floated away. Solid Citizen West grimly stuck out a paddle and Pickering climbed back into the canoe over the bow.

Nobody said much. Pickering divested himself of his dripping clothes and tried to dry out. It was growing dark in the deep Brule valley. Pete seemed unaccountably depressed but Pickering buoyed him up with words of good cheer. We hurried to the canoe dock and quit the stream. The whitethroats were hitting it up as we drove back over the trail to the main road through the Norway pines and the peace of a beautiful summer sunset spread over the land.

We dropped Pickering at his hotel. Thoughts of the lost fish were still in our minds but the topic had become taboo, so greatly hurt had Pete seemed at the turn of events. As Pickering was about to leave, with another bellhop lugging his accessories and impedimenta, Pete suddenly stuck out his hand to say good-by.

"Pick," said Solid Citizen West, with a twinkle in his eye. "I'm sorry you lost that fish."

"Yes?" said Pickering, expectantly.

"I've got a confession to make," said Pete. "I really believe you didn't deserve to catch that trout after what you said about my river."

"I knew it," said Harold Gregg Pickering without flinching. "I got just what I had coming to me."

"Sure," breathed Solid Citizen West, as though a load had been lifted from his mind.

"And what's the confession?" asked Pickering.

"I tipped you in on purpose," declared Solid Citizen West. "Did I do right?"

"You did," answered Harold Gregg Pickering.

GEESE! GET DOWN!

Again, this one has never been published in book form. I can't imagine why not. It's a rollicking good Me and Joe about a whopper of a goose shooting day. The so satisfying ending; dumping the two Thanksgiving day geese in front of his wife.

The story hits home to me. My beloved Parker shotgun is a 16-gauge. I've killed many geese with it (Brant mostly which come down easy, and a few Canadas which take a lot of killing.) When I moved to Canada goose heaven, the Parker was quickly retired in favor of big 12s. With steel shot, especially, you could fire the 16 all day at Canadas over 50 yards and the shot would just bounce off their feathers.

Frosty mornings on the Rock County prairie of Wisconsin the wild geese fly to the cornfields from Geneva. Koshkonong and Delavan Lakes, and there are autumn ground fogs, so that those who crouch in goose pits may study the phantom billows and marvel at such morning magic. The endless squadrons begin coming to the stripped fields a little after daylight. Deliberate and majestic, like long, crawling strings in the distance, they float over the shrouded prairie and fill the sky with wild, haunting music.

So it was yesterday morning. Or did it just seem like yesterday morning? We shall not quibble. Time is of no importance where the gray honkers are concerned.

In the south, over the farm lands, ragged flocks of mallards traded back and forth. Straight north were wisps of clouds. They were lazy, streamlined clouds blown smooth by the night winds. If these things were not enough to occupy the watchers in the pits, there was the fat red sun in the east, rising lazily over low mists to flood the plain with that recurring miracle which we call daylight.

Piercing the fog at this witching hour were the tall silos of Wisconsin's richest farming country. Over there where the honkers were making wild music, a barn loomed. Yonder in a gentle dip, smoke rose from a chimney and a farmhouse rode at anchor in the fog. Just to the right of it was the church steeple — it was a steeple until the morning wind rolled away the fog to reveal a windmill tower.

As all men know, this is a fine place for hunting, or for just watching the sun come up. Farmers are lucky people to be abroad on that lovely plain in the early morning. Near a field of tardy winter rye, Earl May of Milwaukee had spread his big cork goose decoys, cunning replicas, fashioned in the winter nights when a man's thoughts keep turning to last year and the year to come. With Earl in the pit was this reporter. Earl, who is a moose of a man, but shoots a 16-gauge withal, paid tribute to the day's beginning, and sized up the situation:

"Those from the right are Geneva and Delavan honkers. The ones from the left are Koshkonong boarders. How many would you say are in the air now?"

"Do you mean in sight?"

"Right. Within sight of us this minute."

"Two thousand and that's a wild guess."

"I'll say three, and I don't care if we never fire a shot."

He leaned on the edge of the pit, dug almost five feet down in the heavy, rich soil of this famous prairie, and studied the traceries in the sky as the geese trailed from water to favored cornfields.

The day before, Earl had dug that pit. He, with Ed and Frank Larkin, hunting farmer brothers, had dug it on a gentle, round-topped ridge in a 40-acre field. Aside from the bulging ridge where the blind was sunk, the field was almost as flat as a floor.

The brothers Larkin and Earl had brought the big farm truck in there and shoveled the dirt directly into it, so as to leave no telltale crumbs of soil sprinkled on the ground. They had been very careful not to trample down the earth and vegetation, and when the pit was dug they built a lid for it, cunningly, of light boards with stubble woven through its frame.

Ten feet away, it took discerning eyes to spot the difference between that pit cover and the field around it. To such extremes must one go to lure the canny Canada close to the decoys. They go further, do these painstaking hunters in Wisconsin's best goose country. They keep a short-handled rake in the pit blind and rake up the downtrodden grasses where they have been pressed down by boots. And woe betide the careless one who is so foolish as to toss an empty shell on to the ground outside the pit!

Black ducks, they say, are postgraduates of the school of experience. Some old baymen here in Wisconsin will swear a black duck has a sense of smell! More cautious heads will reply that it all depends on what kind of soft coal a bayman is burning in his pipe, and also how recently said bayman has been subjected to a thorough dry-cleaning.

At any rate, black ducks are credited in these parts with being smarter than their near kin, the gray mallards; but in all truth, where the black duck's wisdom leaves off, that of the Canada begins.

"If we can't get any honkers to work the decoys," said Earl as the minutes passed, "we can spread some duck decoys in the cornfields. We might catch a greenhead or two in range."

But there was no hurry. It was pleasant to lean elbows on the edge of the pit and study the last of the morning goose flight, even though the birds were landing in cornfields miles away. There is a fascination in just watching geese. The year 1940 was the first in many that had brought Wisconsin some real goose shooting. Early November closing of previous years had found the Canadas just arriving on the prairies in the southern counties, so that 1940's 15-day extension was a joy to goose hunters, many of whom had not even dug a goose pit for several years.

With the extended season the southern tier of counties, particularly Rock and Walworth, saw long-forgotten decoys, solid and silhouette, come out of attics and barn lofts. Goose hunters looked again to their hardest shooting guns, and in the snug little farm trading centers roundabout storekeepers told of No. 2's and BB's being once more in demand.

In all the years of the shorter seasons the flame had burned but dimly. And there had been many protests from farmers and sportsmen: "Please, just a few days' extension of the season on geese alone," for this is one of the few areas in Wisconsin where geese are a sort of autumn religion with the faithful. Old-timers like the Larkin brothers tell of lying in the snow on the ground with white sheets over them and the temperature around zero. They tell of the live-decoy days. There are domesticated Canada honkers on these prairie farms today that are known to be more than twenty-five years old.

The Larkin boys had one gander that they prized especially. It seems this bird got to be a member of the family, and Frank swears he house-broke him, like a dog. He stalked about the farm-yard with a lordly air, allegedly afraid of nothing that flew or walked, including dogs, pigs, men and geese. 'Tis said many an unhappy neighbor's dog, unacquainted with this goose's over-lordship, was put to yelping flight as the old gentleman's pinions caught up with him.

"I'll bet that gander could have broken your leg with his wings if he had caught you right," Frank Larkin recalls.

In the hunting seasons of those old days the patriarch really came into his own. Frank says the old boy was as disappointed as any hunting dog at being left behind. Wild birds lighting out of range of the pit were handled beautifully by the old chap. He was never tethered, for he would not attempt to escape. He would amble slowly over to the shy strangers, lick the biggest gander in the flock and bring the whole band back with him in range!

Neighbors recall the event as a satisfactory settlement of all issues involved. And the old goose? What of him?

The Larkin boys gave him decent burial. Eat that old friend? I should say not! You don't know the Larkin boys!

Talk rambled on as the sun rose, the fog thinned and the Larkin boys started the new combine to rattling in a distant field of soy-beans. Earl watched half the horizon and I the other half. The sun grew warmer. The wind picked up. It was to be a warm day for late November in Wisconsin.

Abruptly I sensed Earl's languor change to frozen intensity. Often this sudden change in a companion of the blind is sensed before it is seen. You may be sitting there back to back, not touching, and it happens. A halt in the middle of a sentence, the quick stamping on a cigarette, a sharp intake of breath — this is the unspoken language of the blind.

The transition came in seconds' time. I followed Earl's eyes and saw the moving thread in the sky that was taking a different route than the other moving threads had taken.

"Down! Down! We're going to get shooting!"

Sweeter words are not spoken in goose pits. We carefully pulled the light pit cover over our heads and watched the oncoming birds, first by tilting the cover a little, and then as the birds neared by shooting straightening up, through the minute holes in the lid.

The geese were honking like mad, Earl's cork decoys were doing the trick. Let no man declare that well-made cork decoys will not draw Canadas. The flock came over us about a hundred yards high, made a wide swing in back of us and then set their wings and zoomed straight over our heads at the decoys. There is no other spectacle in all wildfowling like this!

It is indeed a shame that so few sportsmen go to the pains of preparing for geese. It does take work. Pit blinds carefully made. Faultless decoys. Far-shooting guns. And long, cold waits. But it is worth it to see those tremendous birds, wings stiffened, black legs straight out, come sailing overhead.

At such a time the very air seems to become a heavier medium than the air that ducks zip through. How could it be otherwise and support such heavy-bodies flyers? Coming in like that, especially after the hunter has worked on ducks, they give one the sensation of entertaining the winged hosts of another planet.

The approach of wild geese to a blind is one of the neatest optical illusions in nature. The geese just keep on coming. You think they are one hundred yards away, and they are two hundred. You think they are fifty yards away, and they are one hundred. There is an illusion in such flight that upsets the calculations of even the veterans, and especially will it upset the hunter keyed to ducks. I have seen this illusion carried out even in motion pictures in which wild geese seem to fly straight into the camera lens interminably, getting bigger and bigger.

The geese, about fifteen of them, were over the decoys, hanging there, it seemed. I saw Earl's right hand dart upward like a snake and fling aside the lid of the blind. He grunted something which must have been intended for "Now!" but sounded more like "A-a-ark!" pronounced through clenched teeth. I saw his little 16-gauge flash to his big shoulder and felt sorry for him with that pea-shooter. But he likes the gun and picks his bird.

Three times the 16-gauge barked, at the same bird, which tumbled. And then Earl was yelling: "Shoot! For God's sake, man, shoot!"

Fortunately, as he yelled, he also removed his right foot from where it pinned down my left foot in the crowded blind, and then I had room to stand and operate the double-barrel 12-gauge.

At the open barrel feathers flew. The goose was getting way out when the tight barrel caught him. Earl May swears that goose was one hundred yards away by then, that it was just a stray No. 2 buck that clipped its right pinion, that the fall of thirty yards to the frozen prairie was what really killed it. Suffice it that at this moment the Larkin boys shut off the combine in the soy-bean field a half-mile away, and Ed said later he heard the bird hit the prairie.

Pure luck! Two geese, when we might have had two apiece with heavier armament and a little more care in arranging ourselves in a cramped blind. But two corn-fed geese can be quite a load to haul in from the prairie, and they can take up a lot of room in a pit blind, too. Both were Canadas, mine about 8 pounds, Earl's close to 12.

Genial Ed Larkin came down to the blind shortly after to declare he never saw such awful shooting. That morning this farmer-sportsman released a dozen cock pheasants of his own raising, so that they might go forth and replenish their kind in the neighborhood. While he was completing this job, not far from our blind, Earl May caught sight of a new convoy of Canadas working toward us. Ed sought the nearest cover, which was in the pit. He got in the bottom of it, and I tell you we literally stood on his back in the crowded blind.

There was Ed Larkin, scrunched down between us, cussing Earl for having such big feet, and there were eight sociable honkers making that long, stiff-winged toboggan slide into our decoys. I recall that as Earl let go with his 16-gauge Ed yelled, "Give it to 'em but get off my hand!" And I remember that once again I got my elbows over the rim of the pit, and by that time Earl had one down and running and I said to myself, "Here's where I make a double!"

But again the open barrel merely dusted feathers and it took the close barrel to knock him down. I vowed by all that was holy to level nothing but a 10-gauge or a super 12 at them next year.

They can be hit. They are not such elusive targets by any means. But the thing is to hit them hard and make them stay hit.

Never shall I forget Earl legging it over the frozen prairie after that runner. The bird took him a half-mile, through fences, across a creek, over plowed fields. When he returned, red-faced and perspiring, with 10 pounds of Canada draped over his shoulder, I struck while the iron was hot: "That 16 is all right for ducks, but not for these birds. I'm none too confident with the 12."

"I love that gun like a brother, and I'll probably never change, but I believe you're right," he replied.

It was nearly noon. The November sun was showing how kindly it could be even four days before the deer season. Ed Larkin returned to the combine in the soy-bean field. Earl and I stood in the blind and talked. It is a great part of hunting, this talk. Nothing was moving except ducks, and we were in no mood to stage an anti-climax duck hunt. So we stayed out the shooting hours in the pit, reaching down now and then to stroke the fat breasts of four great black-legged Canadas.

"I'll be dog-goned if I know what a man would do with more than a couple of 'em," Earl remarked.

I left Earl in the Larkin yard that night, with the combine closing in swiftly on the small square patch of remaining soy-beans. Earl would hunt a few more days there, then haul out for the deer woods, 350 miles north. The next morning he would be out there with Ed, and they would see the eddying morning fog and the windmill that looked like a church steeple and the great gray geese trading over the plain to the feeding places.

"I hope you get a buck," I said, leaving.

"I don't deserve one after this," he answered.

I drove home. Not swiftly, for I was already two hours late and the supper I had said I would be on hand for was long over when finally I arrived, cold and hungry. I put the car away. I hung hunting clothes on the proper hook. I put the 12-gauge in its corner.

The lady who tolerates me said: "Huh! You should have gone duck hunting. Now we'll have to buy a Thanksgiving turkey." Then she added, exercising the right of all women to scan the time card: "We had a swell supper, but all I can give you is leftovers. After all, you're two hours late . . ."

She was sitting in a chair in the living room, bent over some mysterious chore with a needle which we goose hunters never quite come to understand. I retrieved the two Canadas from the vestibule by the kitchen door and, while she sat there with her back to me, tossed them over her head to her feet. Thump! Thump!

Let it be reported that she dropped the needlework in the chair. I know, for later I sat on it and felt the needle. But that was long after I had cleaned up on the finest late-evening emergency supper that any goose hunter ever had — and no leftovers either, gentlemen.

UPON THE EARTH BELOW

Talk about treasure! I don't know how anyone could write a better story than this one. The winning August rain, the scare of the slippery clay roads, the long night vigil with the rain pelting down. Glamour. Sheer joy. The feel of something big and cold and wet, a giant trout, of course, caught by the never-give-up Mr. President.

And the prophetic "Get ready, my friend, I am just brushing by to settle the dust and wash away today's spent wings." Right out of Ecclesiastes.

There is something about rain . . . A night in summer when the clouds can swell no more and shrink from threatening battlements to ragged shreds over Wisconsin, I often get up from my chair, go to the big closet and speculate over the implements of trout fishing there. Indeed, there is something about rain. Especially a warm rain, spilled over a city or a network of trout streams. It kindles a spark. It presses a button. It is an urgent message from afar to any seeker of the holy grail of anglingdom — trout.

There is the mild August rain sluicing down to the thirsty earth. There are the castellated clouds, fresh from the Western prairie, borne on the hot, dry land wind. And there is your man of the creel and the throbbing rod and the sodden waders going to the window to peer out and plumb the mysteries of the rain and wonder about tomorrow.

It must be that eons ago, when the rain splashed down over the front of a cave door, the muscle-bound troglodyte within went to the opening and stretched out his hand, palm upward. Perhaps he even stood in it a bit, as perfectly sane men will sometimes do. Perhaps that old sprig of Adam, restless by his fire in the dry cave, felt the friendliness of the rain. Perhaps — no troutster will deny it — he felt the drops upon his matted head and wondered about tomorrow.

The rain can beckon a man of the noisy city and draw him to the door or window. Its attraction is so much the greater if it falls at night, when it is a whispering mystic visitor from afar that seems to say "Get ready, my friend. I am just brushing by to settle the dust and wash away today's dead spent-wings."

One night I was sitting alone, restless behind my newspaper. The rain had barely begun. I was feeling its pull. Dark had just fallen, and the rain had come tentatively, like a guest afraid of a cool welcome. It had grown darker, and the rain came stronger. I cast the paper aside and went to the door.

All of the lush buoyance of August was in the night wind that came through the screen. To my nostrils came the scent of wet turf, and in the sparkling lines of rain that penciled down in the porch light I seemed to see the exuberant waters where the trout dwell.

I stared out. The lightning flashed on and off. Two pine trees by my door tossed and glistened, I was lost there for minutes contemplating the beauty of the night.

Also, I knew what the rain would do for certain trout waters. Some of them it would raise; some would even go over their banks. Others, mothered by heavily grown forest country, would take up the water slowly. The trout would be grateful, as it had been dry and hot for a long time. There would be new feed in the streams tomorrow.

From my dry vestibule, nose pressed to the screen, over which hung a small protecting porch roof, I made out, in one lightning flash, the figure of a man. He was walking slowly and deliberately in the downpour. He came across the street under the corner light, and at the distance of fifty yards I could see that the water had flattened the brim of his hat.

He vanished into darkness, walking toward me. Here, I said, is a man doing what I would wish to do if I didn't give a rip about the crease in these trousers. A man out shaking hands with an August rainstorm. I enjoyed his enjoyment. I could almost feel the warm drops cascading off my nose, the squishing of my shoes and the cool touch of rain on my cheeks.

He came closer, passing the mountain ash trees near my walk, sloshing as slowly and happily as ever. And then, as though he had seen me, he turned up my walk. It was not until he strode into the wan light of the tiny porch that I recognized him — the President of the Old Duck Hunters' Association.

He stood beyond the porch roof in the drip, ginning in at me. "This is it," he said.

"And you're fixing to catch a dandy summer cold. Come in."

He stamped off some of the drops, dashed the water from his soaking hat and sized me up. "A little rain," he lectured, "never hurt anyone. Especially a fisherman. This is exactly what these August trout streams have been waiting for."

I lured him inside.

"How about tomorrow?" he said.

I was not given an opportunity to accept his invitation. He rushed on.

"It's close to the end of the month now. This will be the last warm rain of the season. Next good one we get will be a cold September drizzle. Wait and see. Better get that trout fishin' done while there's time. A trout has got to have new rain every so often . . ."

In the living room the situation hit me differently. The spell of the storm had left me, and now all I could think of was Mister President, dripping on my newly covered davenport, selling me a bill of fishing goods. I laughed. It must have seemed a smug laugh to him, such a laugh as a non-venturesome, dry-shod city prisoner would get off in the presence of a dyed-in-the-wool trout fisherman.

"Laugh and be danged," he snorted. "I'll walk five more blocks in the very fine rainstorm to the door of a real fisherman, and I'll bet you anything he'll not only come along with me tomorrow, but he'll walk home with me in the rain — without an umbrella."

I capitulated, of course. It is always good wisdom to capitulate to a

President of the Old Duck Hunters. I even offered him dry socks and a hot drink and spread his dripping jacket in front of the gas oven. He sat there for a long spell, talking trout, and when his warming drink was finished he strode back into the night, to walk like a man and a trout fisherman in the friendly element.

It was not until the next afternoon that I plumbed his further thoughts about the rain. I wanted to get the whole of his philosophy of tramping through a downpour. I sensed a little of it, but wanted to learn more of what stirs the depths of such as he.

"It's like this," he said, shifting his cigar and leaning over the steering wheel which was guiding us to the Iron River, in north Wisconsin. "Up to yesterday it hadn't rained in weeks. I was getting as dry as your hollyhocks. Every day had been the same. Bright, dazzling sun, same old grind in the office. Monotony.

"Then it rained. I was working late. I watched that storm gather, and the heavier the clouds came in from the west the better I felt. Do you suppose there's anything to this here theory that a little electricity in the air peps up a fellow? I kept working through the rain, getting more done than I had all day. And when I was through I said, 'Now for a good walk in the rain.' Why? I just wanted to. The reason I came to your house first was so I could dry off some before my wife saw me."

I didn't quite get it yet.

He continued: "Don't you ever feel like plunging into a snowstorm, or wading a tough river, or climbing a hill? Maybe it's a way of letting off steam. Or maybe I've fished trout so long I'm getting just like a trout, rushing out from under the bank in a rain to see what the river is bringing down for supper. Could be."

I looked him over. A lean, keen business man, much like many another business man except for the fisherman's garb. Sharp brown eyes, a mouth on the upturned quizzical side, horn-rimmed glasses, a goodly swath of gray in the black hair. Yes, he might have been any other harassed slave of commerce on a fishing recess, but he was not. There was something of the boy about him which most men pretend to outgrow, and, doing so, thus become old.

We drove to the Iron in bright sun, and the President stuffed his faded khaki fishing jacket with the things he would need. He donned waders, rigged up, applied mosquito dope, and, with a final flourish, adjusted the old brown fishing felt with the hook-marred band. Then he was gone, leaving me to climb into gear and ruminate upon a way of life that brings a man to an even three-score with the heart of a boy.

I got into the Iron at a little meadow-like spot not far from Wisconsin's Highway 13. The sun was high. Last night's rain had hardly raised the stream. There was a freshness in the woods that all trout fishermen will recall — the freshness of soaking turf and rain-washed air, and the silver tinkling of a wren and the sweet lament of a white-throated sparrow, I hardly feel that I have been trout fishing if I do not hear this precious bird along the stream.

Things went indifferently for an hour. Fish were rising, but they were the tiny, ubiquitous rainbows, so common in steams that empty into Lake Superior and so laughably pugnacious, coming out to smash a fly like a feather-weight sparring with Joe Louis.

By four o'clock the outdoor stage was being set as it was the previous evening. The black, bulbous clouds in the west, borne into Wisconsin by the day-long prairie wind, were rumbling and flickering distantly, I knew it was only a matter of minutes before the storm would be over the Iron.

But it was a fine time to fish. As the first drops fell I got into a fair rainbow, creeled it and went on hastily, to search other likely corners. From a grassy place in midstream came a big enough brown, enticed out of its scant cover by the lure of new food. Downstream a bit I took two more rainbows. All came to a very, very wet single Royal Coachman.

A wind came out of those plumbeus clouds that stirred the popples joyously, so that their long-stemmed leaves turned upward and revealed the silver gray of their undersides. I could feel that rain going through canvas and flannel to my shoulders. The river was boiling like a kettle. "Fine," said I. Trout were out in it. The President was out in it. I was out in it. Let it come. I looked back, and there, a hundred yards downstream, was the President, hailing me.

I went to him. He was certainly in a hurry. He had his rod taken down, but the line was still strung through the guides.

"Got to get out of here quick," he said. He was short of breath. He had hurried to locate me.

"Get out of here?"

"And I mean right now — clay roads!"

I hadn't thought of that. I got to the car ahead of him. I was remembering stalled cars in Lake Superior's red clay and one nightmare exit from a similar spot where he and I made it out only by wrapping wool socks around the wheels in lieu of chains.

No time to climb out of waders. The rain was sluicing down. We had one chance of getting out of that clay-road country to graveled highway. It lay in the fact that we would be the first ones over the sharply crowned road on which we had come in. We might, by luck and careful driving, bite down with our tires and get hold of traction.

It was nip and tuck. But we made it, thanks to the skillful tooling of Mister President, who is an old hand with slippery clay roads. There were a couple of little hogbacks, however, that we actually slid down.

On the graveled road, he drew up at the side and switched off the motor. It was around 4:30 by then. He pawed in the back seat and came up with sandwiches and coffee. Studying the rain-dashed windshield, he made more trout medicine.

"We'll go back to the Brule, in by George Yale's at Rainbow Bend, and have one more fling at it. Won't have to worry about roads there."

Further trout fishing had been far from my mind, but just when you think the President is in a corner he wriggles out and starts a new campaign. "No hurry," he pointed out. "Sit there and finish your coffee — and here, sit on this old raincoat. I can't have you ruining the upholstery on a new $1,800 automobile."

Ruin the upholstery! Heck, I had been with him in the scrub-oak country one day when those tough-tipped branches made an $1,800 job look as if it had been sandpapered. He wasn't concerned. He was more concerned about two limits of mallards we had taken that day from a hard-to-get-at pot-hole.

"About seven o'clock will be soon enough to hit the Brule," he ventured. "Just a half-hour or hour is all I want. A few good ones ought to be out by then."

We sat and talked. We even had time, between showers, to straighten out some of our hastily stowed tackle, and the heat of our bodies partially dried our upper clothing. We talked as do all trout fishermen confined in an auto — of politics and making money and how to get along with one's neighbors and fishing for trout and waiting in frosty duck blinds at dawn.

Fed and reorganized, we drove slowly south and a bit west to the Brule at Rainbow Bend. It is a favorite putting-in place for the confirmed wader. On the peak of land which juts out into this enticing stream in front of the forest ranger's house we sat for more minutes and watched the sun go down behind threatening clouds. By then it had stopped raining. The President lit a fresh cigar and studied the clouds from the west.

"It'll rain again," he predicted.

Darkness was coming fast. The woods dripped. A few between-the-rain mosquitoes were venturing forth. A whippoorwill sent out an exploratory note.

"What time shall we meet at the car?"

"I don't like this fishing in the dark myself," he explained. "Let's fish for an hour and call it a day."

At this place, where the pines lean over the Brule, he jointed his rod and was off down the path on the right bank.

I put in above the Ranger's station, intending to fish above the old stone dam in a stretch that I respect most highly for its combination of quite fast water and long, deep holes. In late summer when aerated water is preferred by trout, I have found this place to be excellent.

Such evenings are long remembered. Nighthawks swooped and cried above me as I went slowly upstream on the right bank. Before I got to my beginning point my neck and shoulders were soaked again from dripping trees.

It was still light enough to hold the eye of a fly to the graying sky and thread a 1x leader through it. I like this place. I have been very lucky here. I leaned against a great rock while I tied on a floater and studied for the hundredth time the familiar stairway of rapids which lay before me.

One of the best things about trout fishing is going back to a familiar place. Then the woods welcome a man. It is not like being alone on a strange river.

I worked out line over the wavelets at the foot of my rapids, but turned over nothing more than the omnipresent baby rainbows. Hugging the right bank and working farther into the hard flow of this swift water, I did better across in the slack water of the left bank when an 11-inch brown, tempted by a back-circling bivisible in an eddy, smacked it hard and sure.

Very well. They were out on the prod, following the rain as Mister President had judged they would be. They seemed everywhere in that foaming water. And they were not choosy. It was dark enough to invite them to be impetuous, and light enough to make for agreeable fishing.

The fish of that place I remember was a stout brown. It came out of the swiftest water in mid-current, seized the fly and went downstream, all in one swoop. With a four-ounce rod and a 1x leader in that kind of water a solid fish like this one, below a man, has all the advantage. I stumbled downstream after him, played him out in the slack water and slipped him in the rubber pocket of my jacket. I thought then that he might go 18 inches. Anyway, I decided, I would claim that length before Mister President.

By squinting a bit I made out the time — 8:30. The hour was up. I returned to the car in the pines on the hill, put everything carefully away, examined the buster trout gloatingly in the car headlights and composed myself behind the wheel to wait for Mister President. Off in the west there was hardly enough daylight remaining to backlight the pointed spruce tops. Back of me and over me the sky was invisible. A big drop of rain hit the windshield hard. I sensed what was coming.

There was a pause in the small night sounds of the Brule valley. I listened. From far off came the bold, surging roar of rain on leaves. The sound came nearer, rushing through the woods in an ear-filling crescendo. Then the rain hit.

It made a goodly cascade on the windshield. It hammered at the steel car top. It was a million wet drumsticks on the hood. With it came a wild, quick wind, whooping and screaming through the tree-tops. The lights, switched on, revealed steel-bright pencils of rain.

Too bad. The President was down in that rain-stricken valley some-where getting soaked anew. He might have escaped a second wetting had he quit the stream at the appointed time. He might have been sitting there with me in the dry front seat, looking out into it.

I was feeling pretty smug about it. The President is a late-stayer. This time, I thought, he was going to pay the penalty for not keeping an appoint-ment. And then there was that damp, comforting lump in the rubber-lined pocket. I could feel it by reaching a hand down over the back of the seat to where my jacket lay on the floor.

I would take my time about showing him that one. I'd be nonchalant. I'd haul out the little ones first, wait for him to snort at them and then pro-duce the good one. I'd show him. I'd say it was a wonder a man can't depend on his best friend's word. I'd say that when I tell a fellow I'll meet him at such and such a time I meet him then, and don't keep him waiting in a cloudburst.

Time dragged. I am an impatient waiter. Would he ever return? A half-hour passed. Then an hour. I turned on the lights from time to time at imag-inary sounds from the path up which he would come. It was a long, boring, fretful wait.

Just after the legal quitting time of 10 PM, I really did hear boots crunch against gravel. I switched the lights on to light his way, for it was Mister President. He came forward in the downpour. The old brown felt was sag-ging, He wore that unconcerned, listless air of a fisherman who is about to declare, "I gave 'em everything in the book, but they wouldn't play." I opened the car door, and he squished in. Played out, he demanded hot coffee and sipped it while listening to my evening's report.

He lighted up some at the sight of the 18-incher, but said it wouldn't go more than 15. "Maybe only 14¼," he ventured. Nope, he hadn't a thing worth while. That dratted rain! And when it grew dark, he had his troubles in fight-ing the river without a flashlight. He wormed out of wet gear and into dry, gol-durning his luck and the weather. We prepared to drive home.

"I'll take down your rod," I offered, and went outside to where he had leaned it against a fender.

I hastily disjointed it and crawled back behind the wheel, handing the rod joints back to him. Then I discovered I was sitting on something. Something big and cold and wet. Something he had put in my place while I was getting the rod.

I turned around and stared down at the largest just-caught native brook trout I have seen come out of the Brule. Later it went a mite under four pounds — something of a miracle in this day and age, when all men know the big fish of the Brule are invariably browns or rainbows.

Hizzoner was chuckling now. The fish, he explained, hit a No. 4 brown fly that didn't have a name. He had heard it feeding in the dark and rain, and stayed with it for a half-hour until it rose to the fly. He admitted it was the largest brookie he had ever taken in the Brule.

I stared at it as a man will stare at so rare a treasure. I envisioned the battle that took place down in that storm-lashed valley. The lightning must have seen a classic combat that night. I held the fish up and examined it by the dome light. "How long do suppose it is?"

He snorted a triumphant snort from his throne in the rear and shot back: "Put it alongside that 18-incher of yours. The way you figger, it'll go just a yard long — just one yard!"

KENAI, DOG OF ALASKA

This is another first in book form. I include it for a specific reason. MacQuarrie was an unabashed dog lover. He admired loyalty and courage and gentleness in all animals, including his fellow man. But saying he was a dog lover doesn't prove it. But I don't think anyone could read this story about Kenai and not see how deep ran this love. Or admiration. Or respect.

I also love the picture of the 100-pound animal advancing to the society desk of the Journal *and the girls looking for something to climb. Whoever said dogs have no memory is full of baloney. I visited Florida with a Labrador that I had spent much time after quail with. Widgeon hadn't seen me for two years, but I could tell she not only remembered me; she remembered our hunts.*

Someone once said, "Never give your heart for a dog to tear." In a lifetime of owning dogs, I've sometimes steeled myself to obey that injunction, because a dog can hurt you awfully. I don't mean to be cynical. Truth is, I'm not so bullet-proof when it comes to dogs. But it's a real world we live and dwell in. Dogs and people can't live forever. Dog lives, like ours, are mixtures of supreme happiness and deep despair.

The paths of man and dog came together more thousands of years ago than we can say. It must have been when the first wild dog, trembling with terror, or cold, or both — who knows? — crept to a fire that warmed a man. It must have been about that way. The wild dog and the hairy man looked upon each other and found it good. The primeval man's hand reached out in the firelight and touched the dog, and the dog did not run away, but remained. So, surely, it must have been that the great peace between man and dog was made.

Kenai was the first MacKenzie River Husky I had ever seen. I'd seen Malamutes, Samoyeds and Eskimos on the bench and at their work pulling sleds. Then, one October day at Rainy Pass in Ptarmigan Valley, Alaska, on the shore of Puntilla Lake, 140 miles by air out of Anchorage, I met the MacKenzie river dogs.

Imagine a dog the size of a timber wolf, 100 pounds or thereabouts, no bark, just a wolf howl. Not grizzled and gray like a malamute or wolf, but a rich solid red, like a golden retriever. Think of him with wolf forebears to be sure, but with all or most of the wolf traits bred out of him, and in their place a dominant trait that demands the love of humans and returns that love in huge measure.

Those red dogs, about a dozen of them, were the varsity sled dogs of E.G. (Bud) Branham, Alaskan guide, outfitter, aviator, mailman, trapper. Five of us had flown to Rainy Pass to collect caribou, moose and other specimens for the Milwaukee Public Museum.

Chained with the red huskies were ten or more typical malamutes with their masked faces, but not at ease with humans, as were their red cousins. Those big red dogs almost broke their stout chains trying to get at us to say hello. I've seen Samoyeds with that same abounding affection for humans.

We stowed away gear, a lot of it, including 700 pounds of salt for preserving museum specimens. It took a while, and then I found myself in the kennel yard with Bud and the red dogs. He unsnapped the chain leash from one of the biggest, and they had a gay, wrestling get-together.

This was Kenai, the leader of the varsity team. Bud always made it a point to make a fuss over Kenai first. That's one way the dog handlers in Alaska have of letting the other dogs know who the boss man is. They take a promising young dog and do everything but spoil him. I suppose what they are actually doing is building up the leader's ego.

Kenai was nice to everyone, but not demonstrative, except with Bud, whom he worshipped and adored. Yukon, the biggest red dog in the string, about 115 pounds, the strongest dog, pound for pound, I have ever known, would make love to anyone who came along. He'd bare his teeth in a grin and almost turn himself inside out to prove his abiding love for all mankind.

That night after supper in the big room of Rainy Pass Lodge, Bud brought in Kenai — another little act to let the other dogs know who was favored in the string. Kenai lay on the floor trying to be dignified while two three-months-old husky puppies did everything but eat him up.

One day out on the tundra, darkness came sooner than we wanted it. We were five miles from camp, and it was snowing. Bud just gave Kenai his head, and he took us home by the shortest good trail, a new one.

That was the night when, back at camp, his harness off, Kenai flew at Kobuk, a teammate. He put Kobuk on his quivering back and stood over him growling, teeth bared. I didn't know what it was all about until Bud explained.

"He's heard me yelling at Kobuk all day for loafing. And even if I hadn't said a word, Kenai would have known Kobuk was soldiering on the job. He'd have known without even turning his head."

Another day I saw Kenai smell a big herd of caribou more than a mile distant. Later we picked out a trophy bull and collected him. It was Kenai who located that herd by lifting his head at the scent and quickening the pace of the team.

Kenai was given to Bud by a Canadian Mountie at a spot 150 miles up the MacKenzie River from its delta. Bud had flown a fur buyer in there, and in the course of the trip had befriended the Mountie. The Mountie gave him the month-old red puppy in a paper box. Many times, flying back home to Rainy Pass, Bud wished he had not accepted the pesky, squawling pup. But since that day, Bud and the dog have seldom been apart for any length of time.

In World War II, Bud was a lieutenant commander, engaged in sea-air rescue work. Kenai was a lead dog in the Navy, too. He led dog teams up mountain trails after live men and dead men, usually victims of plane crashes. He flew with Bud on routine chores in all sorts of airplanes, and sometimes, when the weather got fancy, Bud Branham figured he and his dog were on their last flight.

Once Bud was flying a famous movie star back from a USO assignment far down the Alaska Peninsula, and the actor offered him $1,000 for Kenai.

The only time I have heard Bud swear was when he related to me his reply to the film star. I have never known of any man-dog twosome to get so close to each other as Bud and Kenai.

Twice Kenai saved the lives of humans. Right after the war, Bud brought with him to Rainy Pass a pretty fair hand in the Alaskan bush, but not quite seasoned enough, as events later proved. Bud permitted his friend to take the Kenai-led red team out on the trap-line. Here's Bud's written account of what happened:

"On his second day out my friend ran into trouble. It snowed hard, and the snow was so deep and soft the team couldn't haul the sled. My friend should have returned to my trap-line cabin. Instead he unhitched the dogs and pushed on for home, with the loose dogs breaking trail.

"With five miles to go to Rainy Pass, he abandoned his snowshoes. Four miles from home he left his rifle behind. It had cleared and turned very cold. It grew dark and my friend left his ax behind. He was tiring, and all of the string except Kenai had raced on home.

"In about another mile my friend fell through the ice and got one leg wet. From there on he was hazy — out of his head at times, because he couldn't recall everything that happened. He remembers sitting in the snow and how good it felt. He wanted to go to sleep. But he remembers Kenai nipping at his hands and face. Kenai led him to Rainy Pass by holding onto the cuff of his parka sleeve. That man worships Kenai."

The other life that Kenai saved was Bud Branham's. That little adventure might well have ended in tragedy. Roughly, this is what happened. When Kenai was twelve years old, he became stone-deaf. That meant a new team leader, a sad day for Kenai and Bud, too. But a lead dog has got to hear, to get voice signals. Bud hit the trap-line with the team and the new leader, leaving Kenai chained up at home.

Two days later Kenai broke loose and followed Bud's trail. He found Bud, who of course had no other course than to let him go along with the outfit. The time was early December. The team hit bear scent, and the new leader, incapable of keeping a string of dogs straightened out, let them pile up in a mess.

Bud knew the bear was ahead. He knew, too, that the bear should have been holed up at that time of year. But often, when feeding on a kill, the bears delay the beginning of their long sleep. Bud tied down the dogs, including Kenai, whom he tied with a light cord. He recalls that when he put the cord around Kenai's neck the old dog thought he was getting into the harness again and was going to lead the team once more.

Not expecting bears out at that time of year, all Bud had with him was a .30-30, and a poor one that he acquired in a trade. Of course, such a gun against a brownie is bad business, but Bud is a pretty nifty shot. He walked ahead.

He found the bear, all right, feeding on a moose kill, but he wished he had not found it. While he watched the bear from behind a rather high snowbank he felt something touch his knee. It was Kenai, trailing the broken neck cord.

Kenai whined, and Bud brought his hand down hard on his muzzle to hold his mouth shut. The dog could not see the bear but the brownie heard the whine and made up his mind in a hurry. No one was going to move in on his banquet. He came for Bud on the run. Bud tried for one shot with the .30-30 but the gun didn't fire. Later he learned that the firing-pin was too short.

Bud made for the nearest tree, a cottonwood. Kenai took in the scene and engaged the bear. The snow was crusted so that the lighter dog could maneuver, and the bear broke through and wallowed. Kenai got his teeth through a hind leg and the bear turned his attention from Bud, in the tree, to the dog. Then, for about an hour, Kenai and the brownie played tag. Kenai, at twelve, was fast enough on that snow crust to outfoot the bear. Bud says Kenai handled that bear as a skillful boxer handles a neophyte. The bear finally had enough of it and went off. Bud got out of the tree, and Kenai came to him, shivering and excited. They got out of that place, Bud watching for trees big enough to hold a man in case the bear came back.

This is the dog that will let any kid on the main street of Anchorage maul him. And this is the dog that never in his life picked a street fight with another dog.

During my stay in Alaska I became very fond of Kenai. I drove him many miles. I had no idea this affection was reciprocated to any extent until the morning we were leaving Rainy Pass by plane for Anchorage and then home to Milwaukee. The yard on the shore of Puntilla Lake was littered with gear duffel bags, packsacks, cased guns and carefully packed big-game specimens, including the bones for the museum mammologists.

Everywhere I went Kenai went with me. He held the tip of my right mitten in his teeth, ever so gently, but insistently. I asked Bud why this show of affection.

"He's saying good-by," Bud explained.

"If I come back here in four days I'd be a stranger to him all over again. Dogs have no memory."

Bud laughed. "Wait and see," he said.

Two months later Bud flew one of his planes from Alaska to Milwaukee, and Kenai was with him, of course. I'll never forget the morning he and Kenai got off the elevator on the fourth floor of the *Milwaukee Journal* building, the editorial room. I saw them get off, but gave no sign of recognition, nor did Bud. He merely told Kenai, "Go find him."

Off went Kenai to the society desk, where five beautiful young ladies looked around for something to climb. No such kind of dog had ever been seen in that big, busy room, or perhaps in any editorial room other than that of Bob Atwood's *Anchorage Times.* Kenai wheeled and went to the city editor, in the middle of the room. He sniffed and peered. The gentleman with the eye-shade was braver than the ladies. He reached out a tentative hand to stroke the dog, but Kenai perceived that this was not the man he wanted.

He went back toward the elevator to the desk of T. Murray Reed, then executive city editor of the *Journal,* now retired. Reed, no coward, got in a few tentative pats, and Kenai left him. My desk was about thirty feet from him. I don't know whether he smelled me or saw me. He came over with no show of emotion whatever and lay down beside me.

No tail wagging. Just a matter-of-fact end to a search for someone familiar that he'd been sent on. That proves one thing: at least one dog in the world can remember a person for two months. Since then I've been kidded by people who have wondered if Kenai found me by my smell — and did I smell the same in Milwaukee as I had smelled two months before in the Alaskan mountains? Could be — just could be.

I'll always remember Kenai because he had the courage to stand off a brown bear, and because he was a great leader and a great bird dog. I'll remember him because he was unbelievably smart. But most of all I'll remember him because he was a dog of absolute loyalty and because he was a tender, gentle dog who took uncommon courage for granted. And because he held a deep and abiding affection not only for Bud but for any man or beast of good-will.

THE LITTLE
FLIGHT

There are three generally acknowledged "best" outdoor stories.

William Faulkner's The Bear *is about a whale of a fight with a black bear and a boy growing into manhood over the course of hunting him.*

A young Ernest Hemingway came back from the Italian front in World War I, wounded and wondering what to do with his life. He went trout fishing in Michigan. Later in Paris cafés he wrote The Big Two-Hearted River, *about his fishing adventures. It throbs with power.*

The Little Flight *here belongs in this company. It presents Mr. President at his best. The touches of humor add lilt. As for MacQuarrie's shooting, well, we've all had those days. In style it is perfect: beginning, middle and superb ending on just the right note. It is a matchless story made better by effortless telling.*

In the autumn in the North there comes a time when a few stupid crickets courageously carry on their idle fiddling, but you can never tell, as you drop off to sleep, whether yon shrilling insect will survive the night of shrivel under the frost-whitened grass. It is a time when high noon may find the bees under a full head of steam and the horizon a-glimmer with heat waves, even though the goldenrod is dead and only the purple asters flaunt their color. It is a time when the season offers damning proof that men with calendars know not what they are doing when they split the year into four arbitrary parts.

Some call it Indian summer, that precious interlude before squaw winter, which is the fake winter that comes with snow and gale and is liquidated around Thanksgiving with a real blast from the north. Some call it the tail end of summer; but whatever it is named, there is no place on the calendar for it. It is too heady with autumn scent for August. It is too warm for October.

This is, as much as anything, the wedding of the seasons, the perfect blend of warmth and chill and sun and frost. It is also the time when the first of the migrating ducks marshal their legions and skim away from old homes. Not of course, on that headlong, hurry-up plunge we call the big flight, but rather on shorter, preliminary jaunts. It is the little flight.

The big flight comes after. It is a compulsory thing, brought about by ice-glazed bays where the rice and wapato and coontails grow. The big one is a stern and frigid business of earflaps and mittens and thrashing arms to keep up circulation. It is the traditional flight that we all know about and read about and look forward to. The little flight is so modest, so untraditional, so unsung, that sometimes it comes through our favorite duck wallows when we least expect it.

But I know a man so firmly grounded in the arts and parts of water-fowling that he could not possibly ignore the little flight, and that man, of course, is the man who is always ready, willing and able — the Honorable President of the Old Duck Hunters' Association, Inc., which stands for incorrigible.

"I tell you," he said to me one early October evening, "there's an early movement of ducks through north Wisconsin and all the Middle Western States that has never been properly recognized."

He was tinkering with the ropes and weights of some thirty of the darn-dest-looking decoys ever known — handmade caricatures fashioned of wood, painted and repainted until the stuff lay on like armor. He had acquired this set of boosters by bribery the minute he learned they were a hundred years old and had been used on the St. Clair River flats, near Detroit, before the Civil War.

He would jerk an anchor cord, find it firm, and toss the ancient cheat into the good pile. The infirm and the injured members of this precious flock he doctored with paint, lamp-black, putty, lead, weights, and even now and then a bit of a soft pine plug to seal up abdominal fissures.

"Say what you will," he continued, "there is a sneak flight of ducks flying down this way that your season's tail-ender misses completely. Call it just a trickle if you wish. Still it's a flight. And I don't mean just summer ducks like blue-wing teal and wood ducks. I mean big gray mallards and bigger black mallards and ringbill and widgeon and sprig. The thing is, you've got to hit it right, and you can't do that hunting just weekends. You might be lucky. And you might not be lucky."

Was there, I inquired, a way a man could tell when this vanguard came along?

"A man would. A good man" — he appraised me — "would have his duck marsh handy by, say fifty miles away, and would have a look at it every day the third week of October, let us say. Yep, that would be the week for these parts. Most of the sky-busters have forgotten about ducks since the locals grew so wary, and a man studying a marsh would know what was coming into it.

He'd notice if they increased suddenly, if they traded over different passes; and if they seemed the least bit tamer than the locals, he'd know what they were — visitors."

So the pilgrimage began. First, there was a veritable expedition in which a trailer and two large barrels figured prominently. Also a skiff, which was hidden in the tamarack of a semi-dry swamp facing a mile-long stretch of giant wild rice, The barrels were rolled, dragged and sometimes carried until the President said, "This is the place. Dig!"

One of the barrels was a large, spic-and-span oil drum, which had been washed out with gasoline. The other was an obese hogshead which had once served as a pickle barrel. I have hated dill pickles ever since; so now you know who drew the pickle barrel.

Excavation began in the dry, shifting sand at the edge of the wild-rice bed. The first two feet were easy. Then we hit water, and it was a race to shovel out sand before water came in. We won, but not before the barrels, side by side, had to be pushed and dug and crammed down through the sand and water. In a good, stiff rain they would pop up like a jack-in-the-box, but the

Old Duck Hunters go nowhere without shovels, and it was always possible to reseat them.

Such were the blinds. You let yourself down into them and braced your back against the inner walls. A mound of sand around their rims, flush with the ground, was trimmed with the native flora, covering your head. The theory was fine. I got so I could stay in one almost twenty minutes! The President, a patient man, could worm down in, adjust his head cover, light his crooked little pipe and stay there for hours, perfectly comfortable.

Once a visiting hunter stepped into one of these blinds and well-nigh broke a leg. The President told him they were porcupine traps and he had better be careful, because they were sprinkled all over the place. The visiting hunter did not again trespass upon the secret shores of Shallow Bay.

The dedication of those barrels occurred after the opening, a period dedicated by the Old Duck Hunters mostly to creeping up to hidden potholes back in the cut-over. The lull had set in. Hunters quit the marshes for other shooting. They were the sky-busters, waiting for the big parade. Ducks, to them, meant a first day and a cold day, and in between not much of anything.

The daily ride to the wild-rice bed continued. When the old maestro couldn't get away, yours patiently undertook the long trip, to report back each night what he had seen come into the marsh over the high hill and through the pass and from down Namakagon River way. The prexy followed these reports diligently, and mostly shook his head. The little flight was not yet in. The trickle had not yet begun.

Then there came a lowering day in the beginning of October's third week and, harkening to my evening report, Mister President opined there should be something to see next evening — "The paper says it's 15 above at Medicine Hat. No sign of it here, but something will move down in front of that wave. We may even catch a bit of the weather here."

Next evening, as I surveyed the tawny rice bed of Shallow Bay in the final rays, there was more of a clatter in the center. And there were more birds dropping in. The music of wild mallards is worth listening to anywhere, but never better than when it comes to the ears over an old, familiar duck patch where history has been made. I drove a little faster on the way home to tell him.

Had there been more moving? Were there more birds coming in recklessly, without preliminary swings? Were there, maybe, some bluebills in the rice with the ringbills and the mallards? And teal around yet? The answers all being met with a nod of Mister President's head, he decreed an early start and plenty of shells — "Especially for you on those high ones. Me, I'll get along with a couple of boxes."

In the morning we had the marsh to ourselves. If anything, the congress of waterfowl scattered over the marsh had increased during the night. That dove-tailed with the weather, for the Canadian arctic front had hopped over the boundary and was whooping through the Dakotas and Minnesota and north Wisconsin. It was cold, and it was going to get colder. You don't have to look at the weather forecast to know that. Years of watching autumn northwesters in that country replace calculation with instinct.

The marsh wasn't frozen over. It might be in another twenty-four hours. And afterward, if the weather softened, it might open up again and stay open, even that far north, as I have seen it, far into November. This, of course, is unusual, but I have even seen that marsh open in December.

The mile of wind-tossed rice stretched out before us. It was almost broad daylight when we had set out the decoys and adjusted ourselves in the blind. The odor of the long-departed dill pickles penetrated into my heavy blanket coat, and the President whispered across; "I can smell you and the barrel from here. On the way home, if we meet someone, pretend you don't know me."

From behind a screen of twigs we peered out. It was going to be long shooting, he said. "Be sure and mark your bird — the cover is tough. Me, I'll drop mine right at the edge of the decoys."

Would he want to place a little bet on the first duck? Say a good 10-cent cigar with a band on it? Would he? Quick as a snake on a sunny rock he snapped me up. "Make it a box of shells. The rules are, any man may shoot when he's a mind to without tipping off the other guy."

Even while he spoke I noted his eyes were not on me, but were directed through the little curtain of leaves. Hawkeyed, he was watching something in the air. I was too late. The long, lean barrel of his automatic flipped at the boom, and a single greenhead plunged almost into the decoys. He was about to sound a croak of victory, but sank quickly into the barrel and pointed out front.

The shot had brought the marsh alive with tip-up feeders. Blacks and mallards mostly, big devils hovering over the fringed rice, uncertain whether to flop back into the feeding troughs below or pick up and move on. A dozen, too curious, wheeled in close, and there was no time to lay a bet. They hung in front of us in a 30-mile wind, not close, but close enough. When they had side-slipped away, three more lay out in the rice, and the President reminded me hurriedly that he always shot 1¼-ounce loads and for me not to hand him is payment any piddling ounce loads that I carried around.

Many of the departing ducks fled over the high hill, and soon we could hear the biddies stridently advertising the succulence of this new paradise. We hauled out the skiff and retrieved the down birds, during which Mister President politely requested me to stay down-wind from him — "There's nothing like a dill pickle, though, with a hot dog!"

Anyway, there were other things to occupy us, not to mention the pickle barrel. It was not easy searching out the fallen birds. When it was done and we were adjusted in the blinds, Mister President, sniffing the heavy odor of salt vinegar and cucumbers which emanated from me, said it was a good thing that ducks couldn't smell, else there would be no shooting on the marsh that day. He also said he wished he had a clothes-pin to hang over his nose. There are few idle moments in duck blinds with the President.

Curiosity got the better of the puddlers over the hill, and they began drifting back into the bigger rice bed. The Bible says that the fool returneth to his folly as the dog to his vomit; and while we would be the last to assert that a mallard is a fool, certainly these mallards were not post-graduate locals. Our blinds were perfect, except for the odor which emanated from mine. There was not a sign of anything above ground but natural growth. Not even the old felt hat of Mister President, the band of which was festooned with twigs.

The day wore on, and it rained. It rained, and I missed ducks. I have missed ducks before and will miss them again, but seldom have I missed them like that. These travelers of the little flight had me stopped cold. Maybe, I thought, it was the light one-ounce loads, but light one-ounce loads will kill ducks, and I knew it. So did the President know it. He borrowed a couple and killed a couple of ducks.

Toward the end of the day I waded the shoreline to get into the high hill behind us and have a look-see. Hundreds of mallards got up from the smaller rice bed when I came too close, and one of these, choosing the hill course, was tumbled with a thump to the soggy, acorn-strewn growth on the hilltop. It felt good to pick one out like that. Too bad the President didn't see it, in view of the performance he had witnessed from my pickle barrel.

The others milled over the rice, against a dark, wet, ragged sky. It was a wild and lovely moment — even lovelier when speedsters running the block-ade at the blind came in range and I heard the deliberately spaced booms of the President's automatic.

Back in the oaks over the high hill there was less rain and wind. The forest floor underfoot was a silent carpet of yellow and bronze. A man can often flush a deer in there after the acorns have fallen. I saw one, a furtive doe quietly slipping away. She never dreamed she was seen. Snowshoe rabbits are already changed from brown to white. I walked back with my lone duck.

"Only one?" snorted Mister President. "I saw a million get out of there — well, two hundred, anyway. That's more'n a million."

"He was the only one that came in range."

Mister President pointed to his own comfortable pile, close to a limit. Just as I was about to insert myself in the pickle barrel my eye caught a piece of shell-box cardboard. The President had stuck it on the rim of the barrel and had written thereon: "TO LET — One smelly old pickle barrel. Only good duck shots need apply. Owner going out of business. Chance for a good man to build up thriving trade."

After the laughter had been swallowed up in the tamaracks and I had missed another bird and the President had declared a halt — "For fear you'll get the habit permanently" — we picked up and headed for the car. Nosing out of the sand trails through the dripping woods, I acknowledged his masterminding anent the little flight.

"But," I insisted, "I can't figure out why I couldn't hit 'em. You suppose that pickle barrel had anything to do with it?"

He snorted and half turned beside me to deliver his dictum with full impact: "Boy, your shooting and that pickle barrel both smell the same to me."

OLD DEACON WOODCOCK

This tribute to that wonderful game bird, the woodcock, appeared in Field & Stream *in 1940 and has been in obscurity every since. Why? No good reason. There was just never enough room for all the good pieces.*

We used to hunt woodcock regularly at Cape May, as MacQuarrie here, following the weather reports to know when cold would push the birds down the New Jersey peninsula.

Strange that this cleanest of all game birds (the French eat the "trail," as suggested) should be tainted in some way to a dog. We hunted with a Weimaraner. She'd pick up the birds (or we would never have known if we hit them) but drop them immediately. Few dogs will retrieve them to hand.

Yet what bird is more delicately flavored and sweet tasting? As MacQuarrie says: "The odor must be a potent one, as odors go in that strange dark limbo of dog scent."

"Another thing about timberdoodles — they're easy to dress. Come to think, some good chefs advise against removing the entrails. H-m-m-m. At that, they're one game bird you might handle that way. Fast, aren't they? Lightning in buff and brown. The immaculate legs — you'd think a bird with his feet in the mud would get his spats soiled like a jacksnipe."

Irrelevant thoughts. I addressed them mostly to the furnace the other night while dressing a brace of birds. Down there in the basement on a duck-picking job you just wade in and let the feathers fly. The same with pheasants.

Or even sharp-tailed grouse. Oh, you may muse a bit over a ruffed grouse.

But woodcock! Any addict knows how it feels to have a limit all his own. I know plenty of steady citizens who will forego a guaranteed limit of ducks to take a long shot on woodcock and later someone will say, "Well, dang it, Joe, they were here yesterday." The furtive little eight-ounce dervish of the thick places has developed a school of gunners in this land who are as ardent and secretive as some of the academicians of the floating fly.

Solid now, the woodcock devotees. Bankers, lawyers, business men, farmers — the warp and woof, no matter what their calling. One of the most devout brothers I know is a barber. Scan the field, and you'll find these specialists whole, sound humans.

I gathered together the daily newspapers for the last four days and checked weather reports. There it was, in black and white, in the little column of weather tables headed "Vital Statistics." Vital is no word for it. Temperatures in Canada had dropped to 14 above. In northern Wisconsin and Minnesota it was almost as cold. Had been four days ago. The weather tables confirmed a timberdoodle wave.

That was a morning! For three unrelenting weeks the area from north Wisconsin down into Illinois had been drifting along through the calendar in a haze of Indian-summer vapors. This morning was different. The wind was northwest. Here at last was an end to Indian summer, which had played hob with hunting men in hundreds of duck blinds. The cocks must certainly be riding the southern edge of that arctic mass.

At my friend's I found him still incoherent, bordering upon the inarticulate. He drank a cup of scalding coffee and burned his mouth, but didn't know it until it was down. He lit his pipe and let it go upside down, then tried to light the bottom of it. He mumbled: "Saw 'em last night again . . . After shooting, went down to look . . . Ouch, my mouth! Got a match? . . . They're everywhere . . . Get down, Friskie . . . Hup! Hup you, Friskie!"

Let it be interposed here that if you have any questions about the ability of a Chesapeake to work woodcock, forget them. In the kennel Friskie came out of that morning there remained some of the nicest shooting setters in the state of Wisconsin, a couple of springers and a pointer. Friskie was nominated for this holiest of holy quests.

Ah, Friskie, will we ever forget that day? The parking of the car in a bog where it slowly settled. "To heck with it! We can pry it out later." The hike into the dense thicket, wrists and fingers tingling in the cold blast from the northwest.

Friskie hunted close in. She does it to perfection. Third in the party was a canny native named Elmer who knew the woodcock answers. We spread over a short front. The going was next to impossible. You do not walk through that stuff. You wade through it, in imminent danger of losing an eye from whipping alders. You drag grape vines until your legs ache.

For a big dog, Friskie made marvelous progress through the tangle. She hesitated, and then rushed in, spaniel-like. The morning really came to life.

Something light as the whisper of a ghost lifted from the dense bottom growth, spiraled up like an animated maple leaf. An etching by an old master. Only more like a motion-picture etching, if you can imagine such a thing.

There he was — all of him. The old Deacon himself! Most mysterious, most gallant of all the upland migrators. Hunched back and long bill. I saw one delicate white leg hang for a minute before being retracted like a plane's landing gear.

Bam! Nitro cracking in woodcock cover has something about it as respectable as a village church bell. It was my gun. Something fell beyond a cluster of white birches. Friskie trembled, staunchly waiting the order to fetch. She had marked the bird well and came in with it promptly.

One flaw marred her otherwise perfect performance. In common with many other dogs she dislikes to hold a woodcock in her mouth. But she did her work neatly, albeit her upper lip curled back as though to avoid too intimate contact with the bird. Ordinarily she delivers to hand, but she drops woodcock at a gunner's feet.

There are plenty of explanations as why dogs "fool around" with woodcock. Only the other day a setter fancier told me something we've all heard many times, "They stink!" he said. I resent that as applied to a woodcock. We charter members of the Old Duck Hunters' Association, Inc., won't have woodcock spoken of like that. But the odor must be a potent one, as odors go in that strange dark limbo of dog scent.

The hunt proceeded. Elmer, a proven woodcocker, picked up the next one. Friskie had been "working the line." That is, hunting for everyone by paralleling us as we waded through. Elmer's bird got up out of my sight, but the exultant "Got 'im!" was plain enough. Friskie retrieved the bird.

Put it down here and now that two good big dogs are proving they are more than retrievers here in Wisconsin and the Middle West. They are the Labrador and the Chesapeake. Men are using them like springer spaniels in the tougher cover. Their legginess is a great help in the cow hobbles. They have plenty of stamina, and those I've seen had nose to spare. One day last fall I hunted pheasants with five strapping Chesapeakes. But that's another story.

We were shooting No. 9's in $1\frac{1}{8}$ loads. A sweet load for Deacon Woodcock. Strong though he is of wing, the Deacon is a pretty finely drawn chap with a thin skin. Heavy stuff is certainly not indicated. Leave your duck loads behind. By all means keep a box of nines handy in that shell box all the time. Two boxes! Remember you can't always pick up nines in a cross-roads hardware store.

I would see my friends every so often. They rose and fell in the brush like ships in a heavy sea. Many a cock that morning used his wise, old head and quick, deft wings to clear the tree-tops and slide down the far side of the cover. I don't recall how many Friskie flushed, but I do remember that without her we would not have flushed half as many. She is careful, has the gun in mind in close cover, and what a nose! Once she missed, came around in time with a noseful, ran in back of me and boosted the Deacon out of a spot I had almost walked over. Elmer collected the bird as it drifted away.

I used to do a lot of ruffed-grouse hunting — pa'tridge, they mostly call 'em here in Wisconsin. I still do it, especially when I can do it as I like it best — down the old forgotten logging roads of the lake states, over which they hauled out the white pine. In those days when the Old Duck Hunters'

Association used to hunt 'em day after day, like eating meals, I always enjoyed the ceremony the Hon. President of the Association performed with grouse.

He would inspect them carefully, stroke the feathers, spread the fan-like tail and finally bury his nose in the rich autumn-brown breast. There's a smell about a ruffed grouse. The same little ceremony he carried out with timberdoodles, but then there would be a certain reverence paid the bird. He'd hold the Deacon, stroke the buff underbody, swing it by the bill, stick it in his pocket and remark: "Pa'tridge can't be beat — or can they?"

"Jack Pine Joe" Stories

It's worth recalling that one of MacQuarrie's duties for about 15 years was filling a weekly outdoor page for the Journal. *I can guarantee you that the search for material for this page was constant and compelling. MacQuarrie countered by creating the "Jack Pine Joe" pieces and filling them with Joe's usually inebriated and unsavory friend and, of course, his outrageous plans and opinions. Hiding behind the dialect and the character, MacQuarrie could think and say most anything he wanted, poke fun where he wanted.*

There are four new ones here. I find Jack Pine Joe grows on me. The first read they are snorting funny. But after a few more reads, they are head-shaking funny. "What fools we mortals be" funny. There's a lot of Jack Pine Joe in us all.

Joe Would Train Badgers as Sewer, Tunnel Diggers

Dear Mak:

Sincet the falcyure uv the Flambeau River to the Sea associashun wich wuz fer the perpuss uv bringing oshen vessuls rite up to Lugerville i hev been devotin my nites in deep thawt fer I am as you no intrusted in developin the manofatchurin industry in these parts.

To insoore thet my latest venchure will be a sucksess I hev takin steps to keep ol man Simpson outn it. As you may recawll it was when he abscondud with the $7.64 thet the On to the Sea projeck blowed up. At thet the On to the Sea projeck had its pints even if it finully wound up as haf pints in Simpsons pockit.

Well sir i hev got suthin bran new this time an i am lettin all my frens in on the ground floor and i wont take no fer a answeer speshully from you an uthers as is owin me boat rent.

Whut i am a-hatchin is a macheenry facktry to turn out excavatin outfits. The idee is ter go out an trap badgers an lern em to dig in a strate line then advertise in awl the big papers. Fer sewer diggin we kin supply em with baby badgers an fer middle sized diggins we kin turn out middul size badgers. Fer the bigger jobs like anuther Panamaw canawl we kin perjuce oversize badgers.

I don't mind sayin they cud hev dug the Holland tunnel at haf the cost with these here badgers. My idee is ter use feel mice ahead uv the badgers to get em a-goin an fit out the badgers with steem gages and compusses to show the preshure an keep the direckshun.

Let me no how menny shares uv stock ye kin handul.

Yourn,
JACK PINE JOE,
The Flambeau Guide.

P.S. We kin also sell em fer posthole diggers. My ridge runner sez he kin trane em to not oney dig the holes but put in the posts.

Brrr! Steam Fruz Solid, But Fingers Got Burned

Dear Mak:

In town tother day to trade a pair o Christmas sox fer some eatin terbacker who do i meet in the store but that danged ole hipacrit an liar my good fren Ol Man Simpson. The ol he goat as usual wuz cuttin a swath in the cheese an crackers an lyin like a trooper. Ye kin lie an get away with it in them big cities like Fifield and Park Falls where the reel hicks live but oncet yer outn the country ye gotta be keerful. It was a tolable cold day an peepul natrally tawked about the wether which Simpson did too claimin thet morning wen he went out to the pump he had ter chop out his whiskers wich got fassened in the pump handle. Still it aint so cold he sez it aint so cold. He sez i mind the time when it went down to 75 below. At Hines camp 41 just beyant the Flambeau bridge where I was scaldin a hog in a horse troff the steem fruz solid. Yessir.

Ye dont say, sez i, cetchin the drift a things. An wusnt it the summer arter thet it got so dry the muskies goin upstreem left a trail a dust? It wuz not sez Simpson tightenin his belt. It wus a wet summer thet yeer. It rained dang hard. I hed a empty oak keg outside the cook shanty an sum days the rain cum down so hard it ran in the bunghole so fat it cuddent run out both ends.

Thet wuz too much fer me but Simpson kep a goin. He sez thet summer it was so all fired damp we had to strain the milk frum the cows to get the minnows outa it. By then I wuz headin fer the door an Simpson wuz just warmin up. Then the storekeeper cum over an charged him fer two pouns a cheese an a box of crackers so he said put it on the bill and went home mad.

Yourn,
 JACK PINE JOE,
The Flambeau Guide.

Jack Pine Joe Expounds on the "Sidehill Gouger"

Dear Mak:

As you no I am not a man given to boastingfulness but in the feeld a natral histry you will fine the name o Jack Pine Joe inscribed amung the inmortuls like Awdabum. Eggasee an Carrie Nashun. Oney tother day a feller wuz talking about a marmota monax and wen I looked I see it was oney a woodchuk which he mistook fer sumthin else.

But what i am gittin at is not woodhuks but sidehill gougers. In my latest lecsure to the Lugerville Academy a Signs an Wildlife Reserch I pinted out sum things about the gouger as is not genrully known. Fer instunce, the gouger native oney in the north has legs longer on one side than tother like peeple livin in Duluth on the hill.

They is right an lef handed gougers an they can travel oney wun direcshun cuz they fall over if you reverse 'em account a them short legs bein on the downhill side. They allus go the same direcshun wich dont make no diffrunce to a gouger cuz he dont care where he goes as long as hes goin.

The imachure gougers live in trees an fly backards in the rain to keep the water outa there eyes. There is no truth to a Rinelander report that the sidehill gouger has its hind legs in frunt an its frunt legs behind. They hev the Hodag in mind wich is switched aroun so bad every time he sees his tracks he cant tell if he just come or just left.

In the intrusts a scientific acrisy I hav set the fourgoing down an also in the hope it will keerect previous Miss Apprehenshuns about the Hodag. I mite add I am gatherin material fer a signtific paper on the gillagalee bur an if eny reeders has awthentick fax on same they can send them to me care a the jurnel.

Yourn,
JACK PINE JOE,
The Flambeau Guide.

JOE BUBBLES OVER ABOUT A MUSKIE THAT DID TOO

Dear Mak:

No dowt you hev heerd me menshun the value o using yer hed an savin yer bak which is a favrit subjek o mine lerned from the heethen chinee who sez you kin skin the slippriest cat by using a littul sweetness an diplomercy.

I giv Buck my ridge runner a lesson in sech tackticks oney las summer as we wuz fishin way over to Grindstone. I recollec the day well cuz it wuz the day arter Louis Spray sawt thet big muskie an I sez where theres wun theres to an we went.

It was so hot the beer got warm afore wed circled the lake moren oncet. Without no beer to wet his whissul Buck didunt hev much enthusiasm fer castin but he kep to it. He casted in the brilin sun an the swet run down an no fish cum an soon I see it wuz time fer brain to show its mastery over brawn.

I hed been heving a mite o stummick trubble offn on an the doc gave me summ little white pills which bubbled like all gitout in a glass o water. They wern't nothin moren seidlitz tablits to me but to the doc they wuz 4 bucks fer the cawl an 2 bucks fer the perscripshun an as they didunt do me no good I decided to get suthin outa the investment.

Hol on there I sez to Buck wile I got out the powders. We wuz over a sunk reef an lookin down I cud see a big ol lunker muskie lyin on the bottum. I dropped the powder rite in frunt uv his nose and as it bubbled away he opened wun eye and lookt at it an then opened tother eye an then he gulped er down without hardly no wash.

In no time at all he begun to swell like a plained pup and he slowly riz up to the surface inflated like a balloon an I reeched fer him with the net. He wuz still frothin at the mouth when we hawled him in an hour later his pitcher had been tuk 50 times as a 50 pounder but when the Seidlitz powders wore off he'd shrunk to 20.

Still an all it was a nice fish an as it was my last stummick pill he took I aint been bothered since.

Yourn,
JACK PINE JOE,
The Flambeau Guide.

Now, in June

You are about to read a Paul Bunyan of a story, a Fifth Symphony of a story. In fact Beethoven should have written this story. Or maybe Mozart.

All the majestic MacQuarrie themes are here. The visceral appreciation. The unending thrill, "I can't take 'em without quaking." The love of familiar places. The understated skills involved. And, let's face it, "I'm for filling frying pans, you understand."

There are hundreds of lines that I love in Gordon MacQuarrie's yarns but Mr. President's calling across the water as they enter the stream lasts with me forever. "I can't figger out how a Scotch Presbyterian like yourself can enjoy anything that's so much fun."

No time is better for trout fishermen than early June. Other months may approach it. They may even excel it now and then. But what I am getting at is that June is the best time for trout fishermen, as well as trout fishing.

Take the President of the Old Duck Hunters' Association, Inc., for instance. This symbolic angler said to me one night in knee-deep June in his back yard, "I can tell by the smell in the air I am going trout fishing tomorrow."

It was a good smell. Flowers were coming up out of brown earth. Insects hummed. The neighborhood was suffused with the odors of lush June. You smelled it and, smelling it, wondered if you would take those stuffy waders tomorrow or just an old pair of pants for wading.

"Yes, sir," said Mr. President, "I can smell trout tonight. I can smell 'em along towards tomorrow night on the Namakagon below Cable. I will just put me in there at Squaw Bend for maybe not more 'n an hour or two. It'll be dusk when the wind dies; so the mosquitoes will help me change flies.

"First, I will eat supper in the car. I will be pretty lazy about it. I will not be hurried, you understand? I will set there a spell. I'll bet I hardly move a muscle until I hear the first whippoorwill. Then after a bit I will jump in below the county trunk bridge and tempt providence and the good brown trout of the Namakagon with large, unscientific come-sundown flies. That is what I will do."

Imagine a man in this feverish age, twenty-four hours beforehand, declaring exactly what he will do twenty-four hours hence, come what will as to weather, business or the current status of his sciatic rheumatism.

"Yep," he reiterated there in his back yard, "I will drive down past McKinney's drug-store there in Cable and over to the river, and just as I'm arriving at Squaw Bend four cars with Illinois license plates will be pulling out. These will be city fishermen who don't know any better than to fish for Namakagon browns in broad daylight. They will be sore at the river. They will tell me there ain't a brown in the river — never was! They will go away from there, leaving it to me just when I want it, as the fishing gets good.

"I'm danged if I can figger out what trout fishermen these days are thinking about. They start at 10 AM, after a good night's rest and a leisurely breakfast. They fish until the six-o'clock whistle, and wonder why they don't get 'em. People like that are not entitled to catch trout. To catch trout, you got to suffer and learn."

He carried out the next day's schedule to a T. He abandoned his business at three, and one hour later came up my front walk in khaki trousers, his eyes snapping. I was only half ready. There had been a slight argument at our house. My wife, who is Mister President's daughter, just sort of hung around and looked abused while I picked up my stuff. That can unnerve people like me.

The President took in matters at a glance and yelped: "For heaven's sake, woman! Get away from that man! Can't you see he ain't soaked his leaders yet?"

Think of it! A man who can talk like that and make it stick! Picking up the final odds and ends, however, I wondered for the hundredth time why he could not command so imperiously in his own house, where he achieves his ends by other means — obsequiousness, if not downright chicanery. It's a smart man who knows when he's licked.

"Trout fishing is not like drinking beer," he lectured as the car sped south and east. "It's more like sipping champagne. A good beer drinker just sits him down and lays into it. You hear the first one splash. But you just sip champagne. You take a tiny leetle bit and smack your lips.

"So with trout. You don't want too many. You want to get the stage all set. You look ahead and figger out every move. You will not be rushed. You are not after a bait of fish. If you are, you would go down to the St. Croix and jerk the derned teeth out of smallmouths. What you are after is to fool a trout, or maybe four or five.

"I'm for filling frying-pans, you understand. But only now and then. More often I'm for picking out a trout so smart he thinks of running for the legislature. There he is, living under the bank by daylight and sneering at the guys, who waste their time working over him when the sun is high. My idea of perfection is to give that guy a dose of sprouts — to teach him a lesson he won't forget, if I can't creel him."

"Then you have some places in mind — "

"I'll thank you not to poke into other people's affairs and also to stay away from that hole two hundred yards below the town road, where the big dead stump sticks out into the river."

"Agreed. In return, will you avoid the fast rip below the island?"

"Why should I fool with half-pounders" he snorted. "Your ten-cent rips are secure against trespass."

We drove under Cable's gorgeous pines, past McKinney's drug-store, which has seen more big browns than most drug-stores, past the sawmill, and thence to the Namakagon at Squaw Bend, which is some place.

"Not exactly slightly known, however," Mister President replied when I raised the question. "Too dog-gone well known. But, happily, not intimately to fishermen who will play its own game."

"Like who?"

"Like me. Me, I wouldn't come down here a-whipping and a-lashing this crick in broad daylight. Oh, mebbe I would on an overcast, windy day. And how many of these do we get in a season? Me, I'd come down here either first thing in the morning or last thing at night. I'd rather do this than mow the lawn, I would . . ."

He wheeled the car across a shallow, dry ditch, and it settled on low, hard ground, off the road. Twenty feet away the Namakagon journeyed by in the last direct rays of the sun. He broke out sandwiches and coffee and forbade me to move out of the car "until the time is ripe."

There was the dear old river. And sure enough, two disgusted fishermen coming to their car, parked near by, who answered a hail with "You can have our share of it."

"Imagine!" snorted the President. "The exalted conceit of people who will fish this creek on a day the sky is so bright it isn't blue, but white! There they go, and fair weather after them. Quitting at seven o'clock. You know, I think this present generation of trout fishermen is afraid of the dark!"

Softly comes the night along the Namakagon. Born in cold, crooked-shored Namakagon Lake, it curves south and west to the St. Croix, its upper reaches trout water, its lower reaches smallmouth water almost on a par with the St. Croix itself.

There it was, just beyond the car windows, gray and ropy in the growing dusk. It ran under the county trunk bridge, surged to the right and lost itself around the corner, where there is a grand series of rips. You just look at that kind of river in June and want to plump right into it.

Not, however, when the President is in charge. We sat and munched. In that far northern corner of Wisconsin, darkness comes slowly in early June. That is a great help to deliberate evening campaigners. Those twilights were made for trout fishermen. They give you time, the President says, "to square off at it."

It was a night to remember, and the Old Duck Hunters remember many such and are properly thankful. June along the Namakagon is a month of heavy perfumes and many birds. No stretch of the Namakagon in the Cable-Seeley country offers more than the Squaw Bend Territory.

Trout waters can be very personal places. The best trout streams are the ones you grow up with and then grow old with. Eventually they become like a familiar shotgun, or a faithful old setter, or a comfortable pair of shoes. You develop a profound affection for them, and you think maybe before you die you will even understand a little about them.

We went downstream, he on the right bank, I on the left. At the putting-in place, high above the right bank, stretches the level top of an old logging railroad grade. The light was waning in the west, and the top of this embankment cut off the sky like a knife. Below this ran the churning river, far noisier and more mysterious than it had been an hour before.

Certainly you must know how it is to come to a place like this. A place you know well. A place where you are on intimate terms with the smallest boulders, where yonder projecting limb once robbed you of a choice fly, where from beneath the undercut banks the big ones prowl by night to claim the larger morsels of the darkness.

Strange and utterly irresistible are such places to trout fishermen. There you had hold of a good one. Here you netted a smaller one. Down beyond the turn in the pool below the old snag pile you lost still another. The spell of approaching night silenced the President, but not for long.

"One thing I can't figger out," he said finally. His voice came to me from a point downstream, drifting over the purring waters in the sweet June air, "How can a Scotch Presbyterian like you enjoy anything that's so much fun?"

He vanished in the gloom like some wise ancient spirit of the river. I heard his wader brogues nick a rock as he stumbled, heard him cuss softly and the river took me in . . .

Though it is early June, the mosquitoes are not bad. One of those rare nights when the pesky hordes fail to discover you there in mid-river. The temperature had dropped quickly from a sunlit 80 or so to below 70, and you know it will be a night for blankets. You know, too, as the water laps at waders that it is the cool, kindly hand of night which chills your river every twenty-four hours and makes it livable for trout.

You are as relaxed, physically and mentally, as you will ever be. The river has reached out like an old friend and made a place for you. You pack a leisurely pipe, and the water about you is lit for a minute, the match hisses in the river and the babbling mystery of the night deepens.

The current plucks at your knees. Your fingers feel in the darkness for the familiar shapes of bass-sized trout flies. A whim will decide which one. From long experience you have learned to hold fingers toward the western sky as you bend on your choice.

What to do? Work the right bank down, foot by foot, with the short, efficient line of the after-sunset angler? Or cover all the water methodically, persistently?

Plop! A Namakagon brown has decided the issue for you. He is down-stream maybe as much as fifty yards, and a good fat plop it is. Just the kind of trout you would expect to come prowling out from the snags on a cool June evening. You know it is the careless fling of a worthy brown, and you are pretty sure he will look at something big and buggy, that he is confident and bellicose.

But just a minute now! You've tried these fish before in the near dark. They come quickly and they go quickly. Once pricked, they standeth not upon the ceremony of their departing. You tighten up a bit. Browns, though more foolhardy by night, can still be very chancy. You do, however, reach around and feel for the net handle, but quickly make personal amends to whatever fishing gods there be. You know it does not pay to be cocky. You know you must study to be humble and alert.

You take it easy in getting to a spot upstream from the fish. You get over to the left bank for your little stalk, and you lift your feet high and put them down easily. You study the vague outline of the branches with which you will have to contend in casting. You take long, hard drags at the blackened pipe, so that the bowl glows hot. You are on edge and ready. You get within thirty-five feet of the place and wait . . .

Plop! Good! He is not frightened. You false-cast with the big fly, wondering how to show it to him. A slack-line drift down over him? Or cross-current cast and a smart retrieve? You decide on the former. It will disturb the water less, and you can come back to the fussier cast later.

You lengthen line, and you know your fly is going over his window. Nothing. Again and again you cast, letting it drift below him and out into midstream. And you retrieve each time carefully, so as not to whip his top water and frighten him. Still nothing. He isn't seeing it.

Very well. You have covered all corners of his window with the dead floating fly. You have shown him Business No. 1, and he wants none of it. Very well. Now for action, à la bass stream. Zip — zip — zip! The fly is brought back over his window in short jerks.

Ka-doong! That was the medicine. He's got it. He's fast and he's heavy and he's going places.

Now, for Pete's sake, take it easy. The leader is sound and the stream is free of stuff, except for the undercut bank. He is bucking like a mule. You strip in a couple of feet, tentatively, and exult at your strategy in showing him an actionable fly, something struggling and toothsome.

He's certainly husky. Those Namakagon busters are built like tugboats. He's sidewise now, below you, in midstream, giving you the works. He has broken water a couple times, He rushes you and you strip in like mad, letting the retrieved line fall where it may in the current.

And then after you have given him Mister President's "dose of sprouts," and you reach around and feel the hickory handle of the net . . .

Like many another after-dark brown on the Namakagon, this one was a good pound and a half. I did not see him until he was in the net, and that is unusual. Generally you see living flashes of fleshy brown out there in the gloom. He was reddish and thick and cold as ice as I removed the fly, tapped him on the head and slid him into the wide, deep jacket pocket I use for a creel.

I was trembling. I can't take 'em without quaking. They get right down under me, and turn flip-flops inside. The pipe was out. The tripped line was bellied downstream. The fly was chewed. It was a pattern evolved by a friend whose stamping ground is the surging river Wolf. A few of its devotees gave it a name a year back — Harvey Alft's Nonpareil — and it has stuck.

I went over and sat on a boulder near the bank. Just one trout — and all that fuss. I sat and wondered, as all men have, if the day would ever come when I could take so small a fraction of a trout stream's population and not develop a galloping pulse.

I have caught more trout that I deserve to catch. And always and forever, the good ones like this fellow put me on edge, send me hippity-hopping to a boulder or the bank to sit down and gather my wits.

Another pipeful helped settle things. I thought, sitting there, another bold trout might betray himself by leaping, but none did. I tested the leader, smoked out the pipe and went back upstream by the left bank. Now the first plan of campaign would be in order — fish the right bank like a machine. Swish-swish. That was the only sound there in the dark as the Nonpareil sailed back and out, back and out. Maybe there would be one or two right in close to the bank, just outside the protecting roots.

There was. Indeed there was. Another golden-bellied Namakagon brown mouthed Harvey Alft's Nonpareil with sure determination and made for midstream and faster water. He was smaller, but lively. I horsed him a bit. You are permitted to do that when you are building up to a brace. A pair is so much better than a loner. Two more were netted through the methodical casting toward the right bank, out from which they lay feeding. And there is little excuse for repeating the old, old story.

It was getting on toward 10 PM, which is the time you quit on trout streams in Wisconsin. I moved downstream to the sacred precincts of Mister President's pool. The whippoorwills were in a dither. A deer splashed at the stream bank and snorted back through the brush. The flat top of the old logging grade was now lit by the stars.

I was proud of my four fish. I showed them to him. He said they were fish that would disgrace no man's skillet. He was sitting on the bank in the dark. His glowing cigar end attracted me. He was a little weary, and I felt a little guilty when he pounded me on the back and then said he had nothing — "but I had hold of one — *the* one!"

Nothing for Mister President. I do not like to wind up trout trips with him that way. And, in all coincidence, I seldom do!

We followed the bank back to the car and pulled off our waders. It was just ten o'clock. He slumped a little over the wheel, for he was beaten and he was tired. And then, before he stepped on the starter, he rolled down a window and took a good, long sniff of the Namakagon's June aroma.

"You know," he said, "I can tell by the smell in the air I am going trout fishing tomorrow."

Man Friday
Folds Up

If you happen to have read The National Sportsman *for October 1935 you might be familiar with this yarn. If not, it will be a new treat for you.*

It is a little different. Usually MacQuarrie does without complaint all the work out of regard for Mr. President's lumbago, bad back, rheumatism, etc. Maybe mild complaint. Here the younger man is played out. Does that stop or even slow Mr. President? Of course! He even takes over the oars himself! You'll find out why and when at the end.

I didn't want to go duck hunting, anyway. Hadn't I just returned from a 500-mile trip through storm and sleet? And hadn't I shot ducks on that trip? And hadn't I driven weary miles through a snowstorm outbound, and skidded back home at fifteen miles an hour after rain hit that foot of snow and froze? And wouldn't I need at least one more night of solid sleep to whet my duck appetite again?

The upshot of it was, of course, that the President of the Old Duck Hunters' Association, Inc., was brewing coffee as I entered his kitchen at 2:30 AM.

"Good morning," he chirped, and then added cheerfully, after a glance at my still sleepy eyes, "You'll probably pass out on this trip."

He looked like a man who had been sleeping well for a year. He rubbed his hands and chortled. His supreme indifference to my plight rankled. After all these years, I pondered, during which I had rowed boats for him, driven cars for him, picked up decoys for him with numbed hands — and now, to treat me thus!

I drank a cup of the scalding concentrate he called coffee. He peered out the window, where another unseasonable snowstorm was blowing, and opined there surely ought to be ducks in the air. Then, as he gathered up his final knickknacks, I went out to start the car. My thoughts were bitter as I fumbled in the dark for the switch.

An hour and twenty minutes later we arrived. Oh, yes, I drove. He didn't like to drive at night, he said he just liked to sleep, which he did, his head cradled against my shoulder, while I pushed a car through another seventy miles of blinding whiteness. By this time you may be learning just how crazy I am. There is no help for this kind of insanity. I'm just a duck hunter and should not be held strictly accountable for all of my actions between October first and freeze-up.

It was a long time before daylight, but the snow had thinned and the lake with its wide beach was plainly visible as we stowed our traps in the boat. "There's bound to be ducks," whispered the President. "Say, you gonna row? My lumbago, you know — "

Me, I didn't care. I was present just from force of habit. Might as well row as sit there and freeze, the President suggested. He always contrives to make these things quite logical.

The set was made. The last wooden decoy was plopped overboard and I rowed the boat to distant cover while the President piled some brush around the blind. Then I crept into it and parked on my shell case. The President has assumed his customary worshipful position before the green brush altar of duckdom that is the blind. I've seen him thus on his knees in a blind for hours. And they say there's no religion in hunting!

"Down!" This command is really an important part in the matutinal ceremony — the equivalent, in a church, of the preacher's "Let us pray."

The President's sharp eye, familiar with the duck highways in those parts, had picked out the first distant birds. They came from the right, high and fast, going some place else — perhaps two dozen of them. They saw our layout, but wheeled abruptly, as though drawn by a stronger inducement, and flew straight away from us. Across our lake they headed, passed over a point of land separating our lake from another, now dried up, circled a few times, and descended.

"There's not enough water in that lake to float a chip," I remarked.

"H-m-m-m," said Mr. President. "That's funny — mighty, mighty funny."

Again, "Get down!" From the same direction came another flock but, before they came in range, they rose even higher and followed the exact course of the first flock. For five months that lake had been nothing but an ugly mud flat; nevertheless, flock after flock ignored our carefully made set-up and headed for its dried-up expanse.

I dozed. Then a couple of bluebills came along, but they were obviously stragglers. The real flight, mostly mallards, was going into the dried lake — so dry that the natives in the past year had finally found a name for it — Dry Lake.

The President began to speculate on moving. I tried to steer him away from the subject. I felt I could not pick up the outfit, row it a half-mile, drag it another mile and more through the woods, and then set up somewhere else. Another burden I have been compelled to bear up under, through the ages, is the President's insatiable desire to move house and go hunt somewhere else. This is always very hard on me. I should be bigger, I can see that, all right. I think I'll go in training for the next season.

"If every mallard in Wisconsin heads in there, I'm not moving," I said, registering what I thought was profound conviction.

The President looked me over as one might examine an old horse before hitching him to the plow. "I guess you'll last the day out," he remarked. "Hell, when I was your age I used to walk four miles every morning down the top strand of a barbed wire fence, barefooted, with a wildcat in each hand! You can't quit on me now!"

"No," said I, "I suppose not."

"Atta boy, buck up," he answered grimly. "I knew you had the stuff!"

It was getting colder. The wind was freshening from the northwest, which means plenty of cold in upper Wisconsin late in October. After a period of gloomy inspection of the farther shore I decided to up and build me a fire, which I did. It was a very nice fire, but just when it began to throw some heat a flock of bluebills came along and I got back into the blind, after a hard run.

We got a couple. I was thinking about getting back to the fire. Suddenly from straight in front came a single mallard, flying low. I saw him first. I couldn't miss — and I didn't. I rushed to pick him up.

Just as I got him the President, who had been skirmishing around, called me.

"Hey!" he cried.

"Wha'?"

"C'mere."

I got back to the fire like a dog let in the house after a cold winter night. The President was standing by the fire, a lunch cloth folded over one arm, waiter style. On a snowy white tablecloth laid across the flat log was the morning repast, steaming coffee, sandwiches. Of such climactical whimsy is the President capable.

However, after the first re-tightening of the fraternal bonds between us, it slowly dawned up me that the President had other uses in mind for me that day.

"I'm really just saving you for the second half," he confessed. I made some formal objection to the idea of moving over to Dry Lake, but a full stomach and warm fire changes one's viewpoint. The President had set the stage well. I began to weaken. I broke down completely after a while, and found myself rowing the boat across the lake to the jack pine jungle while the President presided on the stern sea. Some day I shall write a book devoted solely to stories told by the President while watching some one else row.

Soon I was brushing the jack pine needles out of my face while trying to balance a 70-pound load of decoys, guns, shell cases, and assorted ducking knickknacks. The President, it must be admitted, toted his share but his share should have been bigger than half. The moving idea was strictly his own investment but he was using up my capital on it as well as his own. The one-time lake of lakes that burst upon us as we plunged through the last of the jacks was a sorry sight. It was a lonely waste of mud, where, a few years before, had been three feet of water covering wonderful duck feed. One end seemed to contain a little water.

"Is that water up there?" I asked the President.

"Sure — ducks, too."

I dropped my load, the better to see. As I did, several hundred mallards climbed into the air from the little hole that looked, from where we stood, about the size of a hat. A good half-mile walk brought us to it — perhaps fifty yards across, filled with two feet of water from recent rains.

"I knew that hole was here," said the President. "Caught some good bass in it several years ago on a mousie — remember? And you said it seemed like the deepest spot in the lake."

We built a blind. It took more than an hour. We dug her deep, using a little trench shovel. Under the snow the sand was dry and soft. I dug my side on a slant, with thoughts of sleep in mind. It's the first and only bed I ever dug. To build a blind with the President on hand means hard labor. Nothing but perfection suits him and we did the job right. When we were through it was a perfect windbreak, not more than two feet of jack pine showing above the ground and well placed among other jacks which sheltered us overhead. Any other kind of a blind would have been a waste of time for those mallards, that we knew.

I lay back in the soft sand and slept. It was a glorious descent into the valley of slumber, the blind shielding me from the wind and snow and my heavy hunting coat as the down of silk coverlets against my chin. But it ended with the President's heavy hand on my shoulder.

"S-s-s-shh," he cautioned, crouched low. I followed his pointing mitten, through the blind. In the middle of the mud lake a flock of mallards were circling, uncertain. Our invasion had made them cautious. They passed us en masse, with a few in range, but the President shook his head. He counseled shooting at smaller bunches and he had confidence in his blind.

I slept again. When I awakened the President was getting back into the blind, a pair of mallards in his hand.

"Where'd you get them?" I gasped.

"My boy, I used salt. You don't mean to say you didn't hear me fire those three shots?"

"Not a shot."

All of which indicates how sorely in need of rest I was. I took a walk to wake up. It resulted in a condition that might have been merely suspended animation.

The afternoon waned. So did I. I was hanging together fairly well but it was only my pride in my charter membership in the Old Duck Hunters that was doing it for me. The snow wasn't letting up. Neither was the wind.

We (me — who else?) changed the decoys around at 2:30. I thought of building another fire to inject new life into myself, but decided it was too late. There I was — too tired to enjoy what was going on and not tired enough to quit. Quit? On the President? Such things are not done in the Old Duck Hunters' Association, Inc. I was like a small boy at a party, with a bellyache and his fourth piece of chocolate cake.

My only creditable contribution to the day's bag was made when five mallards swung in close and we got three. The one I dropped was over on my side of the blind. Even the president admitted I killed it. "It must have been an awful easy shot," he muttered.

There was still about an hour of shooting left when the cold, purposeful light in the President's eye was modified to an almost human gleam.

"Maybe we'd better quit," he said, looking at me not without pity, strangely enough.

I knew better than to give him a chance to change his mind, and had the blind knocked into a cocked hat before he could think again. We fished for the decoys, and gathered up the ducks and duffel for the retreat from Moscow. Not many birds, I thought, as we trudged back, but I'd stayed with the President to the finish — I kept the faith.

Through some further hocus-pocus I found myself rowing homeward through a choppy cross sea. I was beginning to feel bucked up when the President, eyeing the snowy squalls, got another notion. This notion was to have one more whirl at our first point of the morning. There was some shooting time left. I remonstrated. I argued. I fought like the Old Harry, but after awhile I was rowing harder on the right oar, to swing the boat to the morning blind.

Subsequent proceedings come to my mind as a half-remembered dream. Mechanically I did my share of setting the cold, wet decoys, and rebuilding the wind-torn blind.

About fifty years after that was completed, I found myself sitting on my shell case in back of the brush blind. Could it be possible I had actually lived through that trek into Dry Lake? And had I survived in good enough shape to be back here at the old stand? And what for, anyway? It seemed I had been staring at or through jack pine and scrub oak boughs for several lifetimes.

The President, alert as a cricket, peered through the swirling snow. Suddenly he rose. Bang! One decisive shot rolled away in the rising wind and a minute later the President picked up a black duck from the edge of the water. I didn't even get off the shell case. For once I was licked. The President didn't let it pass. Said he:

"Any duck hunter who won't even stand up at the report of his partner's gun may consider himself officially dead. I told you I'd do it."

A few minutes later a strange thing was happening. The President of the Old Duck Hunters himself was at the oars, rowing the last leg to the waiting car. I can see him now, grinning at me from the middle of the boat, his collar rimmed with snow, a gleam of victory in his eye. A noble fellow, I thought, as my weary bones sought solace on the wide rear seat. An unselfish, lovable soul, if ever there was one . . .

Not until the next day, when I was able to turn the matter over in my mind, did I determine the reason for that last manly act.

He had the wind behind him.

NERVOUS BREAKDOWN

*Somehow this story says something profound to me. Since I first read it in
Field & Stream in 1944, I must have gone back to it a dozen times or more. It is
always deeply satisfying.*

*I think it's because something like it happened to me. I was in college and
things were coming at me too fast. I retreated to an old house we had at the edge of
the sea. I was lonely and depressed. Didn't know what to do with myself. Ha! That
lasted about two days. Suddenly like Bill Jones here, the hours in a day weren't
enough. There were fish to catch in both ocean and bay, a boat to sail, clams to be
raked, my shedding cart demanded constant attention. The days flew by.*

*No airplane pilot came looking for me. No Mr. Banks called. I just went on
with my life, restored, reinvigorated. The winds and the waves drove whatever was
bothering me away.*

For one thing, there was that confoundedly efficient Miss Benson.
Always at him, she was. "Good morning, Mr. Jones . . . Mr. Smith
to see you, Mr. Jones . . . Will you sign these, Mr. Jones? . . .
Goodnight, Mr. Jones."

What was he thinking of, anyway? Gertrude Benson was the finest sec-
retary in New York. Snap out of it, Bill Jones. You're certainly going balmy in
the head!

He dropped the fishing-camp folder in the waste basket and turned to
his desk. Too old, he thought. Should have done it twenty years ago. But

twenty years ago the kids were hardly more than babies, and there was Mom and a job.

Now that the kids were grown, Mom was coddling him more than ever. Yes, coddling him! Dear Mom, always thinking of someone other than herself. Mom could see no sense in a browse bed — "Will! At your age, sleeping on the ground!"

He picked up the memorandum which Miss Benson had left. Mr. Blake of National Metals at 9:30; Mr. Peddy of Empire Sales at 10; senior committee meeting at 11:00. His gaze strayed to the waste basket. The folder said: "Off the beaten track . . . the last frontier . . . our guides really take you back in there . . ."

Fifty-five years old, with a belly and a half-million dollars. He looked out the window, off across the tops of the tall buildings. Thirty-five years of it, from clerk to a vice-presidency. Mom and the kids were very proud of him. They thought it screamingly funny when he took off a week or two and went fishing.

A pigeon, city vagabond of the species, yet somehow wild and free among skyscraper chasms, landed on the window sill. Miss Benson, who forgot nothing, had spread the daily ration of grain. The bird pecked. His thoughts dreamed away . . .

He could tell Mom he was taking a guide so that she would not worry. There was country up there, country for a man to see. Not with a guide — not this time. This was something he had to do for himself. Last summer Hanson, the guide on the fringes of this country, had told him it was solid wilderness north to the Arctic Circle. He remembered Hanson's grin as he explained: "During the depression, when guiding fell off, I spent a season up in there. Got lost a-purpose. Never had such a good time in my life!"

No, he would not be afraid. He had not been afraid as a boy in Pennsylvania when he had camped out on his own trap-line. He might break a leg. Sure! He might get bumped by a truck in town, too.

Miss Benson found him staring out the window. Brisk, efficient Miss Benson, whose words were as crisp as her tailored clothes. He hated Miss Benson. He wanted to say, "Damn it, Gerty, why don't you leave me alone?"

"Mr. Jones of National Metals to see you, sir."

He wanted to answer, "Tell him to go to the devil." He must have telegraphed the thought to Miss Benson, for she frowned. "I'm tired, Miss Benson," he said. "Mr. Pitcaim knows about this order. I suggest — "

"Yes, sir. I'll see Mr. Pitcaim right away. I hope everything is all right." There was real anxiety in her voice.

He smiled at her and suddenly did not hate her at all It was ridiculous to hate Miss Benson. A brick, she was. Good as a man — yes, better than a man.

"Am I cracking up?" he wondered. It was something he could not quite put his finger on. He wasn't interested in his work the way he had been. The consuming passion to try the impossible was gone. For months he had found himself making an effort to do things. It wasn't like him. Was that why Mom hovered around him? She did hover!

His phone tinkled distantly in the big room. It was Banks, the president. Good old Banks — solid, sensible, old Banks.

"Miss Benson mentioned you weren't feeling well. I don't want to intrude. I'm rather awkward about such things. I'm wondering — "

"Mr. Banks, I have got to get out of here." His own words surprised him. He hadn't meant to say it quite that way.

"I'll be right in," Banks said.

He came, cool and steady as always. He came smiling and walked across the heavy rug. "Fellow," he said, "you don't look good to me." It was like Banks to speak his mind.

"Banks — " He could go no further. He was choked up. Banks put a firm hand on his shoulder. "Spit it out. We've always worked that way."

For five minutes he talked. He talked rapidly, and at times his eyes shone. When he had finished, Banks laughed.

"Fine!" he said. "I'd rather you'd take a guide, but do it your way. I respect your way, as I always have."

He fidgeted. "Banks, is this a nervous breakdown?"

"Some call it that."

"Mom will want to get a doctor."

"I think you've written your own prescription."

"I —"

"Nuts!" said J. Forsythe Banks, leader of industry. "Don't let me see you around here in the next month. Git!"

Mom had been difficult, he thought as the train carried him north out of Duluth. But she had felt better about it when he lied cheerfully and said he was taking a cook as well as a guide.

The conductor came through and eyed him. "Lookin' up timber?"

"Yes. Be sure and wake me at six. I want to see the country."

His eyes were open long before the porter came to jerk at the green curtain of his berth. In the September dawn there flashed by an endless land of prim stunted spruce, pink-gray boulders and lakes that seemed to be waiting for someone to come and use them. He put away the business suit and climbed into store new wool. He had to rip the price tag off the checked flannel shirt.

He transferred personal items to the rough clothing that felt so good, then folded his pin-striped double-breasted suit and handed it to the porter to be shipped back to the hotel in Duluth.

"Yes suh, 'deed, suh. We is about two hours from Nine Mile watertank."

He ate a huge breakfast, for he would not want to stop at noon to boil the kettle.

At the water-tank, where the train stopped, he hurried forward to the baggage car and helped with the unloading of the canoe and gear. The train pulled out. His dunnage beside the water-tank made a formidable pile. A hundred yards away lay the edge of Wabigoon Lake. Long before he had toted all the stuff to the rocky lake shore he was weary. He fastened the tiny motor to the bracket of the 15-foot canoe and set forth. The outfitter in town had insisted on the small canoe. "It's a 60-pounder. A two-man job would break your back on the portages."

He had to stop and trim the load so that the bow dropped. After that his speed increased. From an aluminum fishing rod tube he took out a roll-up map of Ontario. Wabigoon looked pretty big the way he was going, north.

He felt free, yet he was anxious. Could he do all the things as well as Hanson had done them? He went over the outfit item by item. The fellow in the store knew his business. He had told this clerk that he had wanted to go with canoe and paddle. The man had insisted on the tiny motor and ten gallons of fuel.

"If you run out of fuel and have to come home light, throw away everything you don't need, including the motor," he had said.

Yes, the outfitter knew his business. He was traveling six miles an hour in a light chop. Almost 160 pounds of equipment, fuel and man in a craft that weighed 60 pounds. By noon the wind had picked up, but a boyhood sense for water had returned. He caught the knack of running on the lee side of the islands. In the open reaches he learned to jockey the waves by quartering into them and away from them.

In the late afternoon, more than forty miles from the put-in, he chose a spruce-grown island for the night. It had a wind-swept point where the late-season mosquitoes would not be present. The island looked like some ancient sea-faring craft, with spruce trees for masts and sails. He cut the motor and swung in. Just before the nose of the canoe touched land the sharp edge of a rock slashed a six-inch gash in the canvas. He would have to be more careful in landing hereafter.

It took an hour to build a fire, heat the tiny can of marine glue, and "iron on" a canvas patch with heated rocks. He scorched a finger doing it. A blister ballooned up.

He longed for a deep, soft chair to sink into, like one at the club or his easy chair at home. And a highball and the evening paper. And an evening meal on a white tablecloth. He unpacked gear and dived into the woods with an ax for browse.

It was near dark when the silk tent was pitched and the air mattress spread over the browse. The wind went down, and his breezy point attracted its quota of mosquitoes. The sunset was tremendous behind spires of spruce. But he did not enjoy it. He lay down awhile before starting to prepare supper. It had been like that for a long time. He wanted to lie down and look at a job before beginning it. In other days he had just pitched in.

He was hungry. How did guides like Hanson manage things so deftly on the ground? He struggled with the fire, which got too hot and then too cold. He burned his other hand. The loons of Wabigoon struck up their song, and he became definitely lonely and uncertain of himself. Just how smart was he in going away by himself without a guide.

By trial and error he adjusted the reflector baker so that the biscuits got done, though some were doughy and some burned. The dried soup which he spilled into the stew-pan swelled enormously and overflowed into the fire. The tea was more like tannin, steeped too long. He must remember to do that last.

The supper did not taste good. The soup got cold and the tea stayed hot. Washing dishes was a chore. There was no sand on the rocky island with which to scour the dishes. He noted as he washed in the lake that his hands were already creviced with dirt.

Well, he would sleep, anyway. He drew tight the mosquito netting in the tent door and flopped down. He did not sleep. Three mosquitoes had to be hunted down. The browse under his hip was too high and had to be read-justed. When this was done, he was nervously wide awake. He tossed in the sleeping bag. It was after midnight when he dozed off.

A few hours later the flapping of the tent awakened him. The wind was shaking it. There was a bright glow through the green tent. He leaped up. The wind had fanned the embers of his cooking fire, and sparks were flying. Without pausing to put on boots, he grabbed a folding bucket and dashed to the lake. He stubbed his toe and swore. It took a half-dozen pailfuls to extinguish the fire, and by then the wind had torn out the stakes on one side of the tent.

In the dark he replaced the stakes, as deep as he could in the thin soil, and anchored them with rocks. He tightened the ridge rope by lifting the shear poles front and back. The rain caught him as he finished. It came horizontally from the west, cold and stabbing — a fall rain. Inside the tent, he lit the aluminum lantern's single fat candle and lay on his back. He fell asleep from sheer exhaustion.

In the morning he felt as though he had not slept at all. The long water hop of the previous day had brought the reflected sun up beneath his hat brim. His face was painfully burned. The oatmeal he cooked was good, but the taste of powdered milk on it was unfamiliar. Mom, right now, was in the breakfast nook, having the kind of breakfast he wanted. If he were there, she would wheel the car up and honk and he would get in and they would drive away and the traffic cops would wave cheerfully.

As it was, he faced a run with the canoe and then a two-mile portage. He dreaded it. If only Hanson were here to take over!

The portage was worse than he had anticipated. It had been a wet September. There was one low spot of a hundred yards where he waded to his knees, feeling the trail with his boots. The gear was in two packsacks. Then there was the canoe, the motor and the two tins of fuel, each weighing thirty pounds.

As long as he lived he would not forget that portage! Hanson had said that this portage was what kept a lot of trippers from going back in there. Even the good guides did not like it. The sweat ran into his eyes. He drank quarts of water at either end of the punishing trail. Pack straps cut his shoulders. He could not complete the job in the day. He left the canoe and motor until next day and hurried camp in the rain. Just in time, too. A needle-fine rain of the lasting kind came down. He gulped hot soup and eased himself into the sleeping bag.

He slept. He slept like a log. In the morning, still groggy, he put on a rain jacket and limped back for the canoe and motor.

The lake before him had no name on the map. It was just a number put there by a surveyor, Lake One. There were others, named and numbered, stretching beyond to the north. He rigged a casting rod and took a four-pound wall-eyed pike with the third cast. He was using a pork-rind lure, but he felt he might have done as well with a clothes-pin bearing hooks.

In the rain he dressed the fish and baked it in the reflector oven with rashers of bacon. He brewed his coffee carefully and saw to it that the biscuits browned evenly. It all tasted good. He ate it, watching a moose on the far shore of the lake. When he had finished, a Canada jay came to his plate and dined. The bird was unafraid and greedy.

The skies cleared in the early afternoon, and he set off. He portaged out of Lake One to another, Lake Three on the map. The portage was a mere hundred-yard haul-over, up a hogback, down the other side. Without waiting to set up camp he cast the pork rind from the shore. A 10-pound northern took it. He got in the canoe and fished the shore. The water was alive with northern pike and wall-eyed pike. It was a carnival of fishing. He saved one for supper.

There was a white frost in the night. He felt it coming before bedtime so he folded back the canoe tent to make a lean-to and built a roaring fire before it. By the firelight he ate, picking the firm pike flesh from his plate with his fingers and wondering what Mom would say if she could have seen him. Owls were abroad, and beaver were working not far away. He tidied up camp and lay in the sleeping bag. The last thing he remembered was the strong whistle of wings. Ducks on the move . . . He fell asleep.

For a week he stayed at this place. Mornings he killed a duck or two, reaching for them with a .410 as they came low across a pass. There were mornings when he might have killed a hundred. All he wanted was enough to eat. Each morning it seemed colder and the white frost heavier. The birch leaves had been yellowish when he began the trip. Now they were gone. The wild-cherry leaves were brown and drying. Sumac groves were carmine. The song birds were gone except for an occasional flicker. He was busy, and the days passed quicker than he cared to see them pass.

It was while he walked around this lake to retrieve a wave-borne mallard that he realized he was not tired! It was a long walk of three miles to where the wind and waves carried the mallard. He thought it would be better for him to walk it than to take the canoe. He picked up the bird.

Ten days of wilderness had made his trousers gape at the waist. One day he permitted himself the luxury of a shave. To his surprise, his face was not left raw and razor-chopped. The skin had toughened. It had had a chance to heal itself from incessant, hurried scrapings.

His appetite amazed him. He found he was no longer dragging himself to camp tasks. He went at them eagerly and did them efficiently. There was always something to do — too much, in fact. The days were too short. They zipped by. He broke out his camera and renewed an old hobby. He built a table and chair for the camp. He fed the trusting whisky-jacks and stalked the shore-line moose, and counted it a red-letter day when he got close enough to one to touch it with a paddle. He was no longer lonely. There was life and activity all about him.

He pushed north from this camp for a steady week, through many lakes, over endless portages. Almost every night the aurora borealis spread over the heavens. Every morning his boots were stiff with frost. A porcupine gnawed his sweat-saturated paddle, and he spent half a day chopping down a spruce and fashioning another with ax and knife. He was inordinately proud of that paddle. Just as he was proud of the neat patching he put on the tent where camp-fire sparks burned through its walls.

The routine of making camp was so perfected that he could slide the canoe ashore, set up camp, and be eating a meal in a half-hour. He found out that the way to eat bacon and fish in a one-man camp was right out of the frying-pan. It saved doing dishes.

He planned and prepared delicious meals and ate them ravenously. Planked fish, bean-hole beans, hot corn-meal muffins. One day he triumphed with his last can of peaches dedicated to a shortcake. In town it would have been enough for four. He licked up the last crumbs and wished he had another can of sliced peaches.

Thin ice in the portage-trail hollow sent him south. He studied the map and penciled out a great arc of travel that would fetch him back by another route. The Nine Mile water-tower was his goal. He was not sure of the date. He had either lost a day or gained a day somewhere. It didn't matter.

It was on a lake named Papoose that he lost the motor. He had neglected to make fast the safety rope to the bracket, and the thrifty eggbeater went down. A weighted fish line showed seventy feet of water, so he did not bother to drag for it. Many miles of paddling and portaging lay before him. He grinned. This is what he had come for: to see how much of him was left. He grinned with anticipation.

First he unscrewed the outboard bracket, threw it away, and heaved overboard the remaining four gallons of fuel. Then he paddled ashore and went over his outfit carefully. Every item was scanned for weight and utility. When he had finished, everything went into one packsack. On the next portage he went across in one trip with canoe and pack.

For five days he paddled and portaged, eating twice a day, morning and evening. It was hard work, but it was good work. His hands had hardened and his back had stiffened before the loss of the motor. They became harder and stiffer. His palms were calloused. In the evenings when he went ashore he welcomed the wilderness with a weary zest. Every place seemed like home, for he was self-sufficient. He got lost for a day and a half by missing a portage trail, but took a short cut back to the penciled route via a new and shorter portage. He wondered what Mom would say when she found him so lean.

"Will! At your age sleeping on the ground!" He laughed. He knew what he would do when he saw Mom. He would sweep her off the floor, and she would protest. "Will, you fool! Let me down!" It had been fifteen years since he had picked up Mom like that. If Mom grew anxious and tried to hover over him again, he would have to spank her, even if one of her grandchildren was present.

On a long, narrow water which the map said was Burnt-over Lake he started supper one night. A seaplane circled, spotted his tent and landed. It taxied in, and the pilot came ashore. He was a commercial flyer, looking for a lost camper. He explained the man's name was William Jones, and that Jones was two days overdue at Nine Mile water-tank. Railway officials had reported that he had not appeared.

"You can stop looking. How bout supper?"

"But you're not lost," said the flyer, who had studied the shipshape camp and the hard brown man.

"Nope, just tardy. Lost my outboard, and I'm paddling in."

"I'll fly you in tonight in a half-hour."

"That's what you think."

"A Mr. Banks has asked us to find you."

"Good old Banks."

The flyer sat down to a meal of fresh caught wall-eyed pike, baking-powder biscuits with maple syrup, and hot green tea. He was a nice chap. He took off while there was still a little daylight. In forty-five minutes he was on the phone.

"But are you sure he is all right?" Banks demanded.

"I've lived in this country most of my life. If I needed a guide, I'd hire that bird."

"Does he feel all right?"

"Well, he carried a fifty-pound down log to the fire with one hand."

"Did he say when he would reach Nine Mile?"

"Yes, sir. He said he would get there when he was damn good and ready."

There was a pause and a sigh at the other end of the line. Then Banks said, "That's him, all right."

Gallopin' Grasshoppers

This is another story published here in book form for the first time. Again, don't ask me why. It's a gallopin' good story.

That Mr. President is slightly paranoid there can be no doubt. Here without any evidence of any kind, he accuses a friendly preacher of stealing his sock full of grasshoppers. Later on when his tackle turns up missing he will accuse practically the whole town of Superior, Wisconsin, of purloining his favorite, time-tested flies.

So why does everybody love this crotchety old man? That's easy to answer. He's honest and humorous. He's kindly. His wife bosses him around. He's a friend to the end. He's enthusiastic and appreciative. He will never grow old.

A good way to go fishing is thuswise: First acquire considerable familiarity with the waters of a given region. So that you hardly know where to fish from one day to the next. Then build a fishing cabin right in the center of this fishing country. From your own home and castle you can thrust out like a spider from its web into whatever waters suit your mood.

I find it a good thing, for instance, on a chill morning in late August, to reach an arm into the darkness and throttle an alarm clock at about 3 AM. Then I lie in bed for a few minutes and consider where I shall fish that day. Sometimes I know the night before where I shall go. But usually not. On most of these before-dawn beginnings I go alone, so there is no responsibility to set a schedule.

One morning last August, after the alarm clock had been silenced and my wife had said, "The fifth day in a row that thing has rung at this hour!"

— after that, I say, I lay back and made an inventory of available nearby waters.

There was the upper Namakagon River for brown trout, either at Squaw Bend below Cable or farther downstream, near Seeley. There was the Totogatic and its walleyes. The St. Croix — Flowage, Copper Mine dam, Fish Trap Rapids and all. There was the Chippewa Flowage and its muskies. Or any one of several hundred lakes, all within a few hours' drive at the most.

Past humble farms in the cutover, with the rising sun at my right making lonely, ragged church steeples of the spruce tops. Down the dank gullies where fog lingered and strong, wet smells of woodland came in through the ventilating window. Left at the "wide corner" and down the long and gradual steepening grade to the Brule. A slackening of speed for a glimpse of the river as the car rumbles over the iron bridge, and then more speed to make the steep hill beyond. A turn to the right again down the rutted narrow clay road toward Lake Superior.

That is the way to go.

The lower Brule at last. The car in the meadow with the lone spruce near the river bank just where the stream comes roaring under the wooden bridge.

Always this place holds a challenge for me. I like the way the stream flares out from under the dark of the bridge, smashes into the high clay bank and veers off to cascade in a long broken run of two hundred yards before it hits another twist.

A late-foraging coyote yapped from far downstream. The sun was still below the horizon. I pulled on a flannel shirt. This, with waders and fishing jacket, was welcome cover against the chill of the dank, misty valley. In mid-July I have seen ice form in a pail left overnight on the bank of the Brule.

A perfect beginning for a fisherman's day. A beginning to instill confidence.

Attend now to the defeat that can visit even a confirmed worshiper of the Brule like myself.

The river was cold. Not just the early morning cold of summer that any springfed stream can show by renewing itself overnight, but the sharper cold of a later season brought about by shorter days, less sunlight and cooler sunlight.

In rips and eddies and glides and pools I fished for three hours without seeing a sign of fish other than the occasional over-ambitious rainbows five or six inches long. These will bust out at anything not larger than a clothes-pin. Dry flies, wet flies, nymphs. Then that regular weapon of the Brule — spinners.

Seldom have I seen the Brule in poorer humor. It should have been a time when every pool was harboring either rainbows or browns. These make a late-summer run into this river. Rainbows that come into it in the spring by the tens of thousands seem not loath to return again in the fall. This fall run is not so well known, nor so large, but with its mysteries we are not concerned here.

Rather are we concerned with the sudden ending of what should have been four classic hours on a great stream. I was a mile down-river when I chose to quit. I wished I had gone to the Chippewa flowage, or any of the Hayward lakes, or almost anywhere. Anywhere indeed! A shabby way for the Brule to treat me after I had not seen it for a year. Me — who has fished it five hundred times.

I drove back to the town of Brule and bought some bacon, a lamp chimney and a dozen oranges. Bacon instead of trout for a second breakfast. A ———— of a note, my friends.

I went home. I was tired. I was tired for the first time in five days of rising at 3 AM and speeding off a-fishing. I was tired, too, because the Brule had let me down. I fell asleep on a davenport with the sun streaming through the windows and the chatter of women-folk in my ears. That must have been around ten in the morning.

When I awoke, the sun was streaming in a window on the opposite side of the room. Standing over me was the President of the Old Duck Hunters' Association, Inc. The President has a knack of catching me at the wrong moment.

"So, you've been fishing," he began. "Where are the fish?"

"In the ice-box. You'll find some nice bass and walleyes there. Go out and take a look."

"I mean trout-fish. Anyone can fill an ice-box with bass and walleyes around here. They tell me you were on the lower Brule this morning."

He dragged it from me, bit by bit. He compelled me to admit failure, and before I knew it he had transferred my tackle from my car to his and I was being driven at good speed back toward the Brule.

All this was not achieved in dead silence. The President kept up a steady conversation about what he was going to do to those Brule trout.

Halfway there he stopped and reached into the rear for a woolly blanket. Without explaining anything more than that he was going to show me how to catch August trout bait, he spread the blanket near the roadside and began to kick about in the grass.

This was a new one. It developed that he was catching grasshoppers. Quite a number of the 'hoppers that he flushed from the grass were bound to light on the blanket, and before they could extricate their saw-edged legs from the wool he would pounce on them.

"And that isn't all, either," he said. "I've got a grasshopper trap that's got everything beat."

From a pocket he extracted a "genuine silk sock — cost me two bucks a pair" and into this he stuffed the captured 'hoppers. The fine silk weave of the sock seized the 'hoppers and held them as had the blanket. And by feeling the outside one knew just where to reach in and grab a 'hopper.

The lore of Mr. President is cumulative. Though he fished "for fifty years, man and boy," no season passes but that he does not add some useful bit of knowledge to his bulging bag of tricks. He was quite triumphant about this new wrinkle; but when I accused him of reading it in a magazine, he got his back up and said if he had it wasn't "one of those libelous pieces you write about me."

He also said that, just to show me, he would go down into the river where I had met defeat and bring up "not less than a frying-pan of good, fat trout-fish by the time it's dark."

I said that anyone could get trout with a blanket and an old sock full of grasshoppers, but that was an old argument between us and he chose not be belittle himself by reopening it.

He did not drive to the lower river, where I had been that morning, but turned in to the upper river on a little known road patronized by about a dozen of us for quite a few years. He said he had talked with a game warden about the lower river and had been informed that the late-summer run of fish was delayed, "perhaps by this spell of dry weather."

We climbed into waders. As per our usual arrangement at this place, I went downstream to fish back with floating flies. The President went upstream, for he prefers to fish downstream. This he does with wet, dry or any kind of flies. He was never one to stand on ceremony or worship some particular thing just because it had a name.

Halfway to the stream I noticed that I had forgotten my landing net. I returned for it and upon opening the car found the President's silk sock of grasshoppers on the floor of the car, where he had forgotten it. I was about to shout to him when another thought suddenly struck me.

Those 'hoppers might come in handy. When you're up against the President, anything goes. Even grasshoppers in a silk sock. I tucked them in my jacket.

Of the Brule on a warm and cloudy August afternoon much can be said. This particular stretch of water is, I believe, one of the grandest pieces of trout water in the country. The stream is crooked, its shores heavily grown to brush and some good timber. Roaring rapids and wide shallow stretches alternate. The banks, like much of this upper river, are sodden with springs. Deadfalls lie like jackstraws. The river itself is cluttered favorably with water-logged timber and huge rocks, and there are some splendid under-cut banks where browns love to lie. It is not especially hard wading, thus making for that perfection seldom attained by trout fishermen good fishing and easy going.

It was near four o'clock when I entered the stream. My thoughts, as I hiked down the river trail, had been on the President and his dilemma. He would not try the 'hoppers at first. That was not his way. First he would take off his old brown hat and, starting with the big Ginger Quill just behind the bow on the band, go methodically though the dozen or so flies strewn about the brim.

When all these failed and he had grunted his dissatisfaction with each and every one, he would then reach for the precious sock. He would go through his creel, his jacket pockets — there must be fifteen of them — his inside pockets under his waders, and might even retrace his steps some. Then he would try to catch a few. But the President is not so spry as he used to be, nor are 'hoppers too plentiful in the coolish grasses of the Brule valley.

I had him. For once I was going to march back up that steep bank, come darkness, with a fish or two caught with the President's own poison. There was poetic justice in that, after the lickings he had given me here and there in some twelve years of fishing.

Nor did I give the 'hoppers first chance to prove their worth. Not at all. They were to be saved for the emergency which, after the morning's experience, I felt was inevitable.

What the evening hatch was I never learned. There was no sign of any kind of insect over the creek or floating on its surface. My friend the trout fed steadily. He was bold, too. Once I dropped line over him in a way that would ordinarily frighten any feeding trout of his size. However, he kept right on feeding, dimpling the water and sometimes flashing a good broad tail as he dived back.

From a place not three feet behind this good trout two smaller ones, which I had not suspected were there, rose and took my flies. Even this did not perturb the larger fish, and when I left his pool he was still rising steadily. Anyway, I had two trout, both browns, and when I creeled two more a few minutes later in a faster stretch above this pool I began to feel better.

It was now quite dark. The thought of that impudent lunker wallowing before my eyes remained with me.

Then I remembered the grasshoppers. In the excitement of trying to make that big one hit flies I had completely forgotten the grasshoppers, which shows how strong is the force of habit with fishermen.

I made my way back to the pool. Without bothering to remove the 3x

leader I had been using, I fastened a kicking 'hopper to a sparsely tied bivisible — they call it a "club sandwich" up this way. The 'hopper floated away
from me in the thinning light. I was above the big trout now.

There, in the foam-flecked bank pool where even Sid Gordon's matchless wonder had been refused, that big brown smacked the 'hopper. No sooner did he feel the barb than he headed for his snags under the bank. There
was only one thing to do — try to turn him. I succeeded for about two seconds. Then the brown won over the 3x leader, and I went away from there, a
sorrier and wiser man.

To make matters worse, I had lost the precious sock, and I did not
intend to fumble around in the Brule bottom, with darkness coming on, looking for a silk sock full of grasshoppers. It seems there is a retributive god that
watches over the affairs of the President of the Old Duck Hunters. I should
have known better than to swipe his bait.

With my five not-too-large trout in the creel, I clambered up the steep,
root-grown bank to the car. The President had not returned. He never returns
until someone goes and gets him or he gets hungry. I had time to build a
smudge fire, climb out of waders and gear, and smoke a bit on the running-
board before I heard him clamping through the hazel brush. He was cussing.

"And my wife asks me why I don't go to church regularly!" he snorted.
"She asks me why I'm not like other men. Why should I go to church? Why
should I go and listen to a preacher tell me how to be good, when I'm better
than most preachers?"

Inquiry divulged he had encountered a preacher on the stream —
"a new fellow in town, but he seemed a nice sort until he swiped my
grasshoppers."

"A preacher swiped your grasshoppers!"

"Yes, and if it hadn't been for that I'd have shown you the dangdest catch
of trout you ever saw come out of this stream in August. As it was, I got a few
good ones, but if that preacher hadn't swiped them grasshoppers — ."

He showed me his glistening creel with its nine browns, none under a foot
and several over 15 inches. So he had caught those fish and without grasshoppers.

As I have often said, there is a special Providence that directs the fortunes of Mr. President. I decided the thing to do was to say nothing and bear him out.

"I met this sky-pilot up along that grassy stretch below Hall's," he explained. "We sat down and had a smoke, and while I was sitting there a sock inside my wader came to my attention. It was lumped up under my heel; so I took off the waders to get at it.

"To do that, I had to take off my fishing jacket. I did so, and laid it right beside the preacher. Later on, when I reached for the sock of 'hoppers — that was after the preacher had left me — I couldn't find 'em."

"How do you know the preacher took 'em?"

"Well, sir, I was suspicious of him from the first. He was too darned friendly. I'd told him all about my new gag with the blanket and the sock. Yessir, that preacher dipped his hand into my jacket while it was layin' there beside him and just filched them 'hoppers."

It seemed years, but finally there came a moment when I could hold back the whoops that were crowding to my tongue's tip. A moment when self-control had the better of an overwhelming impulse to bay at the moon and slap someone on the back.

"Then how did you get those fish?" I asked.

"Flies. That big wet Ginger Quill was the boss fly today. But man oh man, if I'd only had those 'hoppers!"

So any day now I am expecting a certain preacher to be publicly accosted by the President of the Old Duck Hunters' Association and asked if he ever fished with grasshoppers stored in an old silk sock. And when that time comes, there is going to be one preacher who will learn more than he ever anticipated about the hereafter.

THE BLUEBILLS
DIED AT DAWN

"Long live the bleak bitterness of such a morning. Long live the memory of that churlish dawn." MacQuarrie says here he never wrote a poem, but if he ever does, it will be about ducks.

I submit otherwise. Here the mysteries of migration set him off and if it isn't poetic, I don't know what poetry is. Here he gets going on Mr. President and his eager, young outlook. Maybe, at that, it isn't poetry, the way a college professor would define poetry. Call it rapture. Call it the sweet, Celtic touch, the way Shakespeare dishes out those rhapsodic passages in Romeo and Juliet.

Call it anything you like. It's very rare. And very special.

Autumn came to Wisconsin, but Indian summer lingered. Joe finished digging his new root cellar. Back in the shallows off the big lake the wild rice had long been tawny. Muskrats built big houses. Boxes of shotgun shells, festooned with colored leaves, appeared in the windows of hardware stores. Farmers driving horses to town carried sheepskins against possible chilly weather, now long overdue. Blue-winged teal "took out" for the south. Local mallards and black ducks loitered, but had long since grown wise to blinds.

I fretted over Government weather reports; spent long, bright days in blinds where mosquitoes hummed and ants crawled busily. Would real duck weather never come? Would the northern flight find its way across the northwest corner of Wisconsin? Would Indian summer never end?

Evening conferences with the venerable President of the Old Duck Hunters' Association, Inc., brought no answer to our impatient speculations. Wool-lined mittens, my heavy blanket parka and the President's old brown mackinaw stayed behind when we went hunting. Meager bags of mallards hung from the old curtain pole in the basement cold room. We put on storm windows and wished we hadn't. Coal dealers fumed, and city folk took long walks in the warm red sunsets.

But there came a day. One Wednesday morning the breakfast newspaper carried two inches about an impending storm in Canada. I showed it to the President, but he looked at the blue sky and said the proof was in the pudding. The evening paper told of an intense storm in Canada. The plot thickened.

Next morning was Thursday. The paper screamed in large headlines of a record October blizzard in Manitoba. Trains were stalled, autos marooned. Two feet of snow lay over the wheat stubble. Still the rough weather did not strike Wisconsin. A hurry call to Joe at the lake brought back the report of blue-bird weather and no sign of a flight.

Friday it came. No snow, but a sudden gray gloom out of the northwest. Furnace fires glowed as temperatures dropped. That night, as I drove my car into the garage, the tires crunched through a thin skim of ice in a puddle. I conferred again with the President. It looked better. We read the paper. We called the weather bureau. More cold and high northwest winds, the forecast said.

"We'll chance it," decided Mister President, and Saturday afternoon, provisioned for a week, we drove sixty-five miles under racing gray clouds to the big red cottage on the hill.

It was definitely cold now. Joe, at the lake, wore his old red mackinaw and the tip of his nose was ruddy above the old black pipe in his teeth. Many things to do. Light the fires. Split kindling. Hunt up big oak logs for the fireplace. Sort the gear and place it by the door for an early get-away in the morning.

Joe went away to start the sputtering motor of the light plant. Settled for the night, with water heating over the kerosene stove in the kitchen, the

President advised a reconnoiter. We had no reason to believe our trip was any-thing more than a gamble on the weather.

Out the back door, down the steep hill to the sheltered bay of the big lake. Through the final fringe of willows on the shore, and there, in the last of the waning light, we saw them. Great rafts of bluebills and redheads rest-ed on the leaded swell like flotillas. Far beyond the bay a ragged hole through the clouds gave off a faint glow above the treetops. From far and near came the sound of feeding bluebills.

Joe joined us at the shore. He had been so busy that he hadn't had a chance to look for ducks. A flock of incomers topped the trees beyond and wheeled over, coming to rest like seaplanes.

We shook hands all around. We talked of tomorrow, of the west point on Shallow Bay, of our great good fortune in making a guess and hitting the flight at its peak. When we climbed back uphill to the cottage, a rising wind was shaking the rustling leaves of the scrub-oaks and the Norway pines in front of the cabin were moaning.

The President shuffled the coffee pot on the stove, gave the wick an extra turn and danced a jig. Joe hung the thermometer outside, and the three of us drank a toast to the morrow.

After a while Joe returned to his own cabin. The President and I went to bed, and as we dropped off to sleep the gathering wind had its way with the patient trees. While we slept, strident blasts whooped through the night, broke branches, denuded trees of leaves, laid chilly fingers on land and water in all the north country of Wisconsin. Thus began the most wildly beautiful duck hunt of my life.

No hasty, fumbling get-away for the Old Duck Hunters' Association in the morning. The steady hand of Mister President guides the campaign for the day. Warm feet on an icy floor at 5:30. A figure huddling over the red brick fireplace, and soon a pine knot flares and heat permeates the cabin while another figure wheedles the kerosene stove into action and the scent of cof-fee and bacon and eggs fills the kitchen. The fire is doused, the lights turned out, and the Association plunges into the gusty black tunnel that is the road leading to the boat landing. Far above our heads the tossing trees testify to the strength of the wind, and at the water we feel its full power.

Two men at the oars row into the teeth of the gale. Waves slide by in long, hissing procession, spitting spray on woolen clothes. In the shelter of a lee shore we hit ice — a good half-inch of it. Out again into the open, and our hopes sink, for ice there means that Shallow Bay is frozen and we must make new plans quickly. Sure enough, the bay is a dead expanse in the cold gray dawn. Some cold! Later Joe, who had thought to look at the thermometer, said it read six below zero — the coldest late October on record in those parts.

Now a sudden emergency. Shallow Bay closed. Nothing but Long Point, a spear of sand with deep water on one side and shallow water on the other. Deep off the end where the decoys must go when the wind is northwest. As I handle the storm-tossed boat the President fumbles with the cord on the sack that holds the long-stringed decoys.

Emergency? Never let it be said the ODHA went anywhere unprepared. Those decoy strings are forty feet long. Splash! Splash! A couple go overboard, and I maneuver the boat until all are out. Even as we work, the boat tossing in the trough, a couple of wooden blocks are seen to break their moorings and start for the opposite shore, but we can do nothing except to hope that enough strings will hold to provide a fair set-up.

The peak of our point is fringed with jack-pine. In years when the lake was higher, ice thrust up a bulwark of sand on both sides; so we are partly screened from the wind. Stretching back down the point are more pines and through them a hallway down which we will go, very soon, to build a fire and liven numb toes and fingers.

Day is breaking over the sullen lake. Flocks of ducks skim the horizon everywhere. Before we have located ourselves on our shell boxes in the jack-pines our ears have caught the message of wings slashing by overhead.

The President lights his pipe with difficulty in the howling gale. He pounds his mittened hands. There is no need to talk yet. We know the ducks may — or may not — decoy to those wildly tossing blocks. But the set-up is the best we can make.

A ripping tear draws nearer from above. A flock has spotted the decoys and makes a turn in back of us over the point to come in. They trail slowly into the wind, seem almost to stop in mid-air as the wind catches them. When they are fluttering over the blocks, undecided whether to land or make another wheel, the guns speak. Ducks drop into foam-flecked waters and go drifting off to follow the runaway decoys. We'll pick up everything on the opposite shore later.

No use now to tug the boat from its cover on the beach. Let the ducks go. No hunters will bother us on the opposite shore. We own this lake today. Even a duck hunter won't brave six below for a chance at ducks in this place.

The report of shotguns is whisked away in the wind. Our heavy 12's sound like 20's through ear-flaps, and our heavy clothing protects us from the familiar shock of duck-load recoil. A flock comes straight into the teeth of the wind. No hesitation here. These wind-bandied bluebills see the blocks and make straight for them. They settle in before we know it; but when we stand, they leap into the wind and are up and out quickly with that powerful lifting wind under their pinions.

The shotguns puff, and bluebills fall as chilled 5's strike through feathers. The President says he has had enough for a time and runs back down the hallway in the jacks a hundred and fifty yards to light a fire. Always there is that rite of fire with the ODHA on tough mornings. Under the shelter of an ice pressure ridge of sand he builds his fire, warms brittle fingers and returns.

Long live the bleak bitterness of such a morning. Long live the memory of that churlish dawn. Ducks, of course, are the leading actors in the hunter's drama, but the setting is as important. The real duck hunter never lived who didn't thrill to his early-morning quest, who didn't know, standing there in a blind, that he was close to the heart of things. Let others lie abed and rise three hours later in the full light of day. The duck hunter, probing the secrets of a new day, sees the night retreat, and nothing is so fine as daylight coming and night departing while wings overhead whisper the old and unsolved mystery of migration.

I pity the duck hunter who goes for ducks alone. I pity the duck hunter who has not filled his being with the dawn magic. I pity the one who cares not, or knows not, what he has killed. Maybe that two-pound bluebill had his last meal on a Manitoba marsh. Maybe that brilliant golden-eye with the patent-leather bill was on the edge of the arctic a few days ago.

Where, twenty-four hours ago, was that flock of geese which sends its haunting cry earthward? Where was that same flock this morning when you laced your boots and drained your coffee cup? Somewhere over Lake Superior? Looking down on top of an autumn blow through which, perhaps, the blunt nose of a freighter plunged like a trifling pencil on mountainous seas?

These are thoughts that come to the mind of the wildfowler. Certainly few, if any, of the outdoor sports can rival the dramatic zest of this game. Entirely aside from the immediate lure of the sport, which has to do with decoys, blinds and weapons, there is an extra urge that comes from the quest for birds of passage, flying from their northern homes to the smiling marshes of the southland.

City-worn folk with furrowed brows have heard this music, as has the rustic country lad, crouched on the edge of a marsh with his father's shotgun. There is a great deceit in duck hunting by which men count their sport in terms of "limit bags" and "good shooting." Be not fooled. These same men would greet the rising sun in season though they knew their chances of killing even a single duck were very, very poor indeed.

But we were hunting ducks on a sand point in sub-zero weather. It cannot be said of either the President or me that we looked poetical. The President, who is sharp of feature like a faithful hound, had leaned well on the varnish of his shotgun stock. By nine in the morning we could look across to the other side of the lake and spot a group of small dark objects lined against the distant sand. These were our ducks, tossed ashore by the waves.

Full daylight had shown us by the pallid stillness of Shallow Bay, its surface frozen roughly by the frigid wind. On the far side we could see all that remained of our once perfect blind. Now it was a huddle of wind-beaten scrub-oak. Most of it had been swept off by the gale.

If I must choose among the sports that draw me into the open, it will be duck hunting. No other sport with rod or gun holds so much of mystery and drama. The game comes out of the sky. Perennial messengers to the south, the ducks bring to the gunner a sense of having had a part in the autumn pageant of migration.

With the peaceful beauty of a June trout stream, with the gentle silence of snow-clad north woods in winter, with the warm brown fields of October, I have had much to do. But I have never been so caught up and carried away as when hunting ducks. I never wrote a poem in my life. But if I ever do, it will be about ducks.

That bitter morning amid the bluebills the tobacco in my pipe tasted better. Borrowed tobacco it was, from the pouch of Mister President himself, who smokes a pipe only when in a duck blind and always wonders why the devil it doesn't taste as good in his office. Gloves were little protection against the steady northwest wind, but extra mitts from the inexhaustible resources of the President's packsack thawed my fingers. When the fire back in the jack-pines burned out, the President again revealed his strength in an emergency by lighting an old kerosene barn lantern; and with this between our legs in a small trench and our limbs draped with an old army blanket, we sat out the arctic morning in comparative comfort.

Bluebills are the staple flight duck of Wisconsin. Feeding upon luscious vegetation in a thousand lakes, they store up healthy fat against the long flight south. Willing decoyers, their huddled, formless ranks, smashing into the decoys, have given sport to more Wisconsin flight hunters than any other duck. Hard-flying and husky, they brave the blocks with an abandon that puts to shame the cautious, wheeling mallard. Hard to down, nothing less than 5's or 6's will go cleanly through those close-packed feathers — and then the bird must be caught in the heart of the load.

Of the eerie wildness of that morning, of the guttural call of bluebills on the water, of the low racing clouds that seemed hardly higher than the ragged jack-pines I have keen remembrance. After a while the President detached himself from the comfort of the lap robe and produced, thoughtful soul, a vacuum bottle of hot coffee and sandwiches. It did not take that coffee long to cool.

Between sips and munchings we would set the cups down and reach for shotguns as white-breasted bluebills topped the trees on the far shore and darted over the decoys. A problem not easy to solve is that presented when speeding ducks are almost in and one must set down the cup without spilling and reach for the gun — all in one motion.

Just two men in a duck blind. One a comparatively young man, the other over sixty. Yet as I look back at that morning and the many other mornings I have had with Mister President, I sincerely wonder who is the younger. He has an enthusiasm that I shall never have at his age. He has a sturdy, whip-like strength in his spare frame. He has a gleam in his brown eyes that few younger men have. Perhaps it comes from peering through a smother of snow at incoming ducks.

Or from the full, rounded out-of-door life he has led in his chosen home — northern Wisconsin. I speculated with him once about the possibility of some day settling down in a summer clime. Perhaps a place where there would be a few ducks in the marshes and a few quail in the coverts.

"If I couldn't see a northern winter come, I wouldn't feel at home, and neither would you," he told me.

I know he was right. No matter where I go, I shall always remember his words, for he first planted in me a reverence for the country of my birth, and I am proud of it.

We sat there and talked. About who was going to be the next President of the United States. About a good way to cook mudhens — if they must be cooked. About how many of the neighbors we could invite in for supper with the ducks we'd taken. These things are all accessories to the business of duck hunting.

After a while we picked up the decoys. But that's only a part of the story of picking up decoys with the President. About that time he generally gets a backache, or his corns begin to bother him; so I pick up the decoys. I would not have it otherwise. I will burn my reddened hands in the frosty gray water a hundred times rather than have him pick up the decoys. I want to see, each time, what he's going to think of to get out of the job.

He's gone through neuritis, toothache, headache, hangnails and dandruff. This particular morning it was his boots. They were chafing his heels.

He mumbled something about going to see "a chiropractor; no, osteopath — well anyway a foot-feeler."

But he always "sacks 'em." He wouldn't let me "sack 'em" by myself — you gotta be smart to sack decoys. "Did I ever tell you of the time Chadwick sacked 'em at Fish Lake and put all the dead ducks in the bottom? On the way home we thought the aroma was coming from the live decoys."

Then the row back to the boat landing with the wind at our backs. Decoy sacks, shell boxes and guns are put away in Joe's ice-house on the shore. Up the high hill to the red cabin where Joe has rekindled the fireplace and tidied up the breakfast dishes.

I prepare the noon meal while the President and Joe warm their shins before the fireplace. It is a fine meal. I am proud of it. The President appreciates it so much that he says he will help me with the dishes, but he's going to take just a little nap before starting the job.

Joe departs on some errand. The wind howls bitterly under the sloping eaves of the red cabin. The scratchy scrub-oak branches rub their bare, claw-like tips against the windows. Out on the big lake I can see the whitecaps tossing. From another window, looking down at quiet water, are massed rafts of ducks.

I start in on the dishes as Joe departs. In five minutes the water is boiling and I go into the main room to summon Mr. President. He is fast asleep, his glasses pushed up on his forehead. I remove them carefully and throw a blanket over him.

Then I go back to the kitchen and do the dishes myself.

SET A THIEF . . .

One of the great pleasures of working with these stories is that I get to read them again and again. Each time I find something new. I missed here, for example, the way Mr. President maneuvered the beer truck to his neighbor's temperance meeting. My own decoys are plain plastic. I've painted and repainted them but I never held them in affection as Mr. President does Min and Bill, "a hundred years old and game to the core."

The kind of foolery friendship between Mr. President and his neighbor (and MacQuarrie) is at the heart of these stories. Not much today is heartwarming but these qualify. They brighten the day. They make you feel good.

It was precisely the night for the Old Duck Hunters' Association to be about. The October dusk had been snuffed out by a cold rain. Beneath street corner lights the last of the brown leaves gleamed wet and sad.

The house of the President of the Old Duck Hunters loomed ahead. I sloshed through the downpour toward the driveway at the back door, knowing that one or another of his faithful second-hand vehicles would be there, patiently accepting hunting gear, though its rear springs sagged to the hubs.

A neighbor's dog, shunted out for his final airing, snarled at me as I went along, and then wagged an apology after a sniff of recognition. I went on, and the dog returned to his front porch.

The light from Mister President's back porch hardly lit the space ten feet away. The patient old car was there, droopy toward the rear like an overworked laying hen. I tossed my stuff into the broad space between back seat and back of the front seat. There was a thermos bottle on Mister President's stoop, and I put that in too. I might then have gone in to pay respects to Mrs.

President, but my slicker dripped and I knew she had just polished the floors. So I waited for Hizzoner.

I expected he would issue from the back door with a final armful. Usually it was like that. I would be ahead of him and waiting, and he would come out vowing that I was a half-hour ahead of time, which I usually am.

I got behind the wheel of the car in the semi-darkness and waited. A sound from the back yard of Mister President's next neighbor caught my attention. It was a sound like a man with a burden bumping his knees into a concrete bird bath. Rolling down the window, I confirmed that when Mister President growled, "Blast that bird bath!"

He came furtively toward the car. Over a shoulder he toted a bulky bag. He did not see me. Before stepping around the corner of his garage and into the dim gleam of his porch light he stopped and reconnoitered.

I was in a good spot to watch. The rain-dribbled windshield screened me. Mister President set down his burden and strolled into the light. His sudden transformation from skulking to strolling was superb.

He looked across the street and up the street and down the street. He held out his hand, as though he had just discovered it was raining, though rain had been falling for an hour and he was dripping. Then, still supposing he had not been seen, he ducked back into the darkness, emerged with his burden and with one swoop opened the back door of the car and heaved it in.

It landed on the floor, and there was the unmistakable thump of duck decoys. Of course, he saw me then, and in the dark I caught the twinkle of his eye by the expression of his voice: "I ain't done nothing, have I?"

"Nothing," I echoed, for it is a rule of the Association that the Old Man's wish is the membership's law.

"All you saw me do was come through Norm's yard from Carl's house with a sack. Isn't that right? Answer me now!"

"Yes, sir," I agreed most solemnly.

"There might have been a body in the sack?"

"Yes, sir."

"There might have been fifty pounds of pine knots from Carl's garage?"

"Yes, sir!"

"Or there might have been half a bale of hay in that sack?"

"Even a whole bale."

"Fine. Just fine," said the President of the Old Duck Hunters. "I take it, then, you are ready to swear that you never saw me steal Carl's decoys?"

"Your honor," I replied, "His decoys are not worth stealing."

"I suppose," he said, "the only kind of decoys worth stealing are those highfalutin, brand-new jobs of yours — the ones you keep in separate bags so's not to ruffle those wooden feathers." He snorted. "The boosters in that ragged gunny sack which you did not see me steal are ducks! Ducks with a past. Ducks with a reputation. Not a shot hole in 'em. Old ducks — and anybody knows wild ducks like old decoys better'n new ones."

Mister President was off on a pet subject. He has long maintained that the wooden creatures, many times painted and patched, are superior to more modern decoys, no matter how perfect. He holds that "there is something about those old boys — they've got character."

"Anyway," I said, "I did not see you steal them. I am prepared to swear to it."

"Heaven help us," he replied. "The boy is going to be a hypocrite like me."

"Yes, sir!"

"Shut up!" he barked.

He went up the four steps of his back porch and into the house, where I knew he was saying farewell to Mrs. President. I knew, sitting in the car, that he was stooping under the big lamp to kiss her good-by and that she put down the evening paper to pat his shoulder, and that then he was standing in the archway, grinning at her, and she was saying, "Goodby, you dear old fool."

Now he was beside me in the car, wearing the old brown mackinaw with the threadbare shawl collar. I nosed the big car carefully through the drenched streets of town. The thing has the power of a jeep in low gear. It has creaked and swayed and hauled the Old Duck Hunters to many a rendezvous with bluebill and mallard.

"I've had my eye on Carl's ducks for years," he explained. "He keeps them in his basement. I saw my chance the other day. His wife — you know how squeamish she is — caught a mouse in a trap. I was in the yard and she hollered over to me.

"That was my cue. I went down in Carl's basement to remove said mouse, and at the same time I just opened a handy window and hoisted that sack of decoys right out under a lilac bush."

"Why didn't you ask Carl if he'd loan them?" I suggested, though I knew better.

The President stuffed new tobacco on old pipe tobacco and replied: "Did you ever ask a man to loan his pet fly rod — or his oldest carpet slippers?"

"But your own decoys are as old — likely better."

He contemplated that not more than a split second before answering: "Listen, when you were young didn't you ever steal a watermelon?"

The fact is, of course, that Mr. President's 30-odd ancient decoys, born and raised on the St. Claire River flats, are genuine museum pieces, hoary and racked with age — just the decoys for a man like Mr. President, or any man.

"I'll admit," he allowed, "that Carl's may be a bit younger than mine. But they look good to me. Dang it, they look like old man MacDougal's apples used to look hanging over the side of his picket fence."

He did not add that he and Carl have waged lusty feuds for years. They have kept the whole neighborhood in an expectant ferment. There was the time Mister President set the rabbit snares to exterminate a family of bark-loving snowshoe hares. The snares were not a success, but Carl saw to it that a stuffed wildcat was caught in one and a fur buyer's catalogue in another.

So it has gone, with Mister President claiming a signal victory as of the Sunday afternoon he engineered the beer truck up to Carl's front door. Carl was entertaining the Christian Endeavor Society. He is a teetotaler.

Occasionally Mister President and Carl hunt together, but not as often as formerly. I feel partly responsible for breaking up this relationship since I included myself as a member of the President's family. Carl himself has often accused me: "I saw him first, didn't I?"

We drove south through the rain. Mister President pointed out I was wrong in surmising that the rain might turn to snow. "Wind is off Lake

Superior. It'd have to switch to the northwest to make snow this time of year."

We stopped at a certain log house by a big lake and put up for the night. It is my house, but you would never know it. Most people think of it as the President's. I made a snack of tea and toast while Hizzoner hauled in Carl's stolen treasures and went over their anchor ropes.

Those decoys were wondrous objects. Some were blue-winged teal, some coots, and some were obviously intended to represent mallards. A surrealist would have adored them. Viewing them, I thought longingly of my own exact imitation jobs, correct in so far as it is possible for an artist (not I!) to make them.

"Ah," said Mister President, surveying his loot. "Ah." He stroked them and patted them and snugged their anchor ropes. "Look at that redhead," he said. "Ever see a better shaped head? Round as an apple just above the eyes. And look at this canvasback! See how its maker shaped the bill? Aquiline, by George, the way a canvasback bill is supposed to be."

It was no time for me to butt in. Secretly, however, I decided that if any ducks decoyed to them in the morning it would be because they were delegates to an All Nations convention of ducks.

He arranged them handily in the car for the morning get-away. We slung a boat on top of the dripping car, against the morning business, and before I had finished washing the tea dishes Mister President was sound asleep under the scarlet blankets, the alarm clock close to his ear — the clock that runs only when placed face downward.

It seemed only a matter of seconds later when a voice roared in my ear, "Ro-o-o-l-l out, you 'jacks! Bacon's in the pan and fifteen miles to go!"

No mortal can be so wide awake as the President of the Old Duck Hunters at 4 AM. At that time, when life is supposed to be a lowest ebb, he is at a vigorous peak. I think it is because he gauges every tomorrow as calculatingly as he gauges the rate of a suspicious mallard. At any rate, he is a picture of leisured organization, come morning.

The bacon must be crisp and drained on brown paper. The coffee must be egg coffee, velvet-smooth. The eggs must be barely caressed on their tops with melted butter. The bread must be twice toasted, once to dry it and once to stiffen it into toast all the way through.

There was no time to wash the dishes. Our route led around the lake in the dark rain to the narrow road running south to the Totogatic flowage, This man-made lake in Sawyer County, Wisconsin, has established new and inviting feeding grounds for waterfowl. Some say it is ugly because of the drowned trees. The Old Duck Hunters hold that beauty is as beauty does.

The road was a worry. The high-wheeled old power-house of a car needed all it had to get through the clay at hill bottoms and plow up the next incline.

A charming road, this. It penetrates one of the wildest sections of Wisconsin. We went past Smoky Hill fire-tower, past Roy Harmon's deer-hunting rendezvous, over the stone bridge that Hank Koehler built across the Ounce River. Past Porcupine Hotel (another deer camp), past the big stand of hardwood, and so to the Nelson Dam at the foot of the 1,800-acre Totogatic flowage.

Here, the Totogatic River was dammed, so that its hemlock-stained waters were backed up four miles. It is one of four similar water-retention projects in this county, but hunting and fishing men look upon it as a comparatively new field of operations.

Tamarack, popple, pine and spruce were flooded when the waters rose. They stand there now, drowned and dead. The stark trees, with acres and acres of bog, offer the men of waterfowling endless opportunity for cover. Early in the season it is mallards and teal, of course. Later the bull-chested bluebills seem unable to resist the sprawling flowage.

Functioning systematically, the Old Duck Hunters soon had everything in the boat, and were rowing, a pair of oars apiece, south and east to a narrows. Halfway to the place, Mister President called a halt to listen. His sharp ears had caught an outboard's roar above the sound of our rowing. It was coming our way.

"It might be someone wanting our blind," he said without delay. "Bear down on these oars, boy!"

We beat the outboard. As we were splashing blocks overboard the motorboat hesitated before us in the dark. Its occupant sized up the situation and sped on, setting up a half-mile away.

"This here blind," the President explained once we were in it, "is the best on the flowage. That boy who tried to make it is smart, though. He's picked the second best place."

Daylight came somberly over the gray waters. It thrust slantwise through the dead tamaracks. But long before it was time to shoot, the President had made his inevitable second visit to the decoys to rearrange them, as is his way.

"They look different once you're in the blind," he said as he climbed back in.

The wind was at our backs. Before us was a horseshoe of decoys, with the toe of the shoe twenty-five yards from the blind. One arm of the shoe stretched in a long string straight out into deeper water, so that ducks coming in would be guided by the "teasers" over the pocket of decoys which formed the toe of the shoe.

Daylight grew. So did those decoys of Carl's. Some of them looked like gargoyles, and some just looked like tom-fool decoys. A more motley assortment was never spread, with the possible exception of Mister President's own monstrosities.

"I wish," he whispered, "that I'd brought Min and Bill to give 'em just a lee-e-e-tle more oomph."

Min and Bill are two caricatures of decoys, allegedly mallards, named for a cozy pair of live decoys that the ODHA owned in other days. Min has had at least ten coats of paint plastered over her, and Bill as a fissure down the center of his solid back that you can stick a finger into — "but they're a hundred years old, and game to the core."

The lack of Min and Bill worried Mister President until a pair of speculating black ducks sailed by, turned — with astonishment, I think — and flailed right over Carl's comic-strip boosters.

"I told you!" the President exulted. "Those decoys of Carl's are all right. You can't beat old decoys!"

I retrieved the two blacks with the boat, readjusted a couple more of Carl's frauds according to Mister President's shouted directions, hid the boat and climbed back in.

Business was good. To be sure, many a wary black and mallard flared from the stand; but when I complained that it was the fault of the decoys, the President said it was because I had kicked a shell box, or wiggled my head, or because my side of the blind had too much cover sticking up high. "And ducks don't like you like they do me, anyway."

The President described it as "a nice steady day." The advance guard of the bluebill flight was in, tempted to tarry by flowing smartweed, which was at a great peak that season. "Within a matter of days, or perhaps a week, the whole pack of bluebills will be here," the President pointed out.

"That won't be the best shooting," he added. "That kind of shooting is too good. You get your ten ducks too soon, and then you got to go home and put on storm-windows. That's what a conscience will do for you."

It was my job to slide the hidden skiff off the bog and retrieve the ducks that fell. I like it. The Association has decreed that such work shall always be laid out for the rank and file. Mister President swore that day that the job was a privilege. "You just drag that heavy boat off the bog in order to get warmed up, while I've got to sit here and freeze."

The rain kept up. Northeasters from Lake Superior have a way of blowing for three days. It would abate, and then begin again. The president had been right. No snow fell.

We ate our sandwiches, and the flight fell off. It fell off so noticeably that Mister President, standing full length in the blind, could not "look ducks," a technique he claims is very sporting. His idea is that if he exposes himself prominently a duck going by will think there is a fool in the blind and whirl in to make sure.

We stuck it out. At quitting time, when I waded out to recapture Carl's decoys, there was a fair limit of birds. The unknown occupant of the blind down the shore called it quits shortly after. He had done very well, we knew, from watching his birds fall. He came putt-putting in at the Nelson Dam as we were hoisting our boat on to the car.

"I'll be dinged!" said Mr. President. "It's Carl!"

"I never saw nothing," I reminded him.

We helped Carl with motor and skiff. Mister President was especially solicitous of his friend and neighbor. He exclaimed over the nice bag of ducks he had. He said over and over again it was a dog-gone shame we hadn't known who it was up the shore — "then we could have hunted together."

"By George," he said, "it's like old times, getting together like this."

Carl was equally pleased. He said, "By George, it's been a grand day, even if it did rain and I'm wet to the skin."

And so Mister President invited him back to our bailiwick where, over steaming cups of quick coffee, they hearkened back to other days. The two of them killed at least a hundred sharptails on my hearth. They stood again, as of yore, in the snowy cut-over in deer season, agreeing that any man who lit a fire for warmth was a softie.

"I allus hold," Carl declared, "that even a hemlock-bark fire scares deer, even if it doesn't give off smoke."

They were a precious pair. I left them to stir up a hot meal in the kitchen. Through the window I noted that Carl's boat had slipped sideways it its trailer cradle. I went out to straighten it and pushed his decoy sack back into the center of the boat, where it would ride. The old cord closing the sack broke, and a decoy rolled into the bottom of the boat.

It was Mister President's Bill, crack in the back and all. Dear old Min was only a few layers below him. The whole sack held nothing but Mister President's aging decoys — the silly coots, the skinny teal, the multicolored redheads. All of them were there.

I switched the sacks to the proper owners then and there, and I went back inside and poured those two old frauds the biggest hottest plates of lamb stew you ever saw. They sat there, chewing the rag and sopping their bread in the stew and hunting and fishing and agreeing it was a fine thing, indeed, there was somebody around this camp to wash the dishes and sweep the floor for a man.

Carl departed in the rain, full of hot stew. I got to him as he shoved off, after the President had said his last farewell and trooped back to the fire.

"Where," I demanded, "did you get those decoys I just found in your boat?"

"As long as you know," he said, "I went right in and burglarized them. I did it the day I happened to look out a basement window and saw mine under that lilac bush. There was only one man in the world who would try that; so I went over one morning when nobody was home and just swiped his."

He drove off, but not before I had assured him that his own precious fakes had been restored.

Back inside, Mister President was vastly pleased with himself. "You don't know nothing then?" he quizzed.

"Not a thing."

"I really like those ducks of Carl's. He didn't catch on, did he?

"Didn't have an inkling."

The President of the Old Duck Hunters' Association settled down for a snooze, but before he dropped off he announced, "It takes an old fool to fool and old fool."

THE KITCHEN-SINK FISH

I defy anyone to read this story and forget it! Who can forget Mr. President staring at the frozen MacQuarrie saying, "Fell in on purpose so I'd feel sorry for you." Or MacQuarrie slipping and *bringing Mr. President down. And Mr. President hitching the canoe and putting his son-in-law over the side for the third time, then offering the blue-lipped angler a thermos full of, not hot coffee, but ice water!*

I hesitate to write it as it may bring down the dark devils but I'm not much on falling overboard. I strongly suspect MacQuarrie wasn't as good at it in fact as he is fond of it in fiction. It's a pratfall. It's funny. It's fun.

If it isn't happening to you.

In the month of May, when spring is a blessed fact in most places, churlish Lake Superior declines to be a good neighbor. This greatest of fresh-water bodies hangs on to departing winter by its coat-tails, fights hard to keep its vast ice-fields from withering before the prairie winds. Some days the westerly winds drive the ice-floes beyond sight of land. Then the wind shifts, and back come the chalk-white rafts to jam the bays and harbors and river mouths. When the lake wind is king, its cold will be felt some distance inland.

A strange climate, this. Raw winter in control on the lake shore many a day when, fifteen miles inland, the country is soaking up 70- and 80-degree warmth. At least one newspaper in a lake-shore city has acknowledged this whimsical weather by publishing, daily in spring, the temperature not only of the city but of the interior at a point thirty miles away. Thus lake dwellers learn when they may escape the cold wind in a game of golf, a country ride — or a bit of fishing.

Now, coursing down for sixty-six miles to the south shore of this chilly old lake is the river Brule. Early in the season this estimable trout stream may, in its upper reaches, soak in 90 degrees, while down below, near the lake, the Brule runs through temperatures of 45 or so degrees.

Strange things can happen to a fisherman in Maytime along this storied Wisconsin stream. A man can fish it of a morning near the lake and see ice form in his rod guides. Later, hunting the sun, he can drive to an upper river put-in and get his neck thoroughly sunburned, and wish to high heaven he had left off the long underwear.

You who fish it — and every troutster hopes he will — should be fore-warned so that you may come with clothing appropriate both for late winter and full summer. The only solution is two kinds of apparel. Many's the time I have hit the lower Brule dressed like an Eskimo, and then gone upstream and cooled my feet by dangling them over the side of a canoe.

A good many of the faithful, like the President of the Old Duck Hunters' Association, Inc., are firm believers in celebrating the opening along the more arctic portions of the Brule. There is sound reason for this. At the average opening many of the big, migratory rainbows from Lake Superior have finished spawning and are working back to the home waters.

"A man would be a ninnyhammer," said Mister President to me, "to pass up that first crack at the big ones."

"Habit is a powerful thing," said I.

Well did he know my affection for the upper reaches and its chance for trout, albeit smaller ones, on smaller lures: namely and to wit, dry floating flies, than which no finer device to deceive fish has been conceived in the mind of man.

Anyway, we went fishing on the lower river, come opening day. It was a morning to gladden pneumonia specialists. Emerging from the warm car at the streamside, I was as eager to embrace the flood as I am to get up in a deer camp and light the fire. Braver men than I have quailed at such fishing. I can remember huge Carl Tarsrud, stellar Brule fisherman, six feet four of Viking stamina, declaring in John Ziegler's gun repair shop that he wouldn't have any part of that lower Brule on an ugly first day.

Well, there we were, us Old Duck Hunters, as far asunder in fraternal spirit as ever we were. It made me shiver just to look at that part of the Brule. We were down below Armstead's farm, north of the town of Brule. There were snowy patches in the hollows, the day was gray, and from the lake blew a searching cold.

The Rt. Hon. President was lively as a cricket. His brown eyes snapped. He had buckled into waders while I was pulling on extra socks — reluctantly. For him the birds were singing and the sun was shining. In him the flame of the zealot burns with a fierce light. He went to the river whistling. I followed in a dampened frame of mind.

Against the rigors of the day I had seen to it that there was a full quart thermos of scalding coffee in my jacket. I knew, too, that the President was similarly fortified, from the bulge in his own jacket. As I waded out into the rocky stream it came to me that, if worst came to worst, it was always possible to go ashore, light a fire, and drown my woes guzzling coffee.

Hizzoner had no thought of coffee at the moment. He hastened away down the little path on the left bank and embraced the current a hundred yards below me. This was duck soup for him. You knew, watching even at that distance, no shiver passed through his wiry frame, and you thought, disgusted, what frightful fanaticism possesses a man who thus cleaves to his private poison under any conditions.

I remember how cold I got. I remember how my hands got blue, how I dreaded changing flies or plucking with numb fingers for lethargic angleworms in the bait can. I remember how the river cold bit through waders and wool and drove me, time and again, to perching on stream rocks. I remember how I thought wader pockets would be handy things to have, and how I pressed hands into armpits to restore warmth.

But, best of all, I remember the big splash I made when worn hobnails betrayed me and I bounced, more horizontal than vertical, off a flat rock into four feet of water. Then the river claimed me completely, so that my under wools and my outer wools were soaked and only a wild grab saved my hat from drifting away.

Ah — the coffee! And the warming fire! A big one. And may the devil fly away with every rainbow trout in the lower Brule, for all of me. They weren't hitting anyway. Blessed coffee. Blessed fire.

Now for a match. Whazzat, no match-safe? Had I left it home this evil day, after toting it for years and years? I had, verily. Oh, foolish man. Oh, bitter cold. Well, the coffee, then. And quick, Henri, for there's a man freezing to death! Ah — a whole quart, scalding hot!

I unscrewed the aluminum top and gazed into a container in which the fragile glass shell had broken into a million pieces. Those old, smooth hobs on my wading brogues had not only half drowned me, but had delivered the thermos to mine enemy, the rock.

A pretty pickle. In ten minutes I'd be ready for an oxygen tent. I have fallen into many a river and many a lake. Annually I achieve swan dives, jack-knifes, half-gainers and standing-sitting-standing performances. I am an expert faller-in. Poling a canoe up Big Falls on the Brule, I can, any day you name, describe a neat parabola and come up dripping with only one shin skinned. On my better days I can weave back and forth in exaggerated slow motion until the waters finally claim me.

Be assured, gentlemen, you are listening to no raw beginner at the diving game. But that one down below Armstead's farm really won me the championship of the Brule that season. That one was an even more convincing demonstration than one of several years before, when I fell head first out of a duck boat and went home by the light of the moon, strictly naked, my underwear drying on an oar.

"For two bits," I said, thinking of Mister President, "I would go look him up and give him a taste of it himself." It was just then the trail bushes parted, and there he was, dry as a bone, grinning like a skunk eating bumble-bees, the tail of a big rainbow projecting from his game pocket. He took me in at a glance.

"Fell in on purpose so I'd feel sorry for you and we'd go to the upper river, eh?"

So much for sympathy from this Spartan who, when he falls in, keeps right on a-going. Nevertheless he produced his hot coffee and dry matches. While the fire roared and I draped clothing on bushes, he told me about the fish. "Down by those old pilings. Salmon eggs. I went downstream with him forty yards. He was in the air half the time."

Then he noticed that his ghillie was, in fact, in the blue-lipped stage. He took off his jacket, threw it around me and pushed me closer to the fire, throwing down birch bark for me to stand upon. It seemed to me there lurked in his eyes a twinkle of sympathy, but I can never make sure about that with him. It may be deviltry. He built a drying frame for the wet clothes, and when an hour had passed and I was back into them, half dry and very smoky, he relented completely. He went the whole hog.

"Well, come on. You'll never get completely dry down here. I've got my kitchen-sink fish anyway."

The President thus describes the whale which he must annually stretch out in the sink before calling in the neighbors.

So it was that we pulled out of the lower Brule valley and drove south. In the town of Brule he stopped the car and went into a store with his now empty thermos bottle.

"A man has got to have coffee to fish," he said.

It was only around noon, and this far up the Brule valley the sun was shining. South we went over familiar trails: the ranger's road past round-as-a-dime Hooligan Lake, the county trunk, past Winnebojou where three hundred cars were parked and thence to Stone's Bridge where Johnny Degerman presided. Up there it was 75 above. There was a strong, gusty wind beating downstream. It was summer, and a few minutes before we had been in winter.

Let it be said here that on opening day along the Brule people who like to be alone will do best to stay above Winnebojou. Along this portion of the creek, for some twenty miles, most of the banks are owned privately, and ingress to same is not to be had at every turn-in gate along the county roads that parallel the stream. But the problem can be solved by going to Stone's Bridge, the common jumping-off place for upper river explorers.

If it is feasible to divide any river into two parts, the division may be effected on the Brule by nominating the Winnebojou Bridge as the equator. And connoisseurs of the difference between fact and fancy should be told, right here and now, that people who really know the creek will always refer to this particular spot as the Winnebojou Wagon Bridge, and you can figure out yourself when the last wagon crossed any bridge anywhere.

Still that is its traditional name. Upstream from it lie several million dollars' worth of real estate and lodges, including the fabulous Pierce estate of 4,400 acres. Downstream from it are the precincts of Tom, Dick and Harry and, let it be added, the best places for getting the big rainbows in the early run.

It was so warm up there at Stone's Bridge that Johnny Degerman, Charon of these waters, had his shirt open all the way down the front.

"Mr. Degerman, I believe," said the President in his best manner.

"Go to hell, the both of you," said Mr. Degerman, who was being bothered some by mosquitoes.

"Mr. Degerman!" the President reprimanded.

"I saved a canoe," said Johnny. "Thought you might be along. Could have rented it for five bucks. And all I get from you birds is a buck."

"Mr. Degerman," said the President, "your philanthropy moves me to the extent of promising to pay one buck and a half for said canoe."

"Lucky if I get the buck," said Johnny, who is a charming fellow. "And say, if you're smart, you'll show them something wet and big and brown. Carl Miller has been knocking their ears off with a big home-made Ginger Quill."

"Enough!" cried Hizzoner. "First you insult me, and then you rub it in by telling me what to throw at 'em. Gimme a canoe pole. I mean give him one. My back ain't so strong today."

So it was that the old Duck Hunters went forth abroad upon the bosom of the Brule and Mr. Degerman called after us, "I may pick up some chubs for you off'n the bridge, in case you don't connect."

We were too far away for the President to do more than look back at Johnny with what must pass as a haughty stare.

It was certainly a day. There was that downstream breeze, which means warmth. There was the smell of a million cedar trees. There was a good canoe under us, and ten miles of red hot river before us, and hundreds and hundreds of cedar waxwings letting on they were glad to be alive.

You know how it is. The signs are right. You feel history is in the making. You take your time buttering up the line. You are painstaking about soaping the surplus grease off the leader. You lay on the anti-mosquito kalsomine. You light a leisurely pipe and don't give a rap what happens tomorrow or the day after.

His nibs exercised seniority rights by occupying the bow with a rod the first hour. It was not too eventful. Small trout could be had for the casting, willing wallopers, mostly rainbows and brookies, which fought with terrier impudence. The worthier foes were lurking under the banks and in the deep holes. The only memorable excitement in five miles was a dusky native of about 16 inches which came out from under a brush heap to take the President's wet Cowdung.

For long years those upper Brule brookies have intrigued the ODHA, Inc. We do not credit them with too much sense. But accuse us not of sacrilege, for we love them dearly. We love them so much that we wish they had more — well, foresight. In a hitting mood they are fly-rushers, showoffs, and that is the trouble. More common caution and less eagerness to lick the world would save many of them useless flops in the bottom of a willow-walled hereafter.

"Did I ever tell you about the Olson boys?" said the President at lunch at May's Rips. "They were taking out pine on a forty near Foxboro, and it was a whale of a big forty, because they got about a million feet off it one winter.

"Anyway, one morning, the kid — I forget his name — woke up late in the camp and began dressing. He couldn't find his socks, which is what happens to anyone who wakes up late in a well-regulated logging camp. So he says, says he: 'Some low-down, no-good miscreant without the decency of a weasel swiped my socks! Was it you, Pa?'"

There was more. Of Jack Bradley's aniline-dyed pigeons which he sold to visiting trout fishermen on the Big Balsam in the old days as holy birds of India. Of the same Jack's famous kangaroo court, where fishermen were sentenced for ungraceful lying. Of times along the storied Brule when lumberjacks took out brook trout by the bushel on red-flannel-baited hooks. And there were tales of Old Mountain, the Brule's mythical gargantua, a rainbow trout whose ascent of the stream raised the water two feet; of his sworn enemy, the Mule, another rainbow, almost as big. That sort of thing didn't catch many fish, but along the Brule you are likely to feel it doesn't make any difference, one way or another.

We sat there, with our backs against cool cedars, and watched the river hustle by. Sometimes a canoe drifted past and a lazy hand would be raised, or a lazier Chippewa would exert himself for a minute, poling up the not-too-formidable fast water of May's Rips. But mostly we just sat and studied foam-flecked water spill down the rips, arrow into a water spear-head at the bottom and carom off to the left. It was almost three o'clock when the President leaped up.

"I don't know why in time I go fishing with you," he declared. "The day is almost over, and I've got only one kitchen-sink fish."

"Gimme," said I, "another doughnut — and shut up, will you?"

But the spell was broken. Mister President was on his feet and there was a river to fish. I took the stern paddle, for it was my turn, and the canoe slid down May's Rips, under the rustic bridge, past the Pierce hatchery outflow, through the wide-spread and down threatening Big Falls, which looks worse than it is, but is bad enough.

Big Falls is just a good fast rip of river, almost completely arched by graceful cedars. You see it from the upstream side as hardly more than an inviting dark tunnel in the cedar forest wall. You see a little lip of curling water; and then when you are right on top of it and your eyes are adjusted to its darker light, you see it as a downhill stretch of roaring water, and unless you are good at twisting canoes around right-angled corners you may have trouble at the end, where it goes off to the left.

Big Falls is just another rapid to a good Brule Chippewa boatman. But neither the President nor I qualify in that respect. We are fair, just fair. On good days, when we are not too tired, we can, with care, bring a canoe back up Big Falls, a stunt the Chippewas do with a passenger — usually sitting, tensed, in the bottom. Well, Big Falls has licked me more often than vice versa, but I am resigned to winning up to about the eighth round, after which I fall in, or out, and grab the bow of the canoe and tow it the rest of the way.

We got down easily, and in the slack water the President said: "Hold 'er! Hold 'er and give me my waders."

For once, I had thought, we were to hit the upper river without recourse to long halts while Mister President climbed in and out of waders. It was not to be so, however. He had his same old scheme in mind: to tie up the canoe and wade the fast water below the Big Falls. He is a man who holds that the best way to catch trout is to meet them on their own terms, afoot.

Below Big Falls the Brule is touch-and-go wading in many spots. It goes down and it twists. It shoots between banks of huge gray cedars, and in places the trees almost meet overhead. Its bottom is rock-strewn. Its current is swift. Here, you would say, is a hunk of river that would be at home in the mountains.

Big fish have come out of that water. Springs seep out of the banks, and watercress flourishes in the sodden places where the river and terra firma contest for control. All of it — river, bank and trees — are forest sponge, and through this rolls gin-white water over knobby bottoms.

I saw Hizzoner get down to business with salmon eggs and spinner. I went at it myself with Degerman's recommended Ginger Quill. Oh, there were fish. There are always frying pan fish in this stretch. Mostly rainbows, here and there a brown that forgot to wait until night, and some brooks. In such swift water things can be very exciting with nothing more than a foot of fish on a line.

I saw the good fish — the No. 2 kitchen-sink fish — hit. It was Mister President's salmon eggs he coveted. A rainbow tardy in its return from waters so far upstream. But there was nothing tardy about the way it whacked the salmon eggs. These fish conjure up a kind of electrical insanity when they feel cold steel.

Hizzoner gave it the butt and yelled. I climbed out on the bank and went down there to view the quarrel. It was getting on toward evening. The river chill was rising.

Mister President's rod — the one with the long cork grip to ease the hand — got a workout that day. Above the rapids he yelled, "For the love of . . ."

The rest of his conversation was swallowed by river sounds, for it is so noisy in those rips that you can smile at a partner, call him a no-good stiff and he will actually think you are complimenting him. However, I gathered that the President desired that I make a pass at the big rainbow with a little metal-rimmed net which I carried. His own deep-bellied net was back in the canoe.

The fish was a good, standard, spring-run Brule job. Maybe around five pounds. Six pounds, possibly. My net was no instrument for him, but that's what I thought Hizzoner had ordered, and I went to work, all eyes on the fish.

He let him leap, up and down and across. There is no stopping these fellows when they start. Not for nothing do they wear that red badge of courage along the lateral line. When they get tired of plowing the top water, they just lie like stubborn terriers holding to a kid's skipping rope and tug — jerk! jerk! jerk!

Mister President was bellowing over the roar of water. I did not hear him. I was intent on getting that little net under the fish. The rainbow was brought close. I saw him a few feet from me — a hard, swift bullet of a fish, ready for another dash.

My time had come, and I swooped. I swooped with the net and missed.

Only in nightmares do I recall it clearly. The rim of the net touched that walloper somewhere, and with one powerful twist he was off and away, a shadowy torpedo heading for deep water.

I was a bit downstream from his nibs. I worked back toward him so that I could hear what he had been shouting. Coming closer, I heard: "I was telling you all the time to go back to the canoe and get my net, dern ye!"

That must have unnerved me, for when I got near him a foot slipped. I reached out for support, got hold of Mister President's shoulder and both of us went down.

To this day the Hon. President refers to that stretch as "the place where I swam the Brule, and later hanged a man on a handy cedar tree."

It was too late for a drying fire. There were miles of upstream poling ahead of us. We had the Big Falls to negotiate the hard way. So we got in the canoe and started. Mister President took the rear; I worked a shorter pole in the bow.

Halfway up, I knew we'd make it. We synchronized well as a poling team. The old knack was there. We would both heave with the poles at just the right instant, and get a fresh hold on the bottom at the right time. For once, said I, the Big Falls would find me triumphant.

Only one of us made it, and it was not I. With about ten feet more to go, the canoe gave a sudden and unaccountable jerk, not caused by rocks, you understand. Once more yours truly was overboard. That one, as I recall, was a quick back dive, and while I floundered, waist deep, Hizzoner shot the canoe up the last curling lip of the rapids.

To this day he will admit nothing. He declares such occurrences are part of the hazards of the game. He avers maybe his pole did slip a bit when it should have remained firm, that maybe he did shift his feet just a trifle. But as for admitting he put me overboard — "You know I wouldn't do a thing like that."

It was getting dark when I caught up with him at the head of Big Falls. He was grinning and had his recently filled thermos bottle open and ready for me. I wrung out such garments as I could and thanked the stars for that warm coffee. I raised it to my lips there in the dusk, and I was chilled to the core.

It contained only ice-water. Ice-water! Of which I had recently drunk enough to float the canoe. From the semi-darkness came his voice: "I thought you'd get so hot up here on the upper river you'd need a cooling drink."

Later, while warming with the upstream poling job, he said that once he saved a man's life. The man had fallen in a lake and was well-nigh a goner. He fished the fellow out, squeezed out the water and restored him to consciousness with a hatful of lake water dashed into his face. The fellow came around, said Mister President, ran his tongue over his lips where the water lingered and said, "Dang it, you know I never tech the stuff."

So we went home with only one kitchen-sink fish, and I was warm as toast long before we got to Johnny Degerman's dock. Which may have been from exertion with a canoe pole, or may have been from listening to the President of the Old Duck Hunters' Association, Inc.

THE BANDIT
OF THE BRULE

*Now we come to Mr. President at his most outrageous. He will steal and re-
steal MacQuarrie's waders and finally, after they are wholly worn out, offer in a
fatherly affectionate way to trade them for MacQuarrie's hip boots.*

*So why does everybody love this guy? Any number of people have over the
years said they knew someone who was a dead-ringer of him. Always spoken with
warmth. A privilege to know, etc.*

*I dunno. I have no quick answer. Mr. President is fun. Not many people are.
And there's no malice in him. Most people have more than enough malice. And he's
this and that that I have pointed out before. But essentially, I think, as he emerges
though MacQuarrie's fiction he is larger than life. Not fully figure-outable. He's a
head-shaking beloved rascal.*

The President of the Old Duck Hunters' Association, Inc., was
clinging to the lower pantry shelf, head and arms thrust into a top
compartment where he stores fishing tackle. Ignoring my entrance,
he got a new grip, shifted his feel and went on prodding a remote corner.
From time to time he grunted and hoisted a foot, the better to stretch his five
feet and seven inches. He made a desperate effort, almost slipped, and a
Wedgewood saucer crashed to the loor. The President withdrew his head and
said accusingly:

"Now you've done it!"

"Eh?"

"You pushed me. That's why I slipped. Wait until my wife finds out who broke that saucer!"

He glared at me. There is no use arguing with the President of the Old Duck Hunters' Association.

"Don't stand there gawking!" he snorted. "Get a broom — no! Don't throw the fragments in the waste basket. Hide them, you loon. My wife always looks in waste baskets!"

This remarkable man bounded from the shelf, dragging something with him. It was a pair of faded, patched fishing waders. He held them in the light from the window, pulled tentatively and something gave way at a seam.

"Now you've got me excited!" he shouted. "You've ruined a good pair of waders!"

No two square inches of those waders were without evidence of the vulcanizer's art.

"All right, I ruined your waders."

"How can a man fish without waders?"

I suggested he might buy another pair.

"Do you know what those waders cost?" he demanded truculently, and added before I could reply: "Thirty dollars. That's what they cost!"

I knew they cost $18.25 and said so.

"Not on your life. These were made to order. They had to send for 'em."

"Can't they send again?"

"Well, if you want to go to that expense it's all right with me . . . I want to be fair about it. I was going to take just whatever you had in stock. But if you really intend to duplicate these waders, the inseam measurement is — ."

"Come to think of it I have an old pair."

"Old pair!" His manner was bristling. "As if I'd take an old pair. I'll take those your uncle sent you from Scotland. I know he was in jail when he sent them but I'm not particular."

That's how the President got my new waders. He stole across the street to my house and removed them while I mowed the lawn. I saw him sneaking back home with them, the dog tagging along behind. The dog was supposed to be my dog but had found a boon companion in Mister President. He seemed to have found advantages in the President's mode of life that I could not offer.

I was for going over to his house and stealing them back but my wife was against it. She said it served me right — "leaving things around where he can get his hands on them." There wasn't any use making a fuss. I'd have to get along that season as best I could with my hip-high rubber boots.

The President also had my fishing jacket and a box of my flies. I had received the flies as a Christmas present from him but he took them back the day after Christmas because he said I didn't appreciate such things. When I had demurred he turned on me:

"What did you give me for Christmas? Nothing but a little etching of a trout jumping. A fine spirit to show at Christmas! Grasping — that's what you are!"

The first day the President went fishing in my waders he repaired alone to a secret place — "you walk two miles through brush, wade a swamp and hit the stream. Take you there? So every Tom, Dick and Harry in town will find out about this place? Not much!" He returned at midnight and phoned me out of bed.

"Those darned waders you gave me," he commenced. "They're too long in the toes. You know I've got a short foot. When you buy waders it's a wonder you wouldn't think of someone besides yourself. When I get a sock on over them there's a big lump right in the toe. I never saw such da — ."

"Then bring them back. They fit me."

"There you go — always grasping. What's more, there aren't any suspenders or suspender buttons on 'em — ."

There was a weighty pause while he let that sink in; then his voice took on a cheerier note as he continued:

"But I fixed that. At first I held them up with one hand while I fished with the other. That was before I got the bright idea of slashing holes in the tops and rigging up suspenders out of a fly line — ."

I had a sudden suspicion it was one of my fly lines. He confirmed it cheerfully:

"I took that old cream-colored double-tapered line I found in your fishing jacket and cut it up for suspenders. It worked pretty good. Next time you buy waders get some that don't need overhauling on the stream. Damif I ain't sick and tired of wasting good fishing time repairing your stuff!"

He hung up and I lay awake two hours wondering if I'd left anything else lying around that he might have appropriated in his ingenious fashion.

It was not until a week later, on the Cranberry River, that I fully realized how much those waders would cost me ere summer had fled. Returning at night to our parked car the President bade me pull off his and/or my waders. I always have to do that. I have tried for years to skid him along the ground but he anchors himself and I am very likely to fall over backwards myself.

"Them waders — ," he began. "Cheap things. I just barely brushed against a spruce stub and rip! Went the right leg. See? Just above the knee. But it's only a six-inch rip. You can get it vulcanized."

I did. It cost $2.40 for the job. It would have been cheaper if the tire shop man hadn't found three other weak spots and, like a dentist exploring for cavities, reinforced them.

Anyway, I got the waders back. But the President learned, somehow, that I had them repaired and crept into my house one night. That's how he got them back.

I did the best I could on the various trout waters of North Wisconsin in a pair of new tan rubber ducking boots. Good thing I had them. They always shipped water over the tops but they kept a fellow dry for a little while. Their rubber bottoms were slippery on the rocks but it was cheaper using them than risking a wife's disfavor by investing in new waders — "how much money have you spent on that junk already this year?"

Once more that season the President returned my waders for dry-docking. This restoration followed a trip he made up the north shore of Lake superior with a worm-drowning crony by the name of Rudy. They always got brook trout back inland from the lake where the beaver had dammed the streams. Brooks up to a pound and a half. You go in there with the President or Rudy or you don't go at all. Naturally, hardly anyone but the President and Rudy go in there.

The waders looked pretty sick by that time. At the toes where he turned them up to fit his wading brogues, there were marked abrasions. They had been placed too close to a fire to dry out and as a result one leg had acquired a stiff, crepe-rubber appearance. But they still held out water. Especially after I had them re-vulcanized for an even three bucks. Even the tire shop man, who is an expert wader surgeon, shook his head by this time — "They're on their last legs," he said.

I thought sure I could retain them after that second vulcanizing. But the President, after letting a whole week slip by, braced me on a street corner and said in a voice that could be heard a half-block away:

"It's a wonder you wouldn't return things that don't belong to you!"

He got them that night, by stealth. Warning came too late when I heard him tramping back across the street, the dog following approvingly. He was whistling a jaunty air as I saw him pass under the street light on the corner, the waders folded under his arm.

A few days later a friend by the name of Tommy phoned to ask me if he might borrow my waders for a day. He said he knew a place. I told him he could have them if it was all right with Mister President. Through Tommy I learned later that the old rascal had invited him into his house with a bow, that he had produced potable liquid from a place in the basement.

Tommy said he laid the waders in the middle of the floor — "sure, Tommy, you can have 'em. Anything for a neighbor." Then they downed about four tumblers of what turned out to be chokecherry wine from the President's own trees. He said he forgot all about the waders and stayed up until 2 o'clock playing bridge.

Things went along like that as the season advanced. I followed the President faithfully to all the trout holes he knew — and he knows a lot of them. He tours about to these places on weekends, not forgetting to drop in and say hello here and there. For instance, he says hello to the fellow who runs the portable sawmill on the banks of the Namakagon at Squaw Bend and to the fellow who is always waiting at dusk on Stone's bridge on the upper Brule.

I don't know who this last fellow is. It's too dark to see by the time we poke our canoe nose into the dock. But this fellow is always there. He leans over the bridge right near the dock and says "Howdy, boys." Maybe it's a different fellow every time but it sure looks like the same one there in the dusk, with the faint western sky outlining his droopy felt hat and folded arms. I don't think this fellow has any face at all. Anyway, I never saw it. The only part of him I ever saw are the khaki pants and heavy boots that are revealed in the little circle of light the President makes with a flashlight, showing him our catch.

Now when the season is about to close, when the northern maples are reddening and the popples show signs of yellowing, the President prepares for a solemn mission — the last day of the season. This is fully as important as the opening day. It involves a study of the almanac to determine when the sun rises, thus insuring an early start. It also involves an auto packed the night before, two alarm clocks, in case one doesn't work, and considerable prayer that the day will be fair, but not too fair; warm, but not too warm; cloudy, but not too cloudy.

He roused me long before there was a hint of gray in the east and led me, half-asleep to his waiting chariot. There he bade me take the wheel while he crawled in among the duffle in the rear and went sound asleep after commanding: "McNeil's on the lower Brule."

So that was the place he had chosen . . . Good judgement, I mused, as I wheeled through town, across the Nemadji river fill, under the ore dock approach where the laden cars thundered by overhead.

McNeil's . . . Not a bad place for the last day. The browns from Lake Superior have a habit of working upstream in late August. The President, with my now disreputable waders as a pillow, got in a solid two hours of sleep as I drove through the sweet August dawn. It was light when we drew up under the lone spruce in the clearing. River mist marked the pathway of the Brule along the valley as far as we could see. The President grumbled about the waders, put them on gingerly so as not to strain the seams, said he doubted if they'd last out the day, told me to be back at 11 for lunch and stalked off by himself downstream.

After he had departed I prepared myself for the final quest. I put on the inadequate rubber boots and wondered how long it would be before the water would come trickling over their tops. I never attempt to accoutre myself for the river while the President is messing around inside the car. He requires an acre lot in which to get ready. He goes through every jacket, bag, car pocket and corner and takes what suits his fancy, regardless of whose it is. I just sort of stand around hoping he won't see too much. When he is gone I dive in and take what's left.

The most magical place in the world for me at 5 o'clock in the morning on the last day of the trout season is the lower Brule of Wisconsin.

Then autumn has already laid a tentative finger on the country. The steep banks of the Bois Brule play hide and seek in the morning fog. The river is a sullen gray rope, more crooked than at any place on its 66-mile length. Water that was warm a month ago — yes, two weeks ago — seems suddenly frigid, the result of longer, colder nights.

It was a morning of mornings. Always, by some inscrutable legerdemain with the weather gods, the President arranges for perfect weather on final day. He admits he has a special arrangement with the people who prepare weather and will trade a good closing day for, say, rain on the day of the Odd Fellow's picnic.

Above this place we call McNeil's hole, there is a long stretch of fast water — perhaps 400 yards — with a two-foot sheer drop at the beginning of it. There I went and with a gold-bodied brown bivisible sought to solve the mystery of a plunk-plunk that sounded from the middle of a deep run. I'd have bet money that fish would have taken. Getting closer I saw him through the mist, a bold, two-pound brown, feeding steadily, coming clear out of water and plunking back.

No better time. Early morning and late evening are best for browns. They seem less wary then. Middle of the day tactics are not needed. I offered him the bivisible a score of times. I doubt if on any of the casts he saw the tell-tale leader or line. But he wouldn't come. He wouldn't come to anything I had. I did not put him down. I left him plunking there in the corrugated riffle — for what, I never learned.

Upstream a bit two smaller brownies surrendered to the lure of gold and two more came to net from flies dropped right into the churning froth beneath the little two-foot falls. I worked upstream. The sun was climbing. Mist evaporated. A porky swam the creek in front of me. By 11 o'clock weary, hungry, I returned to the car.

The President had been there ahead of me. He had some fish. "Yes, I've got some good keepers — but them damn waders. Look at me! I'm soaking. I feel like a spaniel. Gimme a cup of coffee before I catch my death."

He dried out while we ate. After the meal the President produced two heavy wool blankets and spread them triumphantly in the shade of the car. In five minutes he was snoring. After he got to sleep I managed to swipe one blanket and snoozed myself, with the hum of insects in my ears. It was near 4 o'clock when he awakened me. There he stood, fully clad for the stream—wearing my rubber boots!

The waders, half dried, hung from the big spruce like half a scarecrow. He said:

"I felt sort of conscience-stricken about those waders. Here it is the last day and you haven't had a chance to use 'em. You take 'em."

We went fishing. This time together and downstream. Downstream while the sun dipped lower, the river grew louder, the air chillier. Downstream beyond the rocky stretches to where the holes were really deep. Wet fly water it was and the browns began to hit with considerable zest when the sun was definitely under the horizon.

I was soaked to the waist in no time. The President, by canny manipu-lation, managed to stay dry even in the boots — no mean feat on the Brule. His 9-foot rod with the foot-long cork handle gave him casting distance where I was stymied with my eight-foot rod. He reached into places I couldn't touch.

He took browns. Always we take browns on the last day. Not a rainbow in the stretch. Nor a brookie. But browns, zippy, sparkling devils from the big lake, feeling again the frigid waters of the Bois Brule as they work upstream to spawn, later in the fall.

We were two miles from the car when the President called a halt. We clomped back along the bank, feeling our way in the gathering darkness. Twice we waded the river on short-cuts. Each time the cold river stung into me through those miserable waders.

At the car the President proceeded with the vespers of the Old Duck Hunters', Inc. He rubbed the back of his hand across his mouth and said: "Ah-smack!" He fumbled in the glove compartment, came up with a bottle and poured a drink apiece. After an interval he poured another.

Always there are two drinks. Never more except on special occasions. We sat on the running board and sipped. Gradually there spread through my chilled body a warmer, kindlier feeling toward my fellowman.

I looked down at the waders. The toes were practically worn through. All the seams were either loose or frankly open. The surface was speckled with black rubber patches. At the crotch the outside material was rubbed away to the rubber beneath.

I must have shivered in the cool night breeze for the President poured a third drink. An unexpected gratuity. The President peered into my creel and opined I had caught the best mess of trout. He slapped me on the back and said I was a good fellow. There was about him a hail-fellow note that ordinarily he did not waste on me. He spoke:

"I'm glad I let you use those waders today. They sure are swell waders. I never wore a finer pair in my life. I want you to know just how I feel about them. I'd just a soon part with my wife as I would with those waders, they're that comfortable."

At the moment everything he said sounded logical. I looked again at the shredded waders. I said sure, they were great waders. I said I'd patch 'em and they'd do just fine for another season.

"By all means," said the President. "You'll need those waders next spring. I think you ought to have them. It's only right. Tell you what. I'll make you a deal. Duck season is comin' on and I need a pair of rubber boots like these."

I listened with interest. I was in a mood to say yes to almost anything this great and good fisherman would propose. He leaned toward me with fatherly affection and said:

"I'll swap you the waders for the boots!"

CITY-LIMIT DUCKS

If you have a copy of the May 1932 Field & Stream *around you can read the next story. It's a good one, published here in book form for the first time.*

Two things about City-Limit Ducks *interest me: Geese and shanty boats. When I was a boy on Barnegat Bay the end of the shanty boat era was occurring, although I didn't know it at the time. But little houseboats, "shanties," on a floating hull were commonplace. No rent. No taxes. If you didn't like your environs, tow her to a new spot. Outboards killed shanty boats. Outboards made it too easy for the public to visit and vandalize them.*

MacQuarrie here writes with feeling about Canada geese going past. Know that Canadas were a rarity in 1932. Today they are all over the place, but the great population build-up has been over the last twenty years. Then — as now — majestic grand animals, it was an outdoor event to see (and hear) a flock going over. It's why a Canada marks our wildlife refuges. One biologist put it to me that Canada geese are "the wild in wildlife."

"You needn't drive fifty or sixty miles away from town to get good duck hunting." The President of the Old Duck Hunters' Association, Inc. had the floor, and I perceived that he had a subject of some importance by the light in his eye and the air of conviction he conveyed in biting off the end of a fresh cigar.

"Where you lead I shall follow," I said.

"We've been running off here and there all over upper Wisconsin for years looking for ducks," he went on, "when one of the best duck marshes in the whole state is located right at our front door. I propose to see Superior,

Wisconsin, first this season, and give those ducks on Allouez Bay an opportunity to enroll in the Association."

"How about a boat?"

"Got that arranged last week. Shanty man down on the bay shore says he'll leave his out at the mouth of Bear Creek, with the oars in it, any night I say."

"Good old shanty man! See that he gets an application for honorary membership in the Old Duck Hunters' Association. When do we go?"

"You know me," dictated the President. "Tomorrow." He reached for the telephone and called George, the garage man, whose boy, Tommy, was drafted to tell the shanty man that we would want the boat in the morning. The President was given assurance by George that Tommy, even at the moment, was skedaddling down the clay road to the shanty man's humble domicile with the tidings of our early-morning expedition.

"That's that," said the President. "Be at my house at three all ready to go. It'll take an hour and a half or more to get located in a blind. I haven't shot on the old bay for twenty years. Boy, I remember the day I stood in a clump of bushes and presided — yes sir; presided — at the fall migration of Canadian ducks!"

"Let that rest until the morn," said I. "It's ten o'clock now, and three will come early. But say, come to think, I can't go tomorrow morning — darn it! I've got to be at the office. Whatever made me think tomorrow was Sunday? You'll have to call off George's boy for this trip."

"Can you stay away from the office until 9:30?"

"Yes, but — "

"No remarks from the floor, you'll be back on time. You see that's the beauty of Allouez Bay. That you kill your ducks and greet the day, and you're back at work in due season — a hero among your follow men!"

The President was ready and waiting when I knocked at his door. I threw my gun and shell case into the car. Everything else, including the two sacks of decoys, was already stowed away. A cup of coffee and a few slices of toast, filched from the table of the President himself, and we were off. I had no idea as to how we were to get to the bay. I knew that occasional bags of ducks were killed on Allouez Bay, which forms the easterly end of Superior-Duluth harbor, but had never visited the rice-grown flats.

We parked the car, and as we locked the doors I heard the booming of surf on the shore of Lake Superior. A sullen October northeaster was blowing itself out, and the surf was filling the damp night air with a monotonous, hollow rhythm. Gusts of rain, blown fine by the wind, slapped coldly against our cheeks. Ghostly trees rose on each side of the narrow road in which we had halted. It was the zero hour — that time of least joy to all duck hunters except the very stout-hearted, when the bright fires of optimism are checked until they give but a meager glow. It is then that the morale of the old duck hunters, is made apparent.

"Here!" commanded the President, all business. "Take this sack of decoys and your own stuff. I'll take the rest. It's a half-mile walk to the boat, near the mount of Bear Creek."

That was news. I had envisioned a comfortable ride, a jump right into the boat and a short pull to the rice beds, but it was not to be so. In the darkness, loaded heavily, we wallowed and waded down what was once a road, now mere tracks of water in the red clay. Matters were not improved when we got off the road once and came to a deep, narrow creek. But it was not the right place.

"Little farther on," said the President. "I'm getting my bearings now. This is where the Dutchman used to keep his boats. We'll back-track to the road."

"And where is the Dutchman now?"

"Dead."

"Too bad," said I, and I meant it.

Those decoys were heavy and the loaded shell box and the gun carried awkwardly, but we made it back up a hill, through some brush. One hundred and fifty yards farther on we came upon the shanty man's boat. With his flashlight the President located it, resting bottom side up, with two oars leaning against it. I needn't describe that rowboat for anyone. Everybody knows the kind of a boat your shanty man keeps — God bless him! This one rowed as though it were made of water-soaked mahogany, and it was quite impossible to keep it on a straight course. One oar was longer than the other. The President, as in his wont, perched in the back seat, behind the duffle.

"You know, I can't row and keep an eye out for where we're going," he explained. "Anyway, I'm scared of myself in these fragile little boats. Once I pulled a pair of oarlocks crooked in one of the Dutchman's boats, and I was afraid to go back and face him. That's why I haven't hunted here for twenty years. But now that the Dutchman's gone, I suppose it's safe."

Bear Creek oozes into Allouez Bay by the most tortuous pathway possible. It has practically no current and knows not the straight and narrow path. The boat constantly scraped the banks, but the stream widened gradually and we found ourselves in the more or less open water. The bay is dotted with islands of mud, some of which are covered with bushy growths, and here and there one finds a tree. Beds of wild rice are present wherever the water is shallow enough.

The President ordered a halt while he flashed his light on what I took to be a clump of floating hazel bushes. The light revealed a pathway through the bushes, over which boats had apparently been dragged, and we rowed, pushed and cajoled the boat into its hiding place. It was possible to stand in the once thick growth of the bushes and exert some leverage. A slip meant a wetting in deep water. We cut and laid dead grass over the boat, and fixed up a fairly workable blind.

Allouez Bay is the unused two-mile end of the Superior-Duluth harbor, named for Father Allouez of exploratory fame. That morning we were about in the center of the bay. The harbor itself is formed by two peninsulas, Wisconsin and Minnesota points, projecting approximately 10 miles to meet each other. The Wisconsin point is much shorter than the Minnesota point. Where the Wisconsin point ends is the Superior entry to the harbor from the open lake. Eight miles farther on is another entry, cut through the Minnesota point.

"Get down!" the President hissed.

The first sibilant whispering of wings told us they were on the move. It was almost light enough to shoot. I strained my ears to catch the sound of other flocks. Suddenly the morning was shattered by a fusillade of shotgun blasts that most certainly must have wakened every tired deck-hand on the lake boats lying close by the big ore docks. One shot followed another, from different parts of the bay.

Hunters were spotted all over the shallow bay, in the rice beds, on small quaking islands and behind rows of trees on the larger islands. How they got there we could not explain. We had heard none coming. Perhaps we had been late in getting to the shooting ground. Afterward it dawned on us that the inveterate bay hunter is at it early to preempt the most favored blinds. Our guess, confirmed later by observation, was that there were twenty-five or more hunters scattered over the bay that morning!

"They never used to come like this when the Dutchman was here," muttered the President. "Swell chance with all those birds shooting!"

"Down!" I cried as a handful of butterballs zipped by. They went over our heads like the wind, but saw our decoys and curved back. As they made a sharp turn two hundred yards away two hunters rose from a clump of brush and let fly. The range was impossible, but they had their sport, I suppose. The butterballs sped across Wisconsin point, no doubt to take refuge on the bounding main of Lake Superior.

Ducks were everywhere in the air by this time. Apparently they had come into the bay to feed and rest during the night and escape the storm on the lake. Flocks rose up here and there from all points as the shooting continued. It was long after the first bombardment that we got our first chance. A flock of low-flying bluebills coasted into our decoys, wings spread, without warning. We got two, the others soaring off to receive another baptism of fire. I saw them mount higher and higher to avoid gunfire as they flew back into the bay.

"George's boy, Tommy, killed five mallards here the other morning," said the President, to cheer me up.

"No mallard I ever saw would fly into a spot like this," I remarked.

It is written that the President shall forever lead the way in all things, take the honors of the Association, such as they are, and utterly confound me as a presumptuous whelp. Shortly after I spoke he rose to supreme heights by standing up in the boat and killing a lone greenhead with such thoroughness as to humiliate me sorely.

"Boy," said the President, patronizingly, "if there's mallards in this country, we'll get 'em!"

I thanked him for that "we."

It was while I was putting out the boat to pick up the three dead birds that our real chance came. A flock of big ducks, which must have been canvasbacks from their speed and size, came over with every evident intention of decoying. The President took one shot, but it was long. They had come in such a way as to escape even the long-range endeavors of our mates about the bay and would have offered a fair shot with no favors.

As I was getting back into the blind the honking of geese floated down through the rain scuds — a haunting, anxious call. We made them out — a hundred or more coming high over Wisconsin point. Perhaps they had rested on the lake all night, or, more likely, they had flown all night before the northeaster. Up two hundred yards or so, they circled the bay time and again, as though they were tired and wished to alight, but they were far too canny to come anywhere near range.

Their music filled the air, and every hunter on the bay had turned to watch them. I have never before seen or probably will never again see such a splendid army of geese. Safe above the bay full of hunters they circled. Many moved on, to be lost to view, but several flocks kept swinging in wide arcs, as though tired and anxious to rest in the bay. They seemed reluctant to depart.

It occurred to me that the bay might be a feeding place where they had rested weary wings on long north and south treks before. Their constant presence above gave one a pang of regret that they could not come down safely. Brave fellows, they had won the right to rest if they had flown through the night over Lake Superior.

Over the wide reaches of the tossing lake they had come, bearing ever southward, over the curling combers of the surf at the shore edge, and then over the narrow point to find a haven in the bay behind. But tired pinions are as naught compared to the risk of coming too close to the man with a gun, and most them sailed away inland. The President expressed a devout wish that they might have come nearer and, lacking that, wished them Godspeed. It is easy to remember their coming and their song, which was the melody against the bass accompaniment of the surf. They made a wild and beautiful picture — all the more notable because it was within the corporate limits of a busy city.

A mile away street cars rattled along. In front of us a 600-foot lake freighter, belly deep with ore, backed out of a dock and swung around to clear the entry. Its sonorous blast was strangely incongruous at the time, but served only to heighten our pleasure at the goose flight.

I had my watch out and was about to suggest that we take up the decoys when the President pulled me down in the boat. Through the scraggly brush I made out a short, undulating white line, close to the water.

"Those canvasbacks are coming back," warned the President. "Don't wait for them to swing a second time. Shoot when you see the whites of their eyes!"

Straight for us they headed and I reflected miserably upon my inadequate ability to handle that kind of a shot. But there was no time to learn now. They were upon us. My gun barrel settled upon one, and I pulled it up to blot the bird out of sight over the matted barrel, then fired. It tumbled headlong, not forty feet in front of us. My second shot was a mere aimless and desperate effort to hit something that burst over my head with demoralizing speed. The President's first shot had counted too, but that second shot, necessitating a quick turn and complete readjustment, was too much. My watch showed about seven o'clock. Hunters were standing up in their boats and blinds all over the bay. Occasionally one would get a shot at a high-flying bird.

We came ashore while dock and factory whistles on the bayfront sounded seven o'clock.

"You row back, and you can have two ducks instead of just one," proffered the President. He was already seated on the poop deck, cigar and all, and I had not the heart to disturb his tranquillity.

"Yes, sir," said he, on a generous impulse, "you row 'er back, and you can have both the bluebills!"

But going back was not so bad. From the high spot where the car had been left we looked back and saw, high above the bay, a single flock of geese, still winging in tireless circles. An hour later, with a very red face, I was in the office, and it was hard to believe that we had been a part of a rain-swept bay but a few hours before.

Too Daggone
White

You have to concentrate to catch it but MacQuarrie speeds up when there is a fish on the end of the line. It's true. He's delicious when he waxes poetic. His wonderful themes stay with him tried and true. But when he gets into a fish fight and there is no shortage of them he speeds up. His writing goes taut. Sentences are shorter. The action is real. You can see and feel the fish in its fight for freedom. More importantly, you can live the excitement of you, the angler, fast to a fish and using all your skill (maybe a little luck, here, too) to land it.

And, of course, as in this story, you lose some. Like MacQuarrie says in another place, I have caught more fish than I deserve to catch. But the ones I remember the most vividly are the ones that got away.

In March, along the valley of Wisconsin's surging river Brule, there is a season, half spring and half winter, when ragged patches of snow linger at the feet of patient gray cedars, though the northering sun beats warmly in the tree-tops. Coffee-brown spew, stained from hemlock roots, oozes down the slopes to join the rising low, and there is a great rushing of waters along the sixty-six miles of the Bois Brule. The old river is on the rampage from way up beyond Stone's Bridge clear to the mouth of Lake Superior.

It is a season when discontented fishermen peer petulantly out of windows, beyond dripping eaves, and wonder "if the rainbows are up." When that word is passed, all angling men of parts make haste to get to the river and inspect the annual miracle of 10- and 12-pound fish spawning almost at their feet.

On a windy, warmish-coldish March day 'long about tax-paying time I had occasion to pass the place of business of the President of the Old Duck Hunters' Association, Inc. Mister President was standing in his window with one I recognized immediately as Gus, six-foot-four Norwegian who can and does handle an 8-ounce fly rod as you and I handle one of half that weight. The President hailed me.

"The rainbows are up," he announced, and added hurriedly, "but I can't get down to see 'em till Sunday."

Gus had brought the tidings. He had just returned from the recently dismantled South Shore railway trestle which spans the famous creek near a whistling post and switch block answering to the legendary Indian name of Winnebojou.

"They're up, all right," Gus affirmed. "By yingo, some dandies are laying on the gravel south of the trestle."

Only Gus didn't say it just like that. His Norse accent is something that cannot be reduced to paper. You can sort of play around with that accent, but you can't pin it down. You can give a fair imitation of the way of an Irishman with a word, or a Scotchman, or almost any other good American, but I have yet to see the speech of a Gus set down in black and white in a manner recognizable alike to those who know the Norwegians and the Norwegians themselves.

Suffice it to say that all the good, whole, sound, lusty and gusty Guses pronounce yellow with a "j" and January with a "y." There are other little nuances which this inadequate scribe can only hint at in print. But before we go farther, and to justify and glorify the Guses of this world, let all be advised that when they hear someone saying Yanuary instead of January they should listen closely, for that fellow is more than likely to know a lot about fishing.

There, in the President's garage, the chimes of memory started ringing in Gus' honest head. One thing led to another. Almost before we knew it, Gus was launched on a favorite tale. He began it in the little office of the President's establishment, but halfway through all hands moved into the more spacious showroom to give Gus elbow-room. Striding back and forth among the shining cars, Gus made that tale live and breathe.

Yentlemen, we give you Gus:

"There's yust one bait to use in spring. What is it? Salmon eggs. Yudas Priest, what I could do down there today with one yar of salmon eggs and a Colorado spinner! Of course, it being illegal, you won't find me there, by yingo!

"You take a little spinner and throw away the hooks. Put on big bass hooks. Then, when you've got a fish, you've got him — yes-sir-ee. Anyhow, I was going to mention about that day down by the Dry Landing. It was opening day. Six thousand fishermen from Winnebojou down to McNeil's. I had two small ones, but they were — oh-h, about three pounds apiece, and I ain't going home opening day with sardines!

"There's a pretty good hole down there. I came up to it. Yudas! Sixteen fishermen and sixteen poles! Yiminy! I waited. They tried everything. Salmon eggs, spinners, worms, bucktails, streamers. I waited a good hour, and they all left, one by one. Then I stepped in!"

Yentlemen, when Gus steps in, he steps into places where you and I would need a boat. There, in the showroom, we saw Gus easing himself out into the sacred pool, the water gurgling about his barrel chest.

"I knew that hole, all right," Gus continued. "I hadn't fished it twenty-five years for nothing. There I was. Out goes the first cast. All I had on was three salmon eggs with a spinner above. I let 'em slide down to the end of the hole where the water went faster. Nothing. Once again — "

All this was acted. Not just spoken. Gus strode from car to car. His huge feet thumped the showroom floor. His ruddy face grew ruddier with the zest of impending combat.

"Out I sent it again," Gus went on, eyes gleaming. "Down to the end of the hold. Then — oop! What's that now, eh? Comes on the spinner a little t-i-c-k! Um-hum. So he's there, eh? Um-hum. Yaw. You wait, Mister Rainbow. Me and you are going to do business.

"Third time I cast out and felt the same t-i-c-k. I struck, and nothing happened. A wise one, that rainbow, stealing my salmon eggs. Strategy is what he needs. I put on new salmon eggs and cast again. T-i-c-k.

"Then I got bright idea. Instead of striking, I leaned over."

When Gus leans over, it's like seeing the tower of Pisa tip farther.

"I leaned over and let 'em go down in there again — drift cast. I let 'em go two or three feet beyond where he was ticking it. I knew the fish would follow so as not to miss those salmon eggs. I hoped it would work, by yiminy."

You hope so too, as you listen, but you are pretty sure it will, because Gus has told you the tale a dozen times, and he tells it so well that people clear away furniture to hear it again and again in all its primal splendor. There is Gus, huge arms holding imaginary rod, chest-deep in the flow, swishing between the display automobiles. The air becomes tense. The moment is at hand.

"Yust at the right time I felt the t-i-c-k. I knew he'd followed it downstream. I knew he was turned in another direction. Right there I gave it to 'im and Yudas Priest — "

Gus almost went backward over a projecting bumper as he fought the big rainbow, but he got the trout into the open between two deluxe models and fought it out there, even to the point of standing proudly at the end of the fight, holding the flopping giant aloft in triumph.

Great people, those Guses of the northern parts of our lake states.

Where you find good fishing you'll find plenty of Norwegians and Swedes. They excel at the game, either as commercial or sport fishermen. They are anglers from the word go, and tough as all-get-out. The kind of lads the Big Ten coaches smile at when they report in September for the football team. Plenty of them have lugged the pigskin for Wisconsin and Minnesota, and plenty more of them will, by yiminy!

Gus is not only tall but proportioned. He used to fish with a pint-sized pal whom he carried through the deep holes on his back. Legend hath it Gus would stop from time to time and let his comrade whip the waters from this magnificent perch.

Gus departed. Mister President pulled out his watch. It was 2 PM. He said: "If we jump in the car and run down there right now, the sun will be about right to see the big rainbows either off the South Shore trestle or from the front of the St. Paul Club."

"But I thought — "

"Never mind thinking. My taxes are due tomorrow. My dandruff is bothering me. My chilblains are peeling, and besides I haven't been outdoors to speak of since last duck season. Come on!"

An hour and half later the President firmly fastened the single button of the old brown mackinaw and strode forth upon the creaking ties of the ancient trestle to be present at Act I, Scene I of "The Great Rainbow Drama" or "Why Life is Worth Living for Fishermen."

This first glimpse of the big lunkers from Lake Superior in the Brule is one of the Middle West's most dramatic and visible fish migrations. Smelt along the Lake Michigan shores provide another spectacle. Still another is that amazing run of wall-eyed pike up the Wolf River of Wisconsin from Lake Winnebago in April. You can see those newly arrived rainbows as they come up, whereas the smelt only run at night and the walleyes are deep goers. Hence the charm of this Brule spectacle. I have seen at one time as many as fifty persons staring down into the Brule, forty feet beneath them, from that old South Shore trestle.

You first see the fish as mere wavering shadows. The eye becomes adjusted to the riffle, and from a vantage-point you begin to get their outlines in detail. But the "ohs!" and "ahs!" are reserved for the moment when a big, crimson-streaked female rolls on her side and vibrates from stem to stern, apparently hastening the ejection of eggs. Then the startling color of the fish is plainly visible, after which the fish resumes its equilibrium and once more becomes a wavering shadow.

Of course, no fishing is permitted then. Fishing for those big fellows that sometimes lie by the score in a space no bigger than a large room would be sheer murder. Poachers, netters and spearers once reaped a bountiful harvest from the Brule, but vigilantes from game clubs, working with alert wardens, now keep nightly springtime watchers along the stream. One violator got in so deep that he spent a year in the state prison, perhaps as severe a penalty for a game-law violation as Wisconsin has ever seen.

The rainbow run up the Brule is something more than a movement of a splendid game fish. Poems have been written about it. People come from several hundred miles before the season opens to see the big fellows. Natives know it as a sure sign of spring.

This is related so that you may know what sort of pilgrimage called the President from his daily chores at tax-paying time. Right there on the old trestle the season opened for the Old Duck Hunters' Association. Thus it has begun for thousands of north country anglers. It is not for us here, to record the dragging days thereafter, nor the disorderly heaps of tackle laid out for overhauling, nor the endless remembering and the hopeful boastings that ensued between that day and the chill bright dawn of May 1, when the season opened.

It need be reported only that the Old Duck Hunters were there on time, a delicate achievement in itself, made possible by adjusting the get-away with precise calculation of sunrise time and allowing just so many minutes for breakfast, packing and deep prayer. The only delay occurred when the Association halted for a few minutes on a sticky clay road and helped push one of the brethren from a frost boil that had shattered the road's center. That accomplished, no less than thirty cars plunged swiftly through the wallow, labored out the other side and sped off Bruleward. You've got to see that opening-day assault upon the Brule to appreciate it.

There are places where you can escape the multitude, even on opening day. You can, for instance, go in by canoe on the fifteen miles of water from Stone's Bridge to Winnebojou and not see anyone for miles. But because it is canoe water and somewhat inaccessible, by far the great majority prefers to answer the roll call of the faithful in waders. The President voted against a canoe, and we parked with a hundred other cars in a Winnebojou clearing not far from the old trestle. It was Mister President's idea to elbow right in — "Let's try it and have some fun."

The report must be submitted that it was not a great deal of fun at that particular place. One reach of river perhaps a hundred yards long was accommodating twenty or thirty fishermen. Up-stream the concourse of fishermen diminished, but it was bad enough. These gatherings do produce fun, however. Everyone knew everyone else, and those who did not soon got acquainted. In such a crowd someone is bound to hook a good one or two, but the Old Duck Hunters emerged from the stream at noon — with nothing to show for their labor and planning.

On the sunny side of a twisted cedar the President spread sandwiches, uncorked hot coffee and held council. Halfway through the third sandwich, when I was suggesting we forget the big fellows and go after some fun and small ones on the upper reaches, the President looked up suddenly with more than casual interest.

"On yonder well-worn fisherman's trail," he said, "comes the answer to our problems."

It was Gus. But he was despondent. Even three cups of coffee, which he drank scalding and straight, and liberal applications of sandwiches did nothing to cheer him. He said he had been "all over dis har river" since sunup. First near the mouth, then at Teeportens, down by Judge Lenroot's and at four or five other places. " — and there's a fisherman on every hold between here and Lake Superior, by yingo!"

Had he seen any good ones? He had, indeed. John Ziegler had one close to ten pounds. Carl Tarsrud had two of them, maybe five and six pounds. Clarence Grace hadn't done so badly. All are sure-fire Brule fishermen. Gus said he had seen maybe fifty rainbows of five pounds or over, "but by yiminy, I can't find a hole that hasn't been tramped."

He said he was quitting; that he would come back the following day, when the opening-day crew had departed. It is a fact that this opening-day rush on the Brule fades to practically nothing within a day or two. No Wisconsin stream can match it for the first day. We think the boys like to make a ceremony of it, and then go their many ways on hundreds of miles of other good streams all over the northern end of the state.

Gus was no sooner out of sight when the President swept the luncheon remnants together, grabbed at gear and with his mouth still stuffed urged: "We're following that boy. Hurry! I saw his car over in the grove a minute ago."

No fool, the Hon. President. He explained while we skulked along the trail, trying to appear unhurried, that Gus never in his life quit a stream until it was too dark to fish; that wherever Gus was heading now would be all right with us. And furthermore, that following Gus was perfectly legitimate, as also was Gus' attempt to veil his real intent.

All honest fishermen will understand the code. You get what you're good enough to take, with due consideration for bag limits, the folks you are dealing with and your own immortal honor. We watched Gus back out his car and followed along unobserved on a county trunk running parallel to the river.

In the town of Brule, rainbow-trout capital of Wisconsin, where the famous from Presidents Cleveland through Coolidge and Hoover have passed, Gus halted his throbbing engine long enough to clump into Hank Denny's restaurant. From the bulge of his lower lip when he reappeared, we guessed he had laid in a new stock of "snoosed." Or snuff, if you are unfamiliar with this tidbit. Or, if you are familiar with it, "Norwegian dynamite."

It was easy to trail Gus because of the heavy traffic. He passed the road into the old Banks place and the one down to the N. P. Johnson bridge. We thought he might have turned at these places with the idea of hanging around until fishermen had quit certain holes. But Gus had another spot in mind.

Traffic thinned, and Gus turned left, down a road that we knew well. A road not too safe at that season of frost boils, when red clay seethes and softens.

Gus must have known it was a long shot he was taking. No one else had braved that road during the day. It was ticklish work. You slide down one hogback and bluff your way up the next, wheels flinging red-clay chunks twenty feet high into the popple trees. At the bottom of a steep hill we found Gus mired.

We climbed out. We gave aid. We spoke frankly of our intentions. Gus laughed. Gus always laughs. With me driving and Gus pushing, we made the hill with both cars, slid down the next descent, and there we were, practically on the bank of the Brule.

"Vell," said Gus, chuckling, as we surveyed the river, "I don't know but what it serves me right to sneak away from you and get stuck."

The Brule at this point, only a few miles from the big lake, was yellowed with red clay washed down from eroding banks that stretch along the river some distance back from its mouth. Gus remarked that a trout could use a pair of glasses to advantage. Murky water has never bothered the President much. He holds it gives an angler an advantage, permitting him to work water more searchingly without frightening fish. All things considered, he'll take a roily creek to one gin-clear, and he's not entirely a bait fisherman, either. In its upper reaches, by the way, the Brule runs gin-clear the year round.

The place where we put in is below what is known as McNeil's Hole. The McNeil farm lies along the Brule bottoms. Below a bridge at this point the river bends sharply to the east, then turns again straight north and before caroming off a high bank to the west, idles awhile in a long, deep hold.

The Old Duck Hunters love that place. The biggest steelhead I ever saw actually taken from the river came out of that hole on the end of Mister President's leader. It was a seven-pounder. And I mean steelhead, a fish identified carefully later by E. M. Lambert, superintendent of the fabulous Pierce estate upstream.

Lambert knows a steelhead from a rainbow. But he cannot tell at a glance, and neither can anyone else. All you can do is guess. The steelhead is likely to be whiter, but beyond that the boys who know go into the matter by counting scales. However, this is no place to discuss that. There was work at hand.

I went up-stream and worked down under the bridge and around the corner with salmon eggs and a spinner. No fun? Well, yentlemen, as Gus would say, "There are times when the water is too damn wet for dry flies!"

I creeled a few small rainbows and worked toward the big pool which Gus and the President had fished. The latter had a nice four-pound rainbow — a dark, deep-bodied, typical Brule rainbow with a pronounced crimson sash down his side. Gus was out there waist-deep, working everything in his catalogue for another he had seen "roll like a poorpuss, by yiminy."

"He was white as a ghost," Gus yelled at me from midstream. "Maybe I can get him."

The Old Duck Hunters watched the show. It is always a show to watch Gus. He can wade almost any place on the Brule. That rugged river holds no terrors for him. His powerful legs stand against its brawling push where other legs would wabble and shake. He was using his best formula: salmon eggs and spinner.

You who have not fished the Brule, you who have only read about it, should see it with one like Gus performing in its center. It was getting on toward late afternoon. The warmth of the May sun was being dissipated by the familiar chill that rises from the Brule on the hottest days. Gus stood in almost five feet of water, the yellow flow nipping his wader tops. He nursed the "snoose" in his lower lip and practiced his art.

I saw the fish roll once to the spinner. It was indeed stark white, as Gus had said. A good sign to the layman that it was a true steelhead. The Old Duck Hunters smoked and watched, conscious of imminent drama. Finally it happened.

Gus' rod arm went forward and down — he hooks 'em that way. Then the arm was back up and throbbing, and something hard and white and crazy exploded from the pool, forty feet away. Gus backed toward shallow water. The big white fish ran up-stream and leaped many times. They will do it before you can think. From the pool came a snoose-muffled roar, such a one as Gus' Viking ancestors might have bellowed in a foray on the Irish coast a thousand years ago.

"Yudas! I got 'im!" he snorted.

To which the President of the Old Duck Hunters added fervently, "Yiminy whiskers, Gus, give 'im snoose!"

Snoose it was in the first, second and third degrees. Of the battle, of the raging to and for, of the unbelievable strength in six pounds of fresh-run steelhead, of the great grunts and snorts from Gus, there is little need for setting down. Suffice it to say the fish took Gus down-stream fifty yards, came back into the pool and dogged and bucked and leaped and writhed and rolled on the leader until he was washed up.

All these things have been reported many times. No fish in Wisconsin will exhibit the electric insanity of a hooked steelhead in fast water.

After about twenty minutes there was the ghost-white fish on the tiny shelving sand beach at the edge of the pool, and there were two grand old fishermen shaking hands, and there was an ancient gunny sack extracted from Gus' jacket. Into this the big fish went. The mightiest of Wisconsin trout rivers had once more flashed its beaming smile upon the Old Duck Hunters, Inc.

Indeed, it was a chalky fish. Along the lateral line there was hardly more than the faintest wash of crimson. You looked closely to see it. All the rest of him was white, bluish in places, but white — the sign of the steelhead. A sign we could check later with Emmett Lambert, the Brule's grand old authority, if we so desired. Lambert could take measurements and say what he was. For the present there was only supreme content among the Old Duck Hunters.

Gus dipped a blunt forefinger into the round box and spread a damp layer of snoose under a quivering lower lip. It is something to see a six-foot-four Norwegian trembling. Fact is, we were all trembling. And you will, too, if you ever come to grips with one of those Lake Superior submarines. The President got out his omnipresent thermos bottles and passed around hot coffee. His own rainbow, a nice little fish, was forgotten for the larger one.

A native with a long cane pole and a sad look wended toward us from McNeil's bridge. To his hail, "Anything doing?" Gus extracted the still-writhing steelhead from the sack and held it high over his head by its lower jaws. The native's eyes popped. He was about to say something when the steelhead contorted in a quick spasm, wrenched free and dropped into the pool.

Gus lumbered toward the fish, scooping desperately. The fish rolled and slithered out of his grasp, and then, with new strength, shot like a torpedo for deep water.

No one spoke for perhaps a half-minute. The President's coffee spilled from its cup. I shall never forget the gone feeling that hit me. The native seemed sadder than ever. All eyes were on Gus. For only an instant his face was tragic. Then he grinned. A grin that wrinkled and spread and warmed his great red face and lighted it with something you seldom see on the face of a man in such extremity.

He spoke: "Well, boys, he was a pretty good fish. But damn it, I didn't like his color. He was too dog-gone white!"

Too dog-gone white! That from a fisherman who had felt his heart turn a handspring in his throat. Do you wonder why I love those Norse fishermen?

Yentlemen, this reporter begs a last line: When all the fishing is over for Gus, when he will no longer hear the kingfishers screaming along the stream, when all that remains of him is a magnificent legend of a greathearted fisherman, the Old Duck Hunters will write an epitaph for Gus, and this is what it will be:

"Too dog-gone white."

THE BELATED NEIGHBOR

"All I did was give 'er a little nudge." So sayeth Hizzoner.

Hey! Life is tough. Duck hunting is part of life. So when you can, give something that you want "a little nudge." I say (and Mr. President would, I'm sure, agree) do it!

And do it this way. Help the other fellow. Bail his boat. Dry his shells. See that he gets his ducking spot.

But see that you get yours first.

The dust on the road was so thick that the President of the Old Duck Hunters' Association, Inc., was sorry for the dog and almost sorry for me.

Speeding cars raced across that graveled road because it was a connecting link between two concrete highways, and it was a joy rider's October Sunday.

"If I could afford an automobile," said Mister President, wiping his begrimed face, "I would not monkey around driving this road. I would get on one that went to Mississippi or Manitoba, depending on the season."

At the moment Hizzoner was burdened financially and morally with some 60 automobiles including a half-dozen super-supers, priced F.O.B. Detroit. Or was it Flint? Memory weakens in the face of the irrelevant. Thank heaven it holds up otherwise.

The Old Duck Hunters', Inc., was trudging back from a fruitless quest for partridge. It had been a fourteen-mile thrust on foot into the southern hinterland of Douglas county, Wisconsin. Rumor, via a helpful neighbor, had spread the word of a partridge plenitude. We found naught but popple and hazel brush.

Well, there we were, we and the poor dog, a springer of excellent coat excepting the ears which never looked any better than granpa's buffalo cutter robe. About once in so often a car would honk us into the ditch where we would cower until the dust cleared.

"Dang yuh," the old master accused once, "you have picked the leeward side of the ditch three times hand running."

Jerry the springer was smarter than both of us. At the first faint whine of a hill-leaping car he would fling himself deep into the roadside bush. It had been a dry year. It was fierce.

"I often wish I were a dog," the president said wistfully.

We went on. I had a heel blister. He contended I ought to be in better shape because I had drunk the most water at the farmhouse, five miles back. His good spirits buoyed me. Also was I cheered when he summoned me to the center of the road. Pointing to a gravelly, dusty rut he demanded:

"You know what made that track?"

"No sir."

"That's where my tail has been dragging."

A speeder from the rear started us for cover again. As we hit the hazel brush the oncomer slowed and Mister President yelled from his ditch, "Heaven help us, here comes a gentleman! Here's luck!"

The car drew up slowly and dustlessly. The driver was a lone hunting man with a long cheerful nose and a hunting jacket white as sailcloth from many washings. He hailed Mister President.

He was of course a neighbor and brother of the chase. He was also the brother of the chase who had sent the ODHA on its hideous partridge hunt. The President emerged to make palaver with his great and good neighbor. As in a dream I heard Hizzoner in flagrant fabrication —

"Never saw anything like it . . . Woods alive with partridge . . . Killed a limit apiece . . . Pshaw, we don't want a ride . . . The walk'll do us good . . ."

As the car vanished over a hill I thought of the big bottle of sparkling water I had seen in the back seat.

"I wouldn't ask that scoundrel for the morning dew on his decoys," Mister President snorted. "Did you see him leer at me when I told him about those eight birds we didn't get? He seemed greatly surprised. All I was doing was lying like a gentleman."

Doubtless, I agreed, but insisted I would rather accept one big cool swig out of his water bottle than all the partridge in the North.

This respondent is not one to quibble with our peerless leader. This respondent knows all about the standing feud between this neighbor and Mister President. This respondent recalls the moribund mouse which this neighbor carried in his pocket to a dance. And the itching powder that went with it. And who done it.

The respondent also knows of the time when this suffering neighbor sat for two days on a Washburn county pothole that never saw a duck land in it from one year to the next. And of the slightly turpentined pointer dog, owned by this same victim, and how said pointer embarrassed him before a gallery of the grandest chicken hunters that ever put down a dog on O'Connor's potato field.

"If you ask me," I said, "you are just making trouble."

"Who asked you?"

And now let us forget that partridge chapter and by the license granted to the Old Duck Hunters begin right away with the plot, the day of reckoning, the Old Man's Method and the ceaseless turning of the spheres in their courses.

It is three weeks later and the Old Duck Hunters are snugly billeted in a familiar cabin on the shore of a big lake shaped like a rubber boot.

The curtain rises on a scene of ineffable peace. The supper dishes are done. Tomorrow's gear is sorted and laid in the boathouse on the beach, including the stable lantern and horse blanket for warming Mister President's shins.

The morrow is one we have marked for our very own. Bluebills fetching through northwest Wisconsin by the thousand. A growing wind rattling the oak leaves. A full moon slicing the clouds.

"It'll blow harder tonight," said Mister President. "The moon is full. Duck'll fly under the full moon. There'll be newcomers by morning."

"And we'll have the bay all to ourselves."

"Perchance . . . perchance . . ." He was dozing.

And now, music. Music of the foreboding kind, like just before the dagger fight in "Gypsy Love." The back door of the cabin is thumped with tremendous vigor. I hurry to open it and admit the man with the long, cheerful nose — the same who had lured the Old Duck Hunters to the place of No Partridge.

Now, I say to myself, the Old Boy will let him have it. He will tell him to his long, cheerful nose what he thinks of him. Now he will walk up one side of him and down the other wearing nothing but a pair of river boots with double naught corks.

Quickly and often painfully are the illusions of younger men broken. Those two friendly foes fell on each other like long lost brothers. Mister President made the visitor comfortable in his own chair. He offered him extra socks! He commanded me to man the coffee pot for he was a wayfarer in the night and a friend of long standing.

The long nosed one explained that he was quartered down the lake shore in a neighbor's cabin. He was alone. He had just arrived. He had to get back and put his boat in, fill the motor, look over the decoys. No thanks, no supper, but a cup of steaming coffee . . . well now!

Felicitations flowed like hot fudge. Mister President laid the campaign for Cheerful Long Nose.

"Pshaw, I know these waters like a book. Only place for you to go in the morning is two miles down the shore to the Hole in the Wall."

I wondered if Mister President had lost his mind. The Hole in the Wall is where we were going! And I listened to him saying —

"You get right up there first thing and grab that blind before someone else does."

Long Nose was formally grateful, but it did seem to me that I could detect he had, hours before, decided to appropriate the Hole in the Wall at all costs. He did not say as much. He merely smiled. What you might call the alarm clock smile which says, "OK, brother. If you set your alarm for 5, mine'll be set for 4!"

He went away and Mister President wound his watch. I protested the division of the Old Duck Hunter's hunting grounds without a vote of the lodge. He merely yawned and set the alarm clock carefully by the faithful hands of the thick gold watch.

Under the covers in the other room I knew what to expect next day — Cheerful Long Nose in the Hole in the Wall blind and the Old Duck Hunters making the best of things on a boggy shore a half-mile away. That bog sinks under a man. It is a mere emergency blind. Not a fit place at all for the ODHA to carry out the rites in comfort.

We had built that Hole in the Wall Blind. It was ours. Everyone knew it was ours. And he had willed it away without the blink of an eyelash!

The wind was picking up as I fell to sleep. It was crying high in the pine trees. It would be a blustery daybreak. A squirrel scuttered over the roof . . . or was it a chipmunk? . . . mebbe a handful of scrub oak leaves. Then, soon . . . I slept.

"Oyez, oyez! The Old Duck Hunters' Association is now assembled in due form!"

He was leaning over me, a sharp brown eye looking down and a lean brown hand grasping the red blankets. There is no choice at such times. I got up. Better that than to lie there blanketless and shivering.

Breakfast was ready. He looked as if he had been up for hours. There were red spots in his cheeks. They might have been put there by the wind that was fairly tearing the ridge pole off but he said they were "just from leaning over that hot stove frying you four eggs." He was exceedingly happy for a man who had recently given away the best bluebill blind in north Wisconsin.

Down at the boathouse we rolled out the sinews of war and clamped on the motor in a tossing sea. Heaven bless that motor. Not once on the coldest mornings has it failed. Once it spat defiance to a November that came upon us with six below in the night.

Halfway out of our bay I stopped the motor to listen. The sound of no other motor was heard. There was only the long hissing waves and the wind roaring outside my earflaps. I suggested to Mister President that Cheerful Long Nose was already up there, in our blind. He replied —

"What the hell you worried about that blind for? That guy has got an alarm clock that never goes off until it's too late. Head for the Hole in the Wall. If he shows up we'll move out."

In twenty minutes we had made the Old Duck Hunters' favorite setup of bluebill stool. Outside of the fact that I could write a book about it, it is simple: a long narrow horseshoe of decoys, lopsided where one arm of the layout stretches far and inviting into the bay.

"I believe in being neighborly," said the President as we put gear ashore and tucked the boat beneath over-hanging bank willows. "If he comes along we've got to shove over to that bog. Hope you brought your boots."

There was a good twenty minutes to wait before the hands on the thick gold watch declared the legal moment. Long before the moment the bluebills were dive-bombing the decoys. He waited, watch in hand.

Something was certainly doing. Wings were cutting the air to pieces. The light grew and the 'bills increased. Beyond in the tossing bay we saw ragged lines of black. Hundreds of bluebills sat there, over the densest growths of coontail I knew about.

When Mister President said "Now!" it was mere routine lodge work for the association to rise and knock four bluebills to the water from the bundle of six that smashed by.

It is an elegant thing to perform such duties with coordinated dispatch. Among the Old Duck Hunters there is no such foolish: "I'll tell you when," or "You tell me when." Duck hunting men of the veterans' stripe know when, where and how. It is a kind of synchronization with each man taking his allotted side of the bluebill bundle as it swoops at the decoys. It is best done by two who know each other well.

Picking them up fell to the least membership and while I was at it a dozen tried to sit in the decoys.

The bluebill seeker outside of the northern states knows nothing of this; he is inclined not to believe it. His ducks are educated. But let him once see the scaups lesser and greater as they glide into wooden decoys in northern

Minnesota and Wisconsin and he will know. Too bad so few know. Too bad, too, that brother bluebill takes to eating fishy foods once he gets down a way into the United States. Up there in the northern tier of states he is just a bundle of jam-packed rice and coontail.

Some of them were big birds. Some of them sat among the decoys. Some of them, shot at, would fly 200 yards away, sit down again and look around to say: "What the hell is this anyway?" Which prompted Mister President to declare —

"One of these days when you're scribbling something just put down that anybody shooting at a bluebill on the water is not only a bum sport but a fool. Anybody who can't hit 'em when they get up hadn't ought to have gone hunting in the first place."

They came from the north and from the west. From Minnesota's northern wilderness, and also from Lake Superior, sixty miles straight north of us, where ducks sit by the tens of thousands until the wind gets at them. As I retrieved them the President speculated:

"One of these here experts told me once that if a bluebill's black head is shot with purple he's a lesser scaup; if it's shot with green he's a greater scaup. Now you just show me any 'bill in that pile, big or little, that hasn't got BOTH green and purple in his black head feathers."

I did not show him. I have gone through it all too many times with the President of the Old Duck Hunters. All I know is what I read in the books and what the Old Man says. Both can't be right. And I have too much affection for the book writers to incite them to battle with the Old Man.

The faithful outboard roared forth many times that morning for the pick-up. Once it was to pick up three canvasback, remnants from a big flock that just cut the edge of our decoys.

"Just what we needed," he observed. "There's nothing like a little color to improve the looks of a bag."

By eleven o'clock of that blasty morning we were counting ducks pretty carefully. When the bluebills hit northern Wisconsin in their big years a man with a gun will do well to watch his arithmetic. There is a great difference between ten apiece and twelve apiece. That difference can happen in a five-second flurry. Hence the mathematics, as fixed and certain with Mister President as the hands of his thick gold watch.

The time came for Hizzoner to make a final count and give the signal. He assembled the gear on the shore and I wound in the decoys. Only on the return, facing the bitter northwest wind did I think of Cheerful Long Nose. He had gone completely out of mind in the robust zest of a grand lodge session. Over the motor's roar I asked, "Where'd you suppose he went?"

Mister President shrugged and yelled back, "He ain't got a good alarm clock!"

Battling waves back into our own bay, where it was calmer, I saw on the north shore a tall man leaning over a beached boat. The waves were beating in there hard for the wind had hauled from west to southwest. The tall man was swooping a pail into the boat. I aimed our boat toward him.

The obvious had happened. The boat he was bailing had drifted away in the night. He was a duck hunter and all such required help. Decoys sloshed in the boat bottom. It was spang up on shore. The wind had been so severe that it had shoved sand up around the boat's bottom and sides. A long green shell case was covered with water.

The man with the pail was Cheerful Long Nose and he was in a Bad Way. Every time he heaved a pailful of water overside to lighten the boat two pailfuls came inboard.

The President was the first to leap ashore and help. He waded in water to his knees, above the tops of his old gum rubbers. He lugged decoys. He grabbed the shellbox and emptied the water. He just took charge of things and eventually we towed the belated neighbor back to his landing.

"Darned if I know how it happened," Cheerful Long Nose explained. "When I left you last night I loaded the boat and then hauled 'er up on the beach far as I could. Put the motor handy. Had every darned thing ready."

The President of the Old Duck Hunters offered him a bundle of bluebill, which he accepted.

"If it hadn't been for you two I never could have budged that boat," he went on. "I've always been careful about hauling boats up high on windy nights."

"Yep. . . ?" said Mister President, more sympathetic than ever.

"But I see now what happened. The stern two feet was in water. The wind rose and sloshed water overside. It got heavy and the boat slid off the beach. I hadn't tied 'er."

"I'll be damned," said Mister President.

We saw him off for the Hole in the Wall. It was full noon with the wind still roaring. He would finish out his bag there, we knew. We gave him hot coffee. We took over six boxes of dampish shells and gave him six boxes of dried ones. He darted out of the bay a happy and grateful man.

The Old Duck Hunters climbed the hill.

"I suppose," said the President of the Old Duck Hunters, "that you think I pushed his boat off the beach."

"Certainly."

He heaved a sigh. He pushed on up the hill burdened with gun and shellcase.

"All I did," he said, "was give 'er a little nudge."

THE MYSTERY
OF THE MISSING
TACKLE

Here, at long last, the last laugh is on Mr. President. With Madame President securely putting him in his place.

What makes me laugh about The Mystery *is the way MacQuarrie keeps his character in place. We've all mislaid gear. You'd expect it could happen to Hizzoner. But then you'd expect Mr. President to react like the world was against him, that "some monster in human form" has tried to do him in. You'd expect him to survey others' tackle, inspect their cars on the sly, accuse the Salvation Army and Good Will and even enlist detective friends to aid in the search.*

Mr. President, praise be to Heaven, will always be Mr. President.

This is about the President of the Old Duck Hunters' Association, Inc. and the ten months he lived in a clothes closet.

At first the tale was just so much idle gossip in Superior, Wisconsin, barber shops. That early version said the President dwelt in the closet only by night.

But lusty souls of that far northern city went to work on it, polished it, gave it life and that necessary emphasis which has caused it to survive throughout the years.

In its amended form Mister President was depicted as spending the entire ten months in the closet, presumably wandering with gun and packsack, living off the country, making his bed where night overtook him.

Far be it from me to amend or delete the folklore of Superior. I have too much affection for the city that gave me birth and the Brule river only thirty miles away.

The Brule river really started the whole thing. The Brule river and four handfuls of trout fishing tackle.

The President was sitting in his living room. It was early March. Outside a tardy blizzard off Lake Superior was lashing empty streets.

He leaped out of his chair suddenly, muttered "I wonder if it's there," and ran upstairs, his wife told me later.

She heard him ransacking the large closet in his bedroom. She can tell when he's doing it because he takes a broom handle and sweeps everything off the shelves. Things thump on the floor. He goes through the debris without having to stand on tip-toe.

He came downstairs and told her "It's gone!" She said, "What's gone?" He said "Four big fly boxes, three leader boxes, a fisherman's knife, four loaded reels — "

She said, "Here it is March and the season won't open till May. Begone!"

The upshot was that she joined him in a second search of the suspected closet. He felt vaguely that he had done something with it the previous autumn. He said he had an idea he put the stuff somewhere, like a squirrel stores nuts — "some place where I could put my hands right on it."

He was urged to put his hands on it then and clean up the mess in the closet, but he was so preoccupied he could do neither.

That was the beginning of the Clothes Closet Expedition. The search eventually included the whole house and extended through days and nights, weeks and even months. The neighbors lent a hand at times. A high spot in this friendly assistance was reached one night when they found two bottles of forgotten blackberry wine in an old trunk.

The President got so he could specify the losses glibly. At first the search was confident. Later it went into the suspicious stage when he began suspecting people of stealing the missing tackle. The week before May 1st was an especially trying one. The Salvation Army, the Good Will people, three innocent neighbors and an equally innocent old clothes man were charged with the crime.

The list of departed treasures appeared at headquarters on a police report spindle.

The missing tackle was indeed no ordinary kit of fishing instruments. Each and every fly, wet, dry and streamer, was a cherished classic. There were such carefully distributed baubles as John Ziegler's hand-made black bucktails; several sparsely-tied delicacies of proven worth and scores and scores of others, each of which reminded the President of victory or defeat on the trouty battlefields of North Wisconsin.

The third or acute stage occurred when his sense of loss turned to desperation. That was the evening before the season opened. During this phase he knew it was a plot against him. Even when three suspected neighbors came in and loaned him enough tackle for the morrow his faith in mankind was not wholly restored.

You couldn't get him away from the big clothes closet. He didn't know why, but he was darned near certain "That's where I put it last fall." Often he would stand on the threshold of the closet, poised, hopeful, then go through it automatically, like a combine through a North Dakota wheat field.

However, immediate needs were well supplied by the accused neighbors that opening evening when I came over to pick him up. He had his own rod, waders, in fact, all of the larger items of his tackle. These, with contributed flies, reel leaders, and what not, left him fairly well supplied with equipment.

On the season's first trip up that way anyone in his right mind and in striking distance goes to the Brule. After a night near the river, during which he thought up new places to look when he got back home, we put in downstream.

I recall it as an exceedingly good day. But Mister President's attention was divided. He would sight a friend from afar, climb out of the pool he was working and accost him on the bank with bluff and deceptive friendliness. While he engaged his fellow man in casual conversation his roving eye took in every item of said fellow man's equipment. I don't know how many creels he thrust his hand into, how many fishermen he secretly inspected, how many parked cars he peered into.

A police detective had told him maybe the thief had peddled the tackle to some unsuspecting comrade. Following each inspection he would return to the stream and go about his chores until another suspect hovered into sight.

It is not to be supposed all this work was conducted in a dead silence. Mister President was prepared at any moment to deliver a speech on "the monster in human form who crept into my house and robbed me."

"It ain't," he would say, "that I object to the financial loss. It's just that it can never be replaced. I haven't got confidence in these other flies. Take that old yellow Sally I used to keep in the upper right compartment of the big box. That's caught more native brookies than they've planted in this state in the last year.

"Yes, a yellow Sally. A bass fly, if you please, that I never used on anything but big native trout late in the evening. Worn out? Not on your life! No hackle left on it, if that's what you mean. And the body was unraveling and the wings chewed.

"No sir, that fly was just in the prime of life. Round about the time when the first deer were snortin' in the brush, anxious for a drink after a hot day, I'd lay that yellow Sally up gainst the undercut banks and — socko!"

Still, the first day was one to remember. The Hon. President, even without his precious talisman, creeled a likely mess of good ones and wound up with a five-pounder. Even with this deep-bodied rainbow, tail projecting from his creel, he was loath to admit the virtue of the lure that had done it. It was a small fly rod plug, miniature replica of a larger cousin of bait casting persuasion.

"It took everything I had to make him hit," he explained. "I knew he was there because I'd seen him roll. It took me an hour to make him hit it. Now, if I'd had — "

The self-same plug, to all human eyes except those of Mister President, was the identical gadget he had used in his own kit.

That evening, driving home, he suggested maybe it would be a good idea to move into a new house, because you find a lot of lost things when you move.

It was an angler's evening. The western sky was drenched with red. The roads, though rutted, were dry, a boon indeed to opening day fishermen along the lower Brule. It was an evening to count oneself fortunate with half the weight of trout we bore home. The President said:

"If I move I can stand at the door to keep an eye on the movers."

When the fish were laid out on the kitchen sink to be witnessed, the President omitted his customary proud office of detailing the struggles, each and every one. The visiting neighbors gaped by themselves while he made a couple of swings through the clothes closet.

Things went on that way. There was that day on the Marengo, below Ashland. With the water up two feet, a new batch of Emerson Houghs donated by Ray Schiller gave the lie to those who hold that your brown trout is no fellow to seek with a wet fly, downstream. It seemed to make no difference how you presented it that fine foggy day on the bankful Marengo. The clipped deer hair body with its simple faint wisp of hackle, running deep, medium or on top, stood the Marengo browns on their heads.

It was another day for the books, as was revealed when the car headlights were turned on at evening to illuminate three damp, glistening creels of brown trout. The car bumped and wound away from the rocky, fog-bound crags. Schiller asked me how I liked the Emerson Hough. Before I could reply the President put in:

"Didja ever try a No. 6 Ginger Quill or Hare's Ear in water like that? I used to have some beauties. Someone stole them . . ."

Schiller was sympathetic. He offered replacements from his own stock, but the President decided he could accept such largess only as a last resort — "I'm gonna get that crook if it's the last thing I do."

He was convinced now that the disappearance of the tackle was sheer larceny, the work of some venomous rascal, planned with cold malice to make his days unhappy.

I do not recall a summer when the trout rose more steadily to our flies in an assortment of streams. There were some empty days. At such times the presidential faith in his own departed gear was strengthened. "Now, if I'd just had those little gray midges when the trout were tailing there tonight . . ."

It was a year of copious rains, not too hot, so that trout were not so prone to seek the inaccessible headwaters. A year when threatening droughts were banished by freshening rain and streams ran healthy and bankful right into September.

One day on the gin-clear Clam, of Washburn County, the President almost forgot himself. The Clam, to ye who know it not, can be as sweet a piscatorial problem as you'll find. You see the big browns ahead of you. They look easy — but they aren't. In the time of the shad fly hatch when they go smashing along the surface with mouths open saying "Yaw-skumsh!" they can be had. At all other times their taking is difficult in the extreme.

That day, a cool, heaven-sent Sunday in the midst of a brief heat wave, the President covered himself with glory via a brace of brown spent-wings which spread their unselfish selves on the unruffled Clam most advanta- geously. That day indeed was heard again the "Yaw-skumsh!" reminiscent of shad fly time.

And sitting in the shade of a giant elm at noon with the appetites of honest, hungry men, the President relaxed long enough to finger the spent- wing that hung from his leader.

"That one is sheer poison," he praised. "I gotta get some of those."

He stopped there. Whatever tribute he may have added died a-borning when the lost tackle came to mind. He sighed over a cold beef sandwich and hoped whoever swiped his tackle would come to an unhappy end.

There was that day on the smallmouth end of the Namakagon when one of those plop-plop bugs with a hollow head did all that anyone could expect a bug to do. It didn't exactly swim out and grab any three-pounders in back of the ears, but it had some of them leaping out of the shore growth and timber tangles like kids after a balloon salesman on Sunday afternoon in the park.

Did the President then renounce the long-mourned treasures of his bosom? He did not! He said that one of John Ziegler's mystic black bucktails would have been just the thing that day.

From time to time, coming and going, fishing and getting ready to fish, in boots and in boats, the President pronounced:

"Everything a fly fisherman needed was in those boxes. Anyway, 200 flies. Some I had since I was a kid. Wet flies you could sink without rubbing them in the mud. Dry flies that floated if you just let them smell the cork of the oil bottle. The accumulation of a lifetime. And where are they now? Maybe languishing in some far distant pawnshop."

"With a price tag of four bits on the whole outfit," I added helpfully.

"It may well be," he would conclude with ineffable sadness.

Even far into the duck season His Honor carried the burden of his loss and forever he probed the now well-nigh impassable depths of the clothes closet. He would look at the door of the closet, scratch his head and draw thumb and forefinger over the edges of his mouth in thoughtful preoccupation.

Neighbors inquired from time to time how things were going. The chief of police asked him how he was coming with his detective work. October passed into November, but long before Christmas relatives had decided to do something for him on the Yuletide.

It was the custom of the President to observe Christmas in wholehearted fashion. A circle of fishing relatives invariably convened at the President's home Christmas Eve. Such gatherings were more than fitting family conventions. They were down-right profitable gatherings for the fishing tackle makers.

Always there was a Christmas tree, about the lower branches of which reposed gleaming plugs, reels, knives. A Christmas without these things was no Christmas at all to that crowd.

Christmas Even came 'round and the faithful came and sat and exchanged fishing tackle, socks, flannel shirts, etc. as had been their wont these many years. Mister President's gifts were practically all fishing tackle.

When the last bit of crumpled tissue paper and bedizened ribbon had been picked up, when the under parts of the Christmas tree looked like a sporting goods window in May, Madame President gained the floor. She said she had an important announcement.

"I have," she said with weighted pauses, "found the fishing tackle!"

"Where?" The words rang out like an angel's chorus. The President leaped to his feet. Madame President bade him be patient.

"Just you sit there a moment," said she. "You have accused everyone in this house and everyone in the neighborhood of filching your old tackle. You ought to be ashamed."

The President sank back into his seat.

"Further," she continued, "you have made a shambles of my house. You have practically wrecked that clothes closet for one thing. Aren't you ashamed?"

Mister President hung his head in abjection, but by leaning over a little bit I could catch the gleam in his eye. Finally he made bold to ask Madame President where he might find the tackle.

"I'll lead you to it. I'll lead everyone to it!" she announced.

Eleven people trooped behind her upstairs. She halted before the clothes closet door. Mister President gasped: "Not there!"

"There indeed!" she said. She switched on a light and the havoc wrought in a ten-months' search was made visible to all. Ladies said "Dear me!" and men gazed with envious wonderment.

Hunting and fishing paraphernalia without end was strewn about. It is a big closet, as I have said, but the only way you could get into it was by wading through packsacks, guns, tackle, sweater, shell boxes.

Madame President thrust in an arm and lifted from a hook near the door a pair of old, worn, stained khaki trousers, one pair out of a half-dozen which had outlived their usefulness. The trousers had been obscured on the hook behind a variety of other outdoor clothing.

Both legs bulged like bags. Around the cuffs were tied old neckties to close the bottoms. She shook the pants, holding them aloft for all to see. From the depths came the clink of metal against metal. She upended the pants and poured out on the floor every last item in the late lamented list of tackle.

The President said "Well, I'll be damned!"

Madame President said, "Right where you put them a year ago last fall.

It was that day you wanted to use your fishing jacket for a shell vest because it was warm. Remember?"

The assembled witnesses yipped. They slammed the Honorable President on the back. They suggested he get in there and tidy up the closet.

His treasurers restored, the President regained some of his old form. He piled the tackle neatly and picked up the pants.

"H-m-m-m," he said, inspecting the knots. "Dirty work after all. These knots are granny knots. Everybody here knows I always tie jam knots!"

"Well, then, you would know how to untie a jam knot, wouldn't you?" demanded Madame President.

"That I would," His Honor answered.

"Good! After you get through straightening up that closet untie this jam knot!"

She encircled his shoulders with the pants and knotted them firmly under his chin.

IN THE PRESENCE OF MINE ENEMIES

Sheer delight ahead! Where, oh where, did MacQuarrie find all those biblical quotes? Surely there must have been someone like Chad to start imagination flowing. And a one-armed man to pass the collection plate in church! Outrageous!

As usual someone is trying to outsmart Mr. President. As usual he enlists a wealth of great cunning to outsmart the outsmarters.

That a lot of mallards hit the dust (well, snow) is almost incidental.

The dusk of late duck season was hurrying westward across the sky and slanting snow was whitening the street gutters as I turned into the automotive emporium of the President of the Old Duck Hunters' Association, Inc. The man in the parts department explained that Hizzoner was out on the used-car lot. There I found him, thoughtfully kicking a tire on an august and monstrous second-hand car soon to be taking the Association on its final expedition of the season. "We could try Libby Bay again," he relected. "But the Hole in the Wall will be frozen. Jens says every bluebill on Dig Devil's has hauled his freight. Shallow Bay'd be open at the narrows, but I s'pose Joe's hauled in all his boats. Phoned Hank. He said there's an inch of ice on Mud Lake and she's making fast."

He went over other possibilities. The situation was urgent, for only a few days remained of the season. The widespread below the Copper Dam on the St. Croix? "Might not see a thing 'cept sawbills." The grassy island in the open water of the St. Louis River? "Too much big water to buck in this wind."

Taylor's Point on the Big Eau Claire? "Wind's wrong for it and she's gonna stay in that quarter."

Street lights came on and home-going city toilers bent into the growing storm with collars turned up. One of them crossed the street and tried the showroom door which the parts man had just locked. Mister President called from the lot, "Something I can do for you?"

"Ye're dern tootin!" came the reply. "Open up this dump and let a man get warm."

Mister President grinned. "It's Chad," he said, making haste to unlock the showroom door.

Anyone in that community on reasonable terms with the way of the duck, the trout, the partridge and the white-tailed deer knows Chad just as he knows Mister President. Before the days when I cut myself in as an apprentice, the ODHA had consisted almost solely of Mister President and Chad. In recent years they get together only a couple of times per year on outdoor missions which can be anything from looking up old trout holes to picking blueberries.

But they meet regularly in church, except during the duck season and possibly two or three Sundays in late May or early June when the shadflies hatch. Chad is an especially stout pillar of the church, and passes the collection plate with a stern and challenging eye on the brethren he considers too thrifty.

The belligerent affection which Hizzoner and Chad reciprocate was once amply demonstrated at a Men's Club meeting in the church basement when suggestions were called for.

"Get a one-armed guy to take Chad's job passing the plate," volunteered Mister President.

Chad, who came upon holiness late in life and became so enchanted with Biblical wisdom that he quotes verses every chance, snorted back, "Let him who is without sin cast the first stone . . ."

"The time," Chad announced, "is short."

"There'll be no 14-year-old touring car with California top repaired here this night," declared Mister President. "Tell you what, though — bring it down to the lot and I'll give you $7.50 for it on a new job."

"My son, attend unto my wisdom," said Chad sagely. "Last deer season I was on a drive in back of Little Bass Lake. Found a spring-hole at the edge of a big marsh." His eyes gleamed with what is recognized in church as religious fervor. "No map shows it. Everything else in the country was froze up, and this little spring-hole was open. There's a point of high, dry land poking into it. There's smartweed in there and watercress, and the day I saw it mallards jumped out of it."

"How about the road in?"

"We'll have to walk a mile."

Mister President frowned briefly, but Chad's mustache became a reasonable straight line as he intoned, "If thou faint in the day of adversity, thy strength is small."

"Let's at it, then," decided Mister President.

Quick getaways are no problem for the ODHA in the critical times of the season. At such times decoys are always sorted and sacked, shell boxes full and thermos bottles yawning for their soup and coffee. Against emergency conditions, Mister President also sets the old horse blanket and barn lantern conveniently at hand in the garage, for it is by these implements that he keeps warm in late-season blinds.

A mere accessory to their reunion, I drove the big car while the two cronies smoked and remembered. They agreed I'd come in handy toting gear and that I could be put to use if ice had to be broken. Objections on my part were swept away as Chad patted me on the back and said piously, "The righteous shall flourish like the palm tree."

Fine slanting snow darted across the path of the headlights. With that northwest wind I knew it would not snow much; but should the wind veer to the northeast, then we would be very happy at having the heavy, high-wheeled monster of a car for bucking drifts. It was a little after 9 PM when we disembarked beneath the high oaks which spread over Norm's place on the north shore of Big Yellow Lake, Burnett County, Wisconsin. Norm appeared with a flashlight.

"Might have known it'd be no one but you out on a night like this."

He lit an air-tight stove in an overnight cabin. Chad, police suspenders drooping as he readied for bed, set his old alarm clock with the bell on top for 5 AM. A few minutes were allowed for final smokes and for further recollection of past delights. Chad had started to recall "the night we slept on the depot floor at Winnebojou" when a car entered the yard.

Again Norm emerged, prepared a cabin, and went back to sleep. As is always the way in duck camps, the newcomers pounded on our door for a predawn investigation. As the two men entered, somewhat suspiciously I thought, Chad's face fell for a brief instant, but he made a quick recovery and fell upon the two hunters with vast friendship.

Where were they going to hunt in the morning? Weren't we all crazy for being out in such weather? How's the missus and the children?

Chad volunteered with bare-faced frankness that we were "going down the Yellow River a piece to that widespread just this side of Eastman's." Our visitors alleged they had it in mind to try the deep point in the cane grass across Big Yellow. Mister President and Chad solemnly agreed that sounded like a promising spot — "mighty promising."

The two departed for bed, and Chad cried after them cheerfully, "See you in church, boys!" The moment they were gone Chad seized his alarm clock and set it to ring an hour earlier. "Those fakers aren't fooling me," he snorted.

"Me, either," said Mister President. "Somebody knows something."

"They were with me on that deer drive last fall. Gentlemen, say your prayers well tonight. There's only one spot on that marsh that's really any good, and that's the little spring-hole." He rolled in with a final muttering: "Deliver me from the workers of iniquity."

Within a few minutes the cabin resounded with the devout snores of Mister President and Chad. I lay awake a bit longer, listening to the wind in the oaks, weighing our chances for the morrow and marveling at the hypocritical poise of my comrades in the face of emergency. I knew those two adversaries of ours better than well. One was a piano tuner who, by some transference of vocational talent, could play a tune on a Model '97 that was strictly lethal so far as ducks are concerned. The other was a butcher likewise noted for his wing-shooting and his stoutness in going anywhere after ducks.

Mister President and Chad snored. The snow tapped on the window like fine sand, and then suddenly someone was shaking me in the dark. It was Mister President.

"Get up quietly," he hissed. "We beat the alarm clock so they wouldn't hear it. Don't turn on the light. Don't even strike a match!"

Like burglars we groped in the dark getting dressed and gathering up gear. "How about breakfast?" I asked. Mister President snickered, and Chad's voice came as from a sepulcher in the pitch dark. "Trust in the Lord and do good."

Softly we closed the door behind us and climbed into the car. Mister President got behind the wheel with Chad beside him and me alone in the back seat. The motor roared, headlights blazed and almost simultaneously a light went on in the cabin of our neighbors.

"Step on 'er!" Chad shouted, and the old crate made the snow fly as it leaped out of Norm's yard.

"We've got the jump on 'em," Chad exulted, but did not forget to add: "The righteous shall inherit the land and dwell forever."

It was a wild ride on a wild morning. The snow had stopped when two to three inches lay on the level. That was enough to make for skidding turns on the sharp corners where Mister President kept to maximum speed. We roared up steep hills and kept the power on going down. We passed white barns ghostly and cold-looking in the dark, and at a field fronting a farmstead owned by one honorary member of the ODHA, Gus Blomberg, Chad ordered the car halted. He got out, took something from Gus's front yard that rattled like tin and stuffed it into the car trunk.

"What was it, Chad?" I asked.

"Out of the mouths of babes and fools," he retaliated, poked Mister President in the ribs and roared: "Step on 'er some more! He shall deliver thee from the snare of the fowler!"

I knew part of the road. But after they skirted the base of the long point jutting into Little Bass Lake and took to pulp trails through the jack-pine barrens I was lost. Chad ordered "right," or "left," or sometimes, "Don't forget to turn out for that big scrub-oak."

We labored up a hilltop on a barely discernible pair of ruts, and the big car came to a stop, practically buried in low scrub-oak. Instantly the lights were switched off, and Mister President and Chad listened for sound of the enemy's motor. They heard nothing, but nevertheless hurried with the job of loading up with the sinews of war and heading for the spring-hole.

Only you who have been there know how a 60-pound sack of decoys in a Duluth pack-sack can cut into the shoulders when hands are occupied with gun and shellbox. Chad led the way in the dark and took us miraculously through the better parts of that oak and pine tangle. A half-mile along the way we stopped to listen again, and this time we heard the motor of another car laboring up the hill through the scrub.

"Step on 'er again," counseled Chad, shouldering his burdens. "They haven't forgotten the way in, and that piano tuner can run like a deer!" Chad permitted the use of lights now. We stumbled for what seemed miles until he led us down a gentle slope, and there before us was black, open water, about an acre of it. The omens were good. Mallards took off as a flashlight slit across the water.

"Keep the dang lights on all you want," said Mister President. "Let 'em know we're here fustest with the mostest."

Mister President and I spread his ancient decoys while Chad busied himself on a mysterious errand some distance away. As I uncoiled decoy strings I saw that the hole was a mere open dot in what must have been a large, flat marsh. Tall flaggers hemmed in the open water and stretched far beyond the range of the flashlight.

Mister President and I dug a pit in soft sand on fairly high ground and embroidered the edges of it with jack-pine and scrub-oak. We heard the piano tuner and the butcher push through the cover on the hill at our back, heard them panting and talking in low voices. Chad returned and boomed for all to hear: "Ain't a thing open but this one little patch. Betcha we don't see a feather here today!"

He fooled no one. The piano tuner and the butcher made a wide circle around us. We could hear them crashing through brush and Chad grudgingly allowed, "That butcher can hit the bush like a bull moose." Then we heard them walking across the marsh ice among the raspy flaggers and soon, five hundred yards across the marsh from us, came the sound of chopping as they readied a blind. Chad was worried.

"No open water there, but that's the place where the mallards come in here from the St. Croix River. Those muzzlers are right in front of a low pass through the hills. Them mallards come through there like you opened a door for 'em."

There was at least an hour's wait to shooting time. The two old hands puttered with the blind. They rigged crotched sticks to keep their shotgun breeches away from the dribbling sand of the blind's wall. They made comfortable seats for themselves, and finally, as was their right by seniority, they wrapped the old horse blanket about their knees, with the lantern beneath, and toasted their shins in stinking comfort.

Long before there was any real light, ducks returned to our open water, and the ODHA, waiting nervously, sipped coffee and made a career out of not clinking the aluminum cups. In that blind with Mister President it was almost worth a man's life to kick a shell-box accidentally in the dark. Chad briefed us: "When the time comes, don't nobody miss on them first ones, 'cause our friends over there are situated to scare out incomers. That is, in case they get a shot. Praise be, neither one of them are cloudbusters."

As the zero hour approached Mister President produced his gold watch and chain, and the two of them followed the snail's pace of the minute hand.

"Good idea not to jump the gun," said Chad. "No use to break the law."

To which Mister President added: "Might be a game warden hanging around, too."

"Now!"

As Mister President gave the word Chad kicked his shell-box and stood up. The air was full of flailing wings. I missed one, got it with the second barrel and heard three calculated shots from Mister President's automatic. I also heard Chad's cussing. He had forgotten to load his corn-sheller. The air was a bright cerulean blue until his city conscience smote him and he said remorsefully, "Wash me and I shall be whiter than snow."

With daylight the wind shifted from northwest to northeast and the snow began again, from Lake Superior this time. That kind of snow at that season is not to be trifled with, for northeasters can blow for three days and fetch mighty drifts. I picked up the drake mallard I had downed and the three birds Mister President had collected in his methodical way. The two old hands agreed that none of the mallards were locals, but "Redlegs down from Canada — feel the heft of that one!"

There was a long wait after that first burst of shooting. Obviously there were not many ducks left in the country. The original ODHA comforted themselves with hot coffee and thick sandwiches. From time to time one of them ascended the little knob at our rear to look across the snowy marsh and observe operations over there.

Chad came back from a reconnaissance and exclaimed. "She's workin', glory be."

The words were hardly out of his mouth when five mallards materialized out of the smother, circled the open water and cupped wings to drop in. As they zoomed in Mister President and Chad picked off a drake apiece, and when the wind had blown them to the edge of the ice I picked them up.

"You got him broke pretty well," Chad observed.

"Fair, just fair," grunted Mister President, squinting through the snow. "He's steady to wing and shot, but a mite nervous on incomers. Needs more field work."

Shortly before noon I climbed the hill myself for a look across the marsh. Through the snow over the high flaggers I could make out the dark green blob that was the jack-pine blind of the butcher and piano tuner. We had not heard a shot from the place. As I watched, six mallards, mere specks at first, approached the marsh from the direction of the St. Croix River. They were coming through the low hill pass just as Chad had said they would. Normally they would have flown almost directly over the distant blind.

Some distance from the blind I saw them flare and climb, then swing wide around the edge of the marsh and sail straight into our open hole.

From my vantage-point I saw the two old hands rise and fire, and three ducks fell.

Mister President called up to me: "Pick up that one that dropped in the scrub, will yuh?"

"We'd better keep careful count," Chad suggested. In a few minutes he dropped two more that tried to sneak into the water-hole.

"I'm through," he announced. He acknowledged his limit with a thankful verse: "Thou hast turned for me my mourning into dancing."

The afternoon moved along. The snow increased, and when limits were had all around we finished the last of the soup, washed it down with the now lukewarm coffee and picked up. It was high time we were moving. A good six inches of snow was on the ground. There were steep, slippery hills between us and the main road.

Back at the car, we turned the behemoth around. Parked just to the rear of us was the conveyance of the piano tuner and the butcher. It was a modern job with the low-slung build of a dachshund, but in maneuvering out of the place Mister President's locomotive-like contraption broke out a good trail.

Mister President and Chad were jubilant as the big car was tooled carefully over the crooked road to Norm's where we picked up gear left behind in the unlighted cabin hours before and said goodby to Norm — "until the smallmouth take a notion to hit in the St. Croix."

Homeward-bound. Chad's best Sunday basso profundo broke into a sincere rendition of an old hymn which emphasizes that "He will carry you through," and Mister President joined him with a happy, off-key baritone. We halted at the curb in front of Chad's house, and he emerged from the car laden with mallards and gear and smelling of horse blanket and kerosene.

"We sure fooled 'em," said Mister President.

"Thou preparest a table for me in the presence of mine enemies," Chad intoned, and went up his walk to the door.

At Mister President's back door I helped him with the unloading. What, I demanded, was the thing Chad had removed from Gus Blomberg's front yard?

"Well, sir," said Mister President. "It was a device calculated to do the undoable and solve the unsolvable. I couldn't have done better myself." He sat down on a shell-box on his back steps the better to laugh at his partner's cunning.

"You know," he said, "when he stuck that thing out there just in the right place, he came back to the blind and told me, 'Mine enemies are lively and they are strong.'"

"What was it?" I insisted. "All I know is there was something out there that made those mallards flare."

Hizzoner picked up the shell-box, his hand on the door knob, and said, "It was Gus Blomberg's scare-crow, and I'm surprised you haven't figgered it out."

"All I could guess was that it was something made of tin cans. I heard 'em rattle."

"Gus Blomberg," said Mister President, "always drapes tin cans on his scarecrows soste they'll rattle in the wind. Good night to you, sir — and don't forget to come over tomorrow night and help me pick these ducks."

The Day I Burned
the Oatmeal

That there is a deepening love between the author and his boon companion there can be no doubt. This story goes to emphasize that love. For suddenly the old man pits himself against a raging storm. MacQuarrie, the younger man, surges to the rescue. Barely in the nick of time.

Then, rescue complete, safety accomplished, isn't it like Mr. President to ignore all else and complain about the quality of the oatmeal?

Looking out the office window, I knew that the President of the Old Duck Hunters' Association, Inc., would be phoning soon. A northwest wind was tearing smoke from city chimneys. Pedestrians on the street below leaned into the blast. Lights gleamed from office windows, though it was only 10 AM. Tracer-bullet snowflakes stabbed at the huddled city.

It was mid-November. The leader of the Old Duck Hunters was right on time with his phone call.

"I'm tied up until noon or after," he said. "I'll meet you at the red cabin some time in the afternoon. If I don't show up, don't wait. Get out there yourself. There'll be ducks moving today."

"But I'd rather wait and go with you."

"Maybe I can make it. But you get out there while this wind is at its peak."

Those were marching orders.

Within an hour I had stowed my gear, including Mister President's favorite emergency ration, which is steel-cut oatmeal. With Jerry, the springer, beside me, I drove the seventy miles to the big red cabin on the hill, around which spread a maze of ducking waters. By the time Jerry and I had turned off the main road the snow was coming in sheets.

Jerry, a faithful 45-pound lump of old-fashioned dog, was restless in the storm. His nose-prints were all over the car windows by the time I climbed the last sandy hill to the big red cabin. I made things ready indoors while Jerry investigated one of the grandest November storms I ever saw.

I swept out the cabin. It hardly needed it; but the Old Duck Hunters make a fetish of keeping things shipshape, in a blind or in a kitchen. The red cabin is one of our put-ins, the summer home of a friend who, after Labor Day, turns the key over to the Old Duck Hunters, in exchange for which he gets an occasional brace of mallards.

I trimmed the wicks of the kerosene lamps and polished their chimneys. Then I built a fire in the red brick fireplace for its companionship. I spread the thick blankets on the two beds, set the kitchen table and kindled the kitchen range to get that oatmeal started. It takes, says Mister President, just three hours of slow steaming to make steel-cut oatmeal as acceptable to a man as to a horse.

In the growing storm I split chunks of lightning-struck Norway pine. Storm-tossed chickadees came to seek out grubs turned up by the ax in the protected space of the wood-yard. Another good sign. When the chickadees come right to the chopping block for food, there is weather afoot.

Jerry came snuffling back to the wood-yard, his back and muzzle caked with snow. He sat safely away from the flying firewood, obviously disgusted with a man who would split wood on such a promising day. Had not he, Jerry, been abroad and seen wondrous things? He followed me in with the last armload of wood. When I slid the worn double-barrel out of its case, he raced for the door. His strong stubby tail wagged into my legs as I leaned over him to turn the knob and face the storm.

By then it was two o'clock. It seemed later, it was so dark. Jerry and I went down the hill to the shore of Deep Lake, a putting-out place for many far-flung duck points. I was hopeful that Mister President would be here. Sometimes he did not bother to drive his car up the cabin hill, but just parked it in the firm sand at the edge of the lake and set out from there.

I was disappointed at not finding him. Jerry kept waltzing about to emphasize the dire need to go hunting — "For heaven's sake, man, what are we waiting for?" But wait I must. A day such as this, after weeks of bluebird weather, was best shared with someone.

The Deep Bay was roaring, although it is partly sheltered. Boats would take a merciless pounding out there, once they got away from the high bank. Ducks whipped over Jerry and me. In the smother I could not make them out clearly, but knew from their short wing-beats that they were deep divers. It was a fine moment, just standing there, but I wished Mister President's car would come lurching down the road toward the beach.

By 2:25 I decided to carry out the marching orders — "Get out there yourself." Jerry was in the boat as I slid it off the sand into pounding waters. He crept to the prow as I started rowing.

I shall not soon forget the wind that cuffed us as we left the shore. The boat — a tough, flat-bottomed job of steel — was seized and tossed by the hungry wind. Even Jerry couldn't take it with his muzzle over the gunwale. He dropped into the bottom of the boat.

My aim was to cross a partly sheltered portion of Deep Lake to a narrows. Once through the narrows, the idea was to push across Shallow Bay, straight into the face of the wind, to a favorite blind which should be ideal with the wind where it was. I am a handy man with the oars, but one glance at Shallow Bay, beyond the narrows' mouth, changed my mind.

Shallow Bay, five feet at the deepest, was a cauldron. Moving water had dug so deeply that the usually clear waters were turgid with gray-green bottom muck, and even aquatic plants, torn from the bottom, were being carried off in the waves.

What to do? If Mister President had been there, two pairs of oars could have been manned and we could have fought across Shallow Bay by sheer force. It was no job for one man. Not that half-mile of inland lake, transformed into something approximating a stormy ocean.

Well, I knew a place where a fellow could get in a little shooting without having to take another turn at the oars. This particular country has that in its favor. In season, whatever the weather, a man can manage to get some place where chances will be at least fair.

The spot I had in mind was a half-mile down the shore from the narrows to another leg of this sprawling lake, where a point thrust out into fairly deep water. There had been no let-up in the storm; so there was only one thing to do: leave the steel boat dragged up at the narrows, don't even bother with the decoys, and hike to that point. With a pocketful of shells I set out.

The wind was crying fury on the point. This point sticks about fifty yards beyond shore growths. Between the last of the trees and the roaring water the only cover was a tiny blind, built there some weeks before. The wind had knocked it into a cocked hat. With jack-pine boughs I built it up a little. The wind was so strong that when a chunk of blind tore away it slapped me across the neck.

While I fussed with the blind, ducks were riding the gale overhead, coming mostly from the northwest and smashing across the point like dive-bombers. Jerry shivered with eagerness at my feet as I got into the partly rebuilt blind. No decoys. Visibility was about seventy yards — sometimes more, sometimes less. The snow was deep enough now to be measured in inches.

Nail 'em, if you can, when they cross. If you see 'em at all . . .

I peered through the barrels to make sure they were free of snow. I was ready for a band of bluebills that came at me. They were in and gone so quickly that I got in only the open barrel, and at the report a single fell in a wide slant on the wind-torn waters off the point. Jerry, no non-slip retriever, just a fellow for tearing in, was after it like a shot.

The wind bounced the duck along at a furious pace, but Jerry had marked it well. Half the time he was out of sight, and it was a relief when I made out his round head thrust out in the final act of grabbing and then saw him turn and fight back to shore. He landed some distance down the beach and presented me with a drake bluebill that likely had dined the evening before on some northern Minnesota lake.

That single gave me pause. If I winged one and it dropped out too far, the dog, with a heart too big for his strength, might paddle out there and never come back. After that I was careful to watch the ducks that came from the windward side of the point and nail them as quickly as possible so that they dropped on land or close to it, thus keeping Jerry from risking his precious neck.

Many a shot is passed up under such restrictions, but that was all right. Tomorrow morning the Association would get out together. The wind might be down then. Certainly the ducks would be around. Jerry had some easy pick-ups. I think he was grateful.

It would have been a nice, stormy afternoon if Mister President had been along. If he had been on time, we could have made it across to Shallow Bay point, a great favorite with both of us in a northwest wind. Over there, I thought, we could have picked them just as carefully, only more birds would be moving around. That is the way it has always been. Had he just come on time, then we might have lit a little afternoon fire in the back of the Shallow Bay blind — one getting warm, the other watching the end of the point.

If he had just been on time . . . Men who hunt ducks know what it means to have that indispensable team-mate on hand when things get too much for one man.

I quit at four o'clock by the wrist watch, a very damp watch, strapped to a damp, chapped wrist. Jerry was hardly more than an animated floor mop, but a happy lad, sniffing and snuffing at my game pocket.

As I hiked back to the narrows it came to me suddenly that one of the other rowboats was gone. If the President had come late he might have taken one and set out alone, I searched for tracks, but could find none. Snow had covered everything. I never could keep track of how many boats that landing beach sheltered; so couldn't even guess if he were out in one.

Just one thing to do — get up that hill and see if he were there in the cabin. God, I hoped he was there, sitting before the fire in the gray sweater vest. Moments like those come back with frightful vividness.

In the warm kitchen the oatmeal was bubbling. The broom stood in its appointed corner. The ticking alarm clock mocked me from its shelf.

I burst through the swinging door into the living room. It was empty!

No one had been there. The fireplace screen was untouched. A stick of Norway pine braced it against the face of the opening, just as I had left it. He was out there on Shallow Bay!

I tore out of there and back down the steep path. Jerry was for coming, but I slammed the door on him. It was all plain now. The Old Man had grabbed a boat and then started off alone across that treacherous, screaming Shallow Bay.

What a sap I had been not to wait for him! I should have realized he would try it. Should have realized that was right where he would go in a northwest blow. Should have remembered what he had always said — "Show me the sea on an inland lake I can't ride out in a good rowboat!"

Down the path I went. I tossed off the heavy hunting jacket. I hit that steel boat a-running and was out in it, rowing.

Away from shore, the wind caught me again. It seemed worse than on my earlier trip. Or perhaps my arms were just weary. I hadn't the faintest idea what I would do if I didn't find him. Maybe he had made the point across Shallow Bay. He could handle a boat — indeed he could. There was comfort in that. Maybe he had landed there and was afraid to try going back in the quartering wind, Maybe . . .

I halted at the narrows. I was heaving like a bellows. There was just one thing to do — catch my breath and get right across to that Shallow Bay blind before it got too dark. The direction didn't worry me so much as the rough water. I could make it across if my rowing arms held out. My heart was hammering.

Then he appeared, and I yelled with relief, a yell that he could not hear in the wind. There he was, rowing for the mouth of the narrows against the wind! He had taken off the old brown mackinaw. His white police suspenders stood out like an x in the fading light, for, of course, his back was to me.

Never in my life has the slivery gunwale of a rowboat felt better in my hands. I found myself over my boots as I hauled him in the last twenty-five feet. His mackinaw floated in the half-filled boat. He picked it up and shook the water out of it. The first thing he said was: "Don't ever mention it to my wife! She'd never let me hunt again."

Then he slapped my shoulder, and between us we hoisted his boat upside down on the sand to empty it — the old ritual of the Association. Ten canvasbacks rolled out of it, and he explained, "I just picked the ones with the longest necks when they came by."

Two pairs of oars whisked us back down Deep Bay and we hurried to the warm cabin. Once inside, I knew that he was trying to hide a great weariness, trying to make light of a bad time. I strung the ducks on the back porch. The wind was rising, if anything, but morning and more of it had little appeal right then.

I poked jack-pine kindling under the kettle where the oatmeal bubbled. Then I swept the hearth, for something to do. Over a bowl of that steel-cut oatmeal he told me what it had been like.

"Halfway over I was sorry I'd started. But there I was, and I made it. I'll bet a thousand ducks passed over that point — in range. Seemed like every web-foot in north Wisconsin was up and moving.

"They'd come busting out of the snow, and I'd let 'em have it. Everything was moving — mallards, redheads, cans, bluebills. Then I picked up and started back."

I helped him pull off his boots and found dry things for him. I brought one of the big blankets and tucked it around his shoulders. He leaned back in his chair before the fire. The warmth from it began to get in its work. The tenseness left both of us, and Jerry's stub of a tail showed he had caught the change in out moods.

I got him a bowl of that precious oatmeal, and he was grinning at me when I handed it to him. I was afraid to say anything. Sentiment of the surface kind is foreign to the Old Duck Hunters. I jiggled the stove lids, piling in more wood. There was supper to get.

And then he yelled like his old self from the other room: "Say, how many ducks did you fetch in?"

"Five, I think."

"H-m-m-m. Ought to be ten. Say, got another dab of that porridge?"

All was well in the big red cabin when I brought the porridge, for he said: "Tomorrow morning we'll go back across Shallow Bay, wind or no wind." Then he added: "Damn it, you burned the oatmeal!"

BABB OF THE BRULE

Two violently competitive fisherman, steadfast old friends, companions of the stream. They bet, as fishermen will, on who will take the biggest fish. Then George Babb, a big man in all ways, lets the old man take the prize. (Only there isn't any prize.)

It's a heartwarming gesture. A gallant act. But be prepared. MacQuarrie is warming your heart now. Because soon he will break it.

"Let us stop and wrap this four-pound rainbow around George's neck," said the President of the Old Duck Hunters' Association with a chuckle.

We were returning from a trout opening on Wisconsin's fabulous and fickle Brule. It was dark and cold. Only the hardiest of the spring peepers sang. The northern lights whirled fluorescent banners. The Old Man got the idea of showing George his big fish while he changed socks in the back seat of the car.

"I'm going to show him this fish."

"Your honor," said I, "Babb will have at least two like it, and his wife will have fifteen, none under a foot."

A wet and sandy wader sock swished alongside my ear. "So you won't stop?"

Very soon we were ascending the front steps of George A. Babb's house.

"It's late, darn near ten-thirty," I whispered.

"Knock!" commanded Hizzoner, both hands around that slab-sided rainbow.

Mrs. Babb opened the door.

"'Where's George?'"

"George!" Her call went up the stairway.

A sleepy "'Who is it?'" came down the stairs.

"It's Al," she explained. "He's got a fish he wants to show you."

"Tell him," said Mister President, "that I want to show him the kind he never catches."

Her voice went dutifully up the stairs again. "He's come to show you up, George, dear."

The bare feet of George A. Babb hit the floor above. Down he came in his night-shirt, tousled and sleepy, but belligerent. There were no formalities between Babb of the Brule and the peerless leader of the Old Duck Hunters. George said, "Produce your minnow."

The rainbow was slid beneath his nose. George took one contemptuous look and headed for the kitchen. He promised en route that presently he would unveil an opening-day catch "fit to take home." He suggested to Mrs. Babb that it was a good time to put on the coffee pot. And he dragged into the living-room, right across the rugs, as mighty an assortment of square-tailed, cold-water fish as this scribe has seen in many a year.

They were in a wash-tub, iced, about two dozen. A few were under a pound. The center of interest was a huge, deep-bellied monster of a rainbow.

"Gargantua!" cried Babb, holding it up alongside Mister President's four-pounder.

"Holy man!" said the President. "It'll go a good five pounds"

"Six and a half!" Babb snorted.

"I guess," said the Old Man, "that I just took in too much territory."

"Like the man who rassled the bear," said George, "you're already yelling 'Stop, or I'll let go!'"

There was vast talk thereafter. George told how he had done it. Salmon eggs and worms with a Colorado spinner early in the day, then big wet flies at midday, and back to bait when the sun rolled under the hill. Mister

President managed to issue a few remarks about his own trophy, taken on a black bucktail just below May's Rips. It was a fine meeting until Hizzoner's natural tendencies took charge.

"Tell you what I'll do," he addressed George. "I'll lay you my rod, the one with the 12-inch cork grip, to your waders that next opening night I'll appear on these premises with a bigger rainbow than anything you'll have in that tub."

The hoots of George A. Babb followed us down the steps.

George Babb was perhaps the most proficient fisherman ever to wet a line in the Douglas County Brule. He is the only trout fisherman I know who once announced he would take trout from a certain place, at a certain time, and did it in the presence of a gallery of picnickers.

He came early to the Brule country from Maine. There is a Babb's Island in the Penobscot River of Maine and one in Wisconsin's Flambeau River, both named for logging-day kin of George's. He followed the woods, then took up barbering, fishing and guiding. Although Babb had all the bristly characteristics of a mad porcupine, he had a tender streak in him from here to there. I saw him quit fishing one good evening when accidentally, with a push pole, he knocked a cedar waxwing nest from a tree, drowning the fledglings, while trying to retrieve a hung fly.

He knew the game from A to Z, and loved to disagree with the experts. He had a voice that could boom out a half-mile across the Brule's Big Lake. His whisper was a buzz-saw. I am pretty sure that once, for a year or so, he held the world's record for a brown trout, a fish of some 16 pounds, taken about 1916. When a President of the United States came for three months to the Brule, it was Babb who was called on to teach him fly fishing.

This, then, was Babb, a man who would wrestle you for a dollar and a half any day and give you his last chew of tobacco. Homeward-bound, I reminded Mister President that he was about to lose his pet rod. Soothed by Mrs. Babb's coffee and unruffled about the future, he said "If there's a fishin' season next year, I'll win."

"Nuts!" said I.

"Wake me up," said he, "when we hit the edge of town. I want to get all my gear in one place so you won't drive off with it."

In the long interim of winter I heard reports of meetings of these two. George would come to town once every so often and stop at Mister President's place of business, mostly to promise Hizzoner that he would have that fly rod, come May First. I heard reports of the two of them locked in mortal combat over fishing tactics, though the thermometer stood at 10 below.

One observer relayed that on a street corner where they met one evening he heard Babb exclaim contemptuously, "That old nine-foot crowbar of yours ain't got but the one tip and that's took a set."

To which our peerless leader replied, "Your own wife told me you bought those waders the year Taft was elected!"

On opening day I found myself at 4:30 AM driving again to the Brule. The Old Man sized up the look of the country as we drove. He said he liked darned near everything that morning. He liked the way the popples were fuzzy when the car lights touched them. He liked the way the season had come belatedly, so that the big migratory rainbows from Lake Superior would still be in the river. He also liked the way the spring peepers were hollering — "like they had a cheer leader."

"But," he continued, "I do not like George A. Babb this morning."

"You're not running out on that bet?"

"Me! I'm just mad at him this morning because I'm sure his darn old waders leak. Ere this day is out his hide will be tacked on the barn door."

I had doubts. Had the field of honor been any of a dozen other north Wisconsin streams, I'd have felt safer about Mister President's rod. Babb knew that Brule like the mink that live along its banks.

There was another reason for concern on my part. Mister President, not at all like himself, didn't know exactly where he wanted to put into the stream. It was not time for confusion. The omens were bad. In fettle, the Old Man would have gone to his chosen place as the bee to the honey tree. He speculated as we drove along.

"I'd hit for the Cloquet bridge, only it might rain and we'd get stuck on those hills. The meadows north of Brule might be all right, but there'll be too many there. Winnebojou is a good starter, but since they tore out the South Shore trestle I don't like the look of it . . ."

It was breaking day. A decision was in order. No inspired directions came from Mister President; so I nudged his ancient car beyond Winnebojou and down a two-rut road. It's a good place if you get to the end of it with auto springs intact.

He took a long time to get into his waders. He dallied over his gear. He let the leader and line slip back through the guides several times before he had it threaded properly. He asserted that the canned salmon eggs you get nowadays are no good. He exhibited all the insecurity of a lamb getting fat in a feeding pen and not liking it a little bit. It was light when we hit the river.

"I suppose," said Mister President, "that by this time his wife has caught all the trout he needs."

"Who needs?"

"George A. Babb, you derned fool!"

He left me there, preoccupied and, I think, skeptical of this day's luck. I hardly knew whether to laugh or suggest extenuating circumstances, such as substituting another rod for the nonpareil nine-footer. I knew, as Mister President vanished downstream, that up the river some distance the wizard, Babb, was working a magic line over excellent trout water.

True, Mister President might hang a hook in the mouth of a monster. And George might meet up with a bad day. It was unlikely, though.

The only warm praise I can speak for that cold morning is that there were no mosquitoes. Back from the river bank in the little hollows there was crisp ice. My wader boots crunched through plenty of it as I went upstream along the bank.

The river does a good bit of twisting here. In a few places it has tried to cut cross lots. These are hard to get around, harder to wade through. The business of lifting first one foot and then the other from these mucky bottomed backwaters served to warm me up. I came to a place where the stream is wadable down its center, with a deep long groove of water under the left bank. Willows tip over it. Perhaps there was something in there.

The routine was followed in the strict early-season tradition for these waters — worms and salmon eggs with spinners and without, then big gaudy flies, then those black bucktails. After four hours all I had was an empty tobacco can which had housed some splendid worms. The river seemed dead. I grew tired of a fruitless campaign beneath the willows, went ashore, lit a fire and stretched.

The sun climbed. The grass beneath me warmed up. I dozed a bit. Then I was suddenly awake, wide awake, for a man was standing over me, tickling my nose with the slightly dried tail of a six-pound rainbow trout. The man was the President of the Old Duck Hunters.

"I've got him!" he exulted. "His waders are practically hanging in my garage this minute. That big one he had last spring was a fluke."

He related that he had found a hole "and stuck with it." He saw the big one roll and worked on him for two hours — "threw a hardware store at him. Finally I dug around and brought up this little wooden wabbler. Bet I showed it to him two hundred times before he took it."

"And when he took it?"

"Then I says, says I, 'George, if those waders leak, you'll have to pay for the vulcanizing!'"

Mister President was indeed jubilant. The contrast with his mood of early morning was impressive. He said he felt so darned good that he would climb the steep hill to the car and bring down a frying-pan — "so I can fry up the little ones you got."

I explained I did not have even one little one, that we did not have a frying-pan in the car, and that he was just trying to rub it in.

"Uh-huh," he said. "Got you both licked." Then he rolled over and fell asleep in the sun.

"While he sought that repose to which he was entitled I tried again along this favorite water of mine. The warmer weather helped. Wet flies attracted interest. I nailed a few — "half a hatful," Mister President said later. "Ain't you ever goin' to catch a fish too big for a creel?"

In the evening we went up the hill out of the steep valley. He sat on the running-board and I pulled off his waders, a ceremony which concludes with the puller being shoved sprawling by the pullee. He permitted me to take down his rod — "and don't leave any rag-tag bobtail of leader wound around the reel."

I cramped the car wheels to get it out of the narrow turnaround, and we started down the two-rut road. Mister President leaned back with the taste of victory in his mouth and chortled, "Wait till you see Babb's face fall."

All the way the Old Man was drinking hot blood, right out of the neck.

"Oh," he said generously, "Babb isn't such a bad fisherman. He'll have some fair fish under the kitchen sink in that dingdanged wash-tub. He'll be in bed when we get there pretending he's asleep and hoping we won't have the heart to bother him. Can't you push this old hack a bit faster?"

He lifted up his voice in snatches of song. One ballad dealt with how tall the chickens grew in Cheyenne. He also gave a sincere rendition of "The Stars and Stripes Forever." But it seemed to me he put his whole best into "The March of the Cameron Men."

Going up the Babb front steps, he was toting that dangling rainbow and humming, "She'll Be Comin' 'Round the Mountain When She Comes." Babb himself opened the door. Mister President got right down to the bricks immediately. "Bring on your fish!" he demanded.

Babb grinned. You knew when you saw his grin that it was an emblem of defeat. He slapped the Old Man on the back and roared: "You've got me this time, cold turkey. I never saw sign of a fish half that big."

"Bring on the waders!" demanded Mister President.

"Put on the coffee," said George.

There was vast talk thereafter. George told how he had done it — salmon eggs and worms with a Colorado spinner early in the day, then big wet flies at midday, and back to bait when the sun rolled under the hill. Mister President managed to issue a few remarks about his own trophy.

The pair of them, well along, gray and grizzled, did a lot of remembering. They went over the history of the Brule from the '90s and the history of Lake Nebagamon from the days when the Weyerhaeusers had their headquarters there. It was late when we left. Babb brought out the waders, still very damp.

"Looks to me like the darned things leak," Mister President sniffed.

"I'll say they do. I gave them a month's wear just today."

"W-e-l-l," said Mister President in a burst of magnanimity, "what do I want with leaky waders? I just wanted to show you, dang you!"

"That you did," Babb admitted.

Mister President went out the door toward the car. I remained behind, for Babb had plucked my coat sleeve. He whisked me quickly to the kitchen. There was the familiar wash-tub, iced. On top of a welter of trout lay a rainbow — such a trout as men dream of — huge, glistening carmine and olive.

"It's nice of you, George," I said before hurrying out to the car. "You know he's getting old."

"Sure, sure," he said. "I am, too.

NOTHING TO DO FOR THREE WEEKS

One of the outdoor's most poignant stories lies ahead. As the title suggests, MacQuarrie goes to his cabin by himself and extols the virtues of being alone.

It is a story of soft wonderment. He putters with gear, fishes some, hunts a little, gathers pine knots and chops wood. Alone, he says, but not lonely.

MacQuarrie is alone because of a terrible reason. He doesn't tell you the reason or in any way ask you to share his grief. The story ran in Field & Stream *in February 1956. MacQuarrie is alone because Mr. President is dead. The two will sally forth with comedy and song no more.*

So he teaches us about life. When the inevitable strikes, put a brave face to it. There are pleasures in being alone. He recounts them, enjoys them. It's only when he calls himself a pine-knot millionaire that he hints at the loss he feels. The lyricism is still there. But it is muted, softened, saddened.

I left long before daylight, alone but not lonely. Sunday-morning stillness filled the big city. It was so quiet that I heard the whistle of duck wings as I unlocked the car door. They would be ducks leaving Lake Michigan. A fine sound, that, early of a morning. Wild ducks flying above the tall apartments and the sprawling factories in the dark, and below them people still asleep, who knew not that these wild kindred were up and about early for their breakfast.

The wingbeats I chose to accept as a good omen. And why not? Three weeks of doing what I wished to do lay before me. It was the best time, the beginning of the last week in October. In the partridge woods I would pluck at the sleeve of reluctant Indian summer, and from a duck blind four hundred miles to the north I would watch winter make its first dash south on a north-west wind.

I drove through sleeping Milwaukee. I thought how fine it would be if, throughout the year, the season would hang on dead center, as it often does in Wisconsin in late October and early November. Then one may expect a lit-tle of everything — a bit of summer, a time of falling leaves, and finally that initial climatic threat of winter to quicken the heart of a duck hunter, name-ly me.

To be sure, these are mere hunter's dreams of perpetual paradise. But we all do it. And, anyway, isn't it fine to go on that early start, the car carefully packed, the day all to yourself to do with as you choose?

On the highway I had eyes only for my own brethren of the varnished stock, the dead-grass skiff, the far-going boots. Cars with hunting-capped men and cars with dimly outlined retrievers in back seats flashed by me. I had agreed with myself not to go fast. The day was too fine to mar with haste. Every minute of it was to be tasted and enjoyed, and remembered for anoth-er, duller day. Twenty miles out of the big city a hunter with two beagles set off across a field toward a wood. For the next ten miles I was with him in the cover beyond the farmhouse and up the hill.

Most of that still, sunny Sunday I went past farms and through cities, and over the hills and down into the valleys, and when I hit the fire-lane road out of Loretta-Draper I was getting along on my way. This is superb country for deer and partridge, but I did not see many of the latter; this was a year of the few, not the many. Where one of the branches of the surging Chippewa crosses the road I stopped and flushed mallards out of tall grass. On Clam Lake, at the end of the fire lane, there was an appropriate knot of bluebills.

The sun was selling nothing but pure gold when I rolled up and down the hills of the Namakagon Lake county. Thence up the blacktop from Cable to the turnoff at Drummond, and from there straight west through those tremendous stands of jack pine. Then I broke the rule of the day. I hurried a little. I wanted to use the daylight. I turned in at the mailboxes and went along the back road to the nameless turn-in — so crooked and therefore charming.

Old Sun was still shining on the top logs of the cabin. The yard was afloat with scrub oak leaves, for a wind to blow them off into the lake must be a good one. Usually it just skims the ridgepole and goes its way. Inside the cabin was the familiar smell of native Wisconsin white cedar logs. I lit the fireplace and then unloaded the car. It was near dark when all the gear was in, and I pondered the virtues of broiled ham steak and baking powder biscuits to go with it.

I was home, all right. I have another home, said to be much nicer. But this is the talk of persons who like cities and, in some cases, actually fear the woods.

There is no feeling like that first wave of affection which sweeps in when a man comes to a house and knows it is home. The logs, the beams, the popple kindling snapping under the maple logs in the fireplace. It was after dark when I had eaten the ham and the hot biscuits, these last dunked in maple syrup from a grove just three miles across the lake as the crow flies and ten miles by road.

When a man is alone, he gets things done. So many men alone in the brush get along with themselves because it takes most of their time to do for themselves. No dallying over division of labor, no hesitancy at tackling a job.

There is much to be said in behalf of the solitary way of fishing and hunting. It lets people get acquainted with themselves. Do not feel sorry for the man on his own. If he is one who plunges into all sorts of work, if he does not dawdle, if he does not dwell upon his aloneness, he will get many things done and have a fine time doing them.

After the dishes I put in some licks at puttering. Fifty very-well-cared-for decoys for diving ducks and mallards came out of their brown sacks and stood anchor-cord inspection. They had been made decent with touchup paint months before. A couple of 2-gauge guns got a pat or two with an oily rag. The contents of two shell boxes were sorted and segregated. Isn't it a caution how shells get mixed up? I use nothing but 12-gauge shells. Riding herd on more than one gauge would, I fear, baffle me completely.

I love to tinker with gear. It's almost as much fun as using it. Shipshape is the phrase. And it has got to be done continuously, otherwise order will be replaced by disorder, and possibly mild-to-acute chaos.

There is a school which holds that the hunting man with the rickety gun and the out-at-elbows jacket gets the game. Those who say this are fools or mountebanks. One missing top button on a hunting jacket can make a man miserable on a cold, windy day. The only use for a rickety shotgun is to blow somebody to hell and gone.

I dragged a skiff down the hill to the beach, screwed the motor to it, loaded in the decoys, and did not forget to toss in an old shell box for a blind seat and an ax for making a blind. I also inspected the night and found it good. It was not duck weather, but out there in the dark an occasional blue-bill skirled.

I went back up the hill and brought in fireplace wood. I was glad it was not cold enough to start the space heater. Some of those maple chunks from my woodpile came from the same sugar bush across the lake that supplied the hot biscuit syrup. It's nice to feel at home in such a country.

How would you like to hole up in a country where you could choose, as you fell asleep, between duck hunting and partridge hunting, between small-mouths on a good river like the St. Croix or trout on another good one like the Brule, or between muskie fishing on the Chippewa flowage or cisco dipping in the dark for the fun of it? Or, if the mood came over you, just a spell of tramping around on deer trails with a hand ax and a gunnysack, knocking highly flammable pine knots out of trees that have lain on the ground for seventy years? I've had good times in this country doing nothing more adventurous than filling a pail with blueberries or a couple of pails with wild cranberries.

If you have read thus far and have gathered that this fellow MacQuarrie is a pretty cozy fellow for himself in the bush, you are positively correct. Before I left on this trip the boss, himself a product of this same part of Wisconsin and jealous as hell of my three-week hunting debauch, allowed, "Nothing to do for three weeks, eh?" Him I know good. He'd have given quite a bit to be going along.

Nothing to do for three weeks! He knows better. He's been there, and busier than a one-armed paperhanger.

Around bedtime I found a seam rip in a favorite pair of thick doeskin gloves. Sewing it up, I felt like Robinson Crusoe, but Rob never had it that good. In the Old Duck Hunters we have a philosophy: When you go to the bush, you go there to smooth it, and not to rough it.

And so to bed under the watchful presence of the little alarm clock that has run faithfully for twenty years, but only when it is laid on its face. One red blanket was enough. There was an owl hooting, maybe two wrangling. You can never be sure where an owl is, or how far away, or how many. The fireplace wheezed and made settling noises. Almost asleep, I made up my mind to omit the ducks until some weather got made up. Tomorrow I'd hit the tote roads for partridge. Those partridge took some doing. In the low years they never disappear completely, but they require some tall walking, and singles are the common thing.

No hunting jacket on that clear, warm day. Not even a sleeveless game carrier. Just shells in the pockets, a fat ham sandwich, and Bailey sweet apples stuck into odd corners. My game carrier was a cord with which to tie birds to my belt. The best way to do it is to forget the cord is there until it is needed; otherwise the Almighty may see you with that cord in your greediness and decide you are tempting Providence and show you nary a feather all the day long.

By early afternoon I had walked up seven birds and killed two, pretty good for me. Walking back to the cabin, I sort of uncoiled. You can sure get wound up walking up partridge. I uncoiled some more out on the lake that afternoon building three blinds, in just the right places for expected winds.

This first day was also the time of the great pine-knot strike. I came upon them not far from a thoroughfare emptying the lake, beside rotted logs of lumbering days. Those logs had been left there by rearing crews after the lake level had been dropped to fill the river. It often happens. Then the rivermen don't bother to roll stranded logs into the water when it's hard work.

You cannot shoot a pine knot, or eat it, but it is a lovely thing and makes a fire that will burn the bottom out of a stove if you are not careful. Burning pine knots smell as fine as the South's pungent lightwood. Once I gave an artist a sack of pine knots and he refused to burn them and rubbed and polished them into wondrous birdlike forms, and many called them art. Me, I just pick them up and burn them.

Until you have your woodshed awash with pine knots, you have not ever been really rich. By that evening I had made seven two-mile round trips with the boat and I estimated I had almost two tons of pine knots. In even the very best pine-knot country, such as this was, that is a tremendous haul for one day; in fact, I felt vulgarly rich. To top it off, I dug up two husky boom chains, discovered only because a link or two appeared above ground. They are mementos of the logging days. One of those chains was partly buried in the roots of a white birch some fifty years old.

No one had to sing lullabies to me that second night. The next day I drove eighteen miles to the quaggy edge of the Totogatic flowage and killed four woodcock. Nobody up there hunts them much. Some people living right on the flowage asked me what they were.

An evening rite each day was to listen to weather reports on the radio. I was impatient for the duck blind, but this was Indian summer and I used it up, every bit of it. I used every day for what it was best suited. Can anyone do better?

The third day I drove thirty-five miles to the lower Douglas County Brule and tried for one big rainbow, with, of course, salmon eggs and a Colorado spinner. I never got a strike, but I love that river. That night, on Island Lake, eight miles from my place, Louis Eschrich and I dip-netted some eating ciscoes near the shore, where they had moved in at dark to spawn among roots of drowned jack pines.

There is immense satisfaction in being busy. Around the cabin there were incessant chores that please the hands and rest the brain. Idiot work, my wife calls it. I cannot get enough of it. Perhaps I should have been a day laborer. I split maple and Norway pine chunks for the fireplace and kitchen range. This is work fit for any king. You see the piles grow, and indeed the man who splits his own wood warms himself twice.

On Thursday along came Tony Burmek, Hayward guide. He had a

grand idea. The big crappies were biting in deep water on the Chippewa flowage. There'd be nothing to it. No, we wouldn't bother fishing muskies, just get twenty-five of those crappies apiece. Nary a crappie touched our minnows, and after several hours of it I gave up, but not Tony. He put me on an island where I tossed out half a dozen black-duck decoys and shot three mallards.

When I scooted back northward that night, the roadside trees were tossing. First good wind of the week. Instead of going down with the sun, Old Wind had risen, and it was from the right quarter, northwest. The radio confirmed it, said there'd be snow flurries. Going to bed that windy night, I detected another dividend of doing nothing — some slack in the waistline of my pants. You ever get that fit feeling as your belly shrinks and your hands get callused?

By rising time of Friday morning the weatherman was a merchant of proven mendacity. The upper pines were lashing and roaring. This was the day! In that northwest blast the best blind was a mile run with the outboard. Only after I had left the protecting high hill did I realize the full strength of the wind. Following waves came over the transom.

Before full light I had forty bluebill and canvasback decoys tossing off a stubby point and eleven black-duck blocks anchored in the lee of the point. I had lost the twelfth black-duck booster somewhere, and a good thing. We of the Old Duck Hunters have a superstition that any decoy spread should add up to an odd number.

Plenty of ducks moved. I had the entire lake to myself, but that is not unusual in the Far North. Hours passed and nothing moved in. I remained long after I knew they were not going to decoy. All they had in mind was sheltered water.

Next time you get into a big blow like that, watch them head for the lee shore. This morning many of them were flying north, facing the wind. I think they can spot lee shores easier that way, and certainly they can land in such waters easily. In the early afternoon, when I picked up, the north shore of my lake — seldom used by ducks because it lacks food — held hundreds of divers.

Sure, I could have redeployed those blocks and got some shooting. But it wasn't that urgent. The morning had told me that they were in, and there was a day called tomorrow to be savored. No use to live it up all at once.

Because I had become a pine-knot millionaire, I did not start the big space heater that night. It's really living when you can afford to heat a 20-by-30-foot living room, a kitchen, and a bedroom with a fireplace full of pine knots.

The wind died in the night and by morning it was smitten-cold. What wind persisted was still northwest. I shoved off the loaded boat. Maybe by now those newcomers had rested. Maybe they'd move to feed. Same blind, same old familiar tactics, but this time it took twice as long to make the spread because the decoy cords were frozen.

A band of bluebills came slashing toward me. How fine and brave they are, flying in their tight little formations! They skirted the edge of the decoys, swung off, came back again and circled in back of me, then skidded in, landing gear down. It was so simple to take two. A single drake mallard investigated the big black cork duck decoys and found out what they were. A little color in the bag looks nice.

I was watching a dozen divers, redheads maybe, when a slower flight movement caught my eye. Coming dead in were eleven geese, blues, I knew at once. I don't know what ever became of those redheads. Geese are an extra dividend on this lake. Blues fly over it by the thousand, but it is not goose-hunting country. I like to think those eleven big black cork decoys caught their fancy this time. At twenty-five yards the No. 6's were more than enough. Two of the geese made a fine weight in the hand, and geese are always big guys when one has had his eyes geared for ducks.

The cold water stung my hands as I picked up. Why does a numb, cold finger seem to hurt so much if you bang it accidentally? The mittens felt good. I got back to my beach in time for the prudent duck hunter's greatest solace, a second breakfast. But first I stood on the lakeshore for a bit and watched the ducks, mostly divers, bluebills predominating, some redheads and enough regal canvasback to make tomorrow promise new interest. The storm had really brought them down from Canada. I was lucky. Two more weeks with nothing to do.

Nothing to do, you say? Where'd I get those rough and callused hands? The windburned face? The slack in my pants? Two more weeks of it . . . Surely, I was among the most favored of all mankind. Where could there possibly be a world as fine as this?

I walked up the hill, a pine-knot millionaire, for that second breakfast.

THE OLD BROWN MACKINAW

Now we get a lesson in life from Gordon MacQuarrie. Mr. President is dead and MacQuarrie hunts and fishes alone. As he says, there is no replacing the Old Timers.

But life goes on. Out of the blue emerges another. A man of incredible energy and action. A friend. A companion. A man of quick wit and fine-honed skills.

MacQuarrie appoints him the new President of The Old Duck Hunters. In the cabin the new Mr. President sleeps with snow hissing on the windows and the fire burning low. MacQuarrie senses that the spirit of old Mr. President is very much alive in the cabin and he drapes the old brown Mackinaw over the new man's shoulders.

Life goes on. And if you are brave enough, strong enough, the flame cannot be diminished.

When the President of the Old Duck Hunters' Association, Inc., died, the hearts of many men fell to the ground.

There was no one like Mister President. When the old-timers go there is no bringing them back, nor is there any hope of replacing them. They are gone, and there is a void and for many, many years I knew the void would never be filled, for this paragon of the duck blinds and the trout streams had been the companion of my heart's desire for almost 20 years.

I made the common mistake. I looked for another, exactly like Hizzoner. How foolish it is, as foolish as it is for a man to try to find another beloved hunting dog, exactly like the one that's gone.

In the years after Mister President's death I fished and hunted more than before, and often alone. There was a great deal of fishing and hunting, from Florida to Alaska, before a man came along who fit the role once occupied by Mister President. This is how it was:

I was sitting in the ballroom of the Loraine Hotel in Madison, Wisconsin, covering the proceedings of the unique Wisconsin Conservation Congress. I became aware that a man carrying one of the 71 labels for the 71 counties of the state was eyeing me.

He held aloft the cardboard label "Iowa" signifying that he was a Big Wheel in conservation from that western Wisconsin county. He looked like Huckleberry Finn and he grinned eternally. One of the first thoughts I had about him was that he probably could not turn down the corners of his lips if he wanted to.

Each time I glanced at him his eye was upon me. This sort of thing is unnerving. Once he caught my eye and held it and grinned harder. I grinned back, foolishly. The beggar burst out laughing. I felt like a fool. He knew it and laughed at me.

Let me give you the picture more completely. In that room sat more than 300 dedicated, articulate conservationists. They were framing, no less, the fish and game code of this sovereign state for an entire year. Not in silence, you may be sure.

Up at the front table on the platform, as chairman of the Congress, sat Dr. Hugo Schneider of Wausau, with a gavel in one hand and — so help me! — a muzzle-loading squirrel rifle in the other. Each time Robert's Rules of Order seemed about to go out the window, Doc would abandon the gavel and reach for the rifle.

In this delightful pandemonium, in this convention of impassioned hunters and fishers and amidst the shrieks from the wounded and dying delegates, Wisconsin evolves its game and fish laws. And if you can think of a more democratic way, suggest it. We may try it.

At one point in the milling commotion and confusion, I saw my grinning friend slip to the floor and on his hands and knees start crawling toward me. By this manner of locomotion he managed to evade the baleful eye and subsequent vengeance of Dr. Schneider, and he crawled up to my chair and handed me a scribbled note. Then still on his hands and knees, he crawled away. The note read:

> I've been reading your drivel for years. See me after school if you want to get some good partridge hunting.
>
> — Harry

Since then I suppose I've "seen him" a thousand times — on trout streams, on lakes, in partridge cover, in the deer woods, in the quail thickets, and yes, in the August cow pastures where the blackberries grow as long as your thumb, and in the good September days when you can fill a bushel basket with hickory nuts beneath one tree.

No outdoor event of its season escapes Harry. He is lean and fiftyish. He is a superb shot. He ties his own flies, one a black killer with a tiny spinner at the eye made from special light material he begs, or steals from dentist friends. On a dare, once he shinnied up a 12-foot pole and came back down head first. Once he made me a pair of buckskin pants. All in all, an unbelievable person.

How natural then, just this last October, that we should rendezvous, not in Iowa County — we save those partridge until December — but at the ancient headquarters of the Old Duck Hunters' Association, two whoops and a holler north of Hayward, Wisconsin.

I got there first. This is not hard for me to do when going to this place. Some things do not change and this is one of those things. It's exactly like it was before the atomic age. On that particular day, late October's yellow shafts were slanting through the Norways on the old cedar logs of the place. A chipmunk which had learned to beg in summer came tentatively close, then scurried away, uncertain now.

All was in order, down to the new windowpane I had to put in where a partridge in the crazy time had flown through. The label was still pasted to the tiny square of glass. I must scratch it off some day but there is always so much to do at places like this.

I went to the shed at the rear to check decoy cords and anchors. When you open this shed door one of the first things to catch your eye is a brown, checked-pattern mackinaw, about 50 years old, I guess. It belonged to the President of the Old Duck Hunters. I like to keep it there. It belongs there.

Flying squirrels had filled one pocket of the mackinaw with acorns. They always do that, but these avian rodents, so quick to unravel soft, new wool for nests, have never chewed at the threadbare carcass of Mister President's heroic jacket. Perhaps this is because the wool, felted and tough, has lost its softness and flavor.

I launched a boat, readied a smaller skiff and screwed the motor on the big boat. I fetched three bags of decoys down the hill and placed them handy. I put an ax — for blind building — in the boat with other gear, and when I got back up the hill to the cabin Harry was there.

On the way — a 300-mile drive — he had hesitated, he said, long enough to slay two pheasant roosters.

"I see," he said, "that you have been here an hour and have killed 'ary a duck or partridge." He explained that he had felt my auto radiator — "She's cooled only about an hour." This man operates like a house detective. I explained that in the remaining hour and a half of daylight I would prepare him a kingly supper.

"An hour and a half of daylight!" He flung two skinned pheasants at me, dashed to his car and returned, running, bearing fishing tackle.

"D'ja soak the boat?" he cried as he passed me. I doubt if he heard my answer for he was soon down the hill and nearing the beach when I replied. Within two minutes he was trolling.

The man never lived who could fill up each moment of a day like this one. Nor was there ever a one who could, once the day was done, fall asleep so fast. He goes, I am sure, into a world of dreams, there to continue the pursuits of fish and game, man's life's blood — well, his, anyway.

I lit the fireplace. No need for the big steel stove, or was there? Late October weather in the north can be treacherous. I laid the big stove fire, to play safe. The provident Harry had made getting supper easy. You take two pheasants and cut them up. You save the giblets. You steam some wild rice for an hour.

It was long after dark when Harry returned. He had a 7- or 8-pound northern and a walleye half as big — "If we're gonna be here for four days, somebody around here has got to bring home the grub."

I set the table fast for fear he would fall asleep. He stuffed himself with pheasant and wild rice and mentioned that he must not forget to tell his wife how badly I treated him. Then he collapsed on the davenport before the fire, and in one yawn and a short whistle he was gone. I washed the dishes.

No, he is not a shirker. Before sleep afflicts him he will kill himself at any job which needs doing, especially if it pertains to hunting and fishing. To prove his willingness for the menial tasks, I recall a deer camp one night when one of the boys brought in a 300-pound bear — dragged him right through the door and dropped him at Harry's feet.

Harry was wiping the dishes, clad only in a suit of new, red underwear. He had sworn to be the first man in that camp to bring in important game, and because now he obviously had not, he turned, dishcloth in hand, eyed the bear casually and remarked:

"Johnny, that's a mighty nice little woodchuck you got there."

Even when I turned on the radio for a weather report he did not awaken. His snores, wondrously inventive, competed with the welcome report of changing and colder weather. Outside the wind was coming along a bit and it was in the northwest. But mostly it was the warm wind hurrying back south ahead of something colder at its back.

Iowa County's nonpareil was bedded down in the far room where his snores joined the issue with the rising wind which keened over the roof. A good fair contest, that.

When I arose I had to light the big heater for the weather had made up its mind. No snow, but a thermometer at 26 degrees and a buster of a wind. I hurried with breakfast because I thought we might have to build a blind on Posey's point. That point, the right one on this day, had not been hunted in the season. When I mentioned the reason for haste he explained:

"Man, I built that blind yesterday. You think I fooled away three hours just catching a couple fish?"

It is not possible to dislike a man like that. Furthermore, I knew this blind would be no wild dove's nest, but a thing of perfection, perfectly blend-ed with the shoreline.

A lot of people in this country think the Old Duck Hunters are crazy when they hunt this lake. We carry so many decoys that we have to tow them behind in a skiff. Fifty is our minimum, half of them over-sized balsas, and a scattering of some beat-up antiques more than 120 years old, just for luck.

Settling himself for some duck blind gossip, Harry began, "I was down on the Mississippi at Ferryville last week. Mallards all over the — "

"Mark!"

A hundred bluebills, maybe twice that, who knows, came straight in without once swinging, and sat. We never touched a feather as they rose. I have done it before and I'll do it again and may God have mercy on my soul.

"This," said Harry, "will become one of the greatest lies in history when I tell my grandchildren about it. I am reminded of Mark Twain. When Albert Bigelow Paine was writing his biography and taking copious notes, he once remarked to Twain that his experiences and adventures were wonderful copy.

" 'Yes, yes,' replied Mr. Clemens. 'And the most remarkable thing about it is that half of them are true.' "

He then set his jaw and announced he would kill the next three straight with as many shots. This he did, for I did not fire. While I was retrieving them in the decoy skiff, another bundle of bluebills tried to join those giant decoys and were frightened off by me. Walking to the blind from the boat, I saw Harry kill a canvasback.

He was through for the day and not a half-hour had passed. Many Badgers will remember that late October day. Ducks flew like crazy from the Kakagon sloughs of Lake Superior to sprawling Horicon marsh, 300 miles away. Only one other day of that season beat it — Wednesday, November 2.

Harry cased his gun and watched. I cannot shoot like Harry, but getting four ducks on such a day was child's play. Many times we had more divers over our decoys than we had decoys. It was pick-and-choose duck hunting. I settled for four bullneck canvasbacks.

Back at the cabin we nailed their bills to the shed wall, and over a cup of coffee Harry said the divers we'd seen reminded him of the "kin to can't day." Then, he explained, the law let a man shoot the whole day through from as soon "as he kin see until the time that he can't see." I knew a place, Oscar Ruprecht's sugar bush, and we drove the eight miles to it.

This chunk of maple is on an island of heavier soil in an ocean of glacial sand, grown to pines. If its owner had the equipment he could tap 5,000 trees. Many know it and hunt it. We separated, for we are both snap shooters, or think we are.

The plan was to meet on a high, rocky bluff where the river Ounce passes by below, on its way to the Totogatic. Here was no dish like that easy duck blind venture. These were mature, hunted ruffed grouse, all the more nervous because the wind was high. On one of the tote trails where Oscar's tractor hauls the sap tank I missed my first bird, then missed two more.

A half-mile to my right two calculated shots sounded, well spaced. Perhaps a double. Ah, well . . . My fourth bird was as good as dead when it got out of the red clover in mid-trail and flew straight down the road. I missed him, too.

Three times more, and later a couple more times Harry's gun sounded. Then two birds flung themselves out of the yellow bracken beside the two-rut road and I got one. When I was walking over to pick it up, a third pumped up and I got it.

It was noon when I got to the high bluff. Deer hunters with scopes on their rifles love this place. From it they overlook almost a half-mile of good deer country in three directions. My sandwich tasted good. I lit a little friendship fire and thought about other days on the river below me. It's a pretty good trout stream for anyone who will walk in two miles before starting to fish.

Harry came along. He'd been far up the valley of the Ounce, bucking fierce cover — no sugar bush tote trails in there, only deer trails. But he had five grouse. We hunted back to the car, and in his presence I was lucky enough to kill my third bird.

It was around 2 PM when we pulled into the cabin. My Huckleberry Finn who I have seen, on occasion, whittle away at a pine stick for 20 minutes without doing anything but meditate, was a ball of fire on this day. He tied into the ducks and partridge. When he had finished cleaning them his insatiable eye fell upon the woodpile.

You can spot those real country-raised boys every time when they grab an ax. They know what to do with it. No false moves. No glancing blows. In no time he had half a cord of fine stuff split and piled for the kitchen range and he went on from that to the sheer labor of splitting big maple logs with a wedge for the fireplace.

He spotted my canoe and considered painting it, but decided it was too cold, and anyway, it had begun to snow a little. Then he speculated about the weather, and when I said I wished I had a weather vane on the ridgepole, he went into action.

He whittled out an arrow from an old shingle, loosely nailed it to a stick, climbed to the roof and nailed it there firmly. I suppose that if I had mentioned building an addition to the back porch he'd have started right in. He came down from the roof covered with snow and said he wished he hadn't killed those four ducks in the morning, so he could go again.

"But, let's go anyway," he suggested. "No guns. Put out the decoys and just watch 'em."

Out there on the point the divers were riding that wind out of Canada. Scores of them rode into and above the decoys. Posey, the owner of the point, came along for a visit and decided we were both crazy when he saw what we were doing. Nevertheless, we had him ducking down as excited as we were when a new band of bluebills burst out of the snow. Only in the big duck years can a hunter enjoy such madness.

Our shore duty at dark that night involved careful preparations against the storm. We pulled up the boat and skiff higher than usual and covered everything with a weighted tarp.

Walking up the hill, I considered how nice it was to have one of the faithful, like Harry, on the premises. He should have been bone tired. Certainly I was. But before I relit the big heater he took down its 15 feet of stovepipe, shook out the soot and wired it back to the ceiling. He carried in enough wood for the remaining three days, stamping off snow and whistling and remembering such tales as one hears in all properly managed hunting camps.

He spied a seam rip in my buckskin pants and ordered me to take them off. While he mended them he complained bitterly about such neglect on my part — "There's nothing wrong with the workmanship on these pants."

He had made them himself, two months before, from two big chrome-tanned doeskins. He just walked into my house one night with a gunny sack containing the skins, a piece of chalk and some old shears his wife used for trimming plants. He cut the pants out, fitted them to me and took them to the shoemaker's shop where he sewed them up and affixed buttons. I never in my life wore pants that fit so well.

This man should have been born in the same time as a Kit Carson or a Jim Bridger. Turn him loose anywhere in his native heath, which is Wisconsin, and, given matches, an ax, a fishhook and some string, he'll never go hungry or cold.

He is a true countryman, a species almost extinct. Each day of the year finds him outdoors for at least a little while. In trout season he hits the near-by streams for an hour or two around sunup. His garden is huge and productive. In the raspberry season you may not go near his home without being forced, at gun point if need be, to eat a quart of raspberries with cream.

He represents something almost gone from our midst. He knows the value of working with his own hands, of being eternally busy, except when sleeping. His last act that snowy evening was to go to his car and return with a bushel of hickory nuts. He set up a nut-cracking factory on a table, using a little round steel anvil he had brought for busting 'em. He had a pint of hickory nut meats when I put the grub on the table.

He almost fell asleep at the table. Then he yawned and whistled and looked out the door and said he was glad it was snowing hard — "Don't shoot at anything but cans in the morning." He flopped on the davenport and was gone to that far-off land where no trout of less than 5 pounds comes to a surface fly and the duck season runs all year.

I tidied up and washed the dishes. I smelled the weather and smoked a pipe. The fireplace light danced on the big yellow cedar beams. The snow hissed against the window. The President of the Old Duck Hunters' Association should have been there.

Maybe he was. At any rate, I went out to the shed and took the old brown mackinaw off its nail and brought it in and laid it over Harry's shoulders. It looked just fine there.

You Can't Take
It With You

We at Sports Afield *had bought this soft, sweet story and were having it illustrated when word came of the author's sudden, unexpected death. We marveled at the fact its highlight is a passage about death. Nowhere else does that grim subject intrude on MacQuarrie's always upbeat frame of mind.*

What can you say? Did some harbinger sweep across his vision? He was of good health and young by the standards of the day. Yet this subject. Strange.

It was too good a tale to let lie fallow. We published it in the February 1957 issue without amplification. To my best recollection we didn't put on notice that the author had died. Or that there would be no more Mr. President stories . . . ever.

But we knew. A glorious era had come to an end.

The President of the Old Duck Hunters' Association finished his repast that Sabbath noon and his wife reminded him that the lawn needed mowing, one martin house had been tilted by the wind and the garden clamored to be weeded.

Mister President walked through the summer kitchen which held a freeze box of treasure, including trout, bass and walleyes. His fishing jacket and tackle were in a neat pile by the door leading to the back porch where the wild grapevine twined. He eschewed it.

He strode out on the back porch and looked across the street at the United States post office where he was postmaster and where he often started working at 6 AM and remained until midnight. For the hundredth time he thought it might be a good idea to sell the post office, a drastic measure which he often expounded on opening days to customers who approved of the idea hilariously.

Bob, the shorthair, and Becky, the springer, galloped up and awaited the word from their lord and master. Perhaps they knew what was passing through his mind. Bob's tail was violently in favor of truancy, for Bob is a direct actionist. Becky, more the opportunist, merely sat and hoped for the best.

Mister President disappointed them both. He took the lawn mower from the garage, lingering there only a few seconds to admire the sleek lines of a 16-foot canoe he was recovering with fiberglass. Within five minutes after the demon mower had begun to roar, three neighborhood urchins appeared from unknown crannies, looking for work, to which they were instantly put.

The three dandiprats, elevation about 40 inches, were signed on as horses, and Mister President explained that they were crossing the plains in a covered wagon and he was the wagon master.

"Gee-jap . . . steady . . . haw! Haw, you red-headed hoss! You wanna push the wagon and all our stores over the bank into the wide Missouri? . . . Steady . . . now, gee-jap."

The three hosses walked the mower up and down, halting occasionally on command of the wagon master to fall on their bellies and shoot it out with bands of Indian raiders.

A lady of considerable dignity, for such a pretty day, approached on the sidewalk.

"Sir!" She fixed the President with a fierce and righteous eye. "What do you mean by disturbing the Sabbath with this uproar?"

Heads poked cautiously out of nearby front doors and upper windows, for this lady was notorious in her determination to police the city of Mineral Point, Wisconsin, in the ways of Christianity as she saw them. The President of the Old Duck Hunters was not unequal to the occasion.

"Madam," he answered, "I plumb forgot it was Sunday, because I've been so damn busy minding my own business."

The lady went on her way, bloody, but unbowed, as screen doors closed softly and a little chorus of giggles floated from front porches beneath the 100-year-old elms. Above the roar of the mower, Mister President called out the marching orders:

"We'll make Alkali Bluff tonight, hosses. Plenty of grass and water for you there. Gee-jap."

The gallant hosses and/or Indian-fighting plainsmen had finished their strength-sapping labors and were ingesting fresh strawberries with thick cream — a quart apiece is the standard ration for all comers to this yard — when I drove my car up the short, steep driveway. The President flew into action.

"It's Geronimo and his band!" he cried. "Wheel the wagons into a circle and don't fire until you see the whites of their eyes."

The three plainsmen covered me with rifles that looked like Model 1873 Winchesters and fired white plastic balls. Mister President bravely directed the skirmish from behind a bowl of strawberries and cream — "Shoot the hosses from under 'em, men. Then we'll tommyhawk 'em and scalp 'em when they're helpless on the ground!"

I advanced from my car waving a handkerchief on the middle section of a glass fly rod.

"Cease firing, men, the poor fellows are whupped."

Although I had recently dined, it was compulsory that I attack my portion of garden-fresh strawberries and cream. The three fighting men of the plains accepted additional helpings and sat there restuffing themselves, victorious and belching.

Mrs. President came out. She was about to cheer the billiard-table appearance of the lawn and saw me, so I had to accept another ladle of giant strawberries and impart the family news and amenities. Mister President volunteered:

"Now, Laura, he came all by himself all this way. Seems when I settle down to serious work somebody's always trying to lure me away."

The lady of his heart remarked that luring him away was about as difficult as persuading a rabbit to eat lettuce, and, for that matter, she would attend to the garden and straighten the martin house on its pole.

Mister President, by main force, imprisoned Becky and Bob in his own car to prevent them from following us, and as we backed down the driveway you could see them staring desperately at us through the rear window. At such a time you can hear a dog calling you unprintable names.

The smallmouth and trout domain we visited that day is part of the southwest corner of Wisconsin — the Driftless Area, as the geologists call it, where glaciers have never advanced or receded, and where a complete river system has been eroded by wind and rain and flowing water until the area is almost perfectly drained. A bucket of water thrown on the ground has only one way to go — downhill — looking for some other water.

In this land of the sky, so-called because hills are high and vistas are far, it has been estimated by Mister President that there are about a thousand miles of creeks and rivers which are predominantly smallmouth bass water, with some trout, especially browns in the upper reaches. I think his estimate is high but fear to challenge him, for he may add up that network of moving water to prove to me it's more than a thousand miles.

Our first stop was at the Fever River, not far from tiny Jenkinville. There we acquired a friend, Mr. Lyle "Fudge" Gates, straight as an arrow and merry as a meadowlark despite the burden of his 13 years. He was trying to catch a grasshopper and thus, eventually, a bass. In about four casts from the bank Mister President caught a 14-incher and presented it to Fudge with his compliments. Fudge took out for home on the dusty town road, clutching the giant to his ecstatic breast.

Gentlemen, I have had some awesome fishing in my time. I have stood on the big boulders alongside the Clearwater River not far from where it leaves Careen Lake, Saskatchewan, and found it almost impossible not to take two grayling on every cast. In that same province I have fished with four others and often all five of us have had on, simultaneously, northerns in the neighborhood of 20 pounds.

And that is fine, just fine. But let me vouchsafe that the pure delight imparted that day to Mr. Fudge Gates by Mister President, with a little black bass from a rather muddy little stream, was strangely satisfying, and appropriate.

At this place the Fever winds through closely cropped pastures holding dairy herds and beef cattle. Banks are trampled and those same banks fairly cry out for someone to come and plant cover on them. But the smallmouths are there. At least they are every time I attend to the local rites with Mister President.

Protocol while fishing with Hizzoner in his own domain demands the use of his tested, proven spinner fly — solid black dressing, red head, slim white rubber streamer tonguing out below the single hook. The spinner will twirl in the least of currents. It is made from a light, white metal used by dentists and it is begged, borrowed or stolen from them for this purpose by the President of the Old Duck Hunters.

I recommend that black spinner fly without reservation. I have seen it, in various sizes, take muskies, northerns, walleyes, trout and bass. Far as I know it is nameless. A more imaginative angler than I would likely have named it long ago. Hizzoner evolved it over a period of years, and if I may speculate about its effectiveness, I would guess that its chief attraction is in that spinner, which whirls like a dervish if you so much as blow on it.

It's a meat-in-the-pan fly-rod lure. Possibly there is something important in that solid black dressing. At any rate, one of the most successful of all the fly-rod men against the rainbows of the Douglas County Brule in Wisconsin was the late John Ziegler — and he put his faith in big, black bucktails.

Mister President, by his own admission, is a high-grader. He passes up a lot of water on those Driftless Area rivers. That means going from riffle to riffle and working the pools below the riffs. The process of high-grading brought a couple more smallmouths, and also Mr. Fudge Gates, who panted back to the streamside in time to get another bass a foot long and depart for home. We went along for the Grant River.

There's a place on this river where a gush of water leaps out of the limestone and falls 30 feet to the river. I stuck a thermometer into that flow and, though the air temperature was in the high 80's, the water was 54 degrees. It's colder than that in the ground, and that water, no doubt, is a solid reason why brother smallmouth tolerates the Driftless Area streams in spite of flash floods, silt and absence of bank cover.

It is surprising that so many miles of good smallmouth waters get so little pressure from anglers. The farmers in this opulent hill country hold down the bridges and the deep holes in an eternal quest for catfish. As for the bass angler, his work is easy. I wish it were harder, and it would be if those bald banks had only half the cover they need.

Mister President high-graded himself three more smallmouths within sight of that squirt of water from the limestone bluff above. He put them back, but said he'd save anything that got up to two pounds.

We moved along to the Platte River, to a place called King's Ford — high right bank, low left bank and the same surprisingly cold water from the limestone hill springs. Both of us picked up trout here — browns, half-pounders — and these we saved. Like the bass, they were found in the holes below the riffs. They are not big enough to be called rapids.

On such days as this, the Old Duck Hunters are not averse to other charms of the Driftless Area. Short excursions into the box canyons along these valleys showed that the wild black raspberries were ripe and edible, that the blackberry crop would be a buster and that the wild grape tangles were bearing heavily after a year when the grapes were absent — and the ruffed grouse were not found at these favored tangles.

The area is dotted with wild crab apple trees. Each time I pass one I remember a day in brown October when the incorrigible Mister President paused before a tree loaded with red ripe crabs. He bit into one, smacked his lips, ate it, core and all.

"Honey crabs," he explained. "Sweetest apple this side of heaven."

Greedily I bit into one, though I should have known better. A more tasteless, a more bitter fruit has not touched the lips of man. How he ate one, for the sole purpose of getting a sucker like me merely to taste one, is something I shall never understand.

It was like chewing alum. And yet, Hizzoner, when he ate his, chewed and smacked and swallowed when his face should have been distorted and tears running down his cheeks. Hizzoner will go to great lengths for a laugh, but it takes a man of considerable will power to get 'em that way.

The Platte River was next, and when the dark began mounting up in the east we had two respectable smallmouths each, a brown trout each and some nice country to survey. We sat on a ledge of limestone and watched a farmer send his dog for the cows. A headstrong heifer sneaked away from the obedient herd, but her tawny nemesis brought her back with his teeth snapping close to her heels — "You do that again, sister, and I'll really bite you!"

No, not wilderness fishing. Not in the slightest. Pastoral is the word for it. No big fish to brag about. No heavy water to breast in waders. Just fishin' in nice country. The farmer whose dog rounded up the cows came over and sat on the limestone for a chat — "I'll tell you, boys. You drop a good, stinky doughball into one of them holes and you're apt to get holt of the biggest dam' catfish this side the Mississippi."

It was all right with the Old Duck Hunters. Hizzoner figured it as an even split — "They get the catfish and we have the fun."

Quail scuttled across the gravelly town road as we pulled out of there and Mister President spoke of autumn days. "The grouse'll concentrate around those grape tangles again, sure's you're born." A considerate conservation commission apportions to this area the longest ruffed grouse season in Wisconsin, extending from mid-October to a few days before Christmas. Forget it if you haven't got a dependable dog, or those hills will murder you.

Within about six miles from home Mister President surmised, "She's probably got the garden weeded and the martin house fixed and it's still early." It was early, for a fisherman, not much after dark. He directed me to drive through a long, two-gate lane. We parked at the end of it and walked about a quarter of a mile through deep grass to the headwaters of what can be nothing but a feeder of the Pecatonica River.

That is all I can say about this place. If it has a name, Hizzoner did not tell me, although I prodded him a few times, just gently. I have found it profitable not to attempt to trespass into the mind of a fisherman.

The stream here was slight, with little widespreads and like the others we had seen that day, largely devoid of bank cover. A fine place for the casting of the night line with a fly rod. Mister President vanished in the dark upstream, and I combed the nearby waters for almost an hour with no luck.

I was at the car waiting for him when he came through the high grass to the lane. He dropped a brown of about three pounds on the floor of the car. "There's browns in there big enough to swallow that one."

Becky and Bob began a two-dog riot when the car burst up the short, steep driveway. Hizzoner quieted them hurriedly. He opened the garden gate and made a swift appraisal. "Not a weed in sight," he whispered. He went to the martin house pole and squinted upward. "Straight as a string."

The back porch light flicked on and the Old Duck Hunters were summoned to sit at a table arranged there of fried chicken and fearsome quantities of strawberries. Any number of people who have been entrapped on that back porch in the strawberry season can testify that when they leave they can be picked up and bounced, like a basketball.

Hizzoner lay back in a porch chair and contemplated the night through the grapevine leaves. Becky and Bob came close, the better to adore him. He sighed.

"Laura," he said, "I can probably find time tomorrow after work to weed the garden and straighten the martin house."

She said, "Huh!" She added succinct and appropriate remarks, for the time was opportune, but I noticed that she mussed his hair and smiled the smile of a wise woman before she left us alone on the porch.

We spoke of the country we had seen. I suggested he should consider himself lucky to be living in the midst of it, but, said I, there would come a day when the old geezer with the big sickle would come along and put an end to our days.

Mister President, challenged, sat bolt upright in his chair. "Let him come," said he. "I've got to have a guarantee from him that he's got some trout and bass water up there in the big yonder — yes, and some first-rate grouse cover and some duck hunting."

"You can't take it with you," I said, which was indeed the obvious reply to this man challenging fate. "Nor, can you send it on ahead. What are you going to do if the Sickle Man tells you he will not bargain?"

There was nothing obvious in the reply that the President of the Old Duck Hunters snapped at me.

"In that case, I ain't going."

MacQuarrie
Obituary

by Dion Henderson

Dion Henderson was a longtime MacQuarrie buddy and a companion on many a chase. He was bureau chief of the Midwest Associated Press, a novelist and story writer for many magazines. His words about MacQuarrie's passing speak for themselves.

A bit of magic is gone from the world this day for those who wear the rod and gun upon their family arms; Gordon MacQuarrie is dead. Let no one doubt that there was magic in him. For twenty years he waved a wand of words in what surely was a steady sorcery, for the world of the wild community is a different place than it was when he came, and different than it would have been without him.

MacQuarrie brought the outdoors to the library literature, and he brought the library to the outdoors. He did it with a magnificent idiom, an enormous zest, a flashing wit and the wry wisdom that remembers the impermanence of man's mightiest edifices.

He entertained, in a thousand stories, but his partnership with Mr. President dealt in philosophy and Jack Pine Joe worked in parables, and from Milwaukee to the Court Oreilles, and from the Mouth of the Peshtigo to the Headwaters of the St. Croix there are those — who know not the terms of Plato nor the scaffolding of analogy — who know what no other man could tell them, and who are the richer for the knowing.

MacQuarrie established the modern school of outdoor writing and it is not too much to say that if Aldo Leopold cut a path for man to follow in making terms with his environment, MacQuarrie lighted it to show the way.

This much, at least, needs to be said upon the passing of a man who became a legend in his own time, who stood tall in two worlds and will remain so, a major figure in American Journalism and in the outdoor world.

But what do you say about a man, colleague and kinsman, who was larger than life, yet who trimmed your Christmas tree and taught your children to sing "Jingle Bells" in Gaelic?

For this really is why you remember him. He labored mightily and was heard in the great halls of the world; there was nothing under the sun that failed to interest him, and he had seen everything under the sun. But you remember that he loved best the simple things — picking blackberries in southwestern Wisconsin, a moment when the great serial armadas of waterfowl climbed the spiral staircase above Horicon, the morning mist rising from the Brule above the bridge, a Saturday night when the bubbling crock of beans was opened.

He cherished craftsmanship, the old men bent over the workbenches who put a little of themselves into each rod and each gun stock and each blued barrel; and he was touched with sadness at the remembrance of things past, for the days and events and values that cannot come again. He loved the wild music of the bagpipes, and the trains of the fierce Scots laments, and he would lean back and say, "Ah, tis a grand bunch of savages we are."

He had the moments of black despair that every writing man has, who has so much to say and so little time and tools that are never so good as he would wish them. And there were the times when you heard the sharp hot lash of the tongue of him and you felt the sadness yourself because no man could ever write all the things that MacQuarrie knew.

But there was magic in him. In the last column he wrote, he said:

> "You're here today and tomorrow you're a little old man in a little old room all by yourself and the worldly goods don't mean much."

In that same column, he wrote of an old man walking alone down a lonely road:

> "...there'd be a doe or two gawking at him on the in-road, a fussy pa'tridge inviting temptation on a mossy down log, a tiny skirl of music from invisible chickadees in the Alders, the crawk of a raven, the flap of a whiskey jack across the old burn . . . it'd be near dark in the clearing at the end of the road and there'd be a yellow glow of lamplight from a window and the smell of woodsmoke . . ."

You can see that there was a grand, brave magic in him. Maybe a little of it remains.

If it does, let the pipes speak loudly for him on this day, for the MacQuarrie of the Isles, the MacQuarrie of the Brule, of the Crex and of all the places that he knew so well and which no one ever will know so well again. Let the pipes speak strongly now the fluted music of wild birdsong, and the drums of the deer's sharp foot on the forest duff in the cathedrals of the pine, and the drone in the high November sky of the grey geese going home. Let these pipes play sweetly for him on this day, in farewell.